Praise for the novels of Kelley St. John

REAL WOMEN DON'T WEAR SIZE 2

"A poignant tale that proves that fun and love come in all sizes, be sure to check out *Real Women Don't Wear Size 2*."

—RomRevToday.com

"Witty, funny, cute, sassy, touching, affirming . . . This is great romance (definitely a hot one) that is a real hoot . . . Kelley St. John has hit the ball out of the park with *Real Women Don't Wear Size 2*."

—Onceuponaromance.net

"An entertaining contemporary romance . . . fans will enjoy the escapades of a woman in love."

—TheBestReviews.com

"A great book to take to the beach or read by the pool . . . if the sun is not hot enough for you, this book will be!"

—RomanceReaderAtHeart.com

GOOD GIRLS DON'T

"Sizzling . . . *Good Girls Don't* is just what the cover claims: a sexy, sassy romance about compromising positions."

—Rendezvous

"Fast-paced, sexy, and ⬚⬚⬚⬚⬚⬚ ⬚⬚⬚⬚⬚ *and the City*."

more...

"*Good Girls Don't* shines, and the novel has found a place on my 'permanent keeper' shelf. Kelley St. John will take the romance world by storm!"

—TheRomanceReadersConnections.com

"A very entertaining contemporary romance novel . . . a sexy and fun read."

—MyShelf.com

"A super-sexy and super-funny charmer of a story . . . St. John takes the rider on a wheelie ride of emotion— from laugh-out-loud to that little choke in your throat, and then back to laughing. FOUR STARS!"

—BooksforaBuck.com

"Will be enjoyed by anyone who likes hot contemporaries."
—RomanceReaderatHeart.com

"A PERFECT TEN! A story with fast-moving action, sincere emotions, and the longing for love that is in all of us . . . a dynamite first novel filled with passion, emotion, and laughs. *Good Girls Don't* pulled out all the stops . . . so what else can I do but give it RRT's Perfect 10 award? I know you will give it one too."

—RomRevToday.com

"A must-have! Fun and sexy . . . I highly recommend!"
—JoyfullyReviewed.com

To Catch a Cheat

a

Cheat

Kelley St. John

FOREVER

NEW YORK   BOSTON

The characters and events in this book are fictitious. Any similarity to real persons, living or dead, is coincidental and not intended by the author.

Copyright © 2007 by Kelley St. John
Excerpt from *The Trouble with Men* copyright © 2007 by Kelley St. John
All rights reserved. Except as permitted under the U.S. Copyright Act of 1976, no part of this publication may be reproduced, distributed, or transmitted in any form or by any means, or stored in a database or retrieval system, without the prior written permission of the publisher.

Cover design by Tamaye Perry
Book design by Giorgetta Bell McRee

Forever
Hachette Book Group USA
237 Park Avenue
New York, NY 10017
Visit our Web site at www.HachetteBookGroupUSA.com

Forever is an imprint of Grand Central Publishing.

The Forever name and logo is a trademark of Hachette Book Group USA, Inc.

Printed in the United States of America

First Printing: November 2007

10 9 8 7 6 5 4 3 2 1

To Mom and to Mom Z.
I've been blessed to have both of you in my life.

Acknowledgments

My thanks and appreciation to:
Beth de Guzman and Frances Jalet-Miller, for their
insightful editorial guidance,
Doug and Gay Duhon, for sharing their
fabulous étouffée recipe,
and Caren Johnson, my incredible agent.

To Catch
a
Cheat

Cheaters never win, but they sure can piss you off.
—MARISSA KINCAID

Chapter 1

Boxers or briefs?" Marissa Kincaid asked, keying in the information for this week's AtlantaTellAll poll. She peered over the top of her computer monitor and wiggled her brows at her two best friends and business partners. "Johnny Depp. What do you say, boxers or briefs?"

"It depends." Amy Brooks leaned her head against the back of the couch and fingered the tip of her brown pony-tail with one hand, while her other palm caressed her son's back. Bo, her three-year-old, stuck his rump in the air as he slept peacefully against his mother's chest. "Johnny Depp," Amy whispered, her mouth curving into an extremely wistful, yet satisfied grin. "Oh yeah, it definitely depends." Smiling against Bo's blond curls, she crossed one long leg over the other and let her blue rhinestone-embellished flip-flop dangle from her foot. "You never can tell what a guy might be hiding beneath his jeans."

"You aren't even talking about Johnny Depp, are you?" Marissa challenged. "You're thinking about Landon." No doubt about it, Landon Brooks was one hot cowboy, and Amy rarely had a thought about any male that didn't somehow come back to her hubby.

"Well, yeah, I was." Amy kissed Bo's crown.

Candi Moody unclipped her hospital badge from the front of her blue scrubs, tucked it in her pocket, and yawned. "Okay. I'm sorry, but after the day I had at work, I really don't need to hear about the hunk you've got waiting at home. And what do you mean, it depends? It's a simple question, and you just have to give her an answer so we can finish this poll, then get some sleep. Some of us have day jobs, you know, and one of us hasn't slept in, oh, two days."

"I have a day job," Amy argued. "Full-time motherhood. And it's exciting, even more than designing sex toys."

Previously a designer of unique vibrators for Adventurous Accessories, Amy had decided to stay home and embrace motherhood with gusto the minute Bo was born. She put her all into motherhood the same way she put her all into her sex toy designs, one hundred percent, and she hadn't regretted the decision one iota. But like Marissa and Candi, Amy hoped their webzine would continue growing in subscribers and that her weekly sex advice column for the site would eventually pay off in spades.

So far, AtlantaTellAll had put a dab of cash in each of their pockets, but their readership was steadily increasing, and Marissa dreamed of the day when she could quit her computer-programming position completely and run the magazine. Then she could be her own boss, work from home, and—she shot a glance at the little boy in Amy's arms—perhaps have a little Bo of her own.

Candi mumbled, "Yeah, I guess you're right. You do have a day job, but at least yours takes a nap every now and then, and probably lets you do the same. Now, come on and give Marissa your answer. We've promised our readers that the polls will go up every Monday. In an hour, we've missed that goal for this week. Johnny Depp, boxers or briefs? Answer."

"I can't," Amy said. "Because it really does depend."

"On what?" Marissa questioned, softly drumming her fingertips against the lower portion of the keyboard while she waited for Amy's answer.

"If we're talking Johnny Depp in *Edward Scissorhands*, then I'd say definitely boxers, but if it's Johnny Depp in *Pirates of the Caribbean*, then briefs."

"A pirate wearing briefs? Are you serious?" Candi rubbed her eyelids with her fingertips then informed Marissa, "My answer is boxers, whether it's freaky Edward or yummy Jack Sparrow."

"Gotcha," Marissa said, stifling her laugh. "Okay, we're using Johnny in *Pirates*, and that rounds out our poll of ten."

Candi stretched her arms in a big V and yawned until her jaw popped. "I'm sleeping over. I'm too tired to drive home, and I'm not due back at the hospital until tomorrow night." She yanked the white scrunchie out of her hair and let her ponytail fall free. Long sandy hair, straight except for the circular indention from the scrunchie, fell past her shoulders as her body sagged back down against the couch. "Man, I hope we have fewer stat patients tomorrow night. Let's hope the fireworks have ended by then, totally. The Fourth of July is havoc on the ER. I can't take another day like today."

Squinting through tired eyes, she asked, "Okay. Before I crash, go over the list one more time."

"Orlando Bloom, Brad Pitt, Adrian Grenier, Viggo Mortensen, Denzel Washington, Tom Cruise, Usher, Jake Gyllenhaal, Matthew McConaughey, and Johnny Depp—in *Pirates of the Caribbean*."

Each week, AtlantaTellAll.com's poll started with their answers, then other women logged on to the site and made their own selections, while a running total displayed the results throughout the week on the home page. Then the AtlantaTellAll message board allowed site visitors to discuss how they had voted and why, and all the while, the number of hits skyrocketed, and the price for advertisers steadily increased, since they priced ads based on site visits.

Additionally, the three women produced juicy info on sex toys, Atlanta gossip, and local events displayed in fun, romantic formats, typically hearts and flowers. Marissa covered the events for singles, since most of the computer programmers in her office were young twenty-somethings without a care in the world beyond the next party. At thirty-two, she was practically ancient around them, but at least she stayed in the know on the party scene and was able to convey that prized info to AtlantaTellAll's readers.

Amy, naturally, answered sex questions and explained the latest in sex toys. Her column, Adventures with Amy, was an instant hit, and she consequently promoted all of her husband's famed massage oils, even including links for purchase. Candi's gossip column, Society Sauce, dished about Atlanta's and Gwinnett's most notable residents, ranging from society queens to athletes. Her trauma nurse position at Grady Memorial had generated several friendships with Atlanta's elite, who happened to find themselves in the ER occasionally and were happy to dish on the culprits who had put them there, typically ex-spouses, lovers, or rivals. All in all, they kept a wide range of interesting topics covered within the roses, lilacs, hearts, and daffodils planted sporadically throughout their site.

Marissa quickly plugged in her own answers to the poll and smiled. "I guess that's it for this week. We've got our gossip, our latest sex product recommendation—"

"Landon's new edible massage oil in caramel apple, right?" Amy asked, while Marissa's mouth watered.

"Yeah," Marissa said, imagining someone licking her like a big, caramel-covered apple. Or even better, taking a bite. She swallowed. "We have our recommendation for shopping—the summer shoe sale at Nordstrom's—and our poll. I think this is going to be one of our most successful ones yet. Boxers or briefs," she mused. She leaned her head forward to stretch the bunched muscles in the back of her neck. Her black bangs hit her cheeks like a dark curtain between her eyes and the computer screen. Funny how the only part of her hair that seemed to grow was her bangs. She'd tried growing the remainder of her black mop into a shoulder-length bob, but as usual, gave up fighting the untamable mess and moved back to the short, dark pixie that had graced her head since she graduated from college. It suited her face, anyway, or so her hairdresser—and her mother—said. And speaking of her mother . . .

"Candi, you're welcome to sleep over, but you know Mom will call at 6:00 A.M. sharp."

Candi groaned. "Mona still does that, does she?"

"Even on my days off."

"Want to unplug the phone?" Candi asked.

"Then she'll show up to make sure I'm breathing."

Candi turned her head and groaned into the pillow. "Gotcha. If I stay, I'll ignore Mona's morning ritual." She frowned. "Bet that doesn't do much for the morning after when you have sleepovers, hmm?"

"Hardly," Marissa admitted. "Not that I've had many sleepovers in a while, so it really doesn't matter. But if things work out with Jamie . . ."

"You know, we could add one more category," Amy said, patting Bo's behind.

Marissa rolled her head from side to side then pushed her bangs out of her eyes. She kept her palm against the top of her forehead so she could massage her temples while she prayed Amy's suggestion wouldn't warrant a poll edit. "I'm almost afraid to ask, but I will. What category?"

"Straight or gay." Amy started to laugh, but then stopped abruptly when Candi shot a look of warning her way.

Marissa knew that look. It was a don't-tell-Marissa-what-you-know look, and it meant one thing. Marissa had to know—whatever it was—and the sooner the better. "What?" she asked.

"Nothing," Amy said, dropping the blue flip-flop from her pink painted toes. She stretched her foot toward the fallen shoe, but jostled Bo in the process. The three-year-old mumbled, "Come on, Mom," then squished his nose as though smelling something rank before drifting back to sleep against her purple Adventurous Accessories T-shirt. Amy gave up on the shoe and forced a smile at Marissa. "Forget it. We don't need any more categories. Hey, have you thought about adding our photos to the site? Did I show you the one I took of you by the pool? Of course, you're probably not planning to put in a bikini shot, huh? Then again, if you look that good in a bikini, why not? I'll have to bring that picture over for you to see. Your hair is all curly in it, too. I wish I could pull off that short, sassy look . . ."

Marissa glared at Amy, doing her best to ramble past the issue at hand and make Marissa forget her comment. It wasn't going to work. "I don't want to talk about photos now." She turned to Candi, who she knew wouldn't be able to sidetrack the issue. "Tell me. What is it?"

"What's what?" Candi asked, but her clenched jaw gave her away.

"What's with that look? And, more important, what does that look have to do with me?"

Amy shifted on the couch, moved Bo to the opposite shoulder, and tossed the other flip-flop. Then she wiggled her feet into the crack between the brown leather sofa cushions and let Bo cover her side like a blanket. "We should tell her," she said to Candi.

"Yes, you should," Marissa agreed. "Tell me what?"

"It's Jamie," Candi said.

Marissa's stomach knotted. Jamie Abernathy was the guy who'd effectively swept her off her feet for the past two weeks. They'd been out four times so far, and Marissa was seriously contemplating moving on to the next step, that is, the horizontal (or vertical—whatever worked) step, on their next date, already scheduled for this Friday. Things had been progressing nicely. Very nicely. Too nicely, she suspected, when compared to her long line of monster mistakes. Unfortunately, Marissa had a knack for dating men of the serial nature. Not serial killers, but serial cheaters. Though she'd wager that both types of "serials" deserved the same punishment. So far, she'd played second fiddle to a mother, an ex-girlfriend, an additional girlfriend, a guy best friend, and a tuba. She didn't even want to *think* about the tuba.

"What about Jamie?" she finally managed, dreading what she'd learn with that simple question.

Amy gave her one of her half-frowns, then pushed her cheeks toward her eyes in a you-do-it gesture to Candi.

Resignedly, Candi leaned over the side of the couch and scooped up her purse, then dug through the contents until she found her phone. "Here," she said, taking on the tone she used when she wanted Marissa to remember that she was the oldest of the three. At thirty-six, Candi had merely four years on Marissa and six on Amy, but occasionally, she still managed to turn all motherly. Right now, evidently, was one of those occasions. "They say a picture is worth a thousand words." She flipped through the photos on her camera-phone, then winced when she got to the one she wanted. "I took this Friday night when I was out clubbing with Fiona, that new nurse at the hospital. She's really cool, by the way. I think you'd like her, and she said she was already hooked on AtlantaTellAll.com even before she learned I was one of the contributors," Candi said, stalling.

"Candi," Marissa warned.

"I'm sorry." Candi extended her hand.

A flood of apprehension, quite similar to the feeling she experienced before throwing up, washed down

Marissa, starting with the top of her skull then fingering down her body with rapid urgency. She stood and reached for the small red and silver phone. Dreading what she knew she'd see, she turned it . . . and let her jaw fall. Jamie was in an intense all-out gropefest with a tall blond, a six-foot-plus blond with a close-shaved beard, an abundance of muscles, and an even bigger abundance of testosterone. "Super."

"He wasn't the one for you," Amy said, ever the optimist.

Raw, burning heat fisted in Marissa's chest, then slowly, steadily spiraled outward. She fought the impulse to throw the phone—it wasn't hers, after all—and wished like hell that she could throw Jamie . . . under a bus. A Greyhound. With a full capacity of passengers. All sumo wrestlers.

"You know, I kind of wondered if he was really straight after your second date," Candi admitted sleepily, snuggling back into Marissa's overstuffed couch. "Amy's right, though, he wasn't the one."

"What about our second date?" What was wrong with their second date? They had gone to the Atlanta Botanical Gardens, and he held her hand as they admired all of the hot colors, cool sounds, and wild abandon of Orchid Daze, the carnivale-themed celebration of orchids.

"He knew the plant profiles," Amy reminded her. "Isn't that what you said? He told you all about them, in detail."

"Yeah. So?" The fingers on Marissa's right hand tapped harder against the edge of the keyboard. If she'd had fingernails, it would've made a more satisfying clicking sound, but given she continually bit her nails into oblivion, she could produce no more than a dull drumming, which, for some reason, made the situation seem worse. And while the fingers of her right hand stung from her determination to make the damn nubs "click," her left hand squeezed the blood-red cell phone currently showcasing Jamie in a tongue-tangle with another hunk as though she could pop him right out of the screen . . . and break his neck in the process.

It wasn't a bad image.

"I'm betting not many straight guys know flower profiles," Candi said, "if any."

"And if they do, they probably don't admit it," Amy reasoned.

Did they actually think their analysis of yet another of her failed relationships would make her feel better? Marissa glanced again at the photo, then snapped the phone shut. If only she could snap Jamie. Like a twig. "How many is that?" she asked.

"How many is what?" Amy asked.

"Cheaters. Men who've cheated on me. How many? And why have they been so damn plentiful?" She'd been around cheating men most of her life, she realized. When she was a child, her father had filled that unwanted bill; and now, cheaters still kept finding her.

"Oh, it isn't you," Candi said, once again in her motherly, yet sleepy-motherly tone. "It happens to the best of us. I mean, look at me and Cal. We were married, what, eleven years, and he cheated three times. Third time's a charm, I always say," she muttered, her mouth smothered by the gold crocheted afghan Marissa's grandmother had given her for college graduation.

"Why *did* you wait until the third time to dump him?" Amy asked. "I always wondered."

"Who says I dumped him? I kept taking his sorry ass back. Believed him every time he said he'd changed. That last time, though, he didn't come back. Ran off with a girl he met at *my* high school reunion. Always hated Betsy in school. Hate her more now."

"He'll do the same thing to her," Amy said. "Wait and see."

"I hope he does," Candi said, her yawn twisting into a snide smile. "I really hope he does. And at the next reunion, I hope she's fat. And single."

"But that's it," Marissa said, tossing the phone at Candi and ignoring her muffled yelp of protest when it pinged against her arm. "They keep doing it, and there's no way for any of us to know which ones are guilty."

"Who?" Candi asked, rubbing her biceps.

"Cheaters," Marissa said.

"Guilty?" Amy's green eyes glittered as she obviously wondered where Marissa was headed in this conversation.

"Yeah." Marissa's mind churned with a new idea, an idea that she liked. Very much. "Guilty. Someone should warn women about serial cheaters. I mean, the cops have databases where you can find the location of sex offenders, don't they? It only stands to reason that women should be able to find out the location, and the background, of serial cheaters. It's a crime, too, but a crime that hasn't been punished. So far."

Candi blinked, apparently trying to grasp this train of thought with her sleep-deprived brain. "Run that by me again."

Marissa clicked keys on the computer and was oddly satisfied that she *could* generate a clicking noise, even if she couldn't do it with her nails.

Amy stood and gently placed Bo on the couch. Then she took the afghan from Candi and draped it over her son.

"Good thing I like him," Candi said, reaching for yet another blanket from the back of Marissa's recliner. She draped the red fleece over herself and frowned. "This one isn't nearly as soft."

Amy simply laughed as she crossed the room and looked over Marissa's shoulder. "Oh, I like where you're heading," she said, eyeing the Word file currently filling up the screen with Marissa's rapidly growing list of bulleted notes. "A poll of cheaters? The biggest cheater of the week?" Amy read aloud.

"Not exactly," Marissa said, collapsing the document to view the home page of their site, then squinting at the screen as she envisioned a new, highly visible icon, one that would prompt a database completely devoted to exposing cheaters. She opened another Internet window. "Hold on while I check a domain name. We're going to build another site. You up to creating a few logos for me?"

"Sure," Amy said. Every now and then, Marissa found an additional use for Amy's wildly creative mind. Not only could she design sex toys and talk about them in her column, but she was an artiste at web graphics. Consequently, the AtlantaTellAll site was gorgeous, due to Amy's creation of the colorful floral theme.

Marissa accessed godaddy.com, entered her desired domain name, and hoped it wasn't already taken.

"I can start on it in the morning," Amy said, grinning. "Bo can play with Petie while I work on the site."

"Petie?" Candi looked at Marissa. "Dare I ask?"

"A miniature schnauzer," said Marissa. "Bo bought him for me today, and he's asleep on my bed."

"You actually bought her a dog?" Candi asked Amy incredulously. "With her crazy work schedule?"

"Marissa said she wanted someone to keep her company when she sleeps," Amy said. "Bo and I saw him in the pet store, and he thought I should buy him for 'Aunt Rissi.' He even named him Petie."

Marissa looked at the sleeping boy, his mouth open in a kisslike pucker and his hand fisted beneath his chin. "You know, it would make more sense for Bo to have his own dog."

Amy swallowed, cleared her throat. "We've been discussing it," she admitted. "But Landon and I thought it'd be better for him to, you know, be around one first."

"And you decided to let me be the guinea pig for this little training period?" Marissa asked.

"You did say that you hated sleeping alone," Amy reminded her.

"And you had to know I wasn't planning on a canine filling the bill."

"I can't believe you bought her a dog," Candi said, then audibly yawned. "But I'm still staying over. No way can I drive home this tired." She looked at Amy. "Why don't you let Bo take Petie to your apartment overnight? That way I won't have to worry with a furball waking me up all night long wanting to play."

"And Bo can practice learning how often to take him out," Marissa added.

"Oh, never mind," Candi huffed, settling into the couch for a good night's sleep. "Petie can stay here. I don't think even your mother's predawn wake-up call will rattle me, and I imagine I can sleep through you, Bo, and Petie, too."

"Good," Amy said. "Then Bo and I will come over in the morning, and I'll work on the site, while he takes care of Petie."

Marissa grabbed a spiral notebook from the side of her desk. "I'll sketch some basic ideas for the design, but you can switch it out however you want. Then while I'm at work, you set it all up. After I get off, and after Candi has had some sleep, we'll add the finishing touches and start our list of cheaters, beginning with everyone who has ever cheated on the three of us, then we'll advertise the dickens out of the cheater database on our site." She waited while the computer churned, then smiled sinisterly when she paid for the new domain through godaddy. "We got it," she said triumphantly.

"Got what?" Candi asked from her cocoon of covers.

"Exactly what we need to make them all pay, or at least be recognized as the pigs that they are," Marissa said. "And as soon as we get the graphics and links working, the world wide web is in for a real eye-opener of a site."

"What's the name?" Candi asked.

"TheGuyCheats.com," Marissa said, as the door vibrated with a steady, familiar knock.

"I like it," Amy said, hurrying toward the door. She opened it, and a six-foot-plus hunk of male entered, cowboy through and through, from the black Stetson on his gorgeous head to the just-as-black Ropers on his feet. Landon Brooks. Amy's husband, and proof that dreams come true. Amy's dreams, that is. "Hey, honey!" she exclaimed, jumping into his arms. Marissa turned away, not wanting to watch the way Amy's hips naturally curved into his thighs, as if she knew what was coming later. "We're going to start a new site to expose cheaters," Amy said, after Landon planted a soft kiss on her lips, then smiled at their son, dozing peacefully on the sofa.

Landon grinned, and Marissa's heart tripped a bit when she recognized that grin as the same cocky smile the three-year-old on the sofa gave her every time he wanted an extra cookie. Oh, yeah, Landon and Amy were going to have to fight the girls off when Bo hit the teenage years.

"You know, from any other women, a database for cheaters would surprise me," he said.

"But not us?" Candi asked, apparently rousing at the entrance of Amy's cowboy.

"Not in the least." He squeezed Amy, then released her with another impromptu kiss before walking toward the couch. "Sorry I had to work late. We were waiting for the numbers on the new massage oil."

"Caramel apple?" Marissa asked.

Landon winked at Amy. "You're advertising it in your webzine?"

"Like the good little wife I am," she said, while her husband laughed.

He scooped Bo into his arms, then looked at Marissa. "Seems he's taken a liking to your blanket."

Marissa saw the tiny fists clutching the fabric. "No

problem. Take it on home, and he can bring it back to-morrow, when he comes to play with Petie."

"I take it that's Petie?" Landon asked, indicating the doorway to Marissa's bedroom, where the small gray schnauzer stood, looking sleepy-eyed and irritated.

"Bo picked him out at the pet store," Amy said. "He said he wanted to give him to his aunt Rissi, so he can help her take care of him."

"I'm betting he had a little encouragement in making that decision," Marissa said, "but I'll take your word for it." She scooped up the puppy. "It wouldn't hurt to take you outside again, would it?" she asked the dog, who merely licked her hands in response.

"Glad Bo could help," Landon said, chuckling. "So, how is my little tiger?"

"He's perfect," Amy said. "And your other tiger is doing fine, too," she added with a mischievous, wicked grin.

"Is that so?" Landon asked. "Well then, I'm thinking we'd best be getting on home."

"I'll see you tomorrow," Amy sang, leaving Marissa's apartment with Landon and Bo in tow. "I've got to get home."

"Sure thing." Marissa followed them toward the door with Petie. She paused at the doorway and listened to Amy and Landon, laughing as they made their way to their apartment . . . and to their bed. What would that be like, to have a guy, a child, and a life like that?

Petie barked softly, reminding Marissa that he'd yet to feel grass beneath his feet and that his bladder was ready for that to happen, while Candi growled from the couch.

"What is it?" Marissa asked, cradling the puppy.

"Nothing," Candi said. "It's just nice to see people so damn happy."

"Yeah," Marissa whispered wistfully. "It is." Then she took the newest male in her life—correction, the *only* male in her life—out to pee.

Who needs a man? Get a puppy; they're much less trouble.
—MARISSA KINCAID

~

Chapter 2

Tuesday morning began like any other morning, with the telephone impersonating an alarm clock permanently set on 6:00 A.M. Marissa stretched in the bed, rolled over, and fumbled with the lavender receiver. The pale purple cordless phone was a new purchase, to match the new violet comforter she had bought last week. At the time, she'd thought the color symbolized romance, and since she expected to have a little—or a lot—of romance with Jamie, she'd made the spontaneous purchase. Hmph. She should make the cheater pay her back for the phone *and* the comforter, since she definitely wouldn't have any romance here with *him*.

And speaking of her new comforter, Marissa scanned the covers for the gray furball that had, at last check, been snuggled beneath her chin. "Petie?" she questioned, while bringing the receiver to her ear.

"Petie?" Mona Kincaid repeated through the line. "You have a guy there, Marissa? Because, well, I know you're thirty-two and all, but I haven't heard you even mention any 'Petie.' And what kind of name is Petie anyway? It sounds like, well, it sounds like a nickname for a body part, and a none-too-manly part at that." She snickered into the phone. "I've told you before, and I mean it. If you'll just call me the night before, you know, when you're going to have morning company, then I won't call."

"Sure you won't."

"Oh, all right. I'd still call, but I'd wait until I was on my way to work and give you a chance to wake up, or at least get up, or whatever else youngsters do in the morning." She paused. "I remember when your father and I first married, he always woke up ready to go. Mornings were extremely . . ."

"Mom, please," Marissa interrupted. It was way too early to think about her parents having sex. Plus, the fact that Mona Kincaid still thought of sex with Marissa's father—and thought about it positively—bothered Marissa more than she cared to admit, since they had divorced two decades ago.

Mona chuckled and took a loud sip of coffee, judging from the slurp Marissa heard over the line. "Well, who is Petie anyway?"

"Petie isn't a man," Marissa explained. "He's a gray miniature schnauzer puppy, a present from Amy. Or rather, from Bo." She lifted the sheets and comforter and scanned the foot of the bed, but the dog was nowhere to be seen. "And right now, he's missing in action."

"Check your closet. Puppies love shoes, and you've got plenty for him to choose from," Mona offered. "Nice ones even."

Super. Leave it to Amy to give Marissa a puppy with a Jimmy Choo fetish. She darted to the closet, flipped the light switch, and squinted inside, fearing what she'd find. Again, no sign of the pup. "Not there," she said.

"Try the bathroom." Mona didn't sound concerned at all about the fact that a semitrained puppy was on the loose in Marissa's apartment. "Remember how Babs always loved playing with the toilet paper? And tampons, for that matter. You know, I've got that picture of her around here somewhere, the one where she had the tampon in her mouth and it looked like she was puffing a cigar. Where is that picture? She was so cute then." Drawers slammed through the line as Mona evidently searched for the bizarre photo of Babs.

Babs. Only Mona Kincaid would name her dog Barbra, after Barbra Streisand, and call her Babs for short. Surely the diva singer wouldn't appreciate the black-and-white boxer with serious gastric problems bearing her name.

"I'll check." Marissa moved to the bathroom and scanned the tile floor, but there was no sign of Petie. Fortunately, there was no sign that Petie had been there either, as in, no puddles or plops, which was good. Very good.

Typically, Marissa kept her bedroom door shut while she slept. She was fairly certain she'd closed the door last night, but it wasn't closed now, and a gap of at least three inches separated the edge from the frame. "Petie?" Marissa called, pulling the door open.

"Still haven't found him?" Mona asked, slamming more drawers. "Hey, there it is. I've got the picture. Lord, that was a cute dog. I really miss her. Tell you what, I'll put the photo on the fridge so you can see it next time you come over." Shuffled paper and snapping magnets filled Marissa's ear as Mona evidently rearranged her refrigera-

tor collage to best showcase Babs with her tampon-cigar.
"Find him?" Mona asked.

Marissa grinned at the dog, more salt-and-pepper
colored than plain gray, she noticed, as daylight filtered
through the wooden slats of the blinds in her living room
and glistened against his coat. His ears pricked at the
sound of her voice, and round black eyes widened as he
raised his head from Candi's stomach.

"Shhh," Candi soothed, and placed a hand on his back,
while he raised his brows at Marissa as though asking if
she were more inclined to play than the woman currently
holding him hostage.

"Yes, I found him," Marissa whispered.

Petie emitted a soft bark and tilted his head, while
Candi squinted at Marissa. "I already took him out twice,"
she said, "but I'm betting he has to go again. I think he
has a bladder the size of a thimble, don't you, Petie?" The
puppy yelped happily, then scurried up her chest to lick
her chin.

Candi turned from the long, silver whiskers brushing
her neck and gently lifted the dog toward Marissa. "Here,
you take him this time. It's the least you can do, since he's
yours and all. He drove me crazy."

"Yeah, I can tell by the way you cuddled him," Marissa
said, balancing the phone between shoulder and ear so
she could take the puppy, then grinning when he darted
another thorough lick across Candi's cheek before shifting his attention to Marissa's forearm.

"Who's that?" Mona asked.

"Candi. She spent the night."

"Candi wants a puppy?"

"Mom asked if you want a puppy," Marissa relayed.

"I just told you, he drove me crazy," Candi said, turning her back toward Marissa and burying her face in the pillow.

"Yeah, Mom, I think she does."

"Do not," Candi said, but Marissa only laughed.

Petie thoroughly licked her arm as she headed toward the door and grabbed the red rhinestone-embellished leash that Amy had evidently purchased to match his collar. After snapping it on, she opened the door and saw Noodle sniffing her sidewalk. "Hello, Mr. Nance."

The elderly apartment manager smiled guiltily, his face cracking into wrinkles with the process, and led the little dachshund away from his preferred "spot."

"Tell Henry I said hello," Mona informed her.

"My mom says hi," Marissa said, putting Petie on the sidewalk then watching as he and Noodle sniffed each other's behinds. *Dogs.*

"Hi, Mona!" Mr. Nance called toward the purple phone, then once again, he worked to lead the little wiener-looking dog away from Marissa's tiny yard. After barking at the retreating Noodle, Petie started his own round of sniffing and, blessedly, christened the backside of a bush as his private area of choice.

"Hold on a second. I've got to put my shirt over my head," Mona said, and Marissa heard the phone thunk against the counter. By the time her mother returned, Marissa and Petie were back inside, with Petie whining at the nurse sleeping on the couch. Candi leaned over, scooped him up, and nestled him in the crook of her arm, where Petie contentedly laid his head.

"Don't say a word," Candi warned, then closed her eyes and apparently drifted right back to sleep.

Marissa continued to the bedroom and chose clothes for the day, a red sleeveless silk blouse and black pants. Computer programmers weren't known for style, but she tried to at least hit the business-casual mark. "So, what's on your agenda today?" she asked, pulling a coordinating belt from the closet. Mona's job as an ad rep at the *Atlanta Journal-Constitution* didn't provide a whole lot of variety to her weekdays, but that didn't mean she didn't want to talk about it.

"We've got some specials running this week for new clients, so I'm betting I'll be swamped. Run an ad two times and get a third insertion free. You should take advantage of it with your webzine. I've been wanting to advertise it for quite a while, and with the special, it's a bargain."

"Always pitching your product, Mom?" Marissa grabbed a shoebox from her closet and removed the black slingbacks. Then she thought about the ad special. Her mother was right; it was a good deal. "You know, I may use that special after all, as soon as we get our new site up and running."

"New site?"

Marissa moved to the bathroom and started the water running in the tub while providing a succinct explanation of Jamie, the guy-loving rat fink, of the subsequent idea she had to start a cheater database, and then finally of how she, Amy, and Candi were going to kick off the new database ASAP. "We'll start it with men who've cheated on us, and Lord knows, I've got plenty to get us going."

"You have had your share, haven't you, dear?" Mona asked.

"I'll say." Marissa tested the water, then adjusted

the temperature for more heat. She liked a scalding hot bath, particularly when she was frustrated. And Jamie's sexual preferences, or the lack thereof, had her feeling frustrated.

"How far back are you going? With the cheaters, I mean. Are you including the ones from college? High school?"

Marissa looked in the mirror and frowned. She *had* encountered more than her share of cheaters, and her mother was right; it had started a long time ago. Way too far back to remember the very first cheater. No, that wasn't true. She *did* remember. "Farther than that," she said. "I'm going to start at the beginning, with that dweeb who backed out on the Sadie Hawkins dance, after it took me two weeks to get up the nerve to ask him, and went to the movies with Donna Pritchett instead. Yeah, I'm going to start with him, Trent Jackson."

"Goodness, dear, that's a bit extreme, don't you think? What were you then—thirteen?"

Marissa grinned. "Yeah, I agree that adding him is pushing it, but think about it; I could list cheaters all the way back to junior high. Shoot, I could even include his yearbook photo. He was so skinny, remember? I mean, it wouldn't be a serious cheater, like the ones I've had as an adult, but adding a thirteen-year-old cheater as the starting point would give the site a little humor, you know?" And, Marissa realized, it would also let her site visitors see that she could poke fun at her situation, even if, deep down inside, she knew she hated the fact that she was a repeat *cheatee*. "Yeah," she said. "I'll start with Trent Jackson."

"Trent Jackson," Mona repeated slowly. "Mercy, that

name sure sounds familiar. Wait a minute. I remember now. Isn't Trent Jackson the guy who owns that other—"

Water pooling around Marissa's bare feet took her attention from her mother's conversation. "Mom, I've got to let you go. My bath is running over."

"Oh, goodness, bye!" Mona squealed.

Marissa tossed the phone onto the counter, slid across the floor to twist the nozzles and turn the water off, then started damage control by tossing towels around her feet. Petie, evidently hearing the commotion and vacating his position on Candi's tummy, poked his silver head around the corner then bolted in to lap at the wet floor. His whiskers converted from white to blond as they grew damp, and Marissa smiled at the cute pup, eagerly helping her clean up her mess and, for the moment, keeping her mind off her eternal string of cheating men.

Hell hath no fury like a woman scorned, and a scorned woman can be great for publicity.
— TRENT JACKSON

Chapter 3

"You realize I don't like what you're telling me," Trent Jackson said, tapping a pen against his desktop while his financial advisor, and consequently, his best friend, tied his hands again.

"I'd say that you *hate* what I'm telling you," Keith Parker said. "But I've still gotta say it. You don't pay me to shoot you bull."

Trent swiveled in his chair to view his computer monitor, prominently displaying the DieHardAtlanta balance sheet. It looked like plenty of money to him. "I know you're the expert and all," he started, then stopped when Keith shook his head and held up his palms. "What?" Trent asked.

"I'm not going to sit here and listen to you tell me that you believe me but are still doing things the way you want. I've been to this dance before, and I'm about sick of the tune. Come on, Trent. You're as smart as they come with computer software and websites, but you don't know shit about your finances. That's what I'm for, and I promise that if you try to take DieHardAtlanta to a print edition now, it won't fly." He held up one finger. "You need more equity." Another finger joined the first. "You need more subscribers." A third finger. "You need more exposure." The fourth finger popped up. "And you need more advertising."

Keith's hand displayed the equivalent of a "fourth quarter's ours" sign. Funny, the familiar gesture had symbolized victory when Trent played football in high school. Right now, however, it indicated defeat. And Trent wasn't used to defeat in business, or anything else. Jacksons didn't lose, and Trent wasn't about to break the family record by trying to increase his business too soon. But he was tired of waiting.

Dropping his palm, Keith gave Trent a semiapologetic smirk. "People aren't going to visit your website if they can't find it. Right now, you're doing okay via word of mouth, but you need other forms of advertising to succeed, and you need money to pay for the ads."

"I've scheduled an ad campaign with the *Atlanta Journal-Constitution*," Trent reminded him, "which you suggested."

"Good. Then let's see how many new subscribers the *AJ-C* nets you. Maybe that'll put you in the right ballpark for starting the print side. The way I see it, your numbers need to quadruple before you take the risk."

An increase of four hundred percent? "You're not serious." Trent's voice was as unemotional as he could muster for the blow Keith had dealt. Quadruple? Did Keith have any idea how long it would take to make a jump like that without some earth-shattering dynamic thrown in the mix? Did he think John Smoltz would suddenly find the site impossible to resist and perhaps emblazon the web address on the back of his Braves jersey? Because *that's* the kind of boost Keith was talking about, and that was the kind of boost Trent had no idea how to obtain.

"I'm dead serious. If you want this thing to make it and come out of the gate strong, the way you indicated when you asked me to analyze this venture, then you really need to heed my advice. Wait and let your numbers increase. They've gone up steadily every month, right?"

"Steadily. That's the operative word," Trent said. "Four hundred percent wouldn't begin to count as steadily. That's warp speed, and you know it. I'd need something huge, and I don't have any white rabbits in my hat." He took a thick breath, let it out. Four hundred percent. To increase circulation that much, he'd need a hell of an advertising campaign. And to have a hell of an advertising campaign, he'd have to use the majority of the money he'd made so far. Therefore, no money for the new business. A lose-lose situation, any way you looked at it, unless he was willing to wait and let things steadily progress, as Keith suggested. It made sense, but it sure didn't make Trent happy. "You know, when my father suggested I always rely on Parker and Parker to steer me in the right direction, I don't think he ever planned on *you* monitoring my every financial move. Hell, when he died, Parker and Parker Financial consisted of your grandfather and your father. I'm sure he assumed it'd be one of them overseeing his legacy."

"Nah, Collin knew I'd take over. Dad told him plenty of times that he was pursuing an extremely early retirement in Florida. Face it, your father knew exactly what he was doing. You can tell yourself different, but you know it's true. He wanted me to help you keep your mind straight. Remember, I was always the kid who saved a portion of his allowance, then began to spend. You, on the other hand, were another story." Keith walked over to the small refrigerator Trent kept in his office, withdrew a bottle of water, and took a big swallow. It sloshed loudly as he drank. Normally, the sound wouldn't have irritated Trent, but right now, every agitated drop bubbled beneath his skin.

Keith wiped his mouth with the back of his hand and shrugged. "But the main thing your father wanted was for his inheritance to be monitored by a Parker, and you've got that." He pointed to his chest. "I'm a Parker."

"A Parker who keeps saying no."

"I haven't exactly said no," Keith reminded. "I said that if you're seriously wanting to start this magazine on your own, without any assets already established by Jackson Enterprises—"

"Assets my father and grandfather generated," Trent interrupted.

"Right. If you're wanting to say that you did this entirely on your own, then I suggest you wait until DieHardAtlanta is a stronger force with proven staying power. You've seen my reports. DieHardAtlanta is doing great, considering you've only had the webzine for six months."

"And in that time my circulation has grown every month," Trent said. He turned to view the Atlanta skyline from his office window. No, from his *father's* office window. This place had been handed to him, too, as *Atlanta Business Journal* suggested in its "Boy With a

Silver Spoon" article. *Boy*. Since when was thirty-three considered "boy" status? Or guys who were six-two? Trent glared at the darkening sky, the clouds cloaking the skyrise buildings like smoky capes. The clouds weren't all that substantial, but they still had the potency to hide those impressive buildings that lurked beneath.

Boy. The word brought back memories of his childhood, when he was eternally hidden by his father's shadow, the skinny kid with untamable hair and glasses whose family happened to own a substantial portion of Atlanta. Could Trent help it if his grandfather had been wise enough—or stupid enough, depending on how you looked at it—to buy land during the Depression, when everyone else was buying food? True, Erskine Jackson nearly starved his family in the process, but now his descendants had plenty to keep them sustained for years to come. But Trent's father had taken the money and made more. And more. And more. Wise investments and more than a little luck, and he tripled the Jacksons' already-substantial portfolio.

Problem was, Trent wasn't the kind of guy to mooch off his father's triumph. He wanted to make a name for himself, the way his father had, and he wanted to do it with money *he* generated. He'd always had an interest in the process of publication, specifically of putting his name on something that would be valued as an informative, yet innovative, form of media. He'd seen the opportunity to do that with the rise of webzine popularity, and he started his venture with DieHardAtlanta, an e-zine devoted to the testosterone segment of Atlanta. Articles focused on the highlights of male adulthood—cars, sports, and women.

So far, the online publication was doing very well, and with minimum overhead incurred producing it on the web, Trent had already turned a nice profit. But the money wasn't the problem; the circulation was. He needed more people already hooked on DieHardAtlanta before he added a print edition. Sure, he could put the magazine on the shelves, but if people weren't primed to buy it, it'd be useless paper. Bottom line, he didn't have enough subscribers to pursue the real goal, adding a DieHardAtlanta print format that would eventually cover not only Atlanta interests, but interests in every large city around the country. And then the smaller cities. And then the world.

Might as well dream big.

But after examining the DieHardAtlanta financials, Keith had confirmed what Trent already suspected. He wasn't ready to run with the big dogs, which really pissed him off. What else did he have to do? How could he get his name out more quickly, without sinking every dime he made into the process?

"I'll give you another bit of advice as well," Keith said.

"Why should you stop now?" Trent's thumb pressed solidly against the side of the pen until he felt the cylinder give. Having no desire to spray ink all over his desk, he put the thing down and waited for Keith's next suggestion.

"You need to get your name out there. People don't only need to know the magazine. They need to know you, Trent Jackson."

"You think last month's article in the *Atlanta Business Journal* didn't get my name out there?" Trent asked. "Or do you honestly think people in this city don't know about Jackson Enterprises?"

"They do, but I'm not talking about Jackson Enterprises,

or even an article that refers to Collin Jackson's son. They didn't even call you by your name, you know."

"Sure they did," Trent challenged. "I read it."

"I did, too, and I read it again last night when I googled you online. You're listed as 'Collin Jackson's son, Trenton Jameson Jackson, also known as T.J.,' and they didn't even include a photo. Not much name recognition, if you ask me, particularly since the only people who called you T.J. were your folks. And that would have been the perfect article to mention your new business venture, but DieHardAtlanta wasn't anywhere on the page. It talked about your father, your grandfather, and the current descendant, who is, according to the journalist, merely living off his inheritance."

Keith was right. As far as advertising Trent's name, that particular article hadn't done it. Great. First he takes a hit by the magazine for being born a Jackson, and then he can't even use the article as a selling point to boost his advertising potential.

"Have you googled your name lately?" Keith continued.

"No. Why should I?" Trent watched the smoky clouds rise above Atlanta's skyline as darkness deepened around the illuminated buildings. The peaks of the architectural beauties claimed dominion once more and screamed to be seen and noticed. The way Trent wanted to be seen and noticed.

"I wondered if I should mention it." Keith leaned back in one of Trent's guest chairs and frowned as though pondering how much to tell. "But I did find your name prominently displayed on one website, not that I think it'll do much to increase your DieHardAtlanta business. But still, it is out there. And there *is* an accompanying photo."

"Where?" Trent asked. Prominently displayed? Wasn't that a good thing? Exactly what they were wanting, in fact? But if it were, then why did Keith have that odd look on his face? The one he always got when the two of them were kids and trying to hide a secret. Like the time they wanted to see how long it'd take Trent's parents to realize they'd dumped an abundance of green Kool-Aid mix in the swimming pool to celebrate St. Patrick's.

"Does the name Marissa Kincaid ring any bells?" Keith asked.

Marissa Kincaid. *Rissi.* Talk about a blast from the past. He hadn't seen Rissi Kincaid since—what?—junior high? But yeah, the name did ring bells, lots of bells. The intriguing girl with the jet-black hair and equally dark eyes definitely gave him a reason to get out of bed and go to school each morning. Rissi Kincaid was sassy beyond her years, and sexy as hell, for an eighth grader. Trent smirked. Did Rissi Kincaid still remember him, too? Obviously she did, or Keith wouldn't have found Trent's name on the Net . . . with Rissi's name? And where? Her blog, perhaps? Or another place?

"Was it classmates.com?" he asked, unable to mask the curiosity piqued by Keith's mention of her name. Rissi Kincaid had moved to Florida after junior high, and Trent never saw her again. Since they didn't graduate from high school together, he hadn't seen her at reunions and therefore had no idea whether her hair was still as wild, or still as black, or whether those almond-shaped eyes and that raspy voice could still make his breathing hitch a notch.

Then again, he was a young, inexperienced teen back

then. Times had changed. But he couldn't deny that there was a definite curiosity spiking at wondering what had happened to Rissi. Had the girl who invaded most of his teenage fantasies turned out as sexy as he'd anticipated? Hell, he should have looked her up, but then again, he hadn't really thought about her in years. Until now. "Or was it a web log?" he asked.

"Google your name." Keith remained seated, but indicated the computer screen, which had converted from the DieHardAtlanta balance sheet to Trent's screen saver, the webzine's logo. The bold image, "DieHardAtlanta" in thick red letters with a collage of sports, cars, and women beneath, disappeared when Trent moved the mouse. He quickly accessed the Google site, entered his name in the search engine, and waited.

Of the results displayed on the page, the only "Trent" and "Jackson" that actually referred to him was the first one, on a site listed as TheGuyCheats.com, and the partial amount of verbiage displayed for the reference inferred that "as you can tell from the photo, my string of cheaters started a long time ago, with a boy named *Trent Jackson* . . ."

"What the hell," he muttered, clicking on the link. A painfully bright conglomeration of red, pink, and white filled his screen, and Trent winced as his eyes adjusted to the colorful invasion. On the left side of the screen, a waterfall of sorts trickled steadily down the edge, a waterfall of what appeared to be . . . hearts? "What is this?"

"That?" Keith couldn't hold his chuckle as he explained. "That is an offshoot of the ever-popular Atlanta TellAll site."

"AtlantaTellAll?" Trent squinted to follow the path of

the continual waterfall. The multitude of tiny pink, white, and red hearts fell aimlessly to the bottom of the screen, where they all cracked open like broken pottery. "What's AtlantaTellAll?"

"I guess you could call it the female counterpart to your DieHardAtlanta," Keith said. "It's a place for women to get all the latest info on events, and gossip . . . oh, and sex."

Trent's brows hitched up a notch. "And you found my name there?" Had one of his former conquests said something about him on the site? And wouldn't that be a good thing? He wasn't the type to brag, but Trent knew damn well that he was good in bed. True, it wasn't exactly the type of advertising he'd planned to use to garner interest in DieHardAtlanta, but hey, if it worked . . .

However, he'd never been in bed with Rissi Kincaid. And *that* was the name Keith had mentioned.

"Like I said, this isn't AtlantaTellAll; it's an offshoot. That site has all of the interesting columns. This one is more of an insightful database. And you're in it."

Trent read the site name again. TheGuyCheats.com. "I'm listed in a cheater database?"

"You're not only listed; you happen to be cheater number one, if you sort them chronologically. If you sort alphabetically, though, you're near the middle." Keith tried, and failed, to keep a straight face.

There were four broken hearts, bright red with thick jagged gaps in the center, lining the right side of the screen. The top heart displayed a guy's photo, a surfer-looking dude with a smile a little too bright and a tan a lot too orange. Beneath the heart was the guy's name, Deke Rivers, and the caption *Cheater of the Day*. His face

looked even more odd with the jagged gap in the center.
The second heart was filled with words, and Trent had to
move back and forth between the broken pieces to read
a Patty Loveless song title. Beneath that heart was the
caption *Song of the Day*. The third broken heart had the
words "Tell Us What You Think" written across the two
halves, and the caption signified *Cheater Polls*. And the
final heart was labeled *The Cheaters*.

Trent clicked on the last broken heart, and a vibrant
red page sprang to life with *Cheater Database* stamped
prominently across the top. Beneath the words, male photos formed a checkered pattern on the screen. And the first
of those photos was Trent. In eighth grade.

The photo, obviously scanned from that hideous yearbook shot, captured the self-conscious adolescent who hid
behind a mop of black waves and glasses. A Harry Potter
type who had yet to realize that he was, indeed, rather
cool. Trent was smiling in the picture, but it was a forced
smile that said he was only doing it because he was supposed to, and he looked like he wanted to be anywhere but
in front of that camera. *That* was the photo Rissi chose to
put on this site? Because there was no doubt that she had
put him on this odd list; the subtitles beneath his picture
identified him as *Trent Jackson, Cheater*, followed with
another line designating Marissa Kincaid as *Cheatee*.

Trent scanned the photos, fifteen of them, five rows of
three head shots. Then the bottom of the screen indicated
over ten more pages of cheaters. He scrolled down the
sidebar to view the other guys on page one and noted that
four of them had the same cheatee, Marissa. No wonder
she was pissed. This was exactly what the feisty girl he
knew in junior high would do to anyone who hurt her;

she'd get even. He'd always admired her spunk and sass back then, but that was before she put him on her cheating list. And why? He'd never even dated Rissi Kincaid, much less cheated on her.

"I'm the first one?" he asked.

"Only because the default sorting method is chronological. You can change that, but I assume most people don't." He smiled. "Click on your photo, heartbreaker," Keith instructed.

"This doesn't make sense," Trent said, moving the mouse again. "She's confused. We never dated. Hell, she left before high school."

"Click the photo," Keith repeated, smirking, damn him.

Trent did, and read the details on the screen.

As you can tell from the photo, my string of cheaters started a long time ago, with a boy named Trent Jackson. I admit that adding him to my personal list of cheaters is stretching it a bit, but hey, I have to start the list with someone, and he is the first guy who broke my heart.

What did he do, you ask? Okay. Picture this. A thirteen-year-old girl in eighth grade is afraid she's going to be the only one who doesn't have a date for the Sadie Hawkins dance. You all know about the Sadie Hawkins thing, don't you? That's where traditional roles are reversed and girls ask guys to the dance. Not an easy task for a girl that age, let me tell you. But I'd been friends with Trent and thought he was a safe bet. I actually thought he had something of a crush on me, so I wasn't surprised when he said he'd go. But then, the week of the dance, I got braces. And wouldn't you know, the night of the dance, after I'd spent the entire day getting ready to go with all of my friends,

Trent Jackson called and canceled. And he went to the movies with Donna Pritchett instead. He may have said my "metal mouth" wasn't a big deal, but I knew it was, and the fact that he went out with Donna and left me to go to the dance alone proved it.

From that point on, my life has been filled with cheaters, as you saw on the previous page. So that's why Trent is here. Now, if you know any other cheating stories about Trent Jackson, please, by all means, dish here. That's what we're here for, to warn the world of cheaters and take preventive measures against future broken hearts.—Marissa

"Hey, at least none of your old flames have posted any comments," Keith said, leaning forward to view the screen from his spot on the opposite side of the desk. "A shame they don't have a more current picture."

"Yeah, a real shame," Trent said sarcastically. Rissi did this? After twenty years?

Keith laughed, then settled back in his chair. "Hell, it isn't really a bad thing. More funny than anything else. I mean, she hasn't even associated you with DieHard Atlanta, so it shouldn't do anything to hurt your business, but I did think you'd want to see it. You know, if they had one of these for women, I could add one to the list, but the rules state male cheaters only." Keith's ex-wife had left him for her boss three years ago, and the guy hadn't quite gotten over it yet. "But that's neither here nor there. What's important is that this site shouldn't hurt your DieHardAtlanta business. It's obviously a site meant to let female cheatees vent their frustrations. And you've got to admit, it's a rather imaginative idea. That Marissa Kincaid must be quite the character."

"She was twenty years ago," Trent said. Obviously she was still as spirited now.

"Well, like I said, this really shouldn't hurt your business. Too bad it isn't an advertising angle we could use to give you the exposure you need for DieHardAtlanta. Kind of hard to publicize that the preteen kid on TheGuy Cheats.com is someone who deserves to have his magazine purchased."

Trent stared at his picture on the screen. An idea played across his thoughts, then the notion began to solidify, and Trent smiled.

"What?" Keith asked.

"Maybe this isn't the angle we were looking for to advertise DieHardAtlanta, and me," Trent said. "But that doesn't mean that we can't use Rissi's unusual database to our advantage."

"Okay, I'll bite," Keith said, his blue eyes intense with anticipation. "What have you got in mind?"

"Watch and see." Trent laughed. This was going to be fun, a chance to do a bit of sparring with an old friend and help his webzine grow in the process. And the fact that the old friend was Rissi Kincaid only made it better. He could hardly wait.

In the same manner that a red tie defines power for males, the red dress defines power for females. Power . . . and sex.
—AMY BROOKS

Chapter 4

Y ou're sure about the red dress?" Marissa asked. She had a time trying to decide which outfit to wear for this interview. If her picture made it into the *AJ-C*, she wanted to look good. Damn good. Smart and confident and successful, like a woman who has everything going for her . . . even if her history of being cheated on was now on the Net for the world to see.

What had she been thinking?

"I'm sure," Amy said. "And it's a little late to change anyway. The reporter and the photographer have already seen you."

Marissa's hand moved toward her mouth, then she shook her head and put it back in her lap. She would *not* be biting her fingernails when the reporter returned. She'd maintain her composure if it killed her, and if her heart kept racing, it just might.

Amy scooted closer to her on the couch, propped her arm on the back, and gave Marissa's shoulder a comforting squeeze. "Calm down. Trust me, this is a good thing. I remember when I was at Adventurous Accessories, the *Atlanta Journal* ran a story on Pinky, and my sales went off the chart. Having them request a feature story on TheGuyCheats.com is pure gold. It's the kind of publicity you can't buy."

Marissa forced a smile. "Pinky" was the G-spot-finding vibrator Amy had developed when she was still employed by the famed sex product company. Obviously, Amy Brooks didn't mind being known for her part in Pinky's success. However, Marissa being known for her part in the success of TheGuyCheats.com meant Marissa being known as a woman who'd been cheated on . . . fifteen times! Not that she'd ever actually counted them, but the *Atlanta Journal* reporter obviously had; she mentioned it when she requested the interview. And was that *really* something Marissa wanted as the feather in her cap? And did it matter now? Because come Sunday, merely three days from now, not only would her cheatee history be on the web, it'd be in print, for all of the *AJ-C*'s circulation to see.

"Candi has been in there for a while," Marissa said, listening to the muffled voices beyond the closed door to her kitchen. The reporter had asked to do the interview at Marissa's office so she could get a feel for the work environment where the three women created the webzine. When Marissa explained that they worked in her apartment, the journalist didn't miss a beat. She asked to interview them here, and Marissa agreed. Now she wondered whether that had been a mistake. This wasn't exactly a professional setting, but then again, many online businesses were run out of homes, right? So it wasn't such a bad thing, was it?

Amy reached for Marissa's forearm and gently tugged it to move her hand from her mouth. Marissa hadn't even realized she'd started biting her nails . . . again.

"Is this not the woman who said she wanted this thing to succeed so she could quit the day job?" Amy asked.

"Yeah," Marissa said, "but—"

"Uh-uh," Amy said, shaking her head and sending her ponytail swinging. "No buts. This is what you wanted, what *we* wanted, and we're going for it. And you have to admit that we're doing it right. We only started the new website two weeks ago, and we've already got the attention of one of the biggest newspapers in the South. What's not to be proud of?"

Marissa thought about that and realized Amy was right. This *was* what she wanted, even if it left her a tad vulnerable with everyone knowing her pathetic dating history. And really, was the fact that everyone would learn about it what was bothering her, or was it the fact that she'd never—not once—ended up the victor in the relationship? Or even the one who left someone else wondering what went wrong? And why the hell hadn't she been? Because she was too nice, that's why. And she was tired of it.

"Whoa, what's up with that?" Amy asked, one dark brow raised in curiosity.

"What?"

"That glare that says you want to hurt someone. Five seconds ago you looked like you wanted to throw up. Care to share what you're thinking, because I'm betting it's good."

A soft knock sounded at the door, and Marissa, sus-

pecting who was on the other side, got up to answer it
without responding to Amy's question. She'd just given
herself a mental kick to the caboose, and that was all that
mattered. She'd do this interview, and she'd let women
everywhere know that no one, not Marissa or anyone else,
deserves to be cheated on. She pulled the door open and
smiled.

"Mama done yet?" Bo asked. He'd obviously just
woken up, and evidently his daddy hadn't done a very
good job at removing his bedhead. Blond curls sprang
outward in all directions, primarily straight up. He cradled
a squirming Petie in his arms while Landon stood behind
them grinning. Amy had volunteered Landon and Bo to
watch Petie during the interview, but evidently, Bo's curiosity had gotten the best of him. He peeked in and gave
Amy a smile so big that Marissa was certain she could see
all his tiny white baby teeth. Lord, he was a cute kid. "Ya
done?" he asked. "Daddy's gotta go to work."

"Not yet, sweetie," Amy said, as the kitchen door
opened and Candi came out. Having come straight from
work to the interview, she wore red scrubs with a matching red scrunchie holding back her long hair. The reporter
seemed even more excited about the fact that one of the
three women producing the webzine worked at Grady
Memorial and asked to interview Candi first. No doubt
she covered Candi's day job as part of her story. Marissa's day job as a computer programmer for Web Solutions wasn't nearly as exciting, but Marissa suspected
they wouldn't cover much of her day job anyway. She
assumed they'd cover her dating history, and suddenly,
she felt quite ready to expose the details of it. To say how
she'd been done wrong and how she was determined to

never let it happen again, to herself or any other woman. The cheater database at TheGuyCheats.com would ensure that, and it had been Marissa's idea. Amy was right. Why shouldn't she be proud?

"Your mom is next," Candi told Bo, "and while she's in there, you and I can play with Petie, if you want. We can go to the playground." She turned her attention to Landon. "You can go on to work. Bo can stay with me until Amy's done. No problem. I'm on the first day of three days off, so I'd love to spend time playing with Bo."

"Sounds good," Landon said, while Amy made her way to the door to kiss her husband bye.

"I'm glad you were able to go in late," she said. "I didn't want to wake Bo up, and I'm sure he enjoyed the two of you playing with Petie this morning."

"That's what he told me," Landon said, smiling at his son, then giving Amy another kiss. "See you tonight." Then he turned toward Bo and the dog. "And I'll see you tonight, too." He ruffled Bo's blond curls, then scratched behind Petie's ears, while the puppy licked his son's chin. "You have fun on the playground with Candi and Petie."

"I will," Bo said, producing another wide smile.

"Ms. Brooks, are you ready?" The pretty blond journalist stood at the kitchen doorway and smiled at Amy. Marissa had already forgotten the woman's name, probably due to her nervousness, but she didn't want to ask her to repeat it. She'd find out when the article ran anyway.

"I won't be long," Amy told Bo, "and then I'll come find you at the playground."

"Okay," the toddler said, appeased. "You ready to go?" he asked Candi, while his mother turned her attention to the reporter.

Marissa waited for the kitchen door to close, then held up a hand to stop Candi's exit at the door. "What's her name? The reporter, I mean," she whispered.

"Vivian," Candi said. "Vivian Moore, I believe."

"What did she ask?"

Candi placed a hand on Bo's small back. "Tell you what, let your daddy help you get some of your toy trucks together so we can take them with us and play in the sandbox. When you get done, I'll be ready to go."

"You may need this when you get to the playground," Landon said, grabbing Petie's leash from a hook by the door and handing it to Candi. "And I'll go get Bo's toys together."

"Thanks." Candi waited for them to leave, then listened for the voices beyond the kitchen door. After she heard Amy talking, she quietly told Marissa, "She asked about my job, then about how the webzine got started, where we came up with the idea for AtlantaTellAll, then TheGuyCheats, that kind of thing. Naturally, she asked about my history with cheaters," she added.

"And?"

Candi shrugged. "I told her the truth, that I've only had one guy that cheated on me, but he did it repeatedly, and unfortunately, we were married at the time. Basically, I told her that Cal was listed in our cheater database and that she could read all about him there. I hope she writes about him, and I hope he sees it," she said. "Shoot, I hope everyone he knows sees it. It'll serve him right."

"Yeah," Marissa said, thinking about the guys she had personally listed on the site. "It'll serve them all right."

"I've got my toys!" Bo called, his little-boy voice echoing from his yard. "Ready to go?"

"I'm ready," Candi called through the open doorway. "Come on, Petie."

Petie lifted his head from his water bowl in the kitchen and, seeing the leash, ran to Candi.

"He's excited," Marissa said.

"Good," Candi answered. "You should be, too." She gave Marissa a thumbs-up, mouthed, "You'll do great," then left.

Fortunately, by the time Amy emerged from her interview, Marissa was completely calm, cool, and collected, and ready to tell the world why she had started the cheater database and how she felt about each of the men listed on the site's pages.

"Have fun," Amy encouraged, leaving Marissa's apartment with a smile on her face and her green eyes glittering in apparent anticipation of playing with her son on the playground. "When you get done, come find us."

"Will do," Marissa said, while the photographer and journalist stepped forward from the kitchen.

"Ms. Kincaid, is this the area where you typically work?" the woman asked, pointing to Marissa's laptop, set up at its traditional perch on the circular table in her breakfast nook.

"Yes. I normally work on the computer in the evenings, when we're brainstorming or beginning one of our polls, but Amy takes over while I'm at work. And we can each add our articles and information online via an administration section of the site." Marissa knew she was rambling, but she couldn't help it. She took a deep breath in, let it out, and attempted to will herself to control her nervousness. She silently repeated Amy's words like a mantra for the day. *This is a good thing. This is a good thing . . .*

"And you spend your days as a computer pro-grammer?"

"Yes," Marissa said, grateful for the easy question.

"Can we get a couple of photos of you working?" the woman continued.

"Sure." Marissa sat behind the computer, then rested her hands on the keyboard and smiled as the photographer pointed his lens in her direction.

"Good. Now, can you bring up your website, please? I'd like to get a shot of you actually working on the site," the reporter continued, scratching some notes on a long, skinny reporter's log.

Marissa complied, opening a web browser and click-ing on AtlantaTellAll from her list of favorites. The floral home page surged to life, and she turned toward the pho-tographer, now behind her, to smile for the camera. She hoped the vibrant colors on the screen showed up well for the photo; Amy had worked hard to create a fun, lively site, and Marissa wanted the photograph in the paper to do it justice.

"And you access the new website, the cheater database site, from this one, correct?" the reporter asked. "Can you show me how you do that?"

"Yes," Marissa said, thinking this interview thing wasn't so bad after all. She moved the pointer toward the only image on the screen that wasn't in the shape of a flower, a bright red heart with a dagger piercing its center. "Visitors can simply click on this icon, labeled *TheGuyCheats.com*, to access our cheater database site."

The photographer snapped more pictures while Ma-rissa clicked on the heart and watched the screen change to the familiar waterfall of breaking hearts.

"I love that graphic," the reporter—Vivian Moore, as Candi had informed her—said. "Can you get a picture of that for me, Carl?" The photographer snapped a few shots, while Marissa grew more comfortable with this scenario. It wasn't bad at all, showing what she, Amy, and Candi had created.

"Tell me about those broken hearts on the side," Vivian said, withdrawing a tape recorder from her purse. "Okay if I tape this? It'll make it easier for me to make sure you're quoted correctly."

"Sure," Marissa said, then she clicked on each of the broken hearts to show the woman the pages for the *Cheater of the Day, Song of the Day, Cheater Polls,* and, of course, *The Cheaters.* The woman seemed particularly interested in the photos of cheaters and asked Marissa about the young boy leading the list, Trent Jackson.

Marissa smirked. "Actually, he's the first guy who ever cheated on me, and even though we were only thirteen at the time, I thought he belonged on the list." She looked at the photo, so different from the others on the first page. "I guess I added him to show that I've been dealing with cheaters for quite a while."

"Why is his photo first?"

"Right now, the photos are listed chronologically, based on the date the cheating occurred. His, of course, is the earliest so far." Marissa used the mouse to move the cursor to the sort field at the top of the screen. "Site visitors can also sort cheaters alphabetically by first or last name," she said. "I'll show you." She started to change the sorting method, but Vivian held up her hand.

"No, that's fine," she said. "I'd rather see an actual

cheater page. Can you select his page?" She pointed to Trent Jackson.

Marissa nodded and smiled. Vivian Moore must have picked up on the humor behind adding Marissa's youngest cheater to the list, and Marissa was glad she had. It would show the *AJ-C* readers that Marissa had a fun side, too. She clicked on Trent Jackson's photo.

"So he's the fellow that started it all?" Vivian asked, indicating the teen photo filling the screen, then nodding toward her photographer to get another shot. Carl took several, his camera clicking wildly with every twitch of his finger on the button. "Do you think that perhaps you blame him for your rough luck with guys ever since, because he initiated the pattern for others to follow?" Vivian Moore smiled sweetly, a little too sweetly, in Marissa's opinion.

Marissa swallowed, blinked. "No, I wouldn't say that I blame him," she said, her confidence sliding a hair.

"But he *was* the first one to do you wrong," Vivian said.

Marissa held her tongue. The first one to do her, and her mother, wrong had been her father. He cheated on Mona, so perhaps *he* had set the cheating pattern in place. But Marissa didn't want *that* going into the interview. Mona would kill her.

"It happened in junior high. Right?" the reporter asked, not even bothering to wait for Marissa's answer to the preceding question. Then she flashed another sickly sweet smile that made Marissa's stomach curdle.

Marissa tossed her own smile back, shifted in the chair, and felt the strap of her dress slip off her left shoulder. Carl took another shot with his camera, and Marissa promptly pushed the strap back in place. "That's true. It was junior high, and I really just added him as a joke. I mean, it was a long time ago." She shrugged, smiled. "I had to start the list somewhere, so I picked Trent." Marissa forced a laugh. Surely they realized the boy cheater was added on a whim, for a fun take on how long she'd been cheated on.

"And do you know what happened to that boy, the one that scarred you for all future relationships?" the reporter continued.

Scarred her? Marissa frowned, and dammit, Carl took another photo. "No, I don't, and I didn't say that he scarred me."

"But do you know where he is?"

Irritated, Marissa shook her head. She didn't know what had happened to Trent Jackson. It hadn't mattered. Soon after that dance, she'd been uprooted, moving at the onset of those all-important high school years. Then she never looked back at the guy who basically created her last memory of living in Atlanta. A memory of the first guy to do her wrong. "I have no idea where he is."

"But you included him in the list."

"As a joke," Marissa said, and truly wished she hadn't even remembered that Sadie Hawkins thing.

"Do you think perhaps you included him because you blame him for the fact that you gravitate toward guys of the serial cheater nature?" the lady continued, and even managed to smile when she asked the bizarre question.

Gravitate toward them? *Gravitate?* "No, I don't blame him, and I also don't gravitate toward cheaters," Marissa corrected, careful to keep her voice steady as her blood pumped fiercely beneath her flesh. "But evidently, *they* gravitate toward me. Maybe," she said, thinking aloud, "maybe I tend to attract cheaters, because that's the only kind of relationship I've ever known. Guys who cheat." The truth of that statement stung, and Marissa winced. Unfortunately, Carl found her response perfect for another photo opportunity.

The reporter's smile broadened a bit, but then she carefully pumped down the volume in her enthusiasm. Why did the lady seem so pleased? And why did Marissa suddenly have the urge to chew her nails?

"I want to thank you for taking the time to talk to me, Marissa," the woman said, surprising Marissa when she stood up from the table and extended her hand. "I think this article is going to be one of my most *insightful* ones yet."

A sigh of relief escaped Marissa's lips before she could swallow it down. It was over. The interview was done, and now all she had to do was wait for the article to run on Sunday and reap the benefits of free publicity. She had no reason to worry, after all. Amy and Candi obviously thought their interviews went fine, and Marissa assumed hers had gone just as well, even if those last few questions made her a bit squeamish. Being uncomfortable during an interview was natural, wasn't it? It didn't mean that the piece would necessarily be bad for AtlantaTellAll, or for Marissa.

Or so she thought.

Trent Jackson reread the email on his monitor and smiled. This was definitely one of those instances where being Collin Jackson's offspring paid off, big-time. Too bad his father's old buddy at the paper hadn't sent the accompanying photographs with the preview of tomorrow's article. Trent was more than curious about how feisty Rissi looked all grown up. But come tomorrow morning, he'd know, courtesy of the front page of the *AJ-C*'s Living Section. In fact, all of Atlanta would know the woman behind the vindictive heart-filled site. More important, they'd know about the boy—now a man—featured on her pages. They'd learn about his name, his webzine, and his plans for a print version of DieHardAtlanta. And they'd also learn about his new, equally vindictive site.

Damn, being bad shouldn't be this much fun. Actually, being bad wasn't what Trent truly enjoyed. He liked to win, pure and simple. And Rissi Kincaid, whether she realized it or not, had issued a direct challenge. It'd been a very long time since Trent had sparred with a worthy opponent. Since his father's death five years ago, Trent had been involved in all of the company decisions. *Involved*, but not in control. Collin Jackson had left a well-oiled machine that could, quite frankly, run itself. The truth of that should have made Trent feel secure in running the organization, but it didn't. He wanted to be a worthy asset to Jackson Enterprises, and he believed his success with DieHardAtlanta would make that happen. What's more, he foresaw this public feud with Rissi Kincaid as having the potential to make it happen.

"Publicity is publicity," Collin Jackson used to say. "Good or bad, if it gets your name out, you've succeeded."

No doubt, Collin Jackson would see this article as primo publicity. Whether he'd dub it good or bad publicity, Trent didn't know. But either way, Collin—like

Trent—would have accepted Rissi's challenge. A Jackson never backed down from a fight.

The last time Trent had had a real business battle was when his father had been alive, and Collin Jackson challenged his teen son in a stock war. They'd started with the same amount of cash and had six months to invest as they chose. Trent's money doubled; Collin's tripled. But at the time, Trent was an inexperienced teen. Now he was a man, a man with plenty of business know-how, and with a man-sized desire to beat his opponent, even if she ended up being as cute as she had been back then.

Catching a glimpse of the clock displayed on the lower left corner of his monitor, Trent decided to see if Keith had called it an early night. He selected the *Forward* option on the email and sent the text Keith's way. If Keith was home, he'd have his computer nearby, and if Keith read this article, it wouldn't take him long before he responded, either by email or by—

The phone rang loudly, and Trent didn't bother looking at the caller identification before answering. "I thought you had a date with Cindy Cooper."

"Turned out Atlanta's newest anchorwoman was more interested in trying to determine how many zeroes are associated with the Parker name than in getting to know the man behind the dollar sign." Keith coughed loudly, probably a result of breathing barroom smoke all night, then continued. "Damn, I'm sick of dating. What I wouldn't give to find one woman who didn't care about my money, and who wasn't so undeniably shallow. It gets old. And they all say the money doesn't matter, but it's right there, dancing in their eyes when they check out the house, or the car."

"Maybe if you didn't live in Buckhead, or if you'd forgo the Jag to pick up your dates, you wouldn't have that problem," Trent said.

"Well, I can tell you one thing. You're sure not going to have any problems with women trying to snag you for life. Hell, they won't touch you with a ten-foot pole after they read this, Jackson money or not."

"You got my email."

"You knew I did when you picked up the phone. And you knew exactly what I'd think of it, too."

"Yeah, but go on, say it."

Keith yawned, then turned it into a laugh. "It's brilliant, a masterpiece of free publicity, if I do say so myself. But the lady is going to be pissed when she sees this."

"I certainly hope so," Trent said, scanning the text once more while he spoke. "Because I'd love to keep up this little feud for a while, at least long enough to put DieHardAtlanta on the map and quadruple my subscribers. This should do it, don't you think?"

"Depends on how many people get into the battle. I'd guess that it'll at least double them, but quadruple may be a stretch," Keith admitted.

"Then I'll just have to keep things interesting and pique curiosity. You'd check out these sites if you read this in the paper, wouldn't you?"

"Sure I would, but you're not dealing with me; you're dealing with Atlanta. However, for a wild hair of an idea, I think you've hit a winner. Tomorrow will tell. It'll tell lots of things, such as how many subscribers you gain from the advertising, and how many women you piss off with your new site. I can promise you that one woman will top the rest, and she's liable to take it out in a heated battle on the web. You're prepared for that, right?"

"I'm more than prepared," Trent admitted. "In fact, I'm counting on it."

Those who aren't willing to be front-page news should never agree to an interview.
— VIVIAN MOORE

Chapter 5

Marissa slowly moved her head on the pillow so she could thoroughly enjoy the sweet, soft kisses on her neck. It'd been a long time since her neck had been cuddled, or any other part of her, for that matter, and she was due. His hair teased her chin as he continued kissing, licking, and nipping the sensitive area between her neck and shoulder. "That . . . tickles," she said, on the verge of a lust-filled giggle.

The tall, dark stranger raised his head, smiled . . . and barked.

Marissa's eyes flew open to view Petie, his ears pointed on alert, long whiskers dangling around her chin, and dark eyes begging in an obvious request to go pee. "We've gotta stop meeting like this," she said to the puppy, now licking her jaw with vigor. "And you realize that you're beating my mother by"—she glanced at the blinding red numbers on the digital clock beside her bed—"twelve minutes."

Petie licked her chin again, then his ears stood even

higher and he whirled toward the bedroom door, putting his furry rump directly in front of her face. He growled menacingly, sounding much more fierce than his fifteen pounds.

"Oh, you're playing tough guy, are you?" Marissa teased, but then tensed when she heard a sound in her living room. She grabbed Petie, still growling, and tucked him beneath her arm. His rumbling snarl vibrated against her skin. Either that, or he was as scared as she was. "Who's there?" Marissa called. "I have a dog, and he's big, and he's mad!"

"I know you do," Amy said, opening the bedroom door. "I gave him to you, remember?" She held up a heart-shaped key ring. "I used my key. Hope you don't mind."

"Of course not," Marissa said on a sigh, as Petie relaxed, squirmed from her arms, and wagged his tail.

Marissa moved her attention from her friend—make that friends, because Candi had appeared directly behind Amy—to the clock. Had she forgotten an activity they'd planned for the day? Sure, they were supposed to get together tonight to work on the updates to the site and next week's poll, but it was barely daylight. "What's going on?"

Amy and Candi sat on opposite corners of the bed, gave each other a you-go-first glance, then smiled at Marissa. Whatever they had to say, Marissa wasn't going to like it. Petie, ignoring this unusual morning visit, whimpered, then scurried to Candi's lap.

"I'm sure he needs to go out," Marissa said, pushing the plush violet comforter to the side as she prepared to take care of Petie's needs. "And when I get back, you better tell me why you're here."

Candi held up a hand, then picked up Petie. "I'll take him. No problem."

Amy glared at her. "Coward," she mumbled under her breath, but Candi merely smiled, then headed out the door.

Marissa was even more curious now. "I didn't forget anything, did I? There's a reason you're here this early?"

Amy inhaled, but didn't get the chance to answer before the phone rang. "I'll get it," she said, snatching the purple receiver before Marissa had a chance.

"It'll be my mother," Marissa said, dumbfounded. What was going on here?

"I know, but I haven't talked to Mona in a while." Amy punched the *Talk* button. "Hello? Oh, hi, Ms. Kincaid. Yes, this is Amy. Uh-huh, she's here." Marissa waited for Amy to turn over the phone. It didn't happen. "You did? Uh-huh, I did, too. No, we haven't talked about it yet. No, she hasn't. Yes, that's why I'm here." Amy glanced at Marissa and smiled a little too broadly. "Right, that's exactly what we thought," she added, still smiling through her words. "I brought Candi with me. Yeah, I woke her up, but she's okay with it."

The strange smile on her friend's face reminded Marissa of another smile that she'd seen recently, the one stretching across the face of . . . Vivian Moore.

"The paper!"

"Crap, she's onto us," Amy blurted into the phone. "I'll call you back later." She hung up quickly, while her face reddened, and her hands clamped down on Marissa's shoulders. "Don't panic."

Oh. My. God. When a woman who has designed sex toys for a living looks like she'd rather die than tell you what the *Atlanta Journal* has printed about you, that's definitely a reason to panic. So Marissa did.

"What—does—it—say?"

"It really isn't too bad, all things considered," Amy said, as the front door slammed, and Petie darted into the bedroom in front of Candi. He waited beside the bed until Candi picked him up and put him near Marissa's feet. Then he promptly flopped down with his tail moving slowly between his outstretched back legs and his pink tongue hanging from his mouth, panting through his excitement at the unexpected company.

"You didn't tell her yet?" Candi accused.

"Mona called," Amy said defensively. "I didn't get the chance."

Candi looked at the clock. "Well, that *is* the reason you got me out of bed at this ungodly hour to come over here. I thought the plan was to beat Mona to the punch."

"Which we did," Amy argued.

"Hel-lo," Marissa said, pushing Amy's hands away from her shoulders and straightening in the bed. She reached toward the nightstand to turn on the lamp. Even with daylight filling the room at a rapid pace, she wanted more lighting when she read whatever had her friends worried enough to beat her mother's morning call. "A little reminder for both of you. The subject of this conversation is in the room and more than ready to see that paper. Who has it? And why were you up this early to get it, anyway?"

"Bo woke up at four-thirty wanting some juice," Amy explained. "By the time I got him back to sleep, I was wide awake, and since I was up, I checked to see if the paper had come." She shrugged. "I wanted to read the article."

"Then after she read it, she called me."

"And now you're both stalling. Where is it?"

Amy lifted her oversized Adventurous Accessories T-shirt and withdrew the folded newspaper from the waistband of her jeans. "I had planned on breaking it to you gently, over Ihop's Rooty Tooty Fresh N' Fruity."

"It's that bad?" Marissa asked. If it called for that much comfort food, then it probably was. "What did she say?"

"Who?" Amy asked.

"Vivian Moore," Marissa said. "The reporter. What did she say?"

"You should ask what did *he* say," Candi said.

"He? Who, the photographer? I thought he was just there for the pictures."

"He was," Amy said, slowly unfolding the paper. "But that isn't the *he* Candi's talking about. Here. It's on the front page of the Living Section. Um, you can't miss it." She turned the paper toward Marissa and squinted in preparation for Marissa's response.

She needn't have panicked. Marissa was too shocked to say a word.

Two things caught her attention like a potent one-two punch. One, the headline. *She Said, He Said.* And two, the photos beneath. Two photos, at least five by seven inches each, claimed the majority of the page.

On the left, a picture of Marissa at her computer, with the photo of the only teenage cheater on the site displayed on her monitor. The red dress, as Amy had promised, looked nice in the color photo, and Marissa was thankful she'd taken the time to have her hair trimmed. The short and sassy cut had the very modern, upbeat appearance of a professional at the top of her game. Beneath her photo, a bold caption read *"Marissa Kincaid Claims He Cheated."*

The picture on the right side of the paper featured a gorgeous man who Marissa was absolutely certain she'd never seen before—you'd have to be dead to forget a guy like that—who also smiled for the camera. Jet-black waves teased a strong forehead and accented seductive, smoky eyes and a megawatt grin that made her chest clench of its own accord. Unlike her photograph, his was taken from the opposite side of his computer, so you couldn't see what he viewed on the screen. Was he looking at her site? Was that what this was about? A guy's take on her cheater database? And even if it was, was that so bad?

Before asking Candi and Amy their opinion, however, Marissa noted other distinctive differences in the two pictures. His had obviously been taken in an office setting, with him sitting at a masculine desk and the Atlanta skyline displayed significantly behind him. In Marissa's picture, there was no denying that she was in a residential setting, a very plain residential setting. Her apartment was nice enough, but it didn't compare to this guy's work locale. Still, that didn't bother her too much. Her goal was to prove she could make a successful living staying at home and being her own boss, and she was well on the way to achieving that goal, right?

But why did the reporter include this guy in her article? And who was he?

Perhaps if she hadn't been so captivated with his looks, she'd have read the caption beneath his photo sooner. Because once she finally glanced down and read the line, she knew exactly who he was, and exactly what she needed to do.

Hurl.

"Oh, no," she said, shaking her head as she read the single line.

"Trent Jackson Claims She Lied."

Then Marissa got it. She looked back at her photo and realized that the image displayed on her computer monitor was the young teen photo of Trent Jackson, his black hair overpowering his skinny face and his self-conscious smile giving him the final touch of a total dweeb package.

Her attention jerked back to the to-die-for hunk in the other photo. *That* was Trent Jackson? Sitting in that plush office and smiling at her as though he owned the world?

Did he?

And as if Amy knew her train of thought, she cleared her throat and asked, "I guess you didn't realize that he was Trent Jackson of *the* Jacksons? As in, Trent Jackson, Jackson Enterprises CEO, huh?"

"The sole owner of Jackson Enterprises," Candi said, adding insult to injury.

"I remember the kids in school saying he had money," Marissa admitted numbly, while Petie, evidently sensing her distress, scampered into her lap and licked her right elbow. "Not now, Petie." Momentarily defeated, Petie lay down and looked miserable, the same way Marissa felt. She handed the paper to Amy. "You read it. I can't."

"Sure you don't want to head to Ihop before you hear it? I mean, I'm hungry, and I can almost taste the strawberry syrup, whipped cream, butter . . ." Candi started, but halted her progress when Marissa sent a hell-no look her way.

"All right then," Amy said, flicking her wrists to snap the paper into place. "Scarred for life by the acts of a thirteen-year-old, Marissa Kincaid, along with her friends Amy Brooks and Candi Moody, has added a new dimension to her AtlantaTellAll.com e-zine. Ms. Kincaid, a computer programmer by day, is very excited about all of the hype this new dimension is generating. Accessible via a red heart pierced by a dagger, Ms. Kincaid's new site, TheGuyCheats.com, is essentially a cheater database." Amy peered over the paper at Marissa, who made every effort to show no expression, then Amy turned her attention back to the article, while Marissa mentally kicked herself for agreeing to the interview.

"First things first," Amy continued reading. "What's a cheater database? According to Ms. Kincaid's business partner Candi Moody, a nurse at Grady Memorial, it's a website where women can report men of the serial nature—not serial killers, but serial cheaters. In other words, women report men who have cheated on them, and may also search a potential date's name to see if he has committed any prior offenses, i.e., whether he's cheated on someone else."

"Good description," Marissa managed.

"Thanks," Candi said, as Amy continued.

"While Ms. Kincaid had the inspiration for the new site, the web design, a waterfall of cascading hearts that break into shards upon impact, came from her other business partner, Amy Brooks, formerly a sex toy designer for Adventurous Accessories and now a stay-at-home mom." Amy paused. "Not a bad description of me, is it?"

When Marissa only stared, Amy flashed a grin, then went back to the page.

"There are fifteen cheaters listed in the *Cheaters* section of the site who personally cheated on Ms. Kincaid. Perhaps she should consider giving these fifteen their own section of the site; she could even dub it *Marissa's Many Monsters*.

"Marissa's Many Monsters?" Marissa repeated, appalled at the reporter's audacity.

Amy gave her an apologetic shrug, then kept reading. "But while all of this is interesting enough, it gets better. Because the thirteen-year-old boy that set the pattern for all future cheaters to follow has a name that you may recognize, or at least a last name you'll know. Jackson. As in, Jackson Enterprises. Yes, the son of Collin Jackson has grown up, and contrary to reports in the *Atlanta Business Journal*, he isn't merely living off his family money. Oh, no, Trent Jackson has started his own e-zine, DieHard Atlanta, which, according to Mr. Jackson, is doing very well. However, he suspects his newest venture, inspired by Ms. Kincaid, will do even better."

Amy stopped reading. "That's the end of the 'She Said' section."

"Uh-huh," Marissa said, feeling sick. "So give me his." Petie tottered up Marissa's side, then licked her chin before settling against her heart. Marissa rubbed his back while she waited for the worst. At least doing something with her hands would keep her from biting her nails.

"Here, you take this one," Amy said, handing the paper over to Candi.

"Now who's the coward?" Candi asked, then began. "While residents of Atlanta may not be familiar with the name Trenton Jameson Jackson, everyone is more than familiar with his business namesake, Jackson Enterprises.

The Jackson family has been a staple in Atlanta since the late 1920s, when Erskine Jackson invested in land in what is now the northern and southern portions of I-285. His son, Collin, took Erskine's assets and invested wisely to further increase the Jackson Enterprises fortune, and now it's time for the grandson, Trenton Jameson, or Trent, to make his mark. Like Marissa Kincaid, Trent Jackson pursued the ever-growing e-zine business as his first venture. Jackson foresees a print edition of the DieHardAtlanta magazine in the near future and is working to establish the equity to pursue that goal on his own, without using the assets of the business his father and grandfather established." Candi stopped reading. "That's impressive, isn't it? That he's wanting to succeed on his own?"

Marissa nodded, but wasn't surprised. One of the things she remembered about the boy in middle school was his determination to do things his own way. That was the reason she assumed they clicked as friends. She liked to stand out, and while he didn't seem to want to stand out, he did like making his own decisions. Obviously he still did.

"Here's the rest." Candi visibly swallowed, then trudged on. "After finding himself featured in the cheater database on Ms. Kincaid's TheGuyCheats.com site, Mr. Jackson decided that he would follow his old friend's lead by starting a similar site, a database where men can access information about women who have a history of being less than truthful. Oddly enough, Mr. Jackson started his site with a page detailing the woman who gave him the idea, Marissa Kincaid. In fact, you can view Trent Jackson's comments about Ms. Kincaid at his new site, an offshoot of DieHardAtlanta.com. The site, aptly titled TheGirlLies.com, is accessible from his original site via an icon of a hand slapped over a mouth (another idea that Jackson says he had in response to Ms. Kincaid's daggered heart icon). And now, when you check out TheGirlLies.com, you will learn that Mr. Jackson is showcasing Marissa Kincaid as the *Liar of the Month*." Candi stopped. "That's the end."

"The hell it is," Marissa said, jerking the covers aside and climbing out of the bed. "Liar of the month? Of the *month*?" She stomped across the room, yanked open a couple of drawers, and removed a T-shirt and shorts, then headed toward the bathroom to brush her teeth and change out of her nightshirt. After brushing her teeth so hard her gums hurt, she emerged from the bathroom. "Our site features a different cheater each day, and he puts me front and center for an entire month?" she asked, while Amy, Candi, and Petie watched her from the bed.

"Appears that way," Candi said. "Though I haven't seen his site yet."

"Me either," Amy added.

"Well, by all means, let's go take a look," Marissa said, as Petie hopped off the bed and scampered toward the kitchen. "I'll feed Petie. You guys bring up the jerk's site."

"I'm on it," Amy said, moving toward the laptop perched on the breakfast nook table.

"I'll make some coffee." Familiar with the layout of Marissa's kitchen, Candi easily found everything she needed and had coffee brewing by the time Petie began chomping on his Iams puppy food. Within minutes, Candi had three tall cups of coffee poured, sugar and cream for Amy, just sugar for herself, and black for Marissa.

Marissa accepted her cup, then she and Candi, carrying the other two, returned to Amy, clicking madly on the computer keys.

"You can't just key in TheGirlLies.com to get to his site," Amy said matter-of-factly. She took her coffee cup from Candi and took a sip as the computer whirred in response to her commands.

"What do you mean?" Marissa asked, peering over Amy's shoulder and seeing the home page of DieHardAtlanta.

"When you enter TheGirlLies.com, the screen that comes up is the one for his original site, DieHardAtlanta. Cool graphics on that site, by the way," Amy added, while Marissa emitted a loud "Hmph."

"Anyway," Amy continued, "he's got it set up so that even if you're only wanting to look at TheGirlLies.com, you can't get there without also viewing DieHardAtlanta. Clever way of manipulating your audience," she noted, then snapped her mouth shut when Marissa snarled.

"But the new site is coming up," Candi said, watching the images on the screen transform, then gasping when Marissa's photo, not the one in the paper, but another one evidently taken by the *AJ-C* photographer, popped into view. "Nice picture," she said consolingly.

Marissa gaped at the image and remembered exactly when Carl had snapped it, when the red dress that looked perfectly businesslike in the other photo had slipped off one shoulder. In this picture, she looked over that shoulder toward the photographer, and he'd cut the computer image off completely, so it looked as if she was purposely posing, seductively posing, for him.

"No way," Marissa said.

"It is a good picture," Amy said. "I don't think I've ever seen one of you that looked so—" She paused.

"Sexy?" Candi added, while Marissa dropped into a chair at the table.

"I look like a slut."

"You look like a model," Amy corrected.

"A trashy model," Marissa shot back, looking at her hair in the picture. Every now and then, her curls got the best of the short cut and caused a stray swirl to christen her temple. Like in the picture. "I look like Betty Boop." All she needed was a sexy pucker and her boobs hanging out of a strapless dress. Wait a minute—one strap was gone. Hell, she was halfway there.

"Oh, my, you do!" Amy said, smiling. Then she turned toward Marissa and miraculously both corners of her mouth faded to a straight line. "Sorry."

"What does he say about me?" Marissa said. "Scroll down to the text."

Amy moved the mouse, then started reading. To herself.

"Read it out loud," Marissa complained.

"Noooo," Amy said slowly, "I don't think so."

Marissa scooted her chair closer to Amy's. "Is it that bad?" She quickly scanned the short paragraph, while her stomach churned. The actual verbiage from Trent Jackson wasn't all that terrible. Basically, he asked site visitors to vote for her as the *Worst of the Worst* liar in his *Liar Polls* section, and he claimed that she didn't tell the entire truth in her depiction of what happened when they were in middle school, so therefore, she lied.

"I told the truth," Marissa said.

"Maybe there's more to it than you realized," Candi offered.

"You are *not* taking his side," Marissa snapped. "Tell me you aren't."

"No," Candi quickly clarified. "I'm just saying that maybe there was more going on with him—oh, never mind. I'm the one who kept taking her husband back when he cheated, remember? Don't listen to me. Obviously, I'm a sucker for a gorgeous smile and to-die-for eyes."

Amy coughed on her coffee. "Trust me, Marissa doesn't want to hear about what a hottie he turned out to be. Not now."

Marissa looked again at the computer monitor, where Trent Jackson's photo resided in the upper left corner of the screen, beside the words "Trent's Liar of the Month." He was a hottie, no doubt about that, but he was also calling her a liar. "It doesn't matter what he looks like," she said. "He's a jerk."

"Exactly," Amy said. "And a cheating jerk."

"You know, maybe it'll help when we have other women responding to his cheater page. We do ask for comments, right? Have we had any hits on Trent Jackson?"

"Not yet," Amy said, collapsing the window displaying Marissa's information on TheGirlLies.com and bringing up Trent's individual cheater page on their site. "But I expect we will after today's article is circulated around town and on the net. The *AJ-C* is on the web, you know."

"Good," Marissa said. "I hope every girl he's cheated on comes forward with a story. We'll show everyone what kind of guy Trenton Jameson Jackson has turned out to be, family money behind him or not."

"That sounds good," Candi said. "But there is one small problem with that scenario."

"What's that?" Marissa said, while Petie, done with his meal, whimpered at her feet.

"Didn't I see a link at the bottom of the section about you on his site?" Candi asked. "A place where guys can post about you?"

Marissa leaned down and scooped up the puppy, her hand shaking slightly as she brought him to her lap. "Amy? Was there a link to post comments about me? Because I didn't see it."

Amy frowned slightly, then swapped the windows on the computer again and shifted the laptop so Marissa had a better view. There, at the bottom of the paragraph about her, was a bright red icon, the same one that was on the DieHardAtlanta site, a mouth with a hand slapped over it. Beneath this icon, though, were the words "Know Marissa? Care to Share?" And following that were two words that made Marissa's blood run cold.

Four comments.

"Go on. Let's see them." Marissa waited while Amy clicked on the link.

The first comment was from Jamie.

First of all, awesome site, Trent! I admit I have been addicted to DieHardAtlanta for quite some time, but this site is even more righteous. Now, for comments about Marissa Kincaid. I dated Marissa a few times, about a month ago. We had some laughs, but the girl copped a serious attitude when she figured out I'm not merely a one-woman kind of guy, or more accurately, when she figured out I'm not a one-man kind of guy either. Speaking of which, what's your preference, man? Do you only play for one team? And if you're also the adventuresome type, shoot me an email sometime. We'll talk.

"I'm not believing it. Jamie asked him out," Amy said, her eyes bulging at the screen.

"Sure looks that way," Candi said with a snicker.

"That's just wrong."

"Well, look at the bright side, nothing really bad was said about you in that one," Amy said happily.

"Keep going," Marissa said, not about to be fooled into thinking there wasn't something negative about her in those other three comments. The fact that she liked her guys to play on the straight team didn't bother her at all; the fact that there were three more comments after Jamie's . . . did.

Amy scrolled down, and the three girls and Petie stared at the second comment, from Gerald Hopkins. Marissa recognized the name, and the accompanying photo he'd posted, immediately.

"The tuba lover," she said.

The photo was of Gerald, playing his tuba in the Atlanta Symphony. His post was short and to the point.

"Oooh, I'll read this one," Candi said. "I remember Gerald. Talk about one of your less-than-finer moments." She cleared her throat. "I also dated Marissa Kincaid, three years ago. It lasted about four months. For the record, she lied to me, so the fact that she's listed on this site doesn't surprise me."

"I lied to him? What's he talking about? I never lied to him."

Candi continued, "For the first couple of months, Marissa acted like she really enjoyed spending time with me and attending my performances with the Atlanta Symphony Orchestra (www.atlantasymphony.org). However, after the third month, Marissa informed me that she couldn't stand the way our dates revolved around my hobby. Hobby? This is my life, and she calls it a hobby? She claimed I cared more about my tuba than her, so she called it quits. Obviously, the woman lied about enjoying those first dates, and obviously, the woman was jealous of a tuba. Need I say more? She needs help. The fact that she started her cheater database with a guy whom she hadn't seen since junior high makes her certifiable. Just my opinion, of course, but I'd love to hear yours. By the way, I'm listed on her website, too. And believe it or not, she even states that I cheated on her with my love of my tuba. Mental, that's the word I'd used to describe her. Mental. Gerald Hopkins, Principal Tuba, AtlantaSymphony.org." Candi looked at Amy. "How about that, he managed to plug the Atlanta Symphony, *and* his tuba, no less than three times."

"It could be worse," Amy said, though she didn't say how.

"I shouldn't have put him in the cheater list," Marissa said. "Really, it was a tuba. It wasn't a female or anything."

"I disagree. Lots of females play second fiddle to inanimate objects. I think it's high time that was classified as cheating, too, and you did it. Bravo," Candi added in a mock British accent. She applauded lightly with her fingertips against her palm and stuck her nose in the air for effect.

Amy giggled. "Actually, I believe it would be playing second tuba, rather than second fiddle, right?"

"Go to the third one," Marissa instructed, while Petie

squirmed in her lap. "And hurry. I think Petie needs to go out again."

"Thimble bladder," Candi said, but she patted Petie's head and gave him an air kiss. He responded with a happy bark and apparently forgot his need to go.

Amy scrolled down the page, then shook her head hard enough to send her ponytail swinging and laughed so hard she snorted. "It's Jamie again, asking Gerald out."

"That guy's the mental one," Candi said, grinning.

Petie, remembering his dilemma, scurried up Marissa's chest and whimpered at her neck. "We've got to go out. Just read the last one quick for me."

"Oh," Amy said somberly. "Well, this one doesn't have much to say."

"Just a second, Petie," Marissa said, warning bells sounding at Amy's curt response. "What does it say?"

Amy shot a glance at Candi, who instinctively leaned in front of Marissa to view the screen. Petie, trapped between the two women, barked for more room.

"Sorry, Petie," Candi said, scooting closer to the table and making it even harder for Marissa to see what was displayed. Then Candi muttered, "That asshole."

"Who?" Marissa questioned.

"Blake," Candi replied, the single syllable holding as much venom as she could muster. Neither Candi nor Amy cared for him, mainly because he'd so thoroughly and completely swept Marissa off her feet, had her thinking marriage and babies and the whole nine yards, then flipped over a flight attendant he met en route to Vegas.

Blake Couvillion. The spicy, sexy Cajun whose name alone still sent a quiver straight to Marissa's core . . . and the one guy to whom she'd actually said the "L" word.

What had he put on Trent Jackson's site? And why would he say anything? She never lied to Blake, and while she did have a page dedicated to him in *The Cheaters* section of her site, she didn't state anything all that bad, just that she'd flipped over him, but he flipped over someone else. Basically, that he cheated. She'd only spoken the truth and really hadn't dissed him too much in the process. So what had he said about her?

Amy bumped her head against Candi's to get a better view, then called Blake Couvillion another choice expletive, a lot more racy and a lot more colorful than Candi's.

"What did he say?" Marissa repeated. She didn't even attempt to look at the screen. From their reactions, she was pretty sure she didn't want to hear it, but she was sure as hell that she didn't want to see it on the world wide web, where everyone else in Atlanta, and all over, could read it, too.

"You sure you wanna know?" Amy asked hesitantly.

"Do you really think I want someone telling me at work instead of hearing it from you?" Marissa stroked the back of Petie's neck and prayed that he could hold his bladder a little bit longer, at least long enough for her to find out if Blake's words were as bad as her friends believed.

"He says you cry during sex." Amy squinted, waiting for Marissa's response.

None came.

"He also says that the crying wasn't why he left, but that he admits it turned him off," Candi said quickly.

It turned him off? But the whole reason that she cried—and it only happened once—was that she *thought* she'd just made love for the first time. Obviously, she was wrong. Dead wrong. Embarrassingly wrong.

How many people would read that?

Easy answer—everyone in Atlanta who got the paper and learned about the site.

"I hear Los Angeles is a nice place to live," she said. "I could probably get a job there, near the beach even, and I bet there aren't that many people in California who will read today's issue of the *AJ-C*." There. She now had a plan. Moving two thousand miles away seemed like a good idea.

"You don't think people in L.A. get the Internet?" Candi asked, then slapped a hand over her mouth as though she could push the horrible words back in.

But she was right. Everyone had a computer, and everyone could read about her on Trent Jackson's site. Even the part that said she cried in bed. Oh, the guys would really be lining up to date her now, that's for sure.

"Candi!" Amy scolded. "That is so not what she needs to hear right now."

"Well, it's true. I can't get away from this, and Trent Jackson knows it," Marissa said. She wanted to hit something—hurt something—preferably him.

"You know," Amy said, smiling sinisterly, "it won't take long before people who've read that article start responding to our site, too. I mean, there aren't any comments about Trent on his personal cheater page yet, but I'd bet money that there will be before the day's over. And we all know that women are so much better at putting exes in their place than men."

A frisson of excitement rippled down Marissa's spine. What *would* women say about Trent? Surely he had something embarrassing on him, too, right? Odds were that a woman he'd done wrong would be totally willing to dish on the guy. How long would it take? Was Amy right? Would Marissa have something on him before the day ended? And if so, how could she use it to her advantage . . . and make him pay?

"You think I'm right, don't you?" Amy asked.

"Maybe," Marissa admitted.

"Well, the way I see it, if we do get something juicy on Trent Jackson, we can either broadcast it like crazy over the Net, or"—Candi looked thoughtfully at Blake's post on the screen—"or, we could bargain with the creep. Tell him we'll remove the offensive stuff from his page, when he removes the crying crap from Marissa's. A trade of sorts. And all we have to do is wait for one of his loves-done-wrong to post."

"I hate to say it, because I'd love broadcasting his dirt, but that might be the way to go, Marissa, especially if you'd rather everyone not know about the crying thing," Amy said.

"Everyone's going to see it anyway," Marissa replied, wishing she were wrong, but knowing she was right.

"At least a bargain would get it off Trent's site," Candi said.

"Yeah, that's true." Marissa cradled Petie, who'd started whimpering again, then stood to take him out. "I'll think about it. But really, men don't typically get bent out of shape over mere rumors. Why would he care? And every time his name gets out there, whether for a good reason or a bad, he's getting publicity."

"That's a good point," Amy said. "But then again, every time your name gets out there, you're getting publicity, too. And so are AtlantaTellAll and TheGuyCheats. It is publicity, and it's free."

"And it's humiliating," Marissa added.

"Yeah, that, too." Candi followed Marissa across the room and grabbed Petie's leash by the door. "But one thing's for sure, you said you wanted excitement in your life, and you've got it now."

"This wasn't exactly what I had in mind," Marissa said, snapping the hook on the end of the leash to Petie's collar. "Are you going out with us?"

"Yeah, I can use some fresh air," said Candi, turning toward Amy, who was still moving the mouse as she flip-flopped between the information on the two sites. "You wanna come?"

Amy shook her head. "No, I'm going to keep an eye on our cheater page about Trent and see if anyone posts a comment. And I'll check our email address for TheGuy Cheats.com, too. I'm betting we get plenty of emails today."

"Maybe all of them won't ask about my cryfest during sex," Marissa said.

Amy took a breath, apparently debating whether to say what she was thinking, then, being a bull-by-the-horns kind of girl, she did anyway. "For the record, I cried, too, the first time Landon and I made love. Was that it? Did you believe you were finally making love?"

Marissa's sigh was breathy . . . and sad. "Yeah."

"Well, hell, I guess I still haven't made love," Candi said. " 'Cause I've never cried once, and Cal and I were married for eleven years. Maybe I'm the one you guys should be worried about." She took Petie from Marissa. "I'm thinking more and more that women should be satisfied taking care of their puppies. They're loyal, they're cuddly, they don't talk back, and they don't cheat."

Amy laughed. "Hey, I have living proof at home that there are perfect guys out there. I've actually got two of them, the big and the small version, so don't go dissing all men. You just haven't found the right ones."

"Still say a dog is the way to go," Candi said, as she and Marissa took Petie out and slammed the door.

Typically, there's no such thing as bad publicity; however,
having all of your exes discuss you on the Internet
may be the exception to the rule.
—KEITH PARKER

Chapter 6

"Ted Turner has over two million acres spread out over
seven states and seems to have plenty of time for all of his
other enterprises as well," Trent said, entering his office
to find Keith waiting. Never one to waste valuable time,
Keith obviously hadn't been deterred when Trent was
fifteen minutes late and had already withdrawn his laptop
and started checking the most recent stats on DieHard
Atlanta. "I'm late," Trent acknowledged.

"No problem. I started billing you when I got here."
A slight smirk played on Keith's face in spite of the fact
that he wasn't lying. Business was business, and if Keith
Parker was here for business, Trent was paying for the
services, whether he showed up for the meeting or not.

"A true friend." Trent removed his tie and tossed it
onto the leather sofa that was centered along one wall.
He'd put a couch in the office simply because his father
had one before, but unlike his father, Trent didn't plan on

spending nights at work. Until last night, he hadn't, but the monthly meeting of the Jackson Properties division had started yesterday at 8:00 A.M. and had still been going strong at midnight. Then this morning they'd started bright and early again and finally—finally—adjourned at a quarter past noon. If that meeting was any indication of things to come, Trent could very well begin spending all of his time in this building.

Not his goal, and definitely not his dream. He wanted to run a successful business, wanted Jackson Enterprises to continue to dominate in all areas, but he wanted a life, too. And he'd prefer to run the business of his choosing, that is, DieHardAtlanta. Unfortunately, corporate responsibilities were forever pulling him in other directions, as they'd done the past two days, when he really wanted to concentrate on all of the terrific press his personal business venture was getting.

"For the record," Keith said, "Ted Turner's properties are primarily used as ranches for bison, with some commercial hunting and fishing thrown in for good measure. Turner works hard to keep that land as pristine as possible, in its natural state. On the other hand, Jackson Properties are primarily located in and around Atlanta, with almost all of the land either already developed or in the development stage. You're talking apples and oranges."

Trent removed his suit jacket and tossed it near the tie, then dropped into the chair behind the desk. "If you're trying to make me feel better, you're doing a lousy-ass job."

Keith smiled, way too broadly for Trent's current mood. "I'm trying to tell you that you're in a different arena here, but even so, the reason Turner has time for so many business ventures is that he hires good people to run each division—"

"I've got excellent people running all Jackson Enterprises divisions," Trent interjected. "Hell, some of them have been here longer than I've been alive. They know the company as well as I do, if not better."

"What I was going to say, if you'd let me finish, is that Turner has time for so many business ventures because he hires good people to run each division, and then he lets them do their job."

"A Jackson has always been involved in all aspects of the business," Trent said. "My grandfather started Jackson Properties, but my father remained a key player in the decisions for that portion of the business; however, he also stayed on top of Jackson Investments, the part that was his passion."

"There," Keith said, nodding. "You've hit the nail on the head. Your grandfather's passion was land, and he did very well in that arena. Your father, however, had a passion for investing, and he pursued that avenue, also doing very well. However, your passion isn't in either of those areas, yet you're trying to stay involved in both of them instead of wholeheartedly going after your own goal, formulating DieHardAtlanta as another worthy branch on the Jackson Enterprises tree."

"I'm not arguing with you," Trent said. "I'm spreading myself thin, I know that."

"Well, at least you're acknowledging the problem. The way I see it, where you're screwing up is trying to keep a finger in all of the pies. Let the capable people running the existing Jackson Enterprises divisions do their thing, and you do yours. Sure, you can stay aware of what's going on in the others, but concentrate on leaving your personal mark on your family's legacy. Isn't that what you want your son or daughter to do one day, if they decide to go yet another route in building the empire started by Erskine Jackson?"

His son or daughter? *His* son or daughter? Trent didn't comment. He had been thinking about that lately, his legacy, his heirs, not that he had any heirs yet. But at thirty-three, shouldn't he at least begin to think about the possibility of procreating? His father had waited to settle down, wanting to get Jackson Investments on its feet and running before he brought an heir into the mix. While Trent was sure Collin Jackson thought that was a good plan, Trent didn't agree. The result of his father's waiting until the time was right was a son who lost his parents way too soon, and a son who intended to start his own legacy—in business *and* personally—much sooner. Problem was, in order to do that, he'd need a woman, and no ordinary woman.

"I mean, tell me. How many hours did this meeting about the Suwannee acquisition take? You started yesterday, right?" Keith continued, completely unaware of the shift in Trent's thoughts, which were traipsing over the many women who'd held his attention momentarily. Several had been ready for commitment, but Trent just couldn't see it, not with any of them. His father always said, "For Jacksons, only the best will do. Don't settle . . . with anything." His father had never remarried after Trent's mother passed away, saying he had had the best, so no other would do. Collin Jackson remained single until he died. Trent had never settled, professionally or personally, but that didn't mean he shouldn't at least start thinking about starting a family, in more than a one-day-when-it's-right kind of way.

Keith frowned, cocked a brow. "You realize I'm charging you for this time, right? And I asked how many hours you spent on the Suwannee deal."

Trent ignored the first question and moved to the second. "Twenty. Sixteen yesterday and four this morning."

"And ultimately, who made the final decision on whether the land would be purchased and developed?"

"The board, but they were naturally very receptive to my input."

Keith nodded and clicked a few computer keys. "And you got your advice from whom? Because, truthfully, land isn't your thing. So who did you turn to for recommendations on the pros and cons of this expensive undertaking?"

"William Stallings," Trent said easily.

"Your president for Jackson Properties," Keith said, not even looking up from his monitor.

"What's your point?" Trent asked, though he knew.

"My point is that if you want to sit through twenty hours of a meeting so you can listen to the ins and outs of why they made their decision, that's fine. Or you could handle things the smart way."

"Which is?"

Keith rolled his head from shoulder to shoulder, cracking his neck with each twist. "If I were to give you my recommendation, I'd tell you to request the minutes and outcome of the meeting, verify that their decisions meet with your approval, and in the meantime, have twenty hours to pursue *your* personal business passion, DieHard

Atlanta. Hell, you might even find time to have some fun on the side, like, say, playing baseball."

Trent shook his head. Keith had been trying to get him to play on his recreational league for three years, but Trent simply hadn't had time. He was glad Keith had found something he enjoyed after his wife left. When Melia turned to her boss, Keith turned to baseball. And women. But while the women had come and gone, baseball remained true, and he sincerely wanted Trent to give it a try.

"We could use a center fielder. You have a good arm."

"I *had* a good arm. Past tense. High school has been gone for a while, and I haven't played since."

"It's like riding a bike."

Trent laughed. "Okay, I'll make you a deal. When Die HardAtlanta really gets going, I'll play ball."

Keith looked over the top of his monitor. "And by the way, your subscribers have doubled since Sunday's article hit the paper, not that you'd know that, since you've been cooped up in that meeting."

Trent's brows edged upward. "Doubled? In two days?"

"Most are clicking through to TheGirlLies.com, but they're still getting a glimpse of DieHardAtlanta en route. You know, I'd be curious to see how many of these hits are female. No way to tell, but I'm betting you've probably got nearly as many women checking to see if their name is on that database as men visiting to see who's there. Really, you should send that Kincaid woman a thank-you card for giving you such an inventive way to boost your readership."

Keith was right. Trent had been so busy with the Su-

wanee deal that he hadn't taken time to check his Die
HardAtlanta stats. Swiveling in his chair, he brought up
the site, then clicked through to TheGirlLies.com. There,
at the top of the first page, was Rissi. Damn, he'd been
surprised when the photographer finally emailed these
shots. The woman still had the feisty spark in those dark
eyes that he'd known as a kid, but now she had something more . . . a sultry sexiness that made Trent wonder
if her voice was still as raspy as it'd been back then. In
middle school, its roughness had bothered her. *"I don't
even sound like a girl,"* she'd said. But what she hadn't
realized was that the Demi Moore/Kathleen Turner quality had intrigued him before he was even old enough to
understand why. Now he knew. It was the sound of a
woman's voice when she was aroused, and it was as sexy
as the woman currently staring at him from the screen. He
examined her, looking over her bare shoulder—the red
strap of her dress having sexily slipped down. Damn, she
looked good. An image flashed across his mind, those lips
curving into a smile, arms teasing him into their embrace,
and Rissi, giving him a taste of the woman the feisty girl
had turned out to be. What would she do if she knew what
he was thinking now?

"She'd probably go into shock," Keith said.

Had Trent actually said that out loud? "What?"

"If you sent her a thank-you card."

Trent swallowed thickly, undid the top two buttons of
his starched white shirt, and loosened his collar. "Right,
complete shock."

"And I wouldn't recommend it anyway," Keith said.
"Particularly with these comments about her on the page.
One guy claims she's mental."

"Mental? Rissi?"

"Then again, this guy apparently spent more time with his tuba than with his date," Keith added, chuckling slightly as he read the posts. "Oh, another one says she cries during sex, but her mother came to her defense. Damn, this is good. You've got your own personal soap opera here, Trent, and it's out there for the whole web to see."

Trent fiercely clicked his own computer keys until he got to the same screen. Then he frowned when he read the comments. "I didn't mean for them to trash her."

"No worries," Keith said. "They're trashing you on her site, too."

Hell. Trent opened another web browser. He keyed in TheGuyCheats.com and waited for the broken hearts to fill the screen. Marissa had added the sound of breaking glass to the waterfall image, and the effect was quite impressive, except Trent wasn't inclined to be impressed at the moment; he wanted to know what had been said about him on her site, and how many of his business associates had seen the posts.

"Nothing terrible," Keith said. "Although one of your former flames, a girl named Robin Grenade, claims your, er, anatomy leaves much to be desired. Oh, and another one, LaDonna Farraday, says you have chronic halitosis and suggests Altoids." Keith tilted his head and questioned, "Grenade? Didn't you ever have second thoughts about dating a girl named Grenade?"

Trent's jaw clenched. If ever a woman deserved the "mental" classification, it'd be Robin. She'd been so fiery mad when he tried to give her the "It's been enjoyable, but it's time to move on" spiel that she'd clawed him like a terrorized feline. His face smarted just thinking about it. And LaDonna? He had only gone out with her once. She was the clingy type, had to hang all over him the entire date, and he'd simply not asked her out again. Chronic halitosis? She sure hadn't seemed to think that when she was trying to ram her tongue down his throat.

"No responses?" Keith taunted.

"None," Trent said. He didn't even open the comments page. Why bother, since Keith was having so much fun reading them to him?

"Well, in case you're wondering, two women came to your defense."

"And who would that be?" Trent asked, perplexed.

"Crazy Irene, for starters."

"Great. My sole stalker shows up for the party," Trent said. Why would he classify Robin as mental, when Irene actually filled the bill? He'd finally asked for a restraining order when the cleaning crew in his building found her going through his trash, and he'd never even dated Irene. She'd worked for him, and he'd said hello a few times, and the woman had lost it. Completely. Keith had dubbed her "Crazy Irene" and, unfortunately, Trent had thought of her in that light for so long that he could no longer remember the woman's last name.

"Irene says you're the kindest man she knows, even if she isn't allowed to talk to you anymore," Keith said with a snicker.

"Swell." Trent closed his eyes and forced his blood pressure to settle back into place. "So who was my second defender?"

"Oh, that would be Mona Kincaid, Marissa Kincaid's mother. She's obviously posting on both sites."

"Mona Kincaid," Trent repeated. He had never met Rissi's mother when he was a kid, or at least he didn't remember meeting her. But the name seemed so familiar . . .

"Yeah, she said that she didn't think it was very nice for those women to say those things about you, and that wasn't what her daughter intended when she started the site. She also says that you sounded like a very nice young man when she spoke to you three weeks ago."

"Three weeks ago?" Trent questioned, searching his brain for a recollection. Three weeks ago? Her name *did* sound familiar. But why?

"That's all she says," Keith said.

Trent tried to make the pieces connect, but they didn't. At all. How did he know Rissi's mother?

"And the older Ms. Kincaid also posted on TheGirl Lies.com." Keith moved the mouse on his computer to transition between the two screens, but Trent, with Rissi's page still displayed on his monitor, beat his friend to the punch.

"I've got it," he said, and read her lengthy comment.

This is Mona, Marissa's mother. While I can understand why Trent Jackson started this site as a retaliation of sorts to my daughter's site, I cannot understand why you boys have to post comments of this nature about my daughter. Because I'm upset with each of you for different reasons, I'll reference each of your posts individually. Jamie—you should be ashamed of yourself. Don't bad-mouth Marissa for not wanting to continue the relationship when you were less than truthful with her about your sexual preference. Even if you do "play for both teams" you should have had the courtesy to tell her that you pinch hit, or switch hit, or whatever it is they call it. I never have been big on baseball. And Gerald, if you think that I, a woman who is a professional in the advertising industry, didn't recognize that you only posted to promote your damn (excuse my French) tuba and that orchestra, then you've got a screw loose. The Atlanta Symphony is terrific, but you need to find a life, too, beyond the tuba, and I was thrilled when Marissa let you—and your tuba—go. Okay, now for the toughie. Blake. What do I say to you? She gave you her heart, and you trampled on it. For that, you're the worst of all. And that's all I'm going to say about that. Wait a minute. One more thing. You crazy nuts who are sending the cases of tissues to my Rissi, stop it. Right now.

"The woman doesn't like anyone messing with her daughter," Keith said. "Amazingly enough, though, she says she understands why you've got her on the site, and even calls you a 'very nice young man.' And you don't remember talking to her?"

Trent turned away from his friend so he could concentrate. He scanned the tops of Atlanta's buildings and watched the way the blistering sun made their edges blur in waves. Oddly enough, the image brought back another day, when he sat in this chair and stared out at those buildings, hazy in the summer heat, and spoke to a woman on the phone. She had the sweetest, most tender voice, and reminded Trent of his mother, particularly when she voiced her opinion on how smart he was to start his own business, to pursue his dream, and then she told him how she could help him make it successful . . . with her current ad special.

"Mona Kincaid. She's the advertising rep at the

Atlanta Journal who helped me set up the DieHard Atlanta campaign."

"You're joking."

"No, I'm serious," Trent said. He'd really liked her and had gone with everything she suggested, and all of the ads had ended up in prime positions in the paper. Consequently, DieHardAtlanta had a substantial increase in hits on the days those ads ran.

"You placed the ads yourself? Why didn't you use your Jackson advertising agents?"

"I'm doing this one on my own," Trent said, reminding Keith of his ultimate goal, to succeed without his family's bank account.

"Right," Keith said, grinning. "And you just happened to get Mona Kincaid for an ad rep. Wonder what her daughter thinks about that?"

"No idea."

"You realize the fight is probably over. She hasn't made any effort to contact you since the article ran, so she's probably decided to lie low," Keith observed. "And while this exposure has done a lot for your publicity campaign, it's still not enough. It would've been good if you could have kept this feud going a little longer, in all honesty."

"Well, in all honesty," Trent mocked, "it isn't over yet."

All's fair in love, war . . . and business.
—TRENT JACKSON . . . AND MARISSA KINCAID

Chapter 7

I told you, Mom, I'm not mad," Marissa said Wednesday morning, yawning through the last word. She, Amy, and Candi had worked on the new site until after midnight, and she really wasn't looking forward to going to work. The fact that her coworkers relentlessly teased her about her Internet battle with Trent Jackson didn't help. Then again, AtlantaTellAll.com had gained more subscribers in the past four days than in all of the previous twelve months combined, so she wasn't going to fret over the embarrassment . . . too much. She was, however, determined to make Trent Jackson pay. Somehow.

"I couldn't let those guys talk about you that way, and on the Internet, for the entire world to see," Mona continued, as Marissa patted Petie's head and snapped his leash on his collar for their morning trip behind the bushes.

"It's fine, Mom." Marissa stepped outside in time to see Amy, on her toes and giving her husband a hot-and-heated farewell kiss beside Landon's black Dodge Ram Dually in the parking lot. Landon's hand cupped her bottom, barely covered by her hot pink satin sleep set. An inkling of jealousy burned in Marissa's chest, but she swallowed it down. She wasn't jealous of Amy and Landon, after all, she was merely envious of anyone who found the right one.

Amy and Landon finished their cuddle session, which was totally beyond a typical public display of affection, then Amy watched him leave and turned to see Marissa.

"That was almost X-rated," Marissa called.

Amy beamed. "Thanks!"

"Tell Amy I said hello," Mona instructed, reminding Marissa that she was still on the line and listening.

"My mom says hi," Marissa relayed, then she steered Petie behind his preferred bush.

"Hi, Mona!" Amy called.

"And tell her that I'm proud of you girls for starting the new site, and for keeping it tasteful. After he put you up as liar of the month, I was afraid you might retaliate, but you proved you're above that type of thing."

Ouch. Marissa hadn't really thought about her mother reading Marissa's new comments about Trent on the site, the exact type of retaliation she was referring to, but undoubtedly, Mona Kincaid would check them out for herself. Might as well prepare her.

"Um, Mom, we did add a bit of retaliation verbiage to the site. I don't guess you've seen it yet."

"O-kay," Mona said, drawing the word out. "So what'd you say?"

"Well, last night we updated the site after a few margaritas and, thinking back, we probably shouldn't have made any modifications then." While bracing for her mother's next question, Marissa applauded Petie for making his business in the right spot. The dog pranced as though totally understanding the praise and completely believing he deserved it.

"What type of updates?" Mona asked.

"Just a few modifications to his personal cheater page," Marissa said dismissively, though she knew good and well that Mona Kincaid wouldn't dismiss it.

Amy waved a hand to get Marissa's attention. "I'm heading in to wake Bo. We're going over to my sister's house to let the kids swim this morning."

"Tell Lettie I said hello," Marissa called, as Amy disappeared into her apartment, and Mona squealed in her ear.

"Marissa Leola Kincaid, what—have—you—done?"

"Oh, you found his page?" Marissa asked.

"I cannot believe you did that to his picture." Mona spat out her disappointment in every word.

Okay, obviously her mother had, thus far, only viewed the updated photo of the young Trent Jackson, embellished with a pointed beard, curled mustache, and horns. If that's what had her yelling, just wait until she saw—

"Ma-ris-sa!"

Marissa waved to Mr. Nance and Noodle, out for their morning walk, then darted into her apartment, just in case Mona Kincaid's scream could be heard beyond her ear. "I guess you read the new remarks."

"That you second that horrendous Robin person's comment regarding his private parts and that you've provided his mailing address, in case anyone wants to send Altoids?" Mona asked. "Yes, I read them. Honey, what are you thinking?"

"It isn't actually his home address. It's the post office box for his business, but that'll do. And what I'm thinking is that this website war is going to get me a lot of business, and that he's getting what he deserves for making me liar of the month."

"And you don't think the boy will retaliate?"

"He's thirty-three, Mom. Hardly a boy." Marissa watched Petie scamper toward the kitchen. He stopped shy of his bowl, turned around, and cocked his head in a now-you-feed-me move. Grinning at him, she obliged, filling his food and water bowls. She left him finishing his breakfast while she booted up her laptop.

"I guess he is a man," Mona said softly. "I need to keep reminding myself of that, because every time I think of him, I see that teen picture you have on your site."

"All you have to do is look at Sunday's paper to see he's changed," Marissa pointed out, and hated the way her chest tightened at the memory of Trent Jackson, all grown up and drop-dead gorgeous. Who'd have imagined such amazing eye candy would come from that skinny kid?

"I know. In fact, I should be able to remember his age from the sound of his voice. He certainly has the tone of a man, a very confident man. I noticed that yesterday on the phone."

Marissa's free hand stopped moving over the computer keys and she tightened the other on the receiver. "What?"

"I said I noticed his confidence in his voice, you know, when I spoke with him."

"Yesterday. *That's* what you said. You said, 'When I spoke to him yesterday.' You talked to Trent Jackson—yesterday?"

"Oh, yes. He wanted to order another of our advertising specials, but this time, he needed to advertise his new website and wanted to pay a little more for premier positioning in the paper. Of course, I gave him the best spot I could find. Top right corner, page two of the Living Section, high visibility."

"He's advertising TheGirlLies.com?" Marissa asked.

"Yes, he is," Mona said matter-of-factly. "You know, I still think you should advertise in the *AJ-C*, too. In one day, you could reach over 1.9 million adult readers in Metro Atlanta . . ."

"That's enough, Mom. I've heard your sales pitch, and you don't need it this time. I'll take the same package Trent Jackson bought, and I'll take his prime spot, too."

"Oh, honey, I already slated that spot for him, but I bet I could put you somewhere else that's equally appealing."

Marissa cleared her throat. "Mom."

"Yes?"

"How close to his ad can you get mine?"

"Well, I suppose I could put it right under his on the same page, but it really wouldn't be wise to put two websites that are virtually in direct competition with each other in the same section. I'm fairly certain that my boss won't let me."

"But we're not in competition," Marissa said sweetly. "I'm advertising a database for guys who cheat; he's advertising a database for girls who lie. See, no competition. You could explain that to your boss, couldn't you?"

"Oh, honey, I feel like you really are playing with fire here."

"I am," Marissa admitted. "But trust me; I'm not the one who'll get burned. So, when does his ad start?"

"Tomorrow, and he bought the three-repeat special. The same ad will run three days in a row, Thursday, Friday, and Saturday. He said he was debating running a larger ad in the Sunday paper, but hadn't made a decision yet."

"Did he send the ad camera-ready, or are you designing it for him?" Marissa asked, bringing up her email for TheGuyCheats.com and seeing Trent's name in her inbox. She clicked on it.

"I didn't design it personally, but one of our graphic guys did. Trent wanted it fairly basic, just the site name and the fact that it's for guys to list women who've lied. Why?"

"Can you ask the same designer to do mine, and make them match?"

Mona didn't answer.

"Mom?" Marissa coaxed.

"If you're sure that's what you want," Mona said. "And if I can get my boss to approve it, but if he doesn't see them as competing, like you said, then there shouldn't be a problem. Dear, is that really what you want?"

"Yes, it is," Marissa said, reading Trent's email, short and sweet.

Okay. I looked at my page on your site. Now maybe you'd like to look at yours. Ball's in your court, m'dear.

"Gotta go, Mom. Talk to ya later."

"I'll call you when I get to work. I'll need your credit card info for the ad, okay?"

"Yeah, fine." She disconnected and accessed the Die HardAtlanta site, while Petie, now done with his breakfast, whined at her chair. She scooted back to allow room for him between her and the computer, then put him in her lap. "Let's see what he's done now," she said to the puppy, as she moved the mouse to select the hand-over-mouth icon for TheGirlLies site.

The home page had a new line across the top of the screen.

Help Trent Create the Perfect Quote for Marissa Kincaid.

"Oh, boy," she said, with equal parts trepidation and excitement. What had he done now? She clicked on the bright-red link and was directed to her personal page on his site. Blessedly, there weren't any additional comments in the comment section—she noticed that right off—but there *was* a new addition, nonetheless. Trent had added a cartoon talk bubble to the right of her mouth. So far, the bubble was blank. However, a small box beneath it gave directions on how to enter the "Perfect Quote" for Marissa. The directions also said that Trent Jackson himself would review all submissions and decide the winner, whose winning entry would be posted in the bubble and who would win a month of free sidebar advertising on DieHardAtlanta.com.

"Well, how about that? He's managed to slam me and advertise his webzine at the same time. Not a bad move, Trent. And you're right. The ball is in my court. But I've already slammed it back in your direction. Of course, you won't learn that until you get tomorrow's paper." She lifted Petie, then laughed while she nuzzled his fur and he licked her chin.

This shouldn't be so much fun.

Trent was still in sleep pants and shirtless when the buzzer on his townhouse intercom announced a visitor Thursday morning. A very early visitor. He'd been up late going through the submissions for DieHardAtlanta, as well as submissions for his "Quote for Marissa" contest, and then had been too pumped up to sleep after seeing the staggering leap his site stats had taken in the past week, especially after Sunday's article in the paper. He'd more than quadrupled his subscriptions to DieHardAtlanta, and the increase didn't show any sign of slowing yet. Keith would be pleased . . . and would finally give the go-ahead for the print version of the magazine. In other words, Trent would achieve his goal. Not bad for a week's work.

Yawning, he ambled toward the annoying sound and punched the button. "Jackson."

"Let me in," Keith said, not one to mince words.

Speak of the devil. Trent buzzed him in, unlocked the door, and headed toward the kitchen to produce caffeine. The digital clock on his coffee maker announced that he'd slept two hours later than usual. Was it really nine o'clock? Thank goodness he hadn't scheduled any meetings this morning.

"Hell, you aren't dressed yet?" Keith asked, entering Trent's place wearing his traditional business attire, starched white shirt, navy pants, red power tie, and a rolled *Atlanta Journal* fisted in one hand.

"Yeah, I'm dressed, decided to go casual," Trent remarked sarcastically. "I do own the company, you know. I can go in late every now and then."

Keith's grin overpowered his face. "That's what I've been trying to tell you. So, you stayed up late working on the DieHardAtlanta site?"

"Both sites. Spent a good deal of time reviewing those articles from the prospective journalists, one for sports in general, and the other specifically for NASCAR." Trent had also spent a good deal of time examining Rissi Kincaid's photo, not that Keith needed to know.

"And?"

Trent swallowed, switched his train of thought from the sexy photo of the sassy lady to the articles. "Both of the reporters are young, mid-twenties, but they've got a way of telling a story that makes you pay attention. Hell, I felt like I was *at* Daytona, the way that kid described it. And the Braves game coverage was equally compelling."

"So you're hiring them."

"Sent them the offers last night."

"I guess that means you checked out your stats? Saw that your subscribers have increased well past that quadruple goal we discussed?" Keith climbed on one of the stools at the bar that separated Trent's kitchen and living room.

"I did. And I'm spending some of the cash to better the product." Trent poured two cups of coffee and slid one Keith's way.

"Don't recall you asking my opinion," Keith said, accepting the steaming mug and taking a big swallow.

"The goal was to quadruple my numbers, and I have, thanks to the attention for TheGirlLies, but I'm going for more," Trent said honestly.

"Which is exactly what I would've recommended." Keith slapped the paper on the counter in front of him. "And as I recall, I recommended the *AJ-C* advertising, too, but I didn't realize the two of you were teaming up."

"Who?" Trent asked, while Keith flipped through the pages in the paper, stopped at one, and turned it toward Trent.

"You're telling me you didn't know about this?"

Two advertisements, the exact same size, four columns by three inches, were stacked on top of each other in the upper right corner of the page. Both had black backgrounds with white letters, and both stood out prominently with the limited text that had been recommended by the advertising rep, aka Mona Kincaid. "Well, I'll be damned. She got one over on me."

"Actually, it's a joint benefit, so she's essentially helping your site, too, whether she meant to or not. I mean, look at it. It's as though the two of you are waving red flags and daring the other to charge first."

Trent examined the bold text, four lines in each ad. His . . .

> **Think Your Girl Is Lying?**
> **Find Out at TheGirlLies.com**
> **Know Your Girl Is Lying?**
> **Turn Her in at TheGirlLies.com**

Then, directly beneath his, hers . . .

> **Think Your Guy Is Cheating?**
> **Find Out at TheGuyCheats.com**
> **Know Your Guy Is Cheating?**
> **Turn Him in at TheGuyCheats.com**

"If she bought the same advertising special that I did, both of these will run through Saturday."

"And interest in DieHardAtlanta will continue to escalate," Keith said, shaking his head in obvious disbelief. "I swear, I couldn't have planned this any better myself. You're sitting on a gold mine with this business feud. How long do you think you two can keep it up?"

"As long as she wants," Trent said, and hoped that

Marissa Kincaid "wanted" for a very long time. In fact, he had tried all night long to think of a way for them to bring this feud up close and personal. No, it didn't feel right to simply call and ask her out; they were something of enemies now, after all. But he did want to see Rissi and find out if there was as much spirit and spark in the in-person version as there was in those photos. He wanted to turn this little battle into an intimate confrontation; somehow, he had to make that happen. And soon. Trent couldn't deny the woman was under his skin, and being a man who was used to getting what he wanted, Trent didn't want her merely under it; he wanted her against it, too.

"I spent some time on her site," Keith admitted. "You ever checked out her webzine, AtlantaTellAll? It's really well done. And last night I realized that one of the site's co-owners is married to a guy on my baseball team."

"The nurse, or the sex toy designer?" Trent asked, curiosity getting the best of him. He'd spent time on Marissa's site last night, too.

"Her name is Amy Brooks, and she's a *former* sex toy designer," Keith said. "She's a stay-at-home mom now. I've even seen her at the games, just didn't realize that she was one of Marissa Kincaid's coconspirators. She always brings their son along—cute kid—but occasionally, she has a couple of friends with her on the bleachers. I'm betting Marissa Kincaid has probably been there, though I can't say for sure."

If Trent had known that Rissi Kincaid had grown up to be so sassy and sexy and could potentially be perched in the stands, he'd have rethought his decision to refrain from baseball fun in favor of more time at work.

"You know, they didn't mention it in the article, but her husband also works for that sex toy company."

"Doing what?" Trent asked, trying to imagine exactly how a guy studied to be a sex toy designer. Surely there wasn't a degree for that, even at the online colleges.

"He's actually pretty high up in the company, over the massage oil division. I know because a lot of our teammates rag him about it, but the cowboy could care less. Plus, he plays a mean shortstop and gets a hit damn near every time, so they're not about to say too much. Besides, he's got a bombshell for a wife, and the two of them can hardly keep their hands off each other."

"Massage oil," Trent repeated, not quite knowing what else to say.

"Has a degree in chemistry," Keith enlightened, "and evidently he's got a talent for scents."

Trent drew in a too-big sip of coffee, let the hot liquid sizzle in his mouth, then winced through the swallow. So, one of Marissa's buddies was married to a chemistry whiz who had a nose for massage oil scents and played a mean shortstop. Why did his role as CEO of Jackson Enterprises, specializing in properties and investments, suddenly seem rather . . . boring?

But DieHardAtlanta wasn't boring. It was exciting, invigorating, and as masculine a webzine as they came. Well, if you weren't talking the ones along the line of *Playboy*, *Penthouse*, and *Hustler*.

And come to think of it, TheGirlLies.com wasn't boring either. In fact, it was gaining him the exposure he needed to achieve his goal, a lucrative publication with his name, Trent Jackson—not Jackson Enterprises—behind its success. But the more Trent thought about it, the more he realized . . .

Until TheGirlLies, his life hadn't been all that interesting or exciting. Hell, his name barely came up on Google, in spite of all the dollar signs on the books at Jackson Enterprises. He'd started DieHardAtlanta, but it really hadn't taken off, and though Jackson Enterprises was flourishing, it'd been prosperous since his grandfather started it in the late 1920s. And without Trent's help. Yes, Trent's true jump in the notable category happened when he started the liar site to taunt Marissa Kincaid. *She'd* put that excitement, that sizzle, back in his veins. Did she even realize it? And did she see Trent Jackson as the kind of guy who could keep her attention, or did she see him as the all-about-business guy he'd been merely a week ago?

If she could get him this energized via a website and some strategic newspaper advertising, what could she do if they spent time together one on one? And what could Trent do to make it happen?

"What?" Keith asked. "I know that look, and you're planning something."

"I want Marissa Kincaid," he said without hesitation.

Keith nodded knowingly. "Yeah, I figured you did, wondered how long it'd take you to realize it." He lifted his mug in mock salute, then downed another swallow of the steaming liquid. "Can't wait to see how you're going to pull this one off."

Trent's mind had already started pondering possibilities. He had a feeling he knew exactly how he'd pull it off. She wouldn't be able to resist. He could make it happen, and he would.

Liars never quit, but they sure have talented tongues.
— Winning Submission, Marissa Kincaid
Quote Contest — TheGirlLies.com

Chapter 8

At some ungodly predawn hour, Mona Kincaid boarded a tour bus headed to Branson for a two-week vacation with forty other folks from the Gwinnett Senior Citizens Center, which was why Marissa managed to sleep until seven, when Petie licked her chin and announced that he had needs, and that she should tend to them pronto.

"You know, you're nearly as bad as my mother," she huffed, climbing out of bed and changing into a T-shirt and shorts. Then the phone started to ring. "Ah, she remembered her cell phone." Marissa had expected as much. Vacation or not, Mona Kincaid always called— maybe not as early, but she called just the same. Ever since the two of them had started life "on their own," after her parents divorced, Mona had started her days with a mother-daughter chat, whether they were under the same roof or not. Marissa reached for the cordless phone and started toward the door with Petie, who paused only long enough to let her hook his leash to his collar. On the third ring, Marissa hit the *Talk* button. "Morning, Mom," she said sleepily, opening the door and letting Petie lead the way. She hadn't even checked the caller ID. She'd known it was Mona.

But she was wrong.

"You know, of all the things I've been called, I don't believe 'Mom' has ever entered the picture."

At the sound of that masculine, confident tone, Marissa's hands involuntarily tightened, along with a few other parts of her anatomy, and Petie yelped when the reaction caused a tiny jerk on his leash. "Sorry, Petie," she mumbled apologetically.

"Petie?" sexy voice asked, while Marissa dashed a peek at the caller ID. Sure enough, there was the proof. *Jackson, Trenton J.*

"My dog," she said, kneeling to rub Petie's soft coat in an effort to formally apologize . . . and because her knees had turned to jelly.

"Ah, so you're expecting phone calls from your mother at the crack of dawn, and you're hanging out with your dog at the same time. Exciting life you live, Rissi."

Marissa's jaw tensed, eyes narrowed. "Obviously, yours is equally exciting, since you spend your time running stupid contests about comic strip quotes—for my picture—and spend your mornings calling women who don't want to talk to you."

"The first part may be true," he said, and she could actually hear the smile in his words, "but the last part, well, I wouldn't be so sure. You do want to talk to me, don't you, Rissi?" he asked, then added huskily, "As much as I want to talk to you."

Okay. That stopped her cold. How was she supposed to argue with a guy who looked like Trent Jackson, intrigued the hell out of her, and admitted he wanted to talk to her? She tried to formulate a sassy response, but he didn't give her time before forging on.

"Saw the winning quote, did you?" he asked.

"I did," she admitted, having viewed the winning entry last night before going to bed. It was amazing she slept, given how mad she'd been. A tinge of that fury for his crazy antics rippled down her spine as she recalled the words in that cartoon bubble.

"I imagine you won't have any trouble getting dates, with all of the males in Atlanta wanting to know if it's true."

"If what's true?" she asked, before really thinking through her question. Obviously, he was talking about the quote, so obviously, he was talking about . . .

"Whether liars really have talented tongues," he said, with no hint of a smile filtering through any of the words.

"I can't believe you put that on your site," she said. "My mother read it! And you know good and well that you have no idea about anything having to do with me, or my tongue."

"Did Mona also read about my inadequate anatomy on your site? Because as far as I know, unless I ran into you at some point in life where I'd really had a good time with the bottle, there's no way you have any idea about anything having to do with me, Ms. Kincaid, and that includes my anatomy. Of course, if you'd like to investigate for yourself, and allow me to investigate your tongue talents—" He let the word hang.

Her throat went dry, and Petie barked. She fought to swallow, and licked her lips. Damn, this was *so* not what she needed to be thinking while talking to Trent Jackson. She tugged gently on Petie's leash to get him to go back inside, but he tugged back, ready to play.

Marissa wasn't in the mood. "Come on," she urged Petie.

"Hell," Trent said, his voice even deeper and sounding genuinely surprised. Then he added, "When and where?"

"Oh!" Marissa shook her head as though he could see her through the line, then she dashed inside, so no one in the parking lot could see her flaming face. Had she just unknowingly propositioned Trent Jackson? And had he accepted?

And was that really a bad thing?

Yes. Yes, it was. She released Petie's leash and let him run through the apartment with it dragging behind him. No time to chase him; she had to straighten things out, and quick, preferably before she gave Trent Jackson, the enemy, directions to her house.

"I was talking to my dog." Not the brightest of responses, but the truth, nonetheless.

"O-kay." He didn't say anything else, and again, Marissa felt compelled to explain. Unfortunately.

"N-no," she stammered. Damn. This was getting worse. "He wouldn't come back inside when I pulled on the leash, after I took him out to pee. Because he has to pee every morning, and I have to get up and take him out. Usually we see Mr. Nance and his Noodle, but they weren't out today."

"His—noodle?" Trent asked, and had the audacity to chuckle.

"I mean, his dog, Noodle," Marissa continued. What was wrong with her? And was she actually sweating? Yes, yes she was. A tiny trickle beaded at her neck and tumbled in a jagged line toward her right breast.

Not good.

"Why did you call me?" she asked.

"I wanted to find out what time you need to be at work."

Okay, not what she was expecting. "Why?"

"Have you been on the Net this morning?" he asked, and her curiosity skyrocketed. What now?

"No," she said, hurrying to the breakfast nook to boot up her laptop. "Why?"

"What's your home page?" he asked.

Strange question, she thought, but she answered. "MSN."

"Perfect. Log on, and tell me what you see."

"This better be good." She entered her password, then waited for the machine to boot.

"It's even better than I thought it'd be," he said, while MSN's home page displayed on her screen.

"What is?" she asked, scanning the headlines at the top of the page. Politics. Trouble in the Middle East. Forest fires in California. What was she looking for? "What's even better than you thought?" she repeated.

"Your voice. It was always raspy in school, and you didn't like it. You said it made you sound like a boy, but I thought it was cool. I just didn't know why I thought it was so incredible back then, but now I do."

Have mercy! What was he trying to do to her? And why was he doing it at 7:00 A.M. over the phone, instead of at night, all night. Wait. This was Trent Jackson, the guy who claimed she lied and even put a clever little quotation on his site about the fictitious allegation. She did *not* care what he thought of her voice.

And she'd just have to keep telling herself that. Over and over and over.

"So, did you find it?" he asked, snapping her back to reality.

"What exactly am I looking for?"

"Okay, so we didn't make the top half of the page, but we're still pretty prominent. Scroll down."

Marissa did, and gasped when she saw the photos from last Sunday's *AJ-C*.

"There you go," he said, as though he could see her through the phone. "Now click on the link. That's what hooked Coleman and Speedy."

Marissa clicked on the link, then let his words sink in. "Coleman and Speedy? The radio DJs? *That* Coleman and Speedy?"

"The very same."

"I love their show," she said automatically, then gasped again when more photos, the ones that didn't make the paper, were displayed. Marissa and Trent, behind their desks in various poses, along with the bold black-and-white dueling advertisements from the *AJ-C*. "What's this about?"

"Read the caption," he instructed, and made her feel like they were in school, with him the sexy instructor and her the more-than-willing pupil.

There she went with a sexual image again. But how did you talk to this voice, to this heavenly handsome man, without thinking of sex? How was she supposed to remember that she did *not* like him? And what was the gist of this MSN story?

She read the headline, in block letters, big enough that it looked like it belonged on a movie marquee.

World Wide Web War.

Beneath the headline was a condensed version of the feud that had started Sunday, merely five days ago, between TheGirlLies.com and TheGuyCheats.com, along with insightful miniphotos of Trent's page on TheGuy Cheats, complete with his horn-embellished teenage face, and Marissa's page on his site, complete with her bubble quote.

"Unbelievable," she said.

"Yeah. I think that may have been one of the adjectives Coleman and Speedy used when they called me this morning."

"They called you? Today? About this?" *No. Way.*

"Yeah, even put me on the air, believe it or not. Seems we're major news, babe. And they want to do an interview with the feuding pair."

Babe? Marissa would've argued with him about the term, but the remainder of his news needed her immediate attention. "An interview? With us?"

"Yeah, that isn't a problem, is it?"

She'd been interviewed by the *AJ-C*, and even with the humiliation that followed, it hadn't gone that badly. Her subscribers for AtlantaTellAll had increased, and her fees for advertising on her site had, too. And now there was the MSN footage. Why shouldn't she do radio? She was getting used to all of this publicity stuff, anyway. Plus, Coleman and Speedy wanted both of them, together. She and Trent Jackson, in the same place, and at the same time.

Marissa couldn't deny that she wanted that, too, merely to see if he looked as good in person, that was all. Not because she actually wanted to be near him.

Uh-huh.

"When and where?" she asked, then remembered a few minutes ago, when he'd asked the very same thing, but talking about something very, very different. Something hot and sweaty and . . .

"At the radio station, in two hours," he said, then corrected. "Make that an hour and forty-five minutes."

"You've got to be kidding," she said, glancing down at her old T-shirt and shorts. She hadn't even showered. "I don't know where the station is, and I have to be at work in an hour and a half."

"The station is in Marietta. I can pick you up, if you want."

"No, I can find it," she said, not wanting to risk attacking him outright if they were in as closed-in a space as his car. And she wasn't even sure what kind of attacking she was talking about—beating him up over the things he'd said on the web, or tackling him in a sexual frenzy over the things he'd said on the phone. The latter had much more appeal. "I want to drive," she added. "But that still doesn't fix the work problem. I'm supposed to be there by nine."

"You're a computer programmer, right? That's what the article in the paper said."

"Yeah, what's your point?"

"So call in and tell them you'll be programming a little later today. It isn't as though it won't wait. Hell, all of the programmers at my company work from home and only come in for staff meetings. Even then it's rare, since we conduct the majority of our staff meetings with video conferencing."

Marissa forced herself not to ask for a job. That'd be the dream position, working from home, where she could have a real life and maybe even raise a family, someday, and still have a steady income while she pursued the dream, the webzine. How cool would that be?

"They can live without you for an hour, can't they?" Trent continued, relentless in obtaining his goal. Was he that determined about everything? Not stopping until he was satisfied with the result? And wouldn't that be . . . nice?

She had to get her mind off sex. It'd help if she'd had sex lately, but she hadn't, so there. She'd just have to concentrate. Hard.

"Sure, they can do without me for a while," she said, and knew it was true. She actually had flex hours, so she could come in as early as she wanted and leave as late as she wanted, as long as she got her minimum eight hours. That had seemed like a really nice perk, until she heard Trent say his programmers worked from home. Probably in their pajamas. Talk about a perk. "I'll meet you at the radio station."

"Then it's a date," he said.

"It's a date," she repeated, then disconnected and looked at Petie, eyeing her suspiciously from the door of her bedroom with his leash trailing behind him and a tab of toilet paper hanging from one edge of his mouth. "You unrolled it again, didn't you?" she accused, moving toward him, then pulling the telltale paper from his teeth. The corner of his mouth remained tugged upward, as though he were smiling. Maybe he was. "All males are trouble," she stated. "And you're no exception."

Amazingly enough, that crook in Petie's smile inched a little higher, as though he knew that if she thought this was trouble, she hadn't seen anything yet.

"You're right," Marissa said, and felt somewhat ridiculous for talking to her dog, but not enough to stop. "I need backup." She picked up the phone and dialed Amy's number.

"Hey, did you know you're on the Yahoo home page?" Amy said, taking advantage of her caller ID and not bothering with a simple hello.

Marissa's throat tightened and her nerves were jittery, agitated by this new tidbit of information. "No. I saw it on MSN, but not Yahoo."

"No kidding? MSN, too?" Amy asked, and Marissa listened to computer keys clicking. "Have mercy, this is incredible. Just think how many visitors we'll have on our site!"

"Yeah, incredible." And just think how many people would be listening to her on the radio in—she glanced at the clock on her microwave—an hour and a half. "Listen, I need help."

"You name it," Amy said, then added, "superstar." Her giggle echoed through the line. "This is almost as exciting as winning the industry award for Pinky."

Nothing like vibrator talk to knock you completely off-balance, Marissa realized, as Amy rambled on and on about her famous creation, nicknamed Pinky. But Marissa had to stay focused, and she had to have someone with her when she faced off with Trent Jackson. She knew her hormones couldn't handle him one on one, for lots of reasons.

"Listen, Trent Jackson just called me—"

"Quit it," Amy interrupted, halting all talk of pink vibrators that lit up like a rainbow and were guaranteed to hit the G-spot.

"No, I'm serious. Evidently, Coleman and Speedy saw some of the press coverage for our website battle and want the two of us on their show, together, today. At nine." Marissa paused. "I need you to go with me, Amy. I can't be alone with him."

"Why? Do you think he's dangerous?"

"No." *Yes. Yes, Yes, YES!* Dangerous for her brain, dangerous for her body, dangerous for her business, and way too dangerous for her deprived libido. Hell, yes, the man was dangerous. "No, of course not," she lied. Again.

"Right," Amy said, unconvinced.

"Okay, the truth. The guy merely talked to me on the phone and I got so turned on! So there."

"Do tell," Amy said, then laughed so hard she snorted. "Oh, man, you've got it for your very first cheater. And you've got it bad."

"No, I don't. It's just that—well, he said that he liked my voice—and then he offered to let me personally check his anatomy to make sure Robin Grenade had lied. Oh, and then he wanted to check my tongue, to see if it was talented, or something like that. I don't know," Marissa blathered. "Everything got kind of, um, muddled."

"Muddled? Muddled!" Amy exclaimed. "Sounds like everything got moving, at warp speed. What'd you do, put on the brakes? And why on earth would you do that? It's been a long time since you've had a proposition like that, and you saw the guy. Have mercy, he's a sex toy walking."

This time Marissa snorted. Sex toy walking seemed an accurate description. "You are so bad."

"Landon says that's why he married me."

"Seriously, though, I'm afraid of what might come out of my mouth if I'm with him in person, and truthfully, I'm afraid of what else my body might involuntarily do, too. I need you to come with me, Amy. Can Landon watch Bo this morning? Or can Lettie?"

"Landon went in early, and Lettie's bringing Ginny over to stay with me for the weekend while she and Bill go to Tybee Island to celebrate their anniversary. I'm afraid I can't help you this time."

"I've got to go alone." Marissa hated how pathetic she sounded, but that was the way she felt. True, she wanted to know whether Trent was as sexy in person, but she didn't want to be alone in that studio with him and his killer smile, bedroom eyes, seductive voice. She tripped all over her words merely trying to talk to the guy on the phone. What would she say in person, and on the air?

"Good grief, I can feel your pulse increasing through the phone. I've never known you to get this worked up over a guy."

Marissa simply waited. It wouldn't take Amy long to remember.

"Well, there was Blake, but that was different."

Bingo. "What was different?" Marissa asked, curious about Amy's take on that particular disaster.

"Easy. You were in love with Blake, but you aren't in love with Trent, are you?"

"I don't even know him anymore."

"Exactly. You're in lust with him, and for now, that's exactly what you need. I say jump his bones and give your body, your mind, the whole nine yards. This is what you need to move forward. And while you're at it, you can show him that liars really do have talented tongues."

"I haven't lied," Marissa said, then felt foolish when Amy's laughter rolled through the line.

"Who cares about the lying? I was talking about the tongue. And it's funny that you went straight for the lying part, but didn't say a thing about not wanting to use your tongue, in whatever way you choose, on Trent Jackson. That says a lot."

"I still don't want to go to the radio station alone," Marissa said, "whether I end up jumping his bones or not. And I sure don't want to even have the slightest hint of 'I want to jump you' on my face when I get to that station. You know Coleman and Speedy; they won't miss anything, and they sure won't miss pointing it out to their listening audience. That's all I need, for Atlanta to know I'm sitting there drooling over the guy who called me a liar. And their station is the one that we listen to at work. When I come in later, my coworkers, mostly male, will know everything I said."

"Will he be drooling over you?"

"What?" Marissa asked, while Petie charged through the living room with his leash and a long stream of toilet paper trailing in his wake. "Oh, shoot, I've got to catch Petie, and then I've got to get ready—if someone will go with me. Is there any way you can go?"

"No, I can't let Lettie down," Amy said, "But Candi is off today. I'll have her over here by the time you're out of the shower. Now go get ready and stop panicking."

"Thanks," Marissa said, vastly relieved, even if she couldn't catch the silver dog with the mischievous twinkle in his eye. She made a lunge for him as he passed, but missed, and ended up hitting the floor with a thud.

"But there's a condition," Amy quickly added.

Marissa gave up on Petie, for now. "What's that?" she asked, breathless.

"When you do decide that you're definitely going to jump his bones, let me know first. I mean, before it happens."

"You've got to be kidding."

"Nope, serious," Amy said.

"Why on earth would I need to let you know first?"

"So I can send you a care package, courtesy of Adventurous Accessories and the Brooks family."

"A Pinky of my own?" Marissa asked.

"Yeah, right. You already have one. Candi found it one night when she was looking for the phone book. You really need a better place to stash your supplies. But I'll send you some of our newer items, guaranteed to please."

Marissa didn't say a word. What could she say? She'd thought her personal Pinky was a secret, but she was learning with every passing day that there were no more secrets in her life. The world already knew about every guy who ever cheated on her, they knew that she cried during sex (even if they didn't realize it was only once), and they knew that she had an ongoing feud with Trent Jackson.

How long till they knew that merely thinking about him made her quiver with desire? And would she be able to hide the lust in her eyes if she was thinking about it?

Petie ran through again, circling wide to keep out of her reach, a silver streak with a white paper tail. She looked at the clock. Merely an hour to catch a dog, de-t.p. her bathroom, and, most important, face Trent Jackson.

Well, she had wanted excitement. Now she had it.

One juicy interview . . . deserves another.
—SPEEDY

Chapter 9

"Can I really do this?" Marissa asked Candi, as the elevator surged upward in the building that housed the *Coleman and Speedy Morning Show*. They might have gone up, but her stomach hovered near the bottom floor. She was going to be sick. Terrific.

Petie issued a bark of encouragement, or Marissa decided to take it that way, from his snug position in Candi's arms. Candi had thought it'd be smart to bring him along, in case Marissa needed an on-air diversion. The suggestion had sounded pretty good at the time, but now Marissa remembered all of the inappropriate dog comments she'd blurted on the phone with Trent this morning, and wasn't certain at all whether this occasion called for a salt-and-pepper schnauzer with a toilet paper fetish. Imagine what Petie could get into in a studio. Or worse, Marissa could ask his opinion; she had been doing that a lot lately. All she needed was to get on the radio, broadcasting live, and let all of Atlanta hear her talking to her dog.

Not in this life.

"Petie is going to sit with you when I do the interview, okay?" she said, and hated that her voice quivered.

"If that's what you want," Candi said, smiling. Well, of course she would smile. *She* wasn't about to do a live radio interview about her cheater website . . . or be in a room with a guy who drove her nearly to insanity, on several levels.

Marissa did a once-over of her reflection in the shiny elevator wall. Her hair had evidently felt sassy this morning, because the stray curl that drove Marissa nuts was, once again, embellishing her left temple. Another Betty Boop day. Yea. Then she examined her choice of clothing. The new white blouse she'd purchased at Macy's was fashionable yet professional, the exact look she wanted. She'd fallen in love with the way one side crossed over the other and then fastened with a black crystal at the hip. Paired with black slacks and black pumps, the shirt gave her the business presence she was after, a woman who would make it in a man's world.

Or did she look like a waiter at Olive Garden?

"It's really cool that they're going to have both of you on together. It's been a while since they've done one of those kind of shows," Candi said, stroking Petie's back while he barked his approval. "Cool, huh, Petie?"

"Those kind of shows?" Marissa asked.

"You know, throwing two opposites together. Don't you remember the two bull riders that were in town for the rodeo a few months back? They brought them on the show and got to talking about how bull riders were sometimes looked at as not the sharpest crayons in the box. Then they talked about the National Spelling Bee taking place that week, and how Speedy had been watching it to try to learn some new words. Next thing those bull riders knew, Coleman and Speedy had convinced them to compete in a live spelling bee, on the air." Candi laughed at the memory. "They had all of these words that had to do with bulls, and nothing remotely easy to spell. It was hilarious. Remember that one guy trying to spell castrated?"

Oh, yeah, Marissa was going to be sick. What was the real reason Coleman and Speedy wanted to interview Trent Jackson and her together? And how long until she found out? The elevator bell dinged and Marissa had her answer. Not very long.

"This is it," Candi said, still smiling, as if she was actually excited. "Thirteenth floor."

"Thirteenth? I thought places skipped the thirteenth floor. Isn't there some kind of unwritten law about that?" Marissa asked, as the elevator doors slid open to reveal the radio station's lobby, empty except for a tall, dark-haired, good-looking man in snazzy business-casual attire who was evidently awaiting their arrival.

Had he heard her comment?

"Thirteen's not so bad," he said, stretching out a hand. "In fact, it's always been my lucky number. Marissa Kincaid, I presume."

Great. She hadn't even entered the recording area and already she sounded like a basket case, a superstitious basket case at that. "Yes."

He placed his palm in hers, then surprised her, covering her outer hand with his other palm with a comforting firmness that somehow made her believe everything would be okay. Would it?

And then he smiled. Marissa's memory was jostled. For some bizarre reason, she remembered the friendly grin from another time, and definitely another place. But where?

"Have we met?" Okay, this would be the precise moment when Coleman, Speedy, and Trent Jackson should magically appear and assume she was hitting on a stranger in the waiting area of the recording studio. Wouldn't surprise Marissa. In fact, providing ammunition to the enemy immediately before a live interview would go along perfectly with the rest of her week.

Fortunately, the guy didn't even flinch at the typical pickup line. "No, we haven't, not officially, that is," he said, "though I know quite a bit about you from Trent, and from both of your sites. I'm Keith Parker, Trent's financial advisor, and even though I haven't met you personally, I do believe I may have seen you a time or two before, at the Gwinnett baseball fields."

Recognition slammed Marissa, which was only right. Healthy thirty-something women didn't typically forget a guy who looked that good in baseball pants. "You're on Landon's team."

"Guilty as charged. And I'll go ahead and admit that I can't field a ball, or hit one, for that matter, anywhere near as well as he can, but they haven't kicked me off the team yet, so I guess I'll do." He turned toward Candi. "I've seen you there, too, haven't I?"

"You're number thirteen. Third base," Candi said breathily.

He raised his brows at Marissa, as though she should've known this as well, but she only remembered the smile. Candi had evidently taken better notice. Much better notice, from the I'm-almost-at-the-drooling-point look on her face.

"This is Candi Moody," Marissa said, snapping the words out to try to bring Candi back into the real world, the one where she wasn't undressing this guy in her mind.

"Right," Candi said, and apparently squeezed Petie when she spoke. His sharp, high-pitched yelp of protest made Marissa jump. "And this is Petie," Candi added, lifting her cradled arms to raise the puppy toward Keith.

At the sound of his name, Petie's ears pricked forward and he emitted a low growl.

"He's trying to protect me from you," Candi informed him, then tenderly rubbed behind the dog's ears. "It's okay, Petie," she soothed. "He's actually Marissa's dog, but he's protective of all of us. I'm kind of partial to him, too."

"Really," Keith said, holding his palm toward Petie. The dog sniffed it suspiciously, then dashed his tongue out for an exploratory lick. Naturally, after the first lick, he licked some more. Keith laughed, a nice laugh that seemed to roll from his chest with ease. "I think he's decided I won't hurt you," he said. "Do you agree?"

"No," Candi said, then blinked a few times and looked helplessly at Marissa. "I mean yes, I agree."

Candi's brown eyes were glazed over, the same way they were whenever she arrived at Marissa's after a twenty-four-hour shift. But then it was due to a lack of sleep. Now, it was due to a lack of sex. Oh, well, wasn't that fitting? Marissa brought Candi along to keep her mind off Trent, and Candi had already lost her senses over his financial advisor.

"Candi," Marissa said sternly. "Where do you think we need to go?"

Candi shifted her entire body away from Keith, as if she were scared to keep looking at those baby blue eyes. Smart move. Marissa had the impression she'd just watched the equivalent of a snake eyeing a bird, except this bird wanted to be eyed. And more than eyed. The fact that Keith Parker looked good in baseball pants—and that Candi knew it—didn't help. But Marissa needed Candi right now, good-looking guy flirting with her or not.

"I imagine we go through there." Candi pointed toward a brown door on the opposite side of the lobby emblazoned with a *Coleman and Speedy* logo in its center, and an "On Air" sign illuminated above the frame. The DJs' logo was popular around town, with the caricature of Coleman in a suit and tie, and Speedy in an "I'm With Stupid" T-shirt, distinctly depicting the two personalities. Mr. Politically Correct, and Mr. Redneck Tech. Right now, Marissa wasn't sure whom she feared more.

"Actually, *she* goes through there," Keith said, indicating Marissa. "They specified only Trent and Marissa Kincaid were to enter the recording booth. Claimed it was because the room was so small, but I'm thinking they want to get you two alone. They're known for surprising their guests, you know."

Ah. Well, there's a guy who doesn't pull his punches.

"I was just reminding Marissa of that," Candi said. "Remember the rodeo guys . . ."

Marissa cleared her throat and interrupted Candi. She didn't want to hear about the spelling bee again. "You don't have any idea what they have in mind?" she asked Keith, petting Petie but eyeing Candi.

"No clue," he said, but his sly smile said he did have a clue and chose not to share.

"Right," Marissa said, huffing out a breath in exaspera-tion. "And when will Trent get here? We're supposed to start in"—she looked at her watch—"ten minutes."

"He's already inside. They said he could go ahead and get started, so he asked me to watch for you and send you in when you arrived." He ignored Marissa's complete loss of color—she could feel it draining from her face—and geared his attention toward Candi and Petie. "Come on, Coleman told me where we can go to listen to the broad-cast, a room down the hall."

"Okay with you?" Candi excitedly asked Marissa, still standing in semishock.

Trent was already in there? Doing what? Saying what? And did she really want to know?

Marissa nodded numbly, watched them turn to leave, and then headed toward her destiny. Or, should she say, her destruction?

"Coleman said not to knock, so go on in," Keith called, reaching toward Petie as he and Candi walked away. Out of the corner of her eye, Marissa saw Petie shift from Candi's arms to Keith's. Super. Now her dog had switched teams.

She stepped inside the room and immediately realized two important facts. One, the recording area was freez-ing, as in you-could-hang-meat-in-here cold. And two, her blouse was thin, as in you-could-hang-Christmas-ornaments-on-her-nipples thin.

Not good.

"Ah, here she is now."

Marissa turned toward the booming perfect-for-radio voice. Coleman, she realized, recognizing the tone that she listened to each morning during her drive to work. He was the more eloquent of the two, with Speedy along for a pinch of redneck comic relief.

Plastering on her best smile, Marissa started down a short hall toward the glass-walled room where Coleman and Speedy sat across from each other at a double desk. Two computer monitors were back to back, with each man viewing his own screen while conversing via a thick microphone hanging from a swing rod in the ceiling. Through the glass forming the back wall, Marissa saw three people, two men and one woman, apparently monitoring the production controls. They all smiled at her, and the woman waved.

Did the woman's face look tense? As though she knew Marissa was walking into a death trap? And where was Trent Jackson?

Marissa opened the door to the DJ area and stepped inside. Wouldn't you know it? The booth was even colder than the outer area, and her nipples were giving Atlanta's most well-known DJs her own version of a private salute.

Scratch that. She was saluting the DJs, but she was also saluting the man now turning one of two cushy recliners, evidently meant for guests, in her direction. How had she missed those chairs? Right, they were hidden by the door. But she should have known Trent Jackson was in here somewhere. Keith, the guy who took her friend *and* her dog, had told her.

"Hello, Rissi," Trent said, those piercing dark eyes deliberately acknowledging her chest, then the rest of her, before he stood. And stood. And stood. He stepped closer, his rock-solid chest behind a crisp white shirt merely inches from her face. Then the musky scent of rock-solid male joined in for effect.

Marissa's head swam. The vision of snake and bird re-emerged. She swallowed, struggled to maintain her wits, and realized she needed to converse. Somehow.

"How tall are you?" she blurted.

Have mercy, she should *not* be attracted to cocky grins, particularly a cocky grin from Trent Jackson. But she was. Attracted. To the grin, and the wavy hair, and the smoky eyes, and the broad shoulders, and the impressive chest, and . . .

"Six-two," he said, extending a hand. She did the same, then he took her palm and held it. Skin to skin. Male to female. Keith's shake had been nice; this one was, in a word, deadly.

Had she actually been cold a second ago?

Coleman cleared his throat, and Marissa jumped at the unexpected invasion. Then she saw the two DJs exchange a knowing look and a nod.

A nod?

"Are we on the air?" Marissa asked, panic-stricken.

"Commercial break," Speedy said, removing his gray earphones and indicating two additional headsets, one red and one blue, on the coffee table between the guest chairs. "But we've got you all set to jump in during the next segment. That blue one is yours. You'll hear our callers and be able to answer them live." Unlike Coleman's, Speedy's voice didn't sound familiar. It sounded deeper than it did on the radio each morning. Deeper, and more intelligent.

"Callers?" Marissa questioned, holding her breath as Speedy swung a huge, intimidating microphone her way.

"Yeah. Trent already covered the basic information

about what your sites do, which went pretty quick, since most folks have already read it on the web. What we're going to do now is let folks call in and ask you guys some questions. Now, go on and have a seat and get comfortable," Speedy said. "This one will pick up both of you." He waited for her to sit in the chair by Trent's, then maneuvered the swing bar so the microphone for guests was directly between them, making it impossible for either of them to speak without looking at the other. Without a doubt, this was the dumbest thing Marissa had ever done.

Trent handed her the blue headset, and she took it, being careful not to let her hand touch his. She'd already learned what that would do and needed no more of it today. Or ever.

"Thanks," she mumbled, pulling the semicircular band apart to snap the cushy round speakers over her ears. Unfortunately, the blocking out of all surrounding sound made her other senses kick it up a notch. For example, her sense of sight started the fun by taking in every magnificent inch of Trent Jackson, talking to Speedy about his headset. Then the sense of smell took control, and Marissa inhaled the full effect of musky male. Her mouth started to water. Fortunately, the senses of touch and taste were not up for grabs.

Speedy moved back to his chair and turned a large knob on the desk. "All right," he said, his voice screaming at her through the headphones. "We're on in five."

Marissa winced at the yelling and realized too late that she should have asked about the volume control on these things. Then she watched with horror as Speedy held up one hand and slowly let the fingers roll toward his palm. Five, four, three, two, one.

The snappy jingle for Coleman and Speedy's show began, and the loudness forced Marissa's eyes to close. Her head would explode before this was over if she didn't figure out how to adjust the volume. She lifted a hand to the earpiece on her right side, and felt the warmth of Trent Jackson's palm over hers. Startled, she looked at him, at that reassuring smile and smoldering eyes, and watched him gently move her hand out of the way, then adjust her volume control.

And now we've added the sense of touch. One more to go. *Oy!*

Trent pointed to the microphone between them as though reminding her they shouldn't speak aloud. "Better?" he mouthed and lifted his dark brows in question.

Marissa swallowed, nodded, and remembered the friend from middle school. One hand inadvertently moved to her mouth, and she prepared to nibble what was left of her nails. With a slight shake of his head, Trent reached toward her again, took her wrist, and moved her hand back to the armrest on the chair. "It'll be okay," he mouthed again, while Marissa wondered what else she could do that would make him touch her again. And soon. Had she really thought this was the enemy? Because he seemed so *friendly.*

"All right, Atlanta, we've got a real treat for you now," Coleman's voice echoed through the headset at a much more desirable tone.

Marissa took a deep breath. Not only was she ill-prepared to answer questions from callers, but she was also ill-prepared to handle Trent Jackson.

"You've had the chance to hear about these unique databases started by Trent Jackson and Marissa Kincaid," Coleman continued. "As Mr. Jackson explained, basically, he designed a place for guys to oust women who lie, and then Marissa echoed that concept with a database for women to identify men who cheat."

Trent nodded in agreement, and Marissa realized she'd just been snowed. *She* wasn't the copycat here.

"Actually, I started the cheater website first," she said, ignoring Trent's smirk and the hey-whatever-she-says shrug he offered the other two males in the room. Why hadn't she considered this? It was a three-to-one ratio, and estrogen was on the losing end. She darted a gaze at the woman in the adjoining room, but the lady was too busy monitoring controls to offer any support whatsoever.

So much for girl power.

"Right, right," Speedy said condescendingly, then gave Coleman another look that Marissa couldn't identify. Obviously there was more going on here than she'd expected, which wasn't a good thing. So this was what Keith had been hinting at when she'd met him in the lobby. These DJs had an agenda. What was it?

And did Trent know?

She jerked her head toward him, eyeing her as if he wanted to throw her on the floor and give her . . . everything she wanted. Oh, man. Yes, she wanted it, but she didn't want it now, and she never wanted it with him. She narrowed her eyes at the smug hunk, raised one corner of her mouth in a snarl, and wished him dead.

He laughed. Laughed! And so did the DJs.

Damn.

"All right, then," Coleman said. "Folks, I'm not sure

if you could hear it in Ms. Kincaid's tone, but trust me;
if you were in the studio now, you would feel the heat of
her animosity toward Trent Jackson, her very first cheater.
And, according to the *Atlanta Journal*, the one who set
the pattern for all others to follow."

"You know, I've seen that look a time or two," Speedy
said. "Whenever my old hound dog, Buzzard, cops an attitude. He's looked at me like that before, usually when
I try to take his pig's ear away. I tell you, sure enough,
you'd better not come between Buzzard and his pig's ear.
You ever bought any of those pig's ear chewies at the
PetSmart, Coleman? Buzzard loves them."

"We are not here to talk about Buzzard, Speedy," Coleman interjected, ever the voice of reason. "Today we're
here to talk to Marissa Kincaid, co-owner of TheGuy
Cheats.com and AtlantaTellAll.com, and Trent Jackson,
owner of DieHardAtlanta.com and TheGirlLies.com, and
consequently, the current CEO of Jackson Enterprises."

With Coleman's last description, Trent flashed Marissa a knowing grin. Did the DJ realize he'd effectively
deleveled the playing field? Trent was a Jackson, of the
Jackson Enterprises Jacksons, and she . . . wasn't.

"Fine," Speedy continued, and somehow gave the word
three syllables. "We don't have to talk about Buzzard, but
you and I may need to talk about something. From the
looks of this woman, she don't want to be in the same
room with this Jackson fellow, much less talk on the air
with him." Speedy really laid the hick accent on strong.
Oddly enough, when she listened to him in the car each
morning, it didn't sound nearly as irritating, but now that
she'd heard him speaking off-air and knew that the guy

wasn't nearly as backwoods as he claimed, the whole fake hick thing got old. Quick.

Then again, was it really his accent bothering her? Or the fact that he was so on-target with his assessment? She didn't want to be in this room, or talk on the air, with Trent. Speedy pegged her right. Thank goodness he couldn't also tell that as aggravated as she was with Trent Jackson, she could still hear his sexy voice from that phone call this morning.

"When and where?"

Suddenly, the woman in the other room popped up her head, and Marissa noticed she also wore a small headset. She pointed to Coleman, gave Marissa an apologetic, flat-line smile, then turned her attention back to the control panel in front of her.

Why was she apologizing? And did Marissa really want to know?

Didn't matter. She was about to find out.

"And we have our first caller," Coleman said, reading something on his computer monitor. "Shelly from Alpharetta. Welcome to the show, Shelly."

"Hi, Coleman," the woman said. "I listen to you and Speedy every morning."

"Ooh, it sounds like we have a first-time caller. Is that right, Shelly?" Speedy asked.

"Yes," the woman said with a giggle.

At that, Speedy pressed a button and a drum roll beat through the silence, followed by cheers and applause. "Welcome to the world of Speedy and Coleman," Speedy said. "Always nice to hear from a virgin caller."

"Speedy," Coleman warned.

"Sorry, couldn't resist," Speedy shot back.

"So, Shelly, you haven't called in before. What made you want to call this time?" Coleman asked. "I'm always curious about what the show can do to encourage folks, like yourself, to participate."

"It's the cheater site," Shelly said. "Is Ms. Kincaid there now? Can she hear me?"

Speedy pointed to Marissa, and Trent reached up and moved the microphone down a little, closer to her mouth than his. Marissa pushed it back to the central location. No way did she want to yell at the callers. She sent another look of warning Trent's way, and he responded by lifting one corner of his mouth in a seductive smile that made her breath catch in her throat.

She was speechless. And Speedy noticed.

"Ms. Kincaid, can you hear the caller?" he asked, then added, "She's quite interested in staring down Mr. Jackson right now, Shelly. Give her a sec."

"I can hear you, Shelly," Marissa said sweetly and debated whether to shift her glare to Speedy. Better not; he was one of the two parties in the room with the most control of this situation.

Marissa sure wasn't.

"Ms. Kincaid, I want to thank you. I'd been dating this guy for a few weeks and heard about your site, so I keyed in his name, and sure enough, there he was, with over twenty posts from women talking about his track record. I don't know if I'd have found out about the kind of guy he really was without your site."

"I'm glad to have helped," Marissa said, and noticed her voice sounded much raspier through the headset. Or did her voice really sound like that? Was that what Trent meant when he said he liked it? She'd kept her attention on Speedy and Coleman while she answered, even though the microphone was directly between her and Trent, but now she darted a glance his way.

He leaned back in his chair, all comfortable and waiting for his turn, apparently not nervous at all, while Marissa's stomach was in knots. At least she had handled the first caller okay. Or she thought she had, until she saw Coleman hold up his hands in a surrender gesture, then continue talking to Shelly, still on the line.

Why hadn't the woman hung up like a good little caller?

"Okay, okay," he said. "Shelly, I have to clarify here. Did you end things with this guy solely on the information you gained from TheGuyCheats.com?"

"Oh, no," Shelly said. "But I found out about his cheating habit there. Then I started asking questions of the other women he dated in the past, learned his pattern, and caught the cheating—"

Shelly's next word was beeped out.

Speedy's cackle trickled through the line on the wake of the cover-up bleep. "Learned his pattern?" he asked. "Oh, this is good. So not only do the cheatees report their cheaters on the site, but you all kind of form a—what would you call it—a posse, maybe? Gang? Clan? Well, whatever you wanna call it, you all get together and figure out how to get back at the guy who has done you all wrong, right? Sounds like something Steven Spielberg might be interested in for a movie, don't you think, Coleman? What would he call it? *Revenge of the Women Done Wrong*? Hey, I'd go see it."

"Sounds good to me," Shelly said.

"You said you learned his pattern," Coleman interrupted. "Can you explain that? Do all cheaters have a pattern?" He tilted his head toward Marissa. "Or is that something you could answer, Ms. Kincaid?"

Marissa swallowed and wished the first call had gone to Trent. "I think men who cheat typically cheat again," she said, careful of every word, and also careful to keep her eyes focused on the microphone, instead of Trent Jackson, lounging in the other chair. "But I'm not sure if that's the pattern Shelly is referring to."

"No, we talked specifics," Shelly said. And again, Marissa wondered why the lady didn't simply hang up. Now.

"For example . . ." Speedy prompted.

"Well, the girl he cheated on before me said that his favorite place to take the 'other woman' was the Fuzzy Duck, a bar downtown. Another of the women he cheated on said the same thing, that she'd found out he'd been to the Fuzzy Duck with someone else while he was dating her. So two nights ago, he said he had to work late, and a friend and I headed down to the Duck. Sure enough, his car was parked in the back. We went in, and helped the lying *[beep]* and his good-for-nothing *[beep]* learn how to wear their drinks and deal with a size-eight stiletto to the *[beep].*"

"O-kay," Coleman said. "And you wanted to thank Ms. Kincaid for her help in making all of that possible?"

"Yes, thanks again," Shelly said.

Marissa's cheeks burned, but she remained silent. What could she say?

"Fuzzy Duck," Speedy said. "I've been there a time or two."

"Doesn't surprise me," Coleman said.

"It's one of those places where you don't want to try to say the name after you've had a few beers, you know. I mean, mix up those consonants and you're in a heap of trouble. You ever thought about that, Coleman?" Speedy said, snickering. "Or don't you get it? Swap the consonants, and . . ."

"What I'd like to get is another caller on the line," Coleman said.

The woman in the back room nodded and fed the next caller through.

~

Chapter 10

You're live with Coleman and Speedy," Coleman said. "And who are we talking to?"

"This is Vic, calling from Douglasville," the deep voice bellowed through the line.

Marissa moved her hand to the volume control and eased it downward. Vic was either in a tunnel, or driving with his window down while placing the call. Either way, the guy was attempting to yell over the sound of traffic in the background.

"Welcome to the show, Vic," Coleman said. "And did you call to talk to one of our guests?"

"Yeah, I've got a question for Trent Jackson."

"Go ahead," Coleman said, then pointed to Trent, who sat up in his chair and brought that to-die-for mouth toward the microphone. Marissa leaned back and turned her eyes away from Trent Jackson and toward the three people working the controls in the other room. No need to stay close to the microphone when it was his turn in the hot seat, and she didn't want to be that close to him anyway. Okay, maybe she wanted to, but she didn't need to.

Act aloof, she silently told herself, *as though nothing he can say or do will affect you in any way, positively or negatively.* She thought of songs, cheating songs. What would tomorrow's song of the day be? And they needed a topic for next week's AtlantaTellAll poll. Last week had been a sexiest-eyes poll, maybe this week they could do sexiest mouth.

Trent moistened his lips, preparing to answer whatever question the caller tossed his way.

Sexiest mouth. *Judge, we have a winner.*

No. What was she doing? Staring at his lips, that's what, and dammit, he noticed. One corner of his mouth eased a little higher in a caught-you-looking grin.

Marissa moved her attention back to the three people in the control room. The woman held up another finger, apparently to indicate to Coleman that yet another caller was sitting at the ready. Oh, joy. How long was this supposed to last, anyway? She did have to go to work today, after all. Maybe she should remind Coleman and his redneck sidekick hick.

"I wanted you to know that I submitted a quote for the Quote for Marissa contest," Vic said, and Marissa closed her eyes and waited for the worst. "The winning quote wasn't mine, but it was a good one."

"Thank you," Trent said, confidence dripping through both words.

Marissa kept her eyes closed. She didn't have to look at the man in the next seat to know he was grinning.

"But I had to call in and ask why you picked the one

you did as the winning quote. Was it because you had personal experience to confirm the fact?"

"The fact?" Trent repeated.

Marissa knew what was coming, and she didn't want to hear it, much less see the thing unfold, so she clamped her eyes closed even tighter and prayed for a miracle.

"Whether liars have talented tongues," Vic said, confirming her fears. "And that liar in particular. I mean, don't take this the wrong way, Ms. Kincaid, but you're one hot number. So I got to wondering if the reason Trent Jackson picked that quote was because he knew that you had a talented tongue. Was that it?"

Marissa's eyes popped open and she shot a look of pure venom to Trent. It was bad enough he put that out on the Net, but to continue that particular lie here would put the final nail in his coffin. Sexy or not, he'd be dead. Soon.

Coleman cleared his throat loudly and raised his brows at his control panel team. "Obviously we didn't field the entirety of Vic's question before we sent that one through."

"I'd like to answer the question," the enemy said calmly.

All eyes in the recording area, and in the outer room, turned to Trent.

"And we'd all like for you to," Speedy said.

"I picked that quote because it was the best one submitted, not because I had any actual firsthand knowledge of Rissi's—I mean Ms. Kincaid's—talented tongue. I don't."

"Okay, I'll buy that," Vic continued, still yelling at a semiscream. "But what about you, Ms. Kincaid? On your site, you second another woman's comment regarding

Trent Jackson's 'anatomy'—I believe that's the way the two of you termed it—so how about you? You have any firsthand knowledge in that area?"

"No!" Marissa blurted, with a little more enthusiasm than she planned. She took a breath and calmed her pulse. "No, I don't. And I'd like to say that my comments were purely in jest, you know. I certainly don't know a thing about his anatomy, nor do I want to," she said, lying through her teeth. "Ever," she added for good measure. Then she smiled at Coleman, Speedy, and Trent. Chalk up one for the girl.

"So you lied," Vic said.

Marissa blanched. "It was a joke," she insisted, realizing she'd been set up, and realizing it about ten seconds too late.

"But you did lie," Vic continued.

"Hey," Speedy interjected. "Looks like there's a good reason that she's listed on the liar database, and that Trent Jackson is on the cheater one. She lied to him, or about him, or whatever, and he cheated on her. Granted, he was only thirteen at the time . . ."

"I didn't," Trent said firmly.

"Sorry, I didn't catch that," Speedy said, winking at Coleman as though he'd personally struck gold. And in the realm of broadcasting, Marissa supposed he had.

"I didn't cheat on her. It was a misunderstanding, and I'm perfectly able to explain what happened back then."

"Go ahead," Coleman said. "I'm betting we'd all enjoy hearing it."

"Yes," Marissa said. "Go ahead."

"No." Trent shifted in the seat, propping an elbow on the armrest nearest Marissa and leaning her way. "No," he repeated, his voice husky, but even though he lowered his voice, it still rumbled steadily through the headset, and over the air. "I do plan to talk to you and explain what happened, but not over the radio. Not with any kind of audience. I'll talk to you alone, just the two of us, in private."

Marissa shook her head. "That's not happening." The thought of being with him in private bothered her more than she cared to admit, or analyze. "I have no desire to be alone with you, for any reason."

"I've never cheated on anyone," Trent said, his voice disarmingly calm, cool, and collected. "Look at those comments on your site, Rissi. Not a one of them said I cheated. They may have said negative things about me, my body, and hey, even my breath." He leaned closer, so close that Marissa had to press her head against the back of the chair to keep his mouth from touching hers. "Rissi, what do you think? About my breath?" He blew a steady stream of deliciously warm, minty air against her mouth.

"It's—fine," she whispered. But her heart wasn't, and neither was her head, or her senses. And she'd wager that the sense of taste was closer than she realized.

"And you can't say anything about my—anatomy—because, as you've said, you don't have firsthand knowledge, do you?"

"No," she admitted, while Trent cupped his hand against the side of his mouth to hide his words from Coleman, Speedy, and crew, and then mouthed slowly, so Marissa couldn't doubt a single syllable . . .

"When—and—where."

"Sorry, we didn't catch that," Speedy said, then relayed to the audience, "I believe these two are sharing some sort of private conversation. Are you discussing, er, anatomy over there?"

"No," Marissa said, pressing her behind into the seat to force another few centimeters between her and the extremely determined male.

"No," Trent agreed, smiling and not budging one iota from his predatory stance. "I was simply pointing out to Ms. Kincaid that I've never cheated on anyone, and that includes her. If she'd ever give me the chance to explain, alone, she'd figure that out."

"And like I said, that's not happening. Now if you'd please move back to your chair," she said, practically pleading. Or panting.

"Sure." Trent eased back to his side, while the warmth covering Marissa's body went away, too. The guy was hot, in lots of ways. Too hot to handle, in her opinion. Or at least, he was too hot for her to handle, and she didn't want to handle any more of him. In fact, she wanted this interview to be over, as quickly as possible.

"Well, Vic, what do you think?" Speedy asked. He waited, looked at the woman in the back room, and saw her shrug, then continued, "I think we lost our connection. Do we have another caller ready?"

The lady nodded, pushed a button, and pointed at Coleman.

"You're live with Coleman and Speedy," he said. "Who are we talking to?"

"Penny," the lady said.

Marissa adjusted the volume on her headset. Unlike Vic, Penny was a soft talker.

"Welcome to the show, Penny," Speedy said. "Where are you calling from?"

"Atlanta."

Coleman nodded. "A hometown girl, and did you call in to talk to our guests?"

"Yes. I have a question for Ms. Kincaid. First of all, I want to say that I love your AtlantaTellAll e-zine. I started subscribing as soon as I learned about it, and I'm thrilled when a new issue arrives in my inbox."

"Glad to hear it," Marissa said, beaming. *Take that, Jackson.*

"And one of my favorite parts of the magazine is the weekly poll. I've voted every time and always enjoy being a part of the decision process."

"That's exactly what we're aiming for," Marissa said, glad the conversation had moved to her e-zine, instead of her cheater database. The questions weren't nearly as difficult.

"So, that's what I want to ask about, one of the polls you had a couple of weeks ago. It was the boxers or briefs poll."

Speedy chuckled, Trent grinned, and Marissa, once again, felt a tinge of nausea.

"That was a popular poll," she said, keeping her voice steady and pleasant. *Don't ruin me here, Penny.* "And we had a lot of fun with it." Was that all Penny wanted to say about it, merely mention how much fun the polls were each week and the fact that the underwear poll had been her favorite? When Penny didn't readily respond, relief washed over Marissa . . . until she heard Penny's actual question.

"So what I want to know is, with Trent Jackson right there next to you, have you determined what category you'd put him in?"

Hell. "Category?" Marissa asked, her voice hitching midword, while the hunk in the other chair sat up a little straighter, pushed his chest out with the movement, and—to Marissa's absolute dismay—glanced at his crotch.

"Go for it," he mouthed.

"Boxers or briefs?" Penny happily supplied.

"No, I haven't put him in a category." Actually, she had, a few categories, in fact. Egotistical, self-centered, arrogant, big-headed—he smirked, and Marissa's insides quivered—hot, sexy, delicious.

Delicious?

"Well, if you had to, which one would you choose?" Penny continued, while Marissa wondered why in the world Coleman and Speedy weren't interrupting, or disconnecting, or something.

"I—don't know."

"I believe that's another one of those discussions that the two of us need to have alone, one on one," Trent said, and winked. Winked!

"Penny, I think that's as good an answer as we're going to get for you this time," Coleman said, then disconnected and turned his attention from his computer monitor to Speedy. "However, I do think that these two could use some time alone to—talk—about things."

"That won't be necessary," Marissa said, glad that the interview appeared to be ending. She smiled, moved her hands to her headset, and added, "But I've really enjoyed visiting with both of you today. And I probably need to go to work now."

"You didn't tell her?" Speedy asked Coleman.

"I thought you did," Coleman said, while Trent leaned

back in his chair again, totally relaxed and grinning. He stretched his long legs out in front of him and crossed them at the ankles.

"Tell me what?" Marissa asked.

"We called Gary Cannon this morning. In fact, I believe he said he'd just hung up from talking to you, after you called to let him know that you'd be late," Coleman said.

"You called my boss?" Marissa slumped back into the chair. This could not be good.

"Yes, and we talked him into giving you the day off, and next week, too, in fact," Speedy supplied.

"Well," Coleman interjected, "he gave you the rest of today off, but next week, he still wants you to work; however, he said you can work offsite."

"Offsite?" Marissa croaked, and yes, that's exactly what it sounded like. A panicked croak.

"See, we've got this proposition for the two of you," Speedy said, and all three people in the control room perked up and peered through the glass at Marissa and Trent to see what they would say or do.

Marissa's thoughts suddenly flew back to those chemistry classes in high school, when you put something under the microscope, added another element, and watched what happened. From the faces on the folks in the control room, Coleman and Speedy were about to add something volatile to the already-unstable composition of Trent/Marissa. And this would be no "like water for chocolate." Oh no, this would be something different entirely.

Like water to acid.

"What kind of proposition?" Trent asked.

"As if you don't already know," Marissa hissed, before remembering they were still broadcasting.

Speedy made the sound of an angry cat, and Marissa wanted to claw him. If she hadn't chewed all her nails to the quick, she would have.

Coleman chuckled triumphantly into his microphone. "Now, now. Mr. Jackson doesn't know any more than you do, Ms. Kincaid, and this is nothing that's set in stone. We simply want to give the two of you the opportunity to have some of that alone time that you obviously need, to straighten things out."

"We don't need alone time," Marissa said, her hand moving subconsciously toward her mouth. She didn't even realize it until Trent's long fingers closed around her wrist, and she jumped as though he had burned her. "Don't touch me," she warned.

He simply eyed the reddened tips of her fingers, shook his head, and settled back in his chair. "I was trying to help you, but trust me; it won't happen again."

"Good," she said, while Speedy gave Coleman the thumbs-up sign.

"But we might as well hear the proposition," Trent continued. "It may be something we want."

"I'm sure it isn't," she said, and wondered whether Candi was waiting outside the door, or if Marissa would have to find her down the hall. She really wanted to leave, the sooner the better.

"I believe you may change your mind, once you hear what we're offering," Coleman said.

"Shoot, that many zeroes would make me stop and listen," Speedy said.

Zeroes? Marissa didn't want to know, really she

didn't. But she found herself holding her breath to hear whether either of the DJs would say more.

Coleman didn't disappoint.

"The station has this corporate apartment," he said, "in Marietta."

Speedy nodded. "We use it for the bigwig guests, and the folks higher up than us on the station's totem pole. You know, when the big dogs come to town for a visit. But, see, next week, it's empty, and we'd like to give the two of you the chance to stay there, do your work on your sites and your day jobs, and get a chance to talk things out." Speedy finished his spiel, then nodded again as though there was nothing to think about.

But there was.

"Not interested," Marissa said. "And I'm surprised my boss agreed to it."

"He said you could work just as well from our apartment as his office. He was particularly interested when we said we'd mention his company, Web Solutions, on the radio each morning."

"I'll bet he was," Marissa said, and thought she heard Trent laugh, though she vowed she would *not* look at him to confirm.

"What do we get if we do it?" Trent asked.

Marissa broke her vow and jerked her head his way, and dammit if her rogue curl didn't twist toward her eye with the movement. She blew it out of the way, and it curled back. "We're not doing it."

"I just want to know what we're giving up, Rissi."

"Ma-ris-sa," she corrected.

"Right, that's what I meant." He purposely turned toward Speedy and away from Marissa, but she saw that tiny clench of his jawline that meant he was suppressing another smile. She hated him. Completely. Totally. And she hated even more her bizarre burning desire to lick that jaw.

"What we're offering is a multimedia campaign that would consist of radio spots, television commercials, and newspaper advertising for a twelve-month period that would total over a million dollars," Coleman said.

"That's all those zeroes I mentioned," Speedy added.

A million-dollar multimedia campaign? For one week of living in an apartment with Trent Jackson? Marissa's mind reeled at the possibilities a million-dollar campaign would offer. That kind of advertising would put her webzine on the map, along with the cheater database. She could increase the price for advertising on the site, get more subscribers, quit the day job . . . and maybe start thinking about that family she wanted one day, the one where she kissed her husband before he left for work each morning, and adored her little boy, or girl, the way Amy adored Bo.

She could have all that, if she could keep her wits around Trent Jackson for one week.

"How many bedrooms?" she asked, and saw Trent's brows hitch up a notch.

"Two," Speedy said.

"And all we have to do is coexist for one week?" she asked, her mind still racing. She could do it, for that kind of media attention, she could. Surely. She'd just stay in her own bedroom and only come out when absolutely necessary, which would preferably be when he was behind his bedroom door. Could she exist on one meal a day? Probably.

"There's a little more to it than that," Coleman said.

Marissa's chest tightened. She should've known it sounded too easy. "Like what?"

"We'll have a list of activities that the two of you have to do, one a day, for the week. Some days you'll have to do something for Trent; some days he'll have to do something for you," Coleman answered.

Speedy added, "And this only goes on during the work week, since that's when we broadcast, so it's five days, instead of seven."

"What kind of activities?" Trent asked, but he didn't sound nearly as worried as Marissa. On the contrary, he sounded intrigued. Which worried her more.

"Why, I happen to have part of the list right here," Speedy said, and clicked a few keys on his computer. "One day you have to cook for Marissa; another day she has to cook for you."

"Can you cook?" Trent asked.

"Can you?" she challenged.

"Alrighty," Speedy continued. "Another day you've got to sit down and talk to each other, find out some answers to questions we provide. No big deal, right?"

Marissa swallowed. So far, so good. She could do all of that without losing her senses.

"Each morning, we'll call the apartment and have the two of you talk on the air, so our viewers can get a feel for how things are going," Coleman said.

"And that's all we need to do?" Marissa asked.

"That's what we're asking you to do," Coleman said, "but there's a condition to winning the ad campaign."

"What's the condition?" Trent asked.

"At the end of the week, you two still have to hate

each other," Speedy said. "It's going to be an honor system kind of thing, but basically, when the week's over, we're going to ask you how you feel about each other. And if you still can't stand each other, you both get a seven-figure ad campaign."

"That's it?" Marissa asked, shocked. She thought there would be more of a catch.

Speedy chuckled. "I'll bet ya a hundred right now, Coleman, that they're together before Wednesday."

Coleman cocked his head and appeared to size up Marissa and Trent. "I'm counting on it before the week's over, but Wednesday's a little soon. You're on."

"The two of you actually believe that the two of us will—" Marissa started, but didn't know how to finish on live radio.

"Yep," Speedy said. "Shoot, we could tell by the posts between you two on your sites that there's a spark there. And I've seen it in the flesh here today. We're merely trying to see if it'll lead to fire."

"Actually, I'd say after watching you two today, there's definitely a fire in store," Coleman said. "We're simply curious to see what kind of fire there is, and I'm sure our listeners are curious, too."

"So whaddayasay?" Speedy asked, as the theme music for the show began playing in the background. "It's about time for the Coleman and Speedy show to pack up for the weekend. Will our listeners be able to get a firsthand account of Cheaters and Liars commingling come Monday morning?"

Trent answered without hesitation. "I'm game if she is."

"And Ms. Kincaid, what do you say?" Coleman asked, while the music began to fade.

"Yeah, whaddayasay?" Speedy asked.

No way, her mind whispered, but her traitorous mouth didn't listen. "Okay."

*Keep your friends close, your enemies closer,
and your dog out of your suitcase.*
— MARISSA KINCAID

Chapter 11

Wow, this is really nice," Amy said, entering Marissa and Trent's temporary residence Monday morning. She carried Marissa's computer bag and walked around the southwestern-themed living room, with its distinct palette of peach and turquoise, and nodded her approval. "I bet it's not as masculine as your roomie would prefer, but I think it's cool."

"Mom, look, a dog," Bo said, pointing to the painting above the sofa. Like the room, the colors were definitely southwestern, with the moon a brilliant peach, the desert shades of orange and flesh, and the howling coyote brilliant turquoise. "Look, Petie," Bo said. He picked up the dog and held him so he had no choice but to look at the painting. "See?"

Petie looked, for a moment, then squirmed in Bo's chubby arms until he turned completely around, then thoroughly licked the boy's neck. Bo giggled. "I like you, Petie."

"He likes you, too," Marissa said, lugging in another box of computer supplies. Why had Gary agreed to let her work from here? And if she could work away from the office, why had he turned her down, every time, when she asked to telecommute?

Because allowing Marissa to work from home didn't get his company's name mentioned on the radio each morning, that's why.

"Where do you want me to set up your computer?" Amy asked.

"In there, I guess." Marissa pointed to the cozy dining room. A round glass-top table with a brass stand was centered in the room, with four white chairs around its perimeter. "Since it looks like my roommate has already taken over the living room." The spacious desk in the living room was covered with numerous files and stacks of papers, several notepads, a cell phone, a cordless phone, a fax machine, and a computer with the DieHardAtlanta logo floating across the monitor as the screen saver.

"Okay," Amy said, unpacking the computer, while Bo chased Petie around the apartment. "So what did Mona say about you moving in here?"

"Believe it or not, I haven't had the chance to tell her. She's only called once since she left for Branson, and I was in the shower when she called. I tried to call her back, but got her voice mail." Marissa shrugged. "I didn't think I should leave a message that I'm now living with a guy I hate."

Amy snorted. "Yeah, you probably should tell her that one in person." She turned on the computer. "I wish Candi could have come. Seems like she's always working."

"She managed to go to Landon's baseball game with

you yesterday, though, didn't she?" Marissa asked. "She told me when she called last night with her ideas about this week's sexiest smile poll. I'm assuming she talked to Keith Parker while she was there?"

"Hmph," Amy said. "He couldn't do diddly squat on the field yesterday, because he kept staring up at the stands at her, and there she was, ogling right back. It was a downright embarrassment for the team." Watching the computer whir to life, Amy concentrated on the monitor and didn't look up.

Marissa knew why. "You loved it, didn't you? Candi losing her head over this guy, and the guy doing the same over her? I wouldn't be surprised if you haven't already given her some of your toys, just in case."

Amy's green eyes glittered with mischief as she peeked over the top of the computer screen. "They were so cute! He's crazy about her, I can tell."

"Uh-huh, Miss Matchmaker. Just remember that Candi's heart has been trampled before, so she doesn't need to rush into anything." Marissa took her attention from the DieHardAtlanta logo to the two bedrooms branching off the living area. She peeked into the one that Trent had already claimed. A king-sized bed took up the majority of the space, with a plush turquoise comforter and over-stuffed pillows covering a span of space in front of the brass headboard.

"You sure we're not talking about *your* heart?" Amy asked, her voice eerily close to Marissa's left ear. Marissa's face reddened, guilty not only of checking out the enemy camp, but also of wondering whether the enemy slept in the buff.

"My heart is fine, and getting used to guys who love

their tubas, or their mothers, or their other girlfriends, or their other men, more than me."

"Right. Ever wondered if you didn't pick those guys on purpose?" Amy asked. "Some people have a fear of success in business, you know. I learned about that when I was working. Maybe some people also have a fear of success in love. And maybe you're one of those people."

Marissa's jaw dropped. "Why would I—" She stopped midsentence when the door to the apartment opened and a sweaty Trent Jackson entered. He wore a black sleeveless T-shirt, black running shorts with a red Nike swoosh at the lower left corner, and a whole lot of muscles. Everywhere.

"Morning," he said, grabbing a towel from a table near the door and wiping his face. He gave Marissa a crooked half-grin, then turned his attention toward the other female in the room. "I didn't know anyone else was coming."

"I'm Amy Brooks," Amy said, obviously not as disoriented as Marissa by the hunk in the doorway. Then again, Amy was used to being around her own heavenly hunk. Marissa wasn't as adjusted to the scene before her, and she needed to figure out what to do about that liability, before she jumped his sweaty bones, and *then* remembered that she hated him.

"The sex advice columnist on AtlantaTellAll," Trent said, and Amy beamed. "And you're married to the guy on Keith's baseball team, right?"

"Not bad," she said, nodding, then winking. "It's smart to know your adversary. Keep your friends close, and your enemies closer, that's what Wanda Campbell, my mother, always says."

Trent grinned, and the effect of that grin on Marissa

was disarming. "You're not the enemy," he said, then added, "and neither am I. Marissa just hasn't realized it yet."

"You know, I'd love to stay and chat with you about that comment," Amy said, apparently having loads of fun, "but I read the rules, and I know that when you two are here, no one else is allowed. And there's no way I want to cause Marissa to miss out on her part of that prize. In fact, I think the rules also said you can't leave the apartment alone after you arrive."

"That's close," he said, "but the rules say we can't leave the apartment alone once *both* of us have moved in. Since Marissa wasn't here when I arrived, I decided to take advantage of the opportunity to go for my morning run." He checked the coyote-shaped clock on the wall. "We don't have anything on the schedule until Coleman and Speedy call at nine, and I got here pretty early, so I figured I was safe."

But am I safe? Marissa wondered. She should have had sex, or at least a good orgasm, before moving in with this mass of testosterone for five days. What was she thinking? Then again, having sex required two people, and she didn't have anyone in mind for the other half of that equation. Well, okay, she did, and she was looking at him, the conceited jerk. An orgasm, on the other hand, could have happened fairly easily, with Pinky's help, but she'd been so nervous about the move and so busy making sure she didn't forget to pack anything . . .

Trent moved to the kitchen, withdrew a bottle of water from the fridge, and started downing it, his throat working in a magically sexy way with every swallow.

Marissa's knees decided to stop working correctly, and

she promptly sat in the desk chair in the living room. Who was she kidding? *A sexual release? As in—one?* It'd easily take a couple, or a few, or heck, a whole night of them, to leave her unaffected by *that*.

"Well, in that case," Amy said, "I guess we should be going."

"We?" Trent asked, twisting the cap back on the bottle and leaning out of the kitchen to scan the living area.

As if on cue, Bo darted out of Marissa's bedroom with Petie at his heels. Petie wasn't barking, however, because his mouth was full.

Marissa's eyes bulged at the bright pink, oddly shaped object hanging out of her tiny dog's mouth and bigger than any of his chew toys. "Ohmygod."

"Is that a—" Trent started, then stopped when Amy held up her palm.

"Don't say another word," she warned. "There's a child present." Then she audibly took a deep breath and, wearing a smile, she turned to her son, grinning at her as though Marissa's dog hadn't just entered the living area, in front of Trent, with a misshapen vibrator hanging out of his mouth. At least the thing wasn't switched on. If it had been, Trent would also have learned that the sucker lit up like a rainbow strobe light when activated.

"Bo," Amy said calmly. "What are you and Petie doing?"

"Playing fetch." A reasonable answer, if the dog were toting a bone, or a stick, or anything but Pinky.

Marissa wanted to die.

"Where did you find that—toy?" Amy asked.

"I jumped on Aunt Rissi's bed and knocked her bag

off. Then that pink bone fell out, and Petie liked it," Bo said, with his trademark toothy grin.

Pink bone. Have mercy.

"I did *not* pack that," Marissa said emphatically.

"No, you didn't," Amy said. "I did." She grabbed the "pink bone" from Petie, then took it to the sink and promptly washed it with soapy water. Only Amy would have no qualms whatsoever about removing a vibrator from a dog's mouth and proceeding to clean it up in the sink, while a sweaty, sexy hunk watched in bewilderment.

"You've never seen one of those before?" she asked, when he continued to look at the thing.

"I've seen my share," he admitted. "But I've never seen one so pink, or so crooked. And I'm wondering why you packed it for Rissi, since she obviously didn't even know it was in her bag."

"Ma-ris-sa," Marissa said, glaring at him.

"*He* called you Rissi," Trent said, pointing to Bo, watching his mother wash the pink bone.

"He's three," Marissa said. "And he's cute."

Trent cocked a brow, and Amy had the audacity to shake her head, as though she knew Marissa had messed up with that one, but Marissa continued, nonetheless. "And when Bo first started talking, he couldn't say 'Marissa' so he called me 'Rissi.' That's it."

"I see," Trent said, but he wasn't looking at Marissa. His attention was on Amy, drying the vibrator with a paper towel before leaving the kitchen and carrying the thing back into Marissa's bedroom.

She returned within seconds, no sign of Pinky.

"Amy, why did you pack that?" Marissa asked.

"And why is it crooked?" Trent followed up.

"Bo, will you go clean up the rest of Aunt Rissi's things that fell out? Just stuff them all back in the bag for me, okay?"

"Okay," he said, trotting back into the bedroom with Petie happily following.

"First of all, it's crooked because it's designed to hit the G-spot, every time. I know because I designed it, and it was the top-selling novelty item at Adventurous Accessories last year."

Marissa opened her mouth, then snapped it shut. What would she say to that, anyway?

"And second"—Amy twisted on her heel to face Marissa—"I packed it in case you got tempted." She shrugged as though this admission wouldn't horrify Marissa, or intrigue the guy in the kitchen.

"Tempted?" he coaxed. "Tempted to do what, may I ask?"

"No, you may not," Marissa said, turning toward Trent. "And would you mind giving us a chance to talk, alone?"

"No problem." He put the bottle back in the fridge, then smiled as he passed the two of them to enter his bedroom. "I have to shower anyway," he called from the other side of the door.

Marissa stared at the closed door.

"You know you're gonna need it," Amy said.

"Yeah, I know. Thanks for packing it," Marissa whispered.

"You have to still hate him on Friday if you want to quit the day job," Amy reminded with a grin. "It's gonna be hard to hate a guy that looks like that and drives you as crazy as he does. I should know; Landon drove me crazy, too. He still does, but in a good way. Oh, I put an extra eight-pack of batteries in the side pocket of your bath-room bag."

"Gotcha," Marissa said, fighting the impulse to laugh. "Tell me something. Is he really that hot, or have I just been too long without sex?"

"Oh, you've definitely been too long," Amy said, while Bo emerged from the bedroom.

"We finished," he said, grinning.

"Good job," Amy said. "And we've got to go now."

"You coming?" Bo asked Marissa.

"Aunt Rissi is going to stay here this week."

"Like a vacation?" he asked, his green eyes alight with excitement.

"Kind of," Marissa said.

"I guess you noticed there's only one bathroom, and it adjoins the two bedrooms," Amy said.

"Yeah, I noticed."

"Use Pinky, often," Amy whispered. "I put her in the nightstand drawer, under a *People* magazine."

"Don't worry. I will."

"Petie's tired." Bo squatted next to Petie's doggie bed, where Petie had already curled up with the majority of his head hidden beneath a front leg. Petie fluttered one eye open at Bo's words, then promptly closed it again.

"Yeah, Petie's tired," Marissa said. Either that, or he was pouting over having his pink bone taken away.

Amy gave Marissa a tight squeeze. "Now, we've gotta get going. Tell Aunt Rissi bye, Bo."

Bo left Petie sleeping and ran to Marissa to get in on the hugging. "Bye, Aunt Rissi."

"Bye, sweetie." Marissa tousled his blond curls as he opened the door.

Amy followed her son, but stopped long enough to state the obvious. "Marissa?"

"Yeah?"

"About what we were saying, you have been too long, but he really is that hot. Even so, if you don't hate him at the end of the week, you can kiss that ad campaign good-bye."

"I know." Marissa waited for the door to close, then hurried to her room. Listening to the shower water running, she opened the nightstand drawer, pushed the magazine aside and grabbed the crooked vibrator. Then she pressed the *on* switch and prayed that Trent Jackson took a long, very long, shower.

While the ultimate cure for sexual tension is sex,
fifteen minutes with Pinky isn't far behind.
—MARISSA KINCAID

Chapter 12

Trent dressed in a black T-shirt and jeans, not his traditional business attire, but then again, his work agenda for the week wasn't anywhere near traditional. And enticing Marissa Kincaid into his bed was a much more intriguing goal than determining how to make the most of a Jackson Enterprises acquisition. Much more intriguing.

He'd spent a lot of time trying to win at business, on his own, without help from his father and grandfather. Thanks to all of the publicity generated by his feud with Marissa, he'd won the battle for DieHardAtlanta. As a matter of fact, after their radio broadcast Friday morning, he'd spent the remainder of that day making the finishing touches and inking the contract to put the print format of his magazine in motion. And if everything continued on schedule, the first print issue of DieHardAtlanta would hit Atlanta newsstands in January. Not bad for a guy who, merely two weeks ago, couldn't get approval for the venture from his financial advisor.

Undoubtedly, he was on the right path to making his mark and winning the game in his business life, but he'd yet to reach the same goal in his personal one. This week, that could change, but not without effort. He didn't care about the seven-figure media campaign; he'd already generated the equity he needed. Winning the DieHardAtlanta battle wasn't the goal anymore; he now had a new objective . . . winning Rissi Kincaid.

He exited his bedroom, noted the closed door to her room and the dog snoozing on the floor. Was this the way it was going to be? *This* was her plan of action for dealing with the electricity between them? Camping out in her room, while Trent and the dog maintained the fort? He sat at the desk and thumbed through his DieHardAtlanta contracts, but his mind was on the woman holed up in her room. Maybe she planned to keep him at bay, but that wasn't how things were going to be, not by a long shot. He grinned, remembering the horrified look on her face when the salt-and-pepper puppy scampered into the living room with that odd-shaped pink vibrator clamped in his mouth. Marissa's buddy, Amy, said it was to keep Rissi from being tempted. *Tempted.* So even Rissi's friends thought that he could tempt her this week, and that she'd need something to combat that temptation. Good to know. Because Trent was going to do more than tempt; he was going to conquer that black-haired, dark-eyed hellion. It'd been a long time since a woman had piqued his interest as much as Rissi Kincaid. He couldn't remember any woman in his past who was so feisty, so intriguing, or so sexy, and he was more than ready for the challenge she presented. *If* she came out of her room.

He checked the clock. Ten minutes until their first

morning show check-in with Coleman and Speedy. Trent
scanned the furnished apartment. He had to hand it to the
station; they were prepared. Obviously, the producers
had put a lot of thought into getting this place ready for
Trent and Marissa's coexistence. It was decent-sized, for
corporate housing, and had all of the necessary conve-
niences to conduct business. Wireless high-speed Internet
allowed Trent and Marissa to stay on top of their regular
business dealings, while a fax machine and speakerphone
provided the means to communicate with the DJs at the
station each morning.

The format for Trent and Marissa's week was fairly
simple. Each morning at nine, they would receive a call
from Coleman and Speedy. The conversation would tran-
spire via the speakerphone on Trent and Marissa's end
and over live radio on Coleman and Speedy's. During the
broadcast, the DJs would provide Trent and Marissa with
their "assignment" for that day and ask for feedback from
the two regarding their cohabitation at the apartment. Obviously, the agenda for the radio station was to get the
two hooked up before the week ended, and therefore keep
their seven-figure media campaign offer. What the station
didn't realize, however, was that their agenda matched
Trent's, to get "hooked up" with Marissa before the week
ended.

The knob jiggled on her bedroom door as she unlocked
it, eased it open, and stepped through. She'd changed
clothes, trading the jeans and T-shirt she had on earlier for
a hot pink tank top and khaki shorts. This was Trent's first
glimpse at long, smooth, tan legs that seemed to go on for
days. While she wasn't extremely tall, no more than five-

seven, her legs would certainly hold their own against those of any runway queen. Trent nodded his approval.

"What?" she asked, crossing the living room and sitting comfortably on the couch. Her dog pried an eye open, then slowly roused and moved toward her. Obviously, he didn't want to miss the opportunity to lounge in her lap. Lucky dog. "Come here, Petie." She leaned over and picked him up, nuzzled him with her cheek, then settled him against her thighs and looked at Trent, still eyeing her. "What?" she repeated.

"I'm simply adjusting to the transition. Merely a half-hour ago, you were ready to detonate, frustrated with this whole situation, and with me. Now, you're all calm and relaxed. It's quite a contrast from the woman who looked like she wanted to die when her dog came out of her bedroom with a vibrator in his mouth."

She tensed, only slightly, but Trent noticed.

"No way. Already?" he asked. So, temptation didn't waste any time.

Those dark eyes widened, and her hand stopped stroking Petie's back. "I don't know what you're talking about."

Sitting in the desk chair, Trent swiveled around to look directly at Rissi. Her cheeks were pink, entire body relaxed and stress-free, lower lip a bit redder than the upper one, as though her teeth had grazed it when she . . . climaxed. "You've been playing with Pinky." It wasn't a question; it was a matter of fact, and the truth of it pleased him immensely. Merely their brief interaction earlier, with Amy, her son, and the dog in the room, and Rissi had needed an orgasm. Just imagine what she'd need if he really turned up the heat. He smiled.

Her jaw dropped, then she glared at him as though she'd like nothing better than to wrap her hands around his throat and squeeze. "It had nothing to do with you, you—you—egotistical son of a—"

The phone rang loudly. "Hold that thought," Trent said, as Marissa gasped in frustration, and he punched the speaker button. "Liars and cheats," he answered, grinning at the woman on the couch turning redder by the second. From embarrassment? Or from anger? He guessed the latter.

Speedy chuckled loudly through the speaker. "Liars and cheats, huh? That fits."

"Thanks," Trent said, never taking his eyes off Rissi.

"It wasn't you," she mouthed.

"Right," he mouthed back, thoroughly enjoying this little game.

"So, Trent, did both of you get moved in okay?" Coleman asked through the line. "And I will remind you that you're on the air."

"Yes, the move went fine. I got here early this morning, and Rissi arrived about an hour ago. We've been fairly busy getting settled, though I'd say she has been more busy than I."

"Ma-ris-sa," she corrected. Those dark eyes burned with fiery heat. She'd kill him for this, and Trent would love every minute of it.

"Is that so, Ms. Kincaid? You're busier?" Coleman asked. "Already started your workday there? We're pleased your boss allowed you to telecommute for our sake."

She cleared her throat. "I've been getting set up for

work," she said, her voice steady, though her eyes still shot daggers at Trent.

"She works *real* hard to make sure she achieves her goal," Trent added, stifling his chuckle. "I'd say she's probably one of the most—hard-working—women I've ever met. Determined to reach her goal, no matter what."

If possible, her cheeks got redder.

"Wow, sounds like you've won him over on your work ethics," Speedy said. "But you two still hate each other? Or is our little game already over?"

"We definitely still hate each other," Rissi yelled toward the speaker. "With a passion."

"She's *very* passionate, from what I've seen," Trent said.

"Is that so?" Coleman asked. "Well, have the two of you discussed Trent's comment on Friday that he actually didn't cheat on you way back when, Ms. Kincaid? I know our viewers are interested in learning what he meant by that."

"No, we haven't discussed it yet," she admitted. "In fact, I don't plan to talk to Mr. Jackson any more than necessary during this week."

Speedy's cackle rang through the speaker. "Well, I'm afraid you're going to have to talk to him a few times in order to do your daily assignments. Today's assignment, in fact."

"Today's assignment?" she asked, while Petie started to squirm in her lap. She placed him on the floor, and he promptly trotted to the door. "Just a second, Petie," she said.

"Petie?" Coleman asked.

"My dog."

"Your dog is there?" Speedy asked. "Coleman, do we even allow dogs at that apartment?"

"Well, Speedy, I'm not really sure. We've never had a reason to ask."

Marissa visibly swallowed, and looked miserable. Trent could tell she really loved that little puppy, and that she didn't want to go through this week without him. He cleared his throat. "It's a small dog, and he's well-trained," he said, and prayed that he was telling the truth. Petie was definitely still in the puppy stage, which meant chewing stage, accidents on the carpet stage, and all of those other negative puppy stages. But he was a cute dog, and more than that, Rissi wanted him here.

"So, if he does mess something up, are you saying you'll pay for it, Jackson?" Speedy asked.

"Yes," Trent answered without hesitation, while Rissi gave Petie a soft smile.

"He won't mess anything up," she said. "He really is a good dog, and right now, he needs to go out."

"By all means, take him out," Speedy said. "We'll just give you today's assignment over the air right quicklike; does that work for you, Coleman?"

"Sure," Coleman said, then added, "Today's is pretty easy, and it'll make our listeners happy, since we've had a multitude of calls from people wanting to know what Trent meant when he said he never cheated on you."

"I know you said you added him as a joke, Ms. Kincaid, but regardless, the two of you obviously have a different recollection of what happened back then, and our listeners want to know why. And that's it, all of today's assignment. Oh, and by the way, this will require talking," Speedy said.

"I know, but if I'm lucky, it won't require much," she said. "And I've got to take Petie out now."

"Not without Trent, you don't," Speedy said with another irritating chuckle. "From now on, the two of you can't go out alone, remember? That's the rule."

Marissa looked as if she wanted to scream, but she didn't. "Well? Are you coming?" she asked Trent.

"Duty calls," Trent said toward the speaker. "So, are we done for this morning's check-in?"

"You're done," Coleman said. "Just be sure to take Petie out before our broadcast tomorrow morning. I've got a feeling that one will take a while."

"Will do," Trent said, disconnecting.

"Oh, no," Rissi said, frowning at the fidgety puppy. He yelped, nudged the door with his head, then yelped again.

"What?" Trent asked.

"I forgot Petie's leash." She scanned the room, either looking for something to use as a leash or willing Petie's to magically appear.

"He can use the patio," Trent said. "There isn't much grass, but it should be sufficient."

She knitted her brows. "What patio?"

"The one through here." He stood and headed toward his bedroom. "Come on. I don't think he's in the mood to wait."

She scooped up the puppy and followed him into his room. "No way."

"What?" Trent pulled the drawstring on the blue curtains until they pleated at one side, then he opened the French doors and waited for Rissi and Petie to pass through.

She did, but she snarled at him as she went. "Your bedroom has a patio? And you were here first. You could've given me this room, if you wanted to, but you picked the best one for yourself. Typical."

Trent held up his palms defensively. "Listen, when I brought my stuff in, I noticed the two bedrooms, one blue and one pink."

"One is turquoise, and one is peach," she corrected.

"Fine. But the way I saw it, one was male; one was female. I opted for male."

"Hmph." She put Petie on the ground, and he trotted directly to the small patch of grass at the left edge of the patio, sniffed, then started doing his thing, while Marissa took in the massive hot tub declaring dominion over most of the deck. Several potted trees branched out over the enormous tub, and Trent had already envisioned the two of them naked beneath their branches. Was Rissi thinking the same thing?

She whirled toward Trent. "Did you grab the blue room because you knew its patio had a hot tub? And the biggest one I've ever seen?"

"Hey, if you want in, I'll share."

"You're despicable."

"That's not what you thought twenty minutes ago." He leaned against the fencing enclosing the small space, crossed his arms, and waited for the battle. Damn, she was cute when she was mad.

"Sure it is," she countered. "I thought you were despicable last week, I thought you were despicable this morning, and I thought you were despicable twenty minutes ago."

Trent merely shook his head. "No," he said. "You didn't."

"I promise you, I did." She marched toward the hot tub, dipped her fingers in and growled. "It's perfect."

"Like I said, I'll share." He smiled. "And do you really expect me to believe you were thinking of how despicable I am when you were fooling around with—what was it again—Pinky?—because I'm betting that you were thinking of me in a way that's not at all classified as despicable. Desirable, yes. Despicable, no."

"You have to be the most arrogant male I've ever met."

"I prefer confident," he said.

She didn't respond, but made a kissing sound toward Petie, who abandoned his sniffing venture and ran to her feet. "Come on," she said to the dog. "I've had enough fresh air." She turned toward the door, and Petie ran inside.

"Go ahead, but we still have to talk," Trent said, "for today's assignment."

Her back stiffened, and she stopped walking. Then she took an audible breath and turned around, her jaw clamped tight and eyes blazing. If it weren't for that cute little curl teasing her forehead, she might have actually looked fierce. As it was, she simply looked sexy. "Let's get it over with," she said, then moved to one of the two wicker patio chairs and sat down.

"Want to call your dog?" Trent asked, moving the other chair to face hers.

"No, he's fine. And this will be better anyway, just the two of us, getting today's assignment over with. By the way, I meant what I told Speedy. I don't want to talk to you any more than necessary."

"Whatever you say. I guess you don't need me to talk to you when you take care of business in your room, huh?"

Her cheeks flared again, eyes narrowed.

"Okay, that was low," he admitted. And fun, not that he'd say that out loud.

"Whether you believe it or not, that had nothing to do with you. Now, let's take care of the assignment." She twisted on the chair cushion, then pulled her legs up to tuck them under her bottom, as though she were totally at ease and ready for anything he threw her way. Trent could see her as a little girl, long black hair in wild curls down her back, sitting the same way on the gym floor when the class waited for instructions in PE. Dare he mention that now? Let her know that she really did make an impression on him way back then? As the feisty girl with the excited dark eyes, so alive and ready for life? Trent looked at those eyes now, still dark and excited . . . but there was something else staring back at him now. And the realization slammed him like a fist to the chest.

Rissi Kincaid was afraid.

Of him? Or something else?

"Like I've said repeatedly, I added you to the database as a joke. I admit I shouldn't have put you on the list, because we *were* just kids, but I didn't lie about what happened back then. And I really would like to get this over with now, if you don't mind," she said saucily.

Trent didn't take time to second-guess instinct. He acted on it, and damned the consequences. "You're right. We should get this over with." He stood from his chair, took a small step to stand in front of her, then leaned closer, bracing both hands on the armrests of her chair while watching those dark eyes widen even more.

"What—" she whispered. "What are you doing?"

"Getting this over with."

His mouth touched hers softly, exploring. He sensed her tense beneath him and vowed to make that go away, at least toward him. He sucked her lower lip, again gently, not wanting to scare her, but to show her that he truly wanted her to feel the impact of this kiss, the impact of what the two of them could share, if she'd stop fighting . . . and let him in.

She moaned, a low, soft sound that eased from her throat, then she opened her mouth and deepened the kiss, her tongue sliding moistly between his lips.

A sound pierced the moment, but Trent was too into the kiss, too into having Rissi Kincaid, to decipher what it was. But the woman beneath him wasn't as lost in the moment, because she jolted with the intrusion, and the next thing Trent knew, she had drawn blood.

Reality bites . . . and so does Rissi Kincaid.
— TRENT JACKSON

Chapter 13

S he bit you?" Keith repeated, while Trent seriously debated whether confiding in his friend about this particular stumbling block in his personal life was the smartest of moves. He ran his tongue over his swollen lower lip, still tasted a hint of metallic blood from this morning's encounter, and nodded. "Oh, yeah, she bit me all right."

Marissa Kincaid had been on the verge of giving in. Trent had sensed her body yielding, the fire inside her sparking to life with that kiss. She'd been very close to forgetting whatever held her back and letting heated desire take control. In fact, Trent would have expected the two of them to be naked and in the hot tub within minutes, at the rate things were heating up. Then Petie decided to check out what was happening on the patio, barked, startled Marissa out of her trance, and the rest, as they say, is history.

Keith's laugh rumbled through the phone. "Well, what did you expect? The woman can't get that multimedia campaign if the two of you get together before the week ends." Keith paused, then asked, "How *would* Coleman and Speedy know whether you got together or not? I mean, surely they wouldn't rely on the honor system when they're talking about that kind of money."

"They're not relying on it at all," Trent said. "In fact, I have a copy of the contract we both signed right here." He lifted it from the desk. "This paragraph follows the section on distribution of prize money, i.e., the advertising campaign," he said. "'If, within the twelve months following the cohabitation period, the two parties are found to be fraternizing as evidenced by photographs and/or reputable eyewitness accounts, then all proceeds accepted shall be refunded to the prize distributors and further prize monies shall be forfeited.'"

"Ah, well, that'll do it," Keith said. "And from her attack on you this morning, we can determine that the two of you probably won't have to worry about 'fraternizing after the cohabitation period.' Hell, you should probably worry more about staying alive until the week ends. Are you sure you were only trying to kiss her?"

"I wasn't trying; I was doing it," Trent said. "And she reciprocated. I think that's what spooked her this time."

"This time? No way, you're going to try again? I think you may have to accept defeat, and in this case, a defeat with the girl is a win for the business. That ad campaign wouldn't hurt DieHardAtlanta's print launch."

"I've already got what I need to move DieHardAtlanta forward. You gave me the go-ahead last week, remember?" Trent dropped the contract back on the desk and turned toward Marissa's closed bedroom door. After their kiss—or bite—on the patio, she'd stormed into the apartment, grabbed her laptop, and headed into the bedroom with Petie following faithfully at her heels. Trent hadn't seen her since, though he had heard her, moving through the bathroom and into his bedroom, evidently taking Petie out. Eventually, though, she'd get hungry, or at the very least, Petie would, and she'd have to show.

For most of the afternoon, Trent had handled business, overseeing a conference call regarding the Suwannee land acquisition and answering the attorney's questions about the DieHardAtlanta contracts, but he'd kept a portion of his attention on that closed door, and the woman behind it.

"You're telling me that the guy so gung-ho about increasing his subscribers isn't interested in winning a seven-figure multimedia campaign that will put the magazine over the top?" Keith asked.

"I wasn't gung-ho about increasing subscribers," Trent corrected. "I wanted to go to print, and I wanted to do that any way I could, without using Jackson Enterprises money. We did that, thanks to the publicity over this web war. The magazine will be top-notch and will hold its own, with or without me winning this radio deal."

"Got to tell you, I'm shocked. I've never known you to throw in the towel on anything, particularly something involving this much money."

"I'm not throwing in the towel," Trent said. "I'm merely going after what I want the most." He heard stirring in Rissi's room. Was she finally coming out?

"Marissa Kincaid?" Keith questioned.

"I told you I wanted her," Trent said.

"So much that you don't care about a seven-figure ad deal?"

Trent heard Petie bark, and then the sound of the two of

them moving in his room. How many times did that dog go out in one day? "The magazine is going to do fine. I've got the equity I need, and we're moving forward. And, for the record, that prize isn't why I'm here."

"Maybe you should tell her that, because I guarantee the prize is exactly why she's there."

"That'll change."

Keith laughed again. "I always knew you were sure of yourself, but do you really think you can convince this woman to give up that kind of deal for you, when she's told you, and all of Atlanta, that she doesn't even like you?"

"She lied," Trent said, but he knew Keith was right; Marissa Kincaid was his biggest challenge, ever. He'd thoroughly enjoyed their battles online and on the radio broadcasts, but this week would be much more fun. An all-out war, up close and personal, where she wanted to hate him, and he wanted to have her.

A loud knock sounded at the door, and Petie started barking from Trent's room. "I'll talk to you later," Trent said. "Sounds like we've got company."

"Keep me posted. Shoot me an email if you can't call."

"Will do," Trent said, disconnecting. He crossed the room and opened the door to find a pizza delivery boy on the other side.

"Compliments of Coleman and Speedy," the skinny guy said, peeking over the top of a thick red bag. "Four larges, cheese, pepperoni, meat lovers, and the works." He grinned, displaying clear braces with red and blue bands. "I guess they wanted to give you a variety."

"There are two of us and a dog," Trent said, moving

out of the way so the kid could bring the pizzas inside. He placed them on the counter in the kitchen and then peered into the living room. "So, where is she?"

"Who?"

"Ms. Kincaid. I listened to the two of you on the radio Friday and then again this morning. Does she really hate you as much as it sounds?" He smiled again, sending a multitude of copper freckles, the same color as his hair, marching across his face.

"She's in her room, where she's been most of the day. But maybe she'll come out for pizza."

The kid snickered loudly, almost cartoonish. "Man, she really does hate you, huh?"

"Appears that way," Trent said, not amused.

"Well, at least that way you both get that prize, huh?" He grinned goofily, then added, "But I've got to tell you, if I were able to stay with a hot chick like that for a week in an apartment, you know, spending all that time alone, I'd have to think about letting that prize go. You gotta admit it, she's hot."

Trent couldn't believe this kid. He was all of nineteen, maybe, and was game to hit on a thirty-two-year-old woman with an admitted dislike for men. He was either ridiculously confident, or ridiculously stupid. Obviously, he had no interest in self-preservation, because when the bedroom door opened—Trent's bedroom door, that is— and Rissi walked out in obvious preparation for battle, the kid only beamed. And why had she exited from *Trent's* room? Should he have thought more about all the sounds coming from the other side of his bedroom door all after- noon? He'd attributed it to her taking the dog out, but now he wondered if there had been more to it than that.

"Ms. Kincaid!" the kid gushed, leaving the pizza bag on the counter and crossing the room to, apparently, touch her. Then he went for a full-blown hug, and Rissi visibly stiffened. When he finally released her, she took a small step back and shot a look of concern to Trent. She was probably wondering why Trent didn't offer to save her from this kid's attack.

Yeah, right.

Trent grabbed a slice of pizza, held it up in mock salute, then took a bite. She'd bitten him, after all. Let her handle her young admirer on her own.

"I was hoping to meet ya," the boy continued. "I paid Trevor five bucks to let me make this delivery, 'cause I thought I might get to see you. This is actually Trevor's route. He's older, twenty-one, but I've been with the company longer. Anyway, I had to tell you that I think, well, I think you're really hot."

When she'd entered the living room, her fuming expression had been intact, but now she merely seemed shocked. She cleared her throat, while Trent continued to delve into the delicious medley of sausage, pepperoni, peppers, and cheese. The works. It was a pretty good pizza, after all. He turned to get a drink out of the fridge and left Rissi to fend for herself. Then he saw Petie eyeing his food bowl. Trent grabbed the bag of dog food off the counter and filled the silver dish. That's right; let her handle her potential stalker; we guys will stick together . . . and eat.

"You really are, you know? Hot, I mean. And I was wondering, well, when this week ends, would you want to give a guaranteed noncheating younger guy a chance . . ."

"I'm sorry," she said, shaking her head as though

waking from a bad dream. "But—" She paused. "I didn't catch your name."

"Bud," he said, pointing to the nametag on his blue-and-red-striped shirt. Obviously, the kid got his shirt to match his braces, or vice versa. How *cute*.

"Bud, you want some pizza?" Trent called from the kitchen.

"No thanks, I get it for free at work, and I've already had some tonight."

"Suit yourself," Trent said, grabbing a second slice, while Rissi visibly panicked. Trent loved it. He grinned and took another bite. The second piece had more pepper than the first, and the open wound on his mouth started to burn. He winced and decided to make her pay. "Bud, you really should think about what you're asking. Ms. Kincaid may give you more than you bargain for. I have it under good authority that she bites."

Bud jerked his head toward Trent, pointing to his lower lip. "You did that?" he asked, turning back to Rissi.

Her dark brows drew together, and that wicked little curl on her temple seemed to hitch forward with the movement. It was a nice look, so Trent gave her a satisfied smile.

"Yeah, I did it," she said. "And if he gets near me a second time, I'll do it again."

"Wow! I've never had a woman who bites," the kid said, complete admiration in every word.

Trent chuckled.

Rissi didn't.

"Listen, Bud," she said. "I know you may not understand this, but I really don't have any desire to be with a man right now."

Trent choked on his pizza. Loudly. And she glared at him. Furiously.

She cleared her throat and continued, "I'm really into my e-zine, and that's going to keep me too busy to date. And, honestly, I believe there's probably a bigger age difference between the two of us than you may realize," she said apologetically, but Bud was obviously prepared for this argument.

"Oh, I don't think that's a problem," he said. "Look at Ashton and Demi."

Rissi's face drained of color, and Trent had to turn away to keep from laughing out loud. He picked up Petie's water bowl and filled it. "Here ya go, Petie," he said, placing it back on the floor. "Might as well have something to eat and drink while we watch the show."

"You're watching a movie tonight?" Bud asked. "Want some company? I could ask Trevor to cover for me."

"Sure," Trent answered. "Maybe you could even sleep over."

"I believe the rules for the contest state that we have to stay here alone," Rissi said, then shrugged. "Sorry, Bud, but I think you're going to have to leave."

Bud shrugged, too. "Well, if you change your mind about seeing a younger man," he said, winking, "then give me a call when the week ends." He withdrew a card from his shirt pocket and handed it to Rissi. "Like I said, it seems to be working out good for Demi."

"I'll keep that in mind," Marissa said, walking toward the door, then opening it for Bud's departure.

"You can keep the hot bag!" Bud yelled toward the kitchen. "The pizza will stay warm for hours in there, and I can come back and pick it up tomorrow."

"Wait," Marissa commanded sharply, then she softened her tone. "Wait right there, Bud."

"You gonna bite me?" he asked.

She didn't answer. Instead, she moved to the kitchen, where Petie was chomping on his dinner and Trent was chomping on pizza, and slid the remaining boxes out of the bag. Trent had already removed the supreme one and was working on his third slice. "Here you go, Bud. I wouldn't want you to have to make another trip," she said, carrying the warm red bag to the kid. "We appreciate you bringing the pizzas."

"Oh, you can thank Coleman and Speedy. They're the ones who paid for them."

"Here you go, Bud," Trent said, reaching around Marissa to hand him a healthy tip.

"Gee, thanks, man."

Marissa didn't even look at Trent. She merely continued facing Bud until Trent slid his arm back, grazing her side in the process, then returned to the kitchen.

Bud left, and the door slammed. Trent waited for the fallout. He didn't have to wait long.

"What do you think you're doing?" she asked, rounding the corner to enter the kitchen.

Trent took another bite, then swallowed. "You know, I could ask you the same thing. Or rather, I should ask what *have* you been doing—in my room?"

She blinked a couple of times, shot a glance toward his closed bedroom door, and looked . . . guilty. "I don't know what you're talking about."

"What should I expect, Rissi? Itching powder in my bed? My sheets shortened? Or what?"

"None of the above," she said, then she scanned

the sides of the pizza boxes and whipped open the one marked *Cheese—plain*. Before Trent had a chance to ask any more questions, she bit into her first slice and slapped another one on a plate.

"Hungry?" he asked, deciding he'd figure out what she'd done to his bedroom later.

She continued chewing an oversized bite, then swallowed. "I'm starving. And a gentleman would have offered me something to eat when he fixed lunch. What was it, anyway? Grilled cheese?" She moved toward the table, sat down, then took another man-sized bite.

"Philly cheesesteak. The station stocked the place well," Trent said, taking the seat across from her. He could get used to this, sitting in the kitchen with Rissi, eating pizza together, while her dog happily ate his meal nearby. This was the closest he'd ever been to domesticated bliss, except for the fact that she had bitten him this morning. To remind her of the fact, he took another bite, and winced.

She stopped chewing, put her slice down, and swallowed. "Your mouth hurts?"

"You did draw blood," he reminded her.

"Well, you kissed me, what did you expect?"

"I expected you to kiss me back," he said easily, then added, "which you did."

"Reflex," she said, then turned her attention back to her pizza.

"Reflex, my ass," he replied, and was rewarded with a guilty smile. "You've got sauce, right there," he said, pointing to one corner of her mouth.

She caught the drop with her tongue, then slid it back inside, while Trent recalled the way that tongue had slid between his lips this morning. "I'm sorry I bit you," she said quickly, "but really, did you actually think I *wanted* you to kiss me?"

"I didn't think anything. I knew."

"You do realize that if we get together this week, or any time in the next twelve months, then we don't get the ad campaign, right?" she asked, finishing off one slice and grabbing the other. "It'd be stupid for us to let anything happen, much less encourage it. Honestly, I thought you were smarter than that."

"So now you think I'm smart."

"A smart-ass," she corrected, and tried to hide her smirk by biting off another piece of pizza. She swallowed too quickly, and her eyes immediately watered, then she started to cough. Her hand flew to her throat, and Trent jumped up from his seat. "Here," he said, raising her arms as she continued coughing.

"Dr-ink," she said.

He released her arms, then picked up his glass and held it to her lips.

Rissi took a few small sips, then slowly shook her head as her coughs subsided. Blinking through the tears, she rubbed her throat and grinned at Petie, concerned enough to leave his food in favor of licking her leg. "It's okay, Petie," she whispered raspily, then she looked up at Trent. "I'm okay now. Thanks."

"I'm not as bad as you thought?" he asked, returning to his seat and then reading the labels on the two unopened boxes. He grabbed the pepperoni one and withdrew a slice. "Want to try something beyond plain?" he asked.

"You're right," she said, finishing off the slice of cheese pizza, then taking another of the same. "You aren't as bad as I thought, and no, I don't want anything else. I like plain."

"Nothing about you says plain," Trent said. He picked a circular piece of pepperoni off his slice and tossed it in his mouth.

She stood, moved to the refrigerator, and withdrew a Coke. Then she popped the top and took a sip from the can. "You know, this meal doesn't seem to fit the image I'm sure most folks have for the CEO of Jackson Enterprises."

"I'm still the same kid you knew back then," he said evenly. "I never have gotten into the overly fancy stuff. The business aspect of the company, well, that's another story. I'm all for that, but the society crap never appealed to me."

"Which is why I'd never seen your name or photograph in the paper until I put you on my site?" she asked as she brought her drink back to the table and sat down.

"That, and the fact that I hadn't done anything news-worthy," he said with a grin.

Trent noted the ease of her posture, the way she was thoroughly enjoying this meal, and him, without any animosity whatsoever, and he liked it. "Ready to call a truce?"

She laughed. "Just because you've ended up being something of a nice guy after all doesn't mean I'm about to give up that ad campaign. And I meant what I told that pizza boy, I don't have any desire to be with a man right now."

"Why is that?" he asked, and then remembered that fifteen of her site's cheaters had cheated on Rissi. No wonder she was gun-shy . . . of all men, Trent included.

"I just don't," she said, and Trent decided to leave it at that, for now. Eventually, though, he'd help her see that not all guys cheat. In fact, he could let her know tonight that his "offense" as a teen wasn't what she thought. And since that was the assignment . . .

"We need to discuss what happened with the Sadie Hawkins thing. I really didn't cheat."

"It was twenty years ago, and we were kids. You don't have to explain." She gave him a smile. "I wish I'd never brought it up."

"But you did, because deep down you thought I cheated back then, and I want you to know I didn't, not really. And besides, we have to talk about it for our assignment."

"I guess you're right," she said, licking sauce from her fingers.

Trent watched her, the way her tongue captured each spicy drop, and his mind took the vision to other, more interesting scenarios.

"You're terrible," she said, stopping the process and grabbing a napkin to finish wiping her hands.

"Maybe, but you're terrible, too, because you knew exactly what I'd think when you started that little finger-licking display." Her cheeks flamed, and he nodded. "See? Guilty."

"Listen," she said, dusting off her hands and taking another sip of Coke. "I kissed you back this morning, okay? I'll admit it. And it was stupid. I *don't* want you."

Trent cocked a brow.

"Okay. Maybe I want sex, but I don't necessarily want it with you."

"Tell me how you really feel," he said, and couldn't

keep from laughing. "And you wonder why all of those guys left?"

Her smirk turned into a sneer. "What I'm trying to say is that I don't even like you. And if the two of us get together, I lose the chance at my dream."

"Your dream?"

"My webzine, remember? AtlantaTellAll.com? I'm wanting it to take off enough that I can quit the day job, find the perfect guy—a guy who doesn't cheat—work from home, and have plenty of babies."

"Plenty?"

"I'm an only child. I always wanted brothers and sisters. You should remember that, since I distinctly remember—oh, forget it."

Trent did remember. "I was like the brother you never had," he said. She'd told him so, when she asked him to that dance way back then.

She snarled. "Let's just get the assignment done. You say you didn't cheat."

"I didn't," Trent said, then held up a hand when she started to speak. "And I want you to hear what really happened. Believe it or not, I didn't even know you'd been upset about that dance thing until I read it on your site. You never said anything."

"I moved the next week," she said. "Trust me, I said plenty, but you weren't around to hear it."

"Well, for the record, I read on your site that you thought I backed out of the dance because you got braces."

"Right."

"Wrong. I didn't care whether you had braces. I backed out of the dance because I didn't want you to see me try to do something I simply couldn't do." He shrugged. "I couldn't dance. That's all there was to it."

She seemed to mull that over, then she chewed her lower lip, which reminded Trent of his. He licked the cut from her morning attack.

Marissa frowned. "I shouldn't have bitten you."

"No, you shouldn't have, and I shouldn't have backed out of that dance back then without giving you the reason."

She smiled. "No, you shouldn't have." Then she tilted her head as though she remembered something, and from the accusation in her eyes, Trent knew he wouldn't like it. "But you did go out with Donna."

"I didn't want to sit home on the night of the dance, so I went to the movies. I'd seen Donna Pritchett that day, and she mentioned wanting to see a movie. Since I was no longer going to the dance, I took her to the movie."

"You stood me up because you couldn't dance, and I put you in a cheater database because of it." She shook her head. "I feel like a fool," she whispered, then those big dark eyes looked directly at him. "I'll remove you from the database, right now." She started to stand, but Trent captured her wrist, then gently guided her back to her seat.

"No, don't," he said. "Then I'll lose all of the great free publicity."

To his relief, she laughed. "Okay, I'll leave it. Besides, it'd seem strange to Coleman and Speedy if I removed it now."

"I don't think it'd surprise them too much, since they're already betting on how long it'll take us to get together.

They'd just see it as a step in that direction, you being nice to me and all."

"But we're not getting together, Trent," she said firmly. "I do want to win that prize, and I don't want to 'get together' with you, or anyone else, right now."

"You said you wanted a guy who doesn't cheat, and lots of kids," he said, obviously before really thinking through the implications of his words.

She blinked. "I barely know you, and that's not what you're offering. You're offering a week of sex."

Trent didn't know what to say, because he wasn't sure *what* he was offering. Sex? Definitely. Beyond this week? Probably. But the whole kit and caboodle and car seats? He looked at the feisty woman and thought . . . *Maybe*.

"What's good about this situation is the fact that we don't want the same thing regarding a relationship, but we do want the same thing regarding our businesses. We want those ad campaigns, which will make it easy to remember why the two of us don't need to let an episode like that kiss happen again. So don't try. And I'll stay clear of you, too. Granted, we're attracted to something about each other, but we've simply got to control that until Friday. Then we'll never have to see each other again, and we can both get our advertising campaigns and both pursue our dreams." She smiled, as though she were thrilled with this perfect solution. "Deal?"

"Hell, no." He wanted to pick her up out of that seat and shake her, or kiss her. Or bite her. Or all three. The little spiel she'd rattled off without preamble sounded like one of the wordy little tirades that accompanied all of the cheater pictures on her site. In other words, she was mouthing off, trying to make light of something that was much deeper than she cared to admit. "No deal," he said.

"What do you mean, no deal?"

"I mean I don't plan to stay clear of you until Friday, Ms. Kincaid," he said, then corrected, "I mean, Rissi. Ris-si," he repeated, when she flinched at the nickname. "As a matter of fact, I'm planning on getting very close, and very personal. I plan to touch your skin, I plan to hear you breathe, I plan to kiss your lips"—he leaned closer, close enough to see her pupils dilate with his words— "and I plan to do more, Rissi. And what's more, you're going to want me to."

"I won't," she said, and had the wherewithal to shake her head slightly with the words. "I'll tell you the truth, Trent. I haven't had the best luck with men treating me right. You know that from my site. Before I get that serious again with a guy, I want to know I won't end up losing another piece of my heart."

Trent swallowed. She'd finally blurted out the truth. She was scared of being hurt again.

Her eyes widened as she apparently realized she'd said more than she intended. "I don't want you," she whispered.

"You do want me." His eyes shifted from hers, to her mouth.

"Your mouth must have healed fast," she said sharply, "if you're ready for another bite."

Trent laughed deeply. Damn, this was fun. "I'm not going to make it that easy for you, Rissi. When I kiss you again, and I will, it'll be because you ask for it, and if you bite, believe me, I'll bite back." He wasn't a fool. Forcing himself on her, particularly when she was so gun-shy of all men, wasn't the way to go. Making her want him so much that she *asked* him to take her . . . was.

At the sound of her gasp, he retreated. "Now, I'm going to take a shower," he said, walking away. "And by the way, I don't lock the door."

"You might as well. I won't be joining you. In anything. Ever."

He didn't turn around, merely stopped at the door to his room and called, "You really are a liar, aren't you, Rissi?"

"I'm going to get that prize," she said. "And if you really wanted it, too, it seems like you wouldn't keep trying to make something happen here."

Trent held his hand on the knob, debated how much to tell, then decided to go for it. What would it hurt if she knew? "You're right," he said. "The truth is, I'm not here because I want the prize, Rissi."

Petie, evidently noticing Trent's location, left his spot in the kitchen and darted toward Trent's feet.

"I bet he needs to go out," she said, looking a little confused from Trent's last statement as she got up from the table and started toward Trent and her dog. "I'll take him, since my room has the patio."

"*Your* room has the patio?" he asked, then he opened the bedroom door, allowed Petie to run through in a frantic pace toward the French doors, and realized why he'd heard Rissi moving about in the rooms this afternoon. She hadn't merely been taking Petie outside, and she hadn't been pulling some sort of prank like shortening his sheets; she had been swapping rooms. The blue room was now completely overpowered by female things. Rissi's things. And none of Trent's. "You moved me to the pink room?"

he questioned, surprised at her gumption, but impressed with it, too. He'd remembered her from their school days as a girl with spunk. Nice to see that hadn't changed.

"It's not pink; it's peach," she said, shimmying past him to go open the patio door for Petie, who ran out as soon as the crack was large enough for him to squeeze through. "And I needed this room for Petie. Sometimes he has to go out at night, and I'm not about to walk through your bedroom in the middle of the night."

"Afraid you wouldn't walk through?" he asked. "Thinking you'd probably decide to stay?"

"In your dreams," she snapped.

"And yours."

She glanced out the patio door at Petie, sniffing the thin strip of grass. "You're the most egotistical man I've ever met."

"You keep saying that, and I'll keep correcting you. I'm confident; there's a difference. I'm confident that you want me, and I'm confident that I'll get what I want this week."

"What did you mean when you said you don't want the prize?"

Trent had known she'd ask, and he was ready. "I meant what I said. I'm not here for the prize, Rissi. What I want . . . is you."

*A man wearing a towel—and only a towel—
should never be trusted . . . or stared at.*
—MARISSA KINCAID

Chapter 14

The phone in the apartment didn't merely ring; it clanged. Loudly. Particularly at 6:00 A.M., when Marissa hadn't slept most of the night due to Trent's *"What I want is you"* comment echoing in her brain until she wanted to scream . . . or run to his room. Neither was a viable option, so she stayed in her bed, completely in hiding, and watched a marathon night of *Rescue Me* on FX. That Tommy Gavin, aka Denis Leary, was one crazy, troubled, and downright warped man. And yet, Marissa found herself drooling over him from her bed. She wanted Tommy Gavin. She wanted Trent Jackson. Both were bad news, deadly combinations of cocky and cool and cute, so both "wants" bothered her terribly.

Clllllllaannnnng.

Marissa blinked again. You'd think Trent could at least answer the phone when he'd inadvertently kept her up half the night. Then she heard the shower, and Petie's loud inhalations as he sniffed the floor. Marissa grabbed the irritating phone from the nightstand and punched the *Talk* button. "Hold on, Petie," she said to the dog, then added a quick, "You hold on, too," to the caller as she crawled off the bed to let Petie out.

She opened the door to the patio, blinked furiously at the blinding light outside, and turned to sneak another look at the clock. It sure didn't look like 6:00 A.M. outside, and that's because it wasn't. "No way. It's eight o'clock already?"

"Yes, dear," Mona Kincaid said through the line.

"Mom?" Marissa said, waking up completely now. "Where have you been?"

"Branson, silly," Mona said. "As if you didn't know. The question is, where have you been? Or rather, why didn't you tell me you were moving in with Trent Jackson? I had to learn from Amy this morning."

"I tried to call you," Marissa said, "and left several messages for you to call me back. Somehow, telling you I was moving in with a guy I despise for a radio station contest didn't seem the right thing to leave on your voice mail."

Mona laughed. "You're right, and I saw where you tried to call on my cell phone, but we've been so busy here." She giggled, then stopped abruptly and cleared her throat. "Sorry dear, something just—got my funny bone."

Got her funny bone? "Mom, have you been drinking?"

"Oh, no, dear. Well, yes, but not this morning. They serve some really nice cocktails at the shows, and I've tried one or two at night, but not today. Anyway, I did try to call your cell phone this morning, but I didn't get an answer."

Marissa visualized the tiny phone, sitting in its charger, in the other room. "It's in Trent's room," she said, then felt the need to explain. "We swapped rooms yesterday, so I could have the one with the patio for Petie to go out, and I left the phone in there. I'll get it this morning, so you'll be able to call me on that number again." Petie darted back into the bedroom, barked happily, then went back outside. He'd really adjusted well to this "going on the patio" scenario. Maybe Marissa should consider fencing in the back area of her own apartment to give him the same independence at home.

"Honey, you still there?" Mona asked.

"Yes. Did you say you talked to Amy this morning?"

"I did. When I called your apartment, then your cell phone, and didn't get an answer on either one, I called Amy to see what was going on. She told me about the radio station contest and gave me this number to try to reach you. She said she was working on answering emails to your new cheater site. Oh, and she told me that she added Denis Leary to the, um, Pick Your Favorite Hottie poll, and then she said that you should be sleeping at three-thirty in the morning instead of emailing her about Denis Leary and *Rescue Me*."

"Amy's full of opinions," Marissa said, smiling. She had missed her regular Monday night chat session with Amy and Candi last night. They'd offered to update the site on their own while Marissa was trapped with Trent. Little did they know, she would've welcomed something to do to keep her mind off the fire he had started in the kitchen, the one that subsequently kept her up all night.

"She does like to talk," Mona admitted. "In fact, she told me that Candi is seeing one of Trent's friends, a guy you two met at the radio station. Amy thinks he's a good match for Candi."

"I don't know," Marissa said. "Amy's always trying to matchmake somebody. Candi's been burned before."

"You never know if it'll work unless you give it a try," Mona said, going for that motherly wisdom tone. "And speaking of giving it a try, what about Trent? I told you before, but I'll say it again. He really seems like a sweetie to me."

"Mom, he isn't even an option. That's the whole point of this week. If I like the guy, I don't get the ad campaign."

"But you do like him."

"He drives me absolutely crazy," Marissa said, and wasn't lying. In fact, the entire situation was driving her bonkers. She couldn't wait until Friday, when she'd get her money and leave, and never see Trent Jackson again. That's what she wanted. *Yeah, right.* She *did want* Trent, but she wasn't about to act on that particular want, and she certainly wasn't going to tell her mother about it.

She did another quick mental comparison of *Rescue Me*'s Tommy Gavin and Trent, and she realized there was a major difference after all. Sure, they were both cocky and cool and cute; she'd already established that. But Mona had touched on the main difference—Trent really was a sweetie. While Tommy was an outright liar and cheat on the show, Trent was the opposite. He'd only given Marissa the truth, even truthfully proclaiming that he wanted her, and he'd also informed her he wasn't a cheater.

And, something else Mona was right about, Marissa couldn't deny that she actually liked him . . . a lot. *But* if she liked him, she lost the ad money. And that he hadn't cheated before didn't mean he wouldn't cheat on Marissa. She did seem to have that effect on men. Come to think of it, how *would* she ever recognize a guy who wouldn't let his heart—and his other parts—wander, if she ever found one?

"Drives you crazy, huh? In a good or a bad way?" Mona asked, pulling Marissa out of her newest quandary with yet another tough question.

"Mom, I really don't have time to talk about this now. We've got to do the morning show with Coleman and Speedy in less than an hour."

"I know, dear. Amy told me how I can listen to it on the hotel's Internet here, so I'll tune in."

"They broadcast over the Internet?" Marissa whispered, then realized that she knew they did. She'd listened to the show through her computer at work, whenever the company PA system was on the fritz. But somehow, that hadn't entered her mind this week, that the entire world wide web could hear each morning's interaction.

"Yes, honey. In fact, Amy said the station will have all of your broadcasts online. I can hear them all with a click of the mouse. Modern technology is amazing, isn't it? Anyway, we're planning to listen to you on the air in just a little bit."

"We?" Marissa asked.

Mona cleared her throat. "Me and my friends, dear. You know I came here with the seniors."

"Surely they've got other things they'd rather do this morning than listen to us on the radio."

"Can't think of a thing, dear. Most of the shows are at night, so this is perfect. Count on us tuning in every morning."

"Great." Marissa moved back to the patio door and gave the little kiss sound that always got Petie's attention. He turned obediently and headed inside.

"Oh, kisses to you, too, honey," Mona said. "I'll talk to you later in the week, okay?"

"Okay," Marissa said, baffled. Later in the week? Her mother had called her daily for as long as Marissa could remember, and all of a sudden a trip to Branson had modified that to a biweekly occurrence? Something was definitely going on with her mother, but Marissa didn't have time to worry about it now. She needed to feed her dog, get her cell phone, and take a shower in—she checked the time—forty minutes. No pressure. Of course, getting a shower was going to be tough if Trent never got out, or if he used all of the hot water. She moved to the bathroom door and banged on it. "Hello! Other people need to use the bathroom, too!"

His rumbling laugh filled the air, and Marissa hated it that her nipples responded with excited bliss. She looked down at them, poking against her thin sleep tank. "Traitors."

She'd barely opened the bedroom door when Petie zoomed past her and ran to the kitchen. He stopped beside his bowl and turned around, ever waiting to be served. Marissa laughed. "You are one spoiled puppy." She filled his food and water bowls, then listened to see if the shower was still going. It was, which wasn't a surprise. The guy obviously liked long showers, or liked making her wait. Probably both.

Fine. She needed to get her phone anyway. Leaving Petie to his breakfast, she crossed the living room and turned the knob on Trent's door. He'd left it unlocked, as if issuing an invitation. She'd wager the bathroom door was unlocked, too, but she wasn't about to try it. Instead, she slipped into his room and tiptoed past the bed to the wall outlet by the closet. The bed was still unmade, and she studied the indention in the pillow from his head. He'd slept right there, merely feet from her room, and he'd admitted that he wanted her. If he were a normal guy, as in one who wouldn't cost her a seven-figure ad deal if she gave in to temptation, then she could have had a really good time in that big pink—or rather, peach—bed last night. But she hadn't. And she wouldn't. It wasn't worth it, because of the ad campaign, a monumental reason not to get involved with Trent Jackson.

But the thought of him on those peach satin sheets . . . definitely had her heart beating a little faster. She stepped closer and ran her fingers down the edge of his pillow. In one of the *Rescue Me* episodes she had watched last night, Tommy Gavin's estranged wife showed up in a trench coat with sexy lingerie underneath. What would Trent do if she came in here at night wearing a trench coat, with something extremely sexy and lacey and black . . .

"Can I help you?"

Damn. Marissa had been so absorbed in staring at Trent's bed, and envisioning herself in it, that she hadn't heard the shower water stop. And she sure hadn't heard the bathroom door open. She jerked her hand from the pillow, slowly turned, and had to clamp her mouth shut to keep her tongue from rolling slap out.

Trent Jackson in clothes was deadly. Trent Jackson in a towel, knotted low on one side and showing way more than she needed to see, was lethal.

"I forgot my phone." She needed to turn around, get the phone, and get out. But instead, she chewed her lip, then her right hand moved toward her mouth in an instinctive gesture, meant to calm her nerves by offering her nubs. But Marissa couldn't even remember how to bite her nails, or how to breathe right. In and out. Yeah, that was it.

His chest was still shower damp, with little droplets clinging to the sprinkle of dark hair at the center. His flat male nipples were dark, too, and she wanted to kiss them.

"Rissi?"

"Uh." There was no way she could get onto him for using the nickname now. In fact, there was no way she could put enough words together to form a sentence right now.

"Ready to forget that ad campaign and give in to what we both want?" he asked, flicking those dark brows and giving her that crooked, sexy smile.

Forget the ad campaign? She blinked. Nope. Yes, he was one tribute to the male gender, all hot and damp and ready to be licked from head to toe, but she wasn't giving in to the temptation. Not today, and not any other day. "No," she said and was glad her vocal cords had decided to cooperate. "I just needed to get my phone." She turned away from the vision in the towel and hurriedly snatched her phone and charger from the wall. Then, without looking at him, she scooted toward the door. "Now that you're finally done, I'm going to take my shower before our broadcast," she said. "And I'm locking the door."

"Good for you," he said.

She made it out of his room and, relieved, took a deep

breath of non-male-influenced air. Then she heard the door creak behind her.

"You forgot this, too," he said.

Bracing for yet another sight of him in a towel, she turned, and saw Trent, smiling—and holding Pinky.

"You might need this," he said.

Marissa stepped back toward the nearly naked man and took her vibrator out of his hand, shivering as his fingertips grazed her palm in the process. "You're evil," she whispered.

He released the vibrator, winked, then turned around and left Marissa gawking . . . as his towel hit the floor.

"Rissi Kincaid, you ain't seen nothing yet."

Twenty minutes later, after a cold shower, Marissa sat next to the man who had all too willingly shown her his magnificent ass-ets and waited for the phone call from Coleman and Speedy.

"How was your shower?" he asked.

Marissa kept her hands busy stroking Petie, nestled comfortably in her lap, so she wouldn't be tempted to slap the smug look off Trent's face . . . "You think you're so cute."

"The question is, do you?" he asked, as the phone clanged to life and Petie barked.

"It's okay, Petie," she said, soothingly rubbing his soft coat. Thank goodness Petie was here. If she didn't have him to keep her mind occupied, at least a portion of the time, then she'd spend every minute wondering if Trent's front view was as good as the back.

Trent punched the speaker button. "Liars and cheats."

Speedy's laughter cackled through. "Gotta love this guy," he said.

"Yeah, he's a real riot," Marissa said.

"Well now, I hear a bit of animosity there," Coleman said. "Is that true, Ms. Kincaid?"

"The prize depends on whether I can hate him for a week," she said. "Trust me, it isn't a problem."

"That's what she claims," Trent added, "but I'm not believing it."

"Is that so?" Speedy asked. "Care to explain that, Jackson?"

"Yes," Coleman said. "I'm sure our listeners would love to hear."

"She wasn't hating me when I kissed her yesterday morning," Trent said.

Marissa sucked in an audible gulp of air. "That's ridiculous! I didn't want you to kiss me."

"Could've fooled me," Trent said, while Coleman interjected.

"You kissed her?" he asked.

"Oh, yeah," Trent said. "Of course, then she bit me."

"You bit him?" Speedy echoed, then howled with laughter. "You know, Coleman, we really should've sprung for video footage of this deal. It'd beat any of those reality shows."

"He deserved it," Marissa said. "He was trying to kiss me, and I wanted him to stop."

"There wasn't any trying to it. I was kissing you, and you were kissing me back, and then you got scared and bit me."

"I'm not scared of you," she snapped.

"Well you're damn well scared of something," Trent said.

"Whoa now," Coleman said through the line. "You're

giving us more than we bargained for this morning, but we don't want to miss figuring out exactly what happened. Marissa, did he kiss you?"

"He tried."

"Okay, and then what?" Coleman continued, his voice slow and easy, even though Marissa knew he was excited about this juicy tidbit that Trent had thrown out for the world to hear. She glared at him. He'd pay for this. As soon as she figured out how to make it happen.

"And then I bit him."

"But she apologized last night, over pizza," Trent said. "By the way, thanks for dinner, guys. And if you send pizza again, make sure the same delivery guy comes. His name is Bud, and Marissa has the hots for him."

"I do not!" she yelled, causing Petie to squirm out of her arms and jump to the floor. He fled the war zone and headed to his doggie bed.

"Okay, okay," Coleman said. "Did anything else happen that we need to know about?"

"I caught her checking out my ass," Trent said bluntly.

"Whoopser, we didn't get that word beeped out," Speedy said.

"What are you talking about?" Marissa asked Trent. Surely he wouldn't tell how she saw . . .

"You, checking out my ass, this morning after I got out of the shower."

She wanted to die. Right here. Right now. "You dropped the towel," she accused.

"Didn't mean you had to look, darling."

"Don't you call me darling. Or Rissi. Or anything remotely resembling a term of endearment," she warned.

Speedy's cackle was nearly constant now. "H-hold on there a minute," he said. "Let me catch my breath."

"Listen," Marissa said. "For some strange reason, he doesn't even want the prize, so he's trying to make it sound like something is happening when it isn't. And that's the truth."

Coleman cleared his throat. "Okay, let me get this straight, because our phones are already lighting up like Christmas trees with callers who are probably as confused as we are. Mr. Jackson, did you try to kiss Ms. Kincaid?"

"I did kiss her," Trent said.

"Fine. And Ms. Kincaid, did you then bite Mr. Jackson?" Coleman continued, like an attorney approaching the witness.

"Yes," she said. No need to elaborate that she actually did kiss him back, until she got her wits.

"And Trent, did you, um, bare your behind to Marissa after your shower?"

"My behind is always bare after a shower. She had the choice to look . . . or not. She looked."

"What woman in her right mind wouldn't have looked?" Marissa said, then flinched when she realized that had just been broadcast over the radio, for all of Atlanta, and her mother, to hear.

"So you liked looking?" Coleman asked.

"I don't like him," Marissa said. "*That's* what we need to concentrate on here. And the fact that he's purposely trying to keep me from winning that prize."

"Is that so, Jackson?" Speedy asked. "Because you know, if she doesn't win, neither do you."

"I don't care about winning," Trent said easily. "That's not why I'm here." And the jerk smiled, then eyed Marissa as if she were a piece of chocolate, ready to be devoured. Damn if she didn't like the image that thought provoked.

But she wasn't about to let him know it.

"Why are you there, then?" Coleman asked. "What do you want, if you don't want the prize?"

"Simple," Trent said, and Marissa braced for his answer to be sent out over the airwaves. "I want Rissi Kincaid."

"Ma-ris-sa," she corrected, then noticed the line had grown silent. For two beats of her heart, she didn't hear a thing but her own breathing, and Trent's.

I want Rissi Kincaid.

Did that sound as intense to everyone else as it did to her? Evidently so, since the DJs were currently MIA. Finally, Coleman came back to life.

"Well, Speedy, this has taken an interesting turn, to say the least."

"I'll say," Speedy said. "Trent Jackson is actually on our side. Looks like the little lady is on her own, huh?"

"It doesn't matter," Marissa said. "I don't want him."

"Liar," Trent said.

"Okeydoke," Speedy said. "Now we're getting somewhere. Liars, cheaters . . . and yesterday's assignment. Let's cover that, while Coleman and I figure out what we're going to do about this new, er, situation. Marissa, did you and Trent determine whether or not he actually cheated on you way back then?"

"Yes, we did," she said reluctantly. "And I already stated that I added him as a joke, so it really doesn't matter that—"

Trent didn't wait for her to finish. "I backed out of the Sadie Hawkins thing with Rissi because I couldn't dance," he explained. "And then, the day of the dance, I met up with another girl and we ended up going to the movies that night. Technically, I don't think I cheated, since I'd already told Rissi I wasn't going to the dance."

"And I agree. Technically, he didn't cheat. But he did hurt my feelings," she added, mainly because she needed some kind of net to brace her fall. Wasn't she now confirming her liar status, joke or not?

"I was thirteen," Trent said. "I didn't have a lot of experience with breaking a date. Admittedly, I handled the situation badly." He paused, then smiled. "Tell you what, I'll make it up to you now . . . somehow." His tone was filled with seduction.

"I don't want you to make it up to me," she said. "I want that ad campaign. And it won't do you a bit of good to go around dropping your towel in front of me, so don't let it happen again," she rattled.

Applause echoed through the line. "You go, girl," Speedy said.

"Obviously, Trent doesn't need a multimedia ad deal to take his business where he wants it to go, but I do," she continued. "He's fine with merely throwing a wrench in my plans, but I'm not about to let him win. I need that ad campaign for AtlantaTellAll and TheGuyCheats.com, and I'll have it when the week ends. Because, like it or not, some girls can live with or without you, Trent Jackson, and I'm one of them."

"Like I said, you're lying, Rissi. You want me, as much as I want you."

"You want Ms. Kincaid?" Coleman asked through the line.

"Definitely."

Marissa fought the frisson of sheer delight that his

word sent through her spine. Had she ever had a guy proclaim in public, much less over live radio, that he wanted her? No, she hadn't. But she also hadn't had one who tried to drive her near bonkers with his sexy talk, seductive looks, and mind games. And how could she know for sure that he wouldn't end up hurting her, like all of the others? Maybe he hadn't cheated back then, but that didn't necessarily mean he wouldn't now. Bottom line, she didn't need another potential cheater. She *needed* that ad campaign.

"Tell me something," Coleman said, then added, "and I'm going to have to word this carefully, since this is a family show, but Trent, I've got to ask . . . this attraction that you've got toward Marissa. Is it purely physical, or is it something more?"

"More," Trent said, at which Marissa laughed.

"You don't even know me," she said. "We were friends twenty years ago, and I didn't even see you again until that article ran in the paper. How can you say it's more?"

"Well, today's assignment may help us determine if it's more," Speedy said.

"What is it?" Trent asked, as though he were actually eager to jump through another of Coleman and Speedy's hoops.

"Glad you asked," Coleman said. "I'm afraid this is another one that's going to require talking, Ms. Kincaid. What we want both of you to do is to find out a little about each other, more than just where you live, your job, and that kind of thing. Basically, tomorrow morning, we want to learn what Trent's hopes and dreams are from Marissa, and what Marissa's hopes and dreams are from Trent. It all depends on the two of you as to how much communicating is required for you to figure that out. And that should give you a chance to connect on a more personal level, beyond the physical."

"And beyond dropped towels and kisses that bite," Speedy added.

"Easy enough?" Coleman asked, ignoring his sidekick.

"Very easy," Trent said. "And for the record, I already know Rissi's hopes and dreams."

"Ma-ris-sa," she corrected, then added, "and how can you even pretend to know my hopes and dreams?"

"You want to hear them?" Trent asked, apparently enjoying himself.

"Sure." She'd spoken the truth. They hadn't seen each other in years, and the brief interactions they had had before moving into this apartment were all fairly heated encounters. Then again, their time in the apartment had also been heated, even physically charged, but nothing at all that would be equivalent to any kind of relationship-building on an emotional level. So what could he know about Marissa's hopes and dreams? Nothing.

Or so she thought.

"First of all, Rissi wants to win this prize, the multi-media ad campaign that will propel her webzine, Atlanta TellAll, to the kind of notoriety necessary for the business to really take off. She wants the business to make enough income to adequately support herself and her two friends, Amy and Candi, who also help run the site. Then—and her boss will have to accept my apologies here—she wants to quit the day job and find a perfect guy. For the record, the only identification she provided for her 'perfect guy' is one who doesn't cheat, though I suspect that she wants much more than that single quality. And last of all, Rissi wants to work from home and have a house full of babies."

Marissa was speechless. He remembered everything she had said last night when she'd rambled on while they chatted over pizza. Every word, nearly word for word, as if her requirements in a man were something he was truly interested in.

Were they?

"You say that you suspect she wants more than that single quality," Coleman said, his voice deep and emotional. "Do you have any ideas as to what that 'more' might be?"

"Yeah," Trent said, "I do. Rissi wants a man who can make her knees weak when he looks at her, a guy who can make her laugh, and make her mad, who lusts not only after her body, but also her feisty spirit, and can hold her arms up when she chokes on her pizza."

Speedy sniffed loudly through the speaker. "Oh, man, I'm gonna cry," he said.

"Well, Ms. Kincaid, I guess I've got to ask. Is he right?" Coleman asked.

"Yes." The word was barely audible.

"And can you tell us his hopes and dreams as well?" Coleman continued.

Marissa shook her head, feeling defeated, and flabbergasted. He really *seemed* to care, but then again, all guys did, at first. "I don't know his hopes and dreams."

"Then that's your assignment for tomorrow," Speedy said. "And Trent, it looks like you're getting off easy, since you've already figured hers out. You can spend your day working, or playing, or dropping towels. Whatever floats your boat." He laughed. "And we did promise that we'd take a couple of callers this morning, so we better hop to that, since we're running short on time. Trent, you want yours first?"

"I've always followed the ladies-first principle," Trent said, nodding at Marissa. "Go ahead, Rissi."

She didn't bother correcting him on the name. He'd already completely robbed her of any fight she had left, and in truth, she was too busy remembering how he'd memorized all her hopes and dreams.

"Okay by you, Ms. Kincaid?" Coleman asked.

"Sure," she said, then turned her attention away from the hunky guy in the other chair to the white speakerphone on the desk. "Go ahead."

"Okay, we have our caller for Marissa. And who are we talking to this morning?"

"Hey, Marissa, it's Jamie."

No way.

"Now, Jamie," Speedy said. "I'm reading our information on you from the log, and it says you're the last guy that cheated on Marissa. Is that right?"

"Yeah," Jamie said. "That's right."

"So we've got the first guy who cheated on her—well, not technically cheated, but hurt her—and the last guy who cheated on her, together on the phone with us now, huh?" Speedy said, then added, "Now, based on the information I'm pulling up on TheGuyCheats.com—neat site, by the way—it looks as though you cheated on Ms. Kincaid with a fellow named Reginald."

"That's right, except he prefers Reggie," Jamie said.

"Reggie," Speedy repeated. "I'll make a note."

Coleman cleared his throat and took over. "Jamie, you said you had something to ask Marissa?"

"Yeah. I've been thinking about everything that went on with us, Marissa, and I really wonder if you didn't see it coming. I mean, most of my friends knew that I, you know, play for both teams. And personally, everyone says that you'd have to be blind to miss it, so I'm wondering if you really did miss it?"

"What do you mean?" Marissa asked, puzzled.

"I mean, do you think that maybe you went out with me *because* you knew it wouldn't work? You know, maybe you suspected that I'd cheat? Maybe not with a guy, but with someone? I mean, it could be that you're one of those girls who really don't want things perfect. Maybe you can only, you know, be happy when you're with someone that you know will cheat."

"That's ridiculous," Marissa said, but she couldn't keep Amy's similar words from tripping through her thoughts: *"Ever wondered if you didn't pick those guys on purpose?"*

"I have to agree with Marissa that it sounds off the wall," Coleman said. "But then again, we do hear of women who have been in abusive relationships, and for some bizarre reason, they continue to gravitate toward men who abuse. Suppose we've stumbled onto a whole new phenomenon, where a woman has been cheated on, and therefore gravitates toward cheaters."

"Hey, you're getting way too deep for me," Speedy said.

"I'd be interested in taking some callers on this topic, but we'll have to cover that tomorrow morning, perhaps at the beginning of the show, before we chat live with

Trent and Marissa. Right now, we need to move on to Trent's caller, unless Ms. Kincaid has anything else to say to Jamie."

"No, nothing," Marissa said. Was she a serial cheater-dater? And did such a thing even exist? She couldn't deny that she'd been mentally pondering the possibility.

Trent's hand reached toward hers, en route to her mouth. "Don't," he mouthed. "He's crazy. You don't date cheaters on purpose."

Marissa had to stare at his mouth to make out the silent words, and staring at his mouth wasn't a good thing. She remembered how good that mouth had felt when he pressed his lips to hers yesterday, hot and sensual and delicious, right up until she bit him. She focused on the tiny crease in his lower lip, evidence of her attack. Evidently, Trent noticed where her attention had turned and grinned. He tapped a finger against it, winked, and mouthed, "Doesn't hurt."

"Okay, we've got our next caller ready," Coleman announced. "Still there, Jackson?"

"I'm here," Trent said.

"We've got Lily on the line, all the way from Clearwater, Florida, where she's listening to us on the Internet. You still there, Lily?"

"Yes," the woman said, and Trent's head jerked slightly; it was only a small movement, but Marissa noticed. Then his eyes widened, mouth flattened, and this time, his word wasn't mouthed. It was quietly spoken, but Marissa was able to hear it.

"Damn."

"And you have a question for Trent Jackson?" Coleman continued.

"Yes, I do. I just found out about this radio station contest this morning, and I still haven't been out to The GuyCheats site, though I plan to as soon as I'm done talking to him. Anyway, I didn't want to wait, because my girlfriends told me that they heard Trent Jackson lying on your program, and I wanted to call in and set the record straight."

"Trent's lying?" Speedy asked. "Well, maybe he needs to go in a lying database, too. Anyone started TheGuy Lies.com yet? Or should Coleman and I get in on that one?"

"Speedy," Coleman warned.

"Just having a little fun," Speedy said. "Go ahead and tell us what the inside scoop is, Lily."

"Well, I didn't hear it myself, like I said, but one of the girls that works with me—her name's Georgia—she said that she was listening to this show last week—I think she said it was Friday—and heard you say it was Trent Jackson, of Jackson Enterprises."

"Right," Speedy said. "And if you want to personally listen to it, click on the previous broadcasts on our home page. But go on, tell us what you want to say to Trent."

"Well, Georgia and I have talked about our previous relationships and all—I mean, I'm happy now, married with a baby on the way—but we've talked about relationships from before, you know."

"Right," Speedy said again, while Trent's face drained of color. What did this woman know? And why did he look so worried about her telling it?

Marissa tried to make eye contact with him, but he kept staring at the speakerphone, as though staring at it would make Lily quit talking, which, of course, wasn't happening.

"But anyway, Georgia heard him say on your show that he has never cheated on anyone. Now, I don't know anything about the lady that was on there saying that he cheated on her, but I do know from firsthand experience that he lied."

"He lied?" Speedy questioned.

"If he said he hasn't ever cheated on anyone, then yes, he lied, because he cheated on me."

"He cheated on you?" Coleman asked.

"Yes, he did. With my sister."

Trent placed his hand on his forehead, then slowly eased it down his face, shaking his head as it progressed. He looked, in a word, guilty.

"Well now, this is an interesting call," Speedy said. "And I guess now we need to let Trent respond."

Marissa's skin prickled as she waited to see what Trent would say. If this woman, Lily, was telling the truth, then that meant that Marissa's fears were reality, and that she was doing it again—finding herself attracted to a cheater. Then again, she was her mother's daughter. And Mona Kincaid had married the king of cheaters, Marissa's father. Evidently, the apple really didn't fall far from the tree.

But if Lily weren't telling the truth . . .

"Well, Trent?" Coleman asked. "Did you cheat? On Lily?"

"Yeah," Trent said, moving his hand from his face and frowning at Marissa. "Yeah, I did."

If you want a woman's attention, confiscate her vibrator.
— TRENT JACKSON

Chapter 15

Trent had heard that the way to a man's heart was through his stomach. He was about to test the theory on a female. However, with the way his luck was going, Rissi might take one look at the hero sub and toss it right back at him, or worse, toss the sandwich *and* the plate.

Since this morning's broadcast, she'd spent the entire day in the breakfast nook with her back facing Trent as he worked at the desk in the living room. If it weren't for the constant banging of her computer keys, and the fact that she did get up occasionally to take Petie out, Trent wouldn't have noticed she was there. But he did notice, thanks to the banging, and thanks to the fact that he couldn't help but notice Rissi Kincaid. She was under his skin, big-time, and he was still determined to have her against it, big-time.

If he had his way, that would happen tonight, whether she realized it yet or not.

He carried two tall glasses of iced sweet tea into the breakfast nook, placed one in front of her and the other on the opposite side of the table. She didn't even look up from the screen. Undeterred, he returned to the kitchen, scooped up the two sandwich plates, and moved back to the breakfast nook. He sat behind his plate, then pushed hers across the table. This time, she peered over the top of the screen in an I-dare-you-to-stay gesture that Trent thought was absolutely adorable. He waved a hand over the plates, filled with the subs, chips, and dill pickle spears, then picked up his sandwich and took a bite.

"I don't want you here," she said, but her eyes darted to the plate beside her.

"Maybe not, but you want that sandwich. Go ahead and try it. I'm a damn good cook."

"You don't 'cook' a sandwich."

"Well, I make a good one, that's for sure," he said, and took another big bite while she watched.

She grumbled, but pushed the laptop aside and picked up the sub. Taking a lady-sized bite, she chewed, swallowed, closed her eyes, and softly hummed her approval.

"Told you," he said smugly.

"You are so cocky," she said, then took another bite, this one not nearly as ladylike.

"Confident," he said. "And what do you do when I'm not around, go without eating? Do you realize it's nine o'clock at night, and you never even stopped for lunch?"

She blinked, then looked at her laptop, apparently to check the onscreen clock. "We had a system crash today, and Gary asked me to work on it, but I didn't realize how much time had passed. No wonder I'm so hungry." She popped a potato chip in her mouth then took a sip of tea. "Thanks for the food, but just so you know, it doesn't mean I'm going to forget that you're a cheater—or that I'll give in to the little tease thing you've been doing."

"Okay," he said, glad she'd opened the door for this conversation. "We're going to have to talk tonight, since you're supposed to fill Coleman and Speedy in on my hopes and dreams during tomorrow's broadcast, but first I want to talk about the 'tease thing' you're talking about, and about what Lily said on the air this morning."

"I don't have to know anything about—"

"Listen, I made you a sandwich. Can you just eat the thing long enough for me to talk?"

"It won't do any good," she said, then sighed. "But you did fix me a sandwich."

"So you'll listen to me, without interrupting?" he asked.

"Until I'm done eating." Although she tried to sound smart-ass, one side of her mouth crooked up a tad, and Trent could see that she really wanted to set her smile free.

"Since you left before the broadcast was over this morning," Trent began.

"Petie needed to go out."

"I thought you were going to stay quiet until you finish eating," he said. "I *can* take that sandwich away, you know."

"Touch it, and you'll end up with a nub where your finger used to be," she said, pulling the plate toward her, picking up the sandwich, and chomping off a big bite.

Trent laughed. Have mercy, she was a pistol. "For the record, don't think I didn't notice that Petie was snoozing in his doggie bed when you woke him up and dragged him to the patio, before we'd finished the interview and, consequently, before I had a chance to answer Lily's accusation."

"So Petie didn't really have to go out, but I'd heard enough for one day, and I'm sure Coleman and Speedy didn't mind. You were the star of this morning's broadcast anyway. You and Lily, that is."

"Are you going to eat and listen, or am I going to have to wrestle your sandwich away?"

"Try it and die," she said, taking another bite. Petie whined from the floor, and she picked off a piece of turkey and tossed it his way. "This really is an amazing sandwich."

"Thanks. Now, what I was about to say, before you rudely interrupted—again—is that while I may have cheated on Lily, it wasn't with her sister, not her biological sister, anyway. She was talking about her sorority sister in college. I met Lily at the University of Georgia, and we went out for a while, I don't know, a month or so. Then I met another girl one night at the frat house, and one thing led to another, and we ended up together. And yes, I cheated on Lily, but I was in college and hadn't really settled down. Those aren't the best of years to use in judging a person's character, you know. Hell, I didn't even remember it until she called in on the show this morning, and honestly, she was dating someone else almost immediately after it happened. It was one of those college things. I cheated, I admit that. But I'm not a 'serial cheater,' as you call them on your site. I cheated once in college. As far as I know, that's the only time, and I really don't plan to cheat on anyone else again."

"Who says cheaters plan it?" she asked, and gave Petie another bite of sandwich.

"Hell, Rissi, are you saying that you're not going to give me a chance to get to know you better based on what happened with Lily?"

She swallowed, tilting her head as though deciding what to say, and then she shrugged in a why-not-tell-you move. "Okay. I'll admit it; I'm attracted to you, *but* I'm obviously attracted to cheaters. And, like it or not, you do now fall in that category, and I don't want to go through that again, Trent. I really don't."

Trent ate some more of his sandwich while trying to determine his next approach. The woman was stubborn, as hardheaded as they came, and yet he wanted her more than he'd wanted anything in a very long time. Call him crazy, but he was going to make her at least give him a chance. Preferably before the week ended. "Okay," he said, "how about a compromise?"

"A compromise?"

"Sex. Why don't we just have sex?"

He didn't pick the best moment for this request. She had a mouth full of tea, and it appeared to take all she had not to spew it in his direction. Instead, she pounded her chest and attempted to swallow. Then, with her dark eyes watering in much the same way they had last night when the pizza took a wrong turn, she squinted at Trent and questioned, "Wh-what did you say?"

"I said sex," he answered, more secure in the proposition than before. This was, after all, a good idea. "Obviously, this living situation is stressful for both of us, particularly since we're both attracted to each other." He paused to let her absorb that, then continued, "You know I'm attracted to you, and you admitted that you're attracted to me."

She covered her mouth with her hand. Was she smiling? Or was she hiding her shock? Well, at least she wasn't biting her nails, which Trent had already defined as her I'm-not-at-all-comfortable-with-this gesture. So, was she comfortable with it?

"Well?" he prompted.

"I'm not going to have sex with you. If you'll remember, us getting together keeps us from getting the prize, and I'm getting that prize."

"Actually, I believe the way the contest is worded, we can't win the prize if we start having a relationship, or if we have one in the twelve months following the cohabitation period. That *is* what it says," Trent said smartly, his idea sounding better by the minute. "But I'm not proposing a relationship. I'm simply proposing sex, something we both want and something that would obviously relieve the tension in this place. You have to admit there's a lot of tension. I mean, watching you bang that keyboard proved to me that you've got your share of stress happening here."

"Our system crashed today, and I had to fix it. That is stressful, but it isn't an everyday occurrence, thank goodness."

"So we have sex tonight, to relieve today's stress," Trent said. "Then if you don't have any additional stressful days during the week, we're done."

Petie barked from the floor, and Marissa tossed him another bite of sandwich.

"I am not having sex with you," she said flatly. "And for your information, there are other ways of relieving stress."

"I don't care how good Pinky is, there's nothing like

the real thing, and you know it." He leaned back in the chair and waited for her next argument.

She didn't disappoint. "I wasn't even thinking about Pinky."

Trent chuckled. "Okay, let's say you can go a day without using Pinky . . ."

"A day? How bad do you think I am? I could go without Pinky for the rest of the week if I had to."

"Care to prove it?" he asked.

She lifted her glass, took a sip of tea, obviously stalling. Trent waited; he was in no hurry. He had all night, and if he played this thing out right, a good portion of the night might be spent getting cozy, or cozier, with Rissi Kincaid.

"Prove it?" she finally asked.

"Yeah. It'd be fairly easy to do. All you need to do is let me be Pinky's guardian for the week. I'll give her back Friday morning, before we leave."

Frowning, she gave Petie more turkey. "Why don't I just give you the batteries?"

"Nice try, but I'm betting you've got more batteries stashed somewhere in your room, and on top of that, I have a feeling a resourceful lady like yourself would probably know how to put Pinky to use, batteries or not," he said, and was royally rewarded when her cheeks flamed with guilt. "Aha, I'm right."

She snarled at him, then got up from the table and started toward her room with Petie trotting alongside. Within a minute, she emerged, sans Petie, who'd apparently taken a trip to the patio. One arm was behind her back, and Trent held out his hand awaiting his prize. Rissi dropped the oddly shaped vibrator into his palm.

Trent stood, crossed the room, and, knowing she watched his every move, unlocked his computer bag and plunked Pinky inside. Then he relocked it, started back to the breakfast nook, and winked. "Okay then. Now that we know you won't be relieving your stress with Pinky, I want to put my offer back out on the table. Sex, with me, without the relationship ties. Just something to help you relieve the tension from your day."

"You'd do that for me," she said sarcastically. "What a giving man you are."

"That's what I'm wanting to show you."

"Uh-huh," she said, nodding. "Well, it isn't happening. Not this week, and not in this life."

Trent leaned forward, placed his elbows on the table, and steepled his fingers beneath his chin. In other words, his negotiating stance, though Rissi had no clue. "Tell you what, I've got another idea that would help you unwind. Granted, it won't work nearly as well as sex, but it'll do, and oddly enough, I'd probably enjoy it as well. Well, not as much as sex, but like I said, it'd do."

She eyed him suspiciously, but curiosity shone through her gaze. "Okay, I'll bite. What's your other idea?"

"A soak in the hot tub."

Her dark brows dipped a notch, as though she were looking for the ulterior motive. Then she ran a hand through her hair and smiled. "A soak in the hot tub sounds good," she said. "But I can do that without you."

"Actually, I'm fairly certain Coleman and Speedy meant for us to share the hot tub. I mean, it may be accessible from your room, but it's obviously for the apartment's occupants, and I'm one of those occupants." He paused, and pretended to be pondering his next words, though he'd known exactly what he would say from the time he started this spiel. "But if you're afraid you won't be able to control yourself in a hot tub with me, I can totally understand . . ."

She laughed, a deep, rich Julia Roberts laugh that bubbled freely and made Trent smile. "Not be able to control myself? Are you serious?"

"Just thinking aloud," he said with an innocent shrug. "Why else wouldn't you let me get in a hot tub with you?"

She backed away from the table and picked up her plate, then she reached over and picked up his. "You cooked; I'll clean. And after I'm done, I'll relieve my tension in the hot tub."

"And?" he asked, watching the way her hips swayed in gray gym shorts as she headed toward the kitchen.

She stuck her head around the corner. "And if you want to get into the hot tub, too, I won't stop you." Then she moved toward the table and grabbed the glasses. "I'm not afraid of you, Trent Jackson."

Trent merely smiled and watched her disappear into the kitchen. "Yeah, darling, but maybe you should be."

*Nothing says sex like a little red dress, except,
perhaps, a skimpy red bikini.*
—AMY BROOKS

Chapter 16

Marissa pivoted from one foot to the other, taking in her reflection in the skimpy red bikini. Why had she let Amy help with the packing? And why couldn't she have brought at least one one-piece suit for this week? She'd packed three bathing suits, and every one of them was equally tiny. Funny, they didn't seem that microscopic when she wore them at her apartment complex. But then, she was concerned with getting a decent tan, not protecting herself from shark-infested waters. In this case, the waters were the ones splashing and bubbling and amazingly warm on her patio. And the shark, well, there was no need to second-guess who filled that bill in this scenario, or wonder whether he'd attack. The question wasn't if, but when. And would she survive?

A rumbling knock on her bedroom door made her jump, and caused Petie to pounce on a pillow. He'd only figured out how to jump onto the bed this week. Previously, he could get down, but not up, and he was currently celebrating another victory of his paws on the comfy square . . . and he was probably celebrating the knock as well, since he knew that meant company.

Company. Shark. Cheater. Hottie. So many nouns to choose from, when it came to Trent Jackson.

"Are you letting me pass through, or have you chickened out already?" he asked from the other side of the door.

Marissa grabbed her sheer black cover-up, whisked it on, and opened the door. Then, as Trent nodded and entered, she realized that she'd been worrying for the wrong reason entirely. Trent Jackson seeing her in a skimpy bikini wasn't the problem. The problem was her seeing him—and that he was hot. Sizzling. Mouthwatering.

He walked right past her to pet the dog on her bed.

"Hi, Petie." He rubbed the scruff of Petie's neck, while Petie's tongue lolled out in contentment. Marissa's tongue was lolling, too, though she was doing her best to control it. Evidently, with this morning's drop of the towel, she'd been too focused on his ass to really take in everything else, as in biceps bulging out nicely, broad and powerful shoulders, a back that was well-sculpted and tan and toned, and then there was the royal blue swimsuit that covered an ass . . . that she remembered all too well.

They really needed to move on to that hot tub. At least he'd be chest-deep in water and mostly covered.

"You ready to go onto the patio?" she asked, and was pleasantly surprised that her voice sounded calm.

"Sure. You coming, Petie?" he asked, walking toward the patio door.

Petie leaped off the bed and scampered outside, totally obeying his nonmaster. Marissa didn't complain. Every minute Trent had his attention on her dog was another minute his attention wasn't on her, and another minute for her to gain her composure before stepping into that bubbling hot water with a sizzling hot man.

Marissa took another glance in the mirror before starting out. She looked cool enough, for someone whose insides were churning wildly. Why had she agreed to soak in a tub with him? As if she didn't know. Because somehow, he'd convinced her that she had a choice: hot sex or hot tub.

Why did she choose the tub again? Oh, right. Because she wasn't going to have sex with Trent Jackson. Now if she kept reminding herself of that, she'd be fine. She started toward the patio door, then remembered there were no towels outside. No way did she want to get out of the tub dripping wet and potentially excited without a towel nearby. And no way did she want Trent Jackson to get out of the tub dripping wet and potentially excited without a towel nearby either. She darted to the bathroom, grabbed two of the oversized turquoise beach towels from a wicker shelf, then headed outside with the determined goal of merely enjoying the tub, rather than enjoying Trent.

No sex with Trent, she silently chanted. *No sex with Trent, no sex with—*

Have mercy, he looked good in a hot tub. He smiled as she neared, and this time, the power of that smile shot all the way to her very center. Not good. She placed the towels on the patio table, then attempted to casually remove her cover-up, but because she was so turned on at the moment, she felt as though she were doing a striptease for the guy staring at her from the tub, and dammit if she wasn't enjoying the way those smoky eyes set her body on fire.

Completely unaware of the sexual tension surrounding him, Petie lounged on the pebbled concrete with his legs stretched out in front and behind him. Nice to know someone was so comfortable with this situation. Marissa stepped over him, then entered the tub and sank into incredibly warm water, all the while aware of Trent watching her every move, her every breath.

"You're making me uncomfortable," she said, edging down so the water covered her shoulders. Mercy, this tub was big. And so was the man in it.

"I haven't even touched you." He propped his arms on the side of the tub as if showing her that he wasn't even making an effort to touch her. "See?" he said, holding up his palms. "My hands aren't even in the water." Then his foot brushed against hers, and she jumped as if she'd encountered a jellyfish in the swirling liquid. The effect was almost the same. A stinging stab through her entire body, coupled with the fear of the unknown—the unknown being what might happen if he did try to touch her, in more than a foot-against-foot kind of way.

"Marissa," he said smoothly. "Do I scare you that much?"

"No," she said, shaking her head as if trying to convince herself it was true. "Of course not."

"Good, because I suggested soaking in the tub to help you relax, but you sure don't seem relaxed now."

"Maybe it's the fact that you asked me to have sex merely fifteen minutes ago," she said. "That's not exactly something I'm accustomed to, someone boldly asking for sex—only sex—with no strings attached."

"Rethinking your answer?" he asked.

"No. Definitely not." *And there you have it; she was unquestionably a liar.*

"Then what?" he asked.

"It's just that all of this is, as you must realize, a bit awkward. And to tell you the truth, I'm kind of shocked at how quickly you jumped from having sex to merely sitting in a hot tub. It's not as though the two go together."

"They could," he said, and his right hand dipped into the water, those long fingers teasing the rippling waves, while Marissa's mouth watered. His fingers shouldn't turn her on, right?

"Stop that," she said.

"Stop what?" He looked genuinely confused, but then his fingers stopped moving on the water, and he smiled. "Oh, honey, if that does it for you, you really should let me help you relax, beyond the tub."

Marissa cleared her throat. "The tub is fine, though I still think it's odd how quickly you moved from having sex to having a soak. They don't go together, as I said. Or at least tonight they don't."

"All right," he said, "I'll tell you, but right now, I'm getting hot." And with those provocative words, he eased forward and dropped off the ledge seat in the tub, completely submerging himself in the hot water, before rising again, his dark hair slicked back and wet and his entire body soaked. He ran a hand down his face. "There. That's better. You should try it. Or are you one of those girls who doesn't get her hair wet?"

Not one to be outdone, Marissa eased forward and dropped beneath the water's surface. The whirring jets rumbled in her ears, hot water covered her completely, and Trent's leg rubbed against hers. This time she didn't jump. Instead, she let her skin touch his and enjoyed the completeness of water and heat and man. It was a wickedly wonderful combination. Reluctantly, she emerged and sucked in a thick breath of air.

"Better, huh?" he asked, while Marissa worked her fingers through her hair and acted as though she hadn't intentionally allowed him to touch her beneath the surface.

"Yeah."

"Good. Okay, so you were asking why the jump from sex to hot tub, right?"

She nodded. "Then we need to talk about your hopes and dreams, and then I'm going to bed."

"Is that an invitation?"

"Nice try."

He laughed, and she enjoyed the sound. This *was* really nice, after all, enjoying his company on the patio, with Petie lounging nearby and the night air surrounding them. More than that, Trent had evidently switched on the twinkling lights that filled the canopy of tree limbs above the patio. Marissa leaned back and stared at the tiny lights, while the pulsating water eased her tension away. Oh, yes, this felt *right*, even if she was with Trent.

"You remember when you were a kid, and your mother would take you through the checkout line at the grocery?" he asked, and oddly enough, he suddenly sounded like the same boy who used to sit and chat with her throughout their entire playground period in elementary school. It was a sweet memory, so Marissa smiled.

"Yeah, but you're really changing the subject here, aren't you?" she asked, still looking at the trees, the sparkling lights, the perfect location for romance. Or for two old friends to chat, which seemed to be the direction this conversation had headed. Worked for her. She couldn't handle much more of Trent's temptation.

"I'm not really changing the subject," he said, then laughed. "Do you think looking at those trees is going to keep your mind off of the two of us sitting in this tub?"

"It's very pretty out here," she said. "You should focus your attention on the trees, instead of on my chest."

"But it's such a nice chest."

"I knew you were looking," she accused.

"Hey, I'm male, what do you expect?" he said, then added, "But okay, I'll join you in your tree watch." The water splashed loudly, as he moved across the tub. Then he was beside Marissa, his right arm grazing her left one, and his hot body edging next to hers.

She fought the urge to shift away, or look at him. "What are you doing?" she asked, keeping her attention on one particular light that seemed to shine a little brighter than the rest.

"I figured the view was better over here, and besides, we're simply talking about when we were kids, you know, as friends. Friends do sit beside each other."

"But friends don't ask to have sex," she countered.

"I guess that depends on who the friends are," he said, his voice right next to her ear. "And for the record, you're right. This is a very nice view."

"You are looking at the trees, right?"

He laughed. "Yeah, but the other view was nice, too. You look good in red, Rissi."

She really liked the way he felt against her, but she wasn't about to let him know. *No sex with Trent, no sex with Trent, no sex with Trent* . . .

"You were talking about the grocery store," she said coolly.

"Yeah, I was. Okay, when you were little and had to go through the checkout line with your mother, what always happened?"

"I wanted candy." An easy answer, every kid wants candy in the checkout line.

"And what did she say?" Trent asked.

"Usually no, but every now and then . . ."

"Exactly. Most of the time you got a no, but every now and then, you'd get that coveted yes, and then there was that internal celebration, that I'm-getting-what-I-want high that only happened when you saw that candy hit the conveyor belt and start heading for the cashier."

Marissa giggled. "You may have grown up, but right now, you still remind me of the kid from back then."

"Give me time. The story isn't over yet, and it has a lot to do with the grown-up," he said, and unless she was mistaken, he inched closer.

She didn't care. She was having fun, enjoying this interesting conversation, and truthfully, enjoying Trent. "Okay, grown-up, keep going."

"So anyway, eventually you try to figure out if there is a way to improve your odds of getting what you want heading toward the cashier. I mean, that is the goal, right?"

Marissa smiled. "Even as a kid, you were a businessman in the making. No wonder you're doing well with Jackson Enterprises; you're always trying to beat the odds. So did you figure out a way to beat the odds of getting candy back then?"

"I think most kids figure it out, eventually. It goes like

this. You ask for that huge, brick-shaped king Hershey bar, you know, the one that kind of rules the candy aisle?"

A hilarious way to describe it, but Marissa could see the monstrous bar, and remembered a few times when she had asked Mona Kincaid for the same thing. "Yeah, I remember asking for it."

"But then, more than likely, with the odds the way they are, what's your mother going to say?"

"No."

"Exactly. So, as a normal kid, you have two options. You can do the whole dying-cockroach fit on the grocery floor . . ."

"The dying-cockroach fit?" Marissa asked, turning her head to view Trent, smiling at her. "I thought you were looking at the trees."

"I was, then I decided to look at something prettier."

"Just tell me what a dying-cockroach fit is," she said, then turned away from the good-looking guy with the intoxicating smile to study the trees. They were much safer than Trent Jackson dealing compliments.

"I'm sure you've seen the dying cockroach. It's when the kid doesn't get his way and he throws himself on the ground at the grocery checkout, flinging arms and legs everywhere while screaming at the top of his lungs."

"You sound familiar with the technique," she said, trying not to laugh at the image of Trent Jackson performing his best dying-cockroach routine as a kid.

"I perfected it," he said, "before I realized that the other option was much more effective."

"Okay, I'm game. What was the other option?"

"When she said no to the king Hershey, I'd pull out the smaller version, the flat one that you use for s'mores, and then add a little pitiful to my tone before asking if I could have the normal chocolate bar, since I couldn't have the big one."

"And?" Marissa asked.

"I got what I wanted, every time," he said with pride.

"Seriously? It worked?" she asked, shifting to look at him again, both because she wanted to look at him and because she wanted to feel the way her body slid against his in the water. She was playing with fire, and she knew it, but at the moment, she couldn't help it.

"Every time," he admitted with a wink. "You ask for the big prize, the one that you're fairly certain is out of your reach, and then when she says no, you go for what you really wanted in the first place. It worked back then, and it works now."

"What do you mean, it works now?" she asked.

His smile claimed his entire face, and he tilted his head to look directly into Marissa's eyes. The effect was breathtaking, or at least it took her breath away. "I asked for hot sex, didn't I? But then I got a soak in the hot tub."

It took less than five seconds for Marissa to get what he said, and then less than one second for her to jerk away from him and splash him hard enough that the water sloshed over the side and soaked Petie. He barked solidly, then scampered inside, away from the battle in the tub.

And it was a battle.

Marissa continued tossing water his way. "You're terrible, Trent Jackson!" she yelled, while he pounced.

"Grab a breath, Rissi, you're going down!" he said, putting his weight on her shoulders and taking her under.

His strong hands held her there, beneath the surface, in the loud, bubbling water, long enough for her to realize that he was in full control, then his fingers moved gently down her arms to ease her to the surface.

She blinked the water from her eyes and, laughing, nudged his chest with her head. "You're awful," she said.

"You won't get any argument from me," he said, then his eyes fell to her mouth and stayed there. "Rissi, let me kiss you."

She shook her head, even though her entire body was screaming yes. "That wouldn't be smart."

"Maybe not," he said, "but it'd sure as hell be fun."

Marissa laughed and pushed away from the hard chest to put some space between the two of them, then she settled on the opposite ledge. She had to try to get them beyond what had just happened, or more important, what had almost just happened, since she'd sensed her resistance waning. She had to keep her mind on her goals, an ad campaign that would propel her business to the top, and a man who didn't cheat. Would she ever find a non-cheater who was half as good-looking, or half as fun, as Trent? Probably not.

Pity.

But in any case, she still had to accomplish tonight's task. She had to get her answers for Coleman and Speedy's quiz session tomorrow morning. "Tell me your hopes and dreams," she ordered.

He splashed her. "After sex."

She splashed him back. "No more bargains, Jackson. Not tonight, anyway."

"Ah, so maybe tomorrow night?" he asked, thumping water at her face as she prepared to argue and causing her to suck in a big gulp. She coughed it away and laughed.

"Do you ever give up?" she asked, while they continued their splash battle.

Finally, Trent caught her wrists, then moved closer to her in the tub. When his face was merely inches from hers, he stopped, eased closer, then kissed her forehead. "I never give up," he said, "but you'll figure that out before the week ends."

"Just tell me your hopes and dreams, and then we'll go to bed."

He cocked a dark brow.

"Our separate beds," she corrected.

He released her wrists and backed away to sit on the opposite ledge. "Suit yourself, though one bed would be more fun."

"Your hopes and dreams?" she continued. "What is it that you want, Trent, more than anything?"

"Right now, or long term?" he asked, exuding sex with every breath.

Marissa didn't have to wonder what he wanted right now. In fact, she'd felt the evidence of what he wanted when they tussled beneath the water. There was no sign of a "shrinkage factor" in Trent's shorts.

"Long term," she said.

"You blushing, Rissi?" he asked.

She knew she was, but admitting it wasn't happening. "Just answer the question. What do you want, long term?"

"You realize that this conversation is about to take a turn away from the fun and into the serious. Is that what you're wanting?" he asked, and those fingers dipped into the water again.

Marissa nodded. True, a shift in conversation might

not have been what she wanted, but it sure enough was what she needed, if she was going to end the night with her bikini intact, as in, still on her body.

"Okay," he said, shrugging. "But really, my hopes and dreams are pretty much the same as any other guy's."

"Fine. Let me hear them. According to Coleman and Speedy, your fans want to know," she said, attempting to sound flippant.

He smiled at that. "*Our* fans, and by the way, after you ditched out early on this morning's interview, Coleman informed me that their ratings have never been higher. He even hinted that if the two of us did end up getting together, the station might swing for one of those reality weddings, something along the line of Trista and Ryan from *The Bachelorette*, or that's the example they gave."

Marissa's mouth fell open. "They didn't."

"Yeah, they did. I didn't actually see that wedding, but from what they were saying, it was really something."

She visualized the wedding. She, Candi, Amy, and Mona watched the entire thing, start to finish, and didn't miss a minute of all the flowers, the ceremony, the cake, the dancing, the shades of pink. Every time Trista cried, they cried. Every time Ryan laughed, they laughed. When the couple kissed for the first time as husband and wife, they applauded and bawled. It was beautiful, magical, perfect.

"You saw it?" Trent asked.

Marissa nodded, rather dazzled by the night's conversations. It had started with sex, then hot tubs, then dying-cockroach fits, then Hershey's candy and now reality TV. Not her usual topics for dates—not that this was a date—but still . . .

Now, to top things off, she was sitting in a hot tub with Trent Jackson, a very sexy Trent Jackson, and talking about weddings. She definitely needed to get this train back on track.

"Well, Coleman and Speedy are simply trying to keep boosting their ratings," she said.

"I guess so," Trent agreed, the tips of his fingers still grazing the water. "But they did say that a poll has been added on their site where people can vote on how long it'll be before we get hitched."

"You're kidding. We don't even like each other."

"Yeah, darling, keep telling yourself that. Seems like the whole listening audience can pick up on the fact that you and I've got some serious sparks flying, whether you choose to acknowledge it or not."

"I've acknowledged it," she said. "Well, to you, I have, but I've also acknowledged that I'm not about to act on it." When he merely smirked, she blew out an exasperated breath. This week was going to be tougher than she had thought, and it wasn't half over yet. "Would you just tell me your hopes and dreams and stop talking about polls and weddings?"

Trent's smirk slid into another heart-stopping smile, but Marissa did her best to act unaffected. "I'll tell you my hopes and dreams, but unfortunately, we'll still have to talk about a wedding."

His hopes and dreams involved a wedding? From any other guy, her heart would melt right now, like a king Hershey bar in the sun, but she wouldn't let it happen with Trent. She couldn't. *No sex with Trent, no sex with Trent, no wedding with Trent . . .*

Where did *that* come from?

"Hopes and dreams," he said. "Okay. I want what my parents had, a marriage that begins with a best friend who will be my closest confidante throughout life, but I want to start earlier than they did. They got a late start, and then they died fairly young. Unfortunately, neither will ever see me with my kids or know how I fared in the business world. In January, if all goes well, DieHardAtlanta will hit the newsstands of Atlanta in print format. I'd always told my dad that I wanted to start a magazine someday, and now I'm doing it, but he won't see the finished product."

Marissa swallowed, her chest constricting with the emotions he was freely doling out in this intimate setting, completely secluded, the two of them, sitting in a hot tub on a patio beneath a canopy of twinkling stars. There was something very special about it all, and she was extremely moved by it. So much so that she didn't speak again, so he continued.

"More hopes and dreams," he said softly, while leaning back and pondering the lights above. "I want to be a young dad, and I guess I'm starting to push the envelope on that dream, but I haven't found that perfect woman yet, and I won't settle for less than a lady who can not only raise my children, but also be my best friend and exclusive lover. Basically, I want a woman who moves my soul, and I want children whom I can adore, simply because they breathe. I want to be a T-ball coach, and a business champion, and a loving, faithful husband." He brought his attention from the trees and focused on her face. "Those are my hopes and dreams."

Marissa didn't let herself think about her response to his words. She simply wanted to show him exactly how he touched her, so she slid off the ledge and moved across the rippling water, then placed her fingertips against his temple and eased them down the side of his face.

"Rissi?" His smoky eyes beckoned her on, and she wasn't about to stop now.

"One kiss," she whispered, then led a finger across his full lower lip. "Because I can't resist."

She softly pressed her mouth to his, then shivered at the warmth beneath her lips, at the realization that she was giving in to him, and that she wanted to, very much, at least enough for one perfect kiss. His mouth opened, and she eased her tongue through, eager to taste him, to connect with him more deeply. His hands tenderly touched her back, then pulled her body closer, until her breasts rubbed his chest and her very center was against his hardness. Rissi let desire take control, pressing against him, deepening the kiss, moaning her contentment with what was happening between them. She ran her fingers through his hair, soft and springy and damp. Exhilarating sensations fired furiously through every nerve, hot water sloshing around them, heated bodies moving against each other, intoxicating hungry kisses . . . so much that Rissi merely rode the desire that had his hands caressing her breasts, then sliding the two triangles of fabric away. He broke away from the kiss and moved his mouth down her neck, while Rissi leaned back and enjoyed this wild abandon. His hand kneaded one breast, while his mouth kissed, licked, and devoured the other bare, sensitive nipple.

Her core clenched in direct response to the attention on her breasts, and she had no doubt an orgasm was in the not-too-distant future. This fact alone caused her brain to join the party. She did *not* need to go this far with Trent

Jackson, and she certainly didn't intend to lead him on, which was what she'd be doing if this went any further.

"Trent," she panted. "This is . . . too much."

His hips, previously pressing against her pelvis, stopped moving. In fact, he stopped everything. His hand, his mouth, his body. And those seductive eyes looked up at her, attempting to bring her body in a more upright position without pushing her center even closer to . . . exactly where she wanted it to be.

He kissed her nipple once more, then moved the two pieces of fabric back into place. Then he slid his hands to her waist and gently shifted her body from direct contact with his pelvis, and turned her so she sat on his lap. "I know," he said, with a crooked, sexy smile. "I'm sorry. I couldn't stop, and you didn't seem like you wanted me to, Rissi."

"I didn't, but I—we can't." With her current position, the entire top portion of her body above the water, the sudden exposure to air made her shiver.

"Here," he said, moving her to sit beside him on the ledge.

The hot water covered her, warming her instantly. "Thanks."

He looked at her and grinned. "I'm sorry I went too far, but you *did* kiss me."

"Yeah, but I never said anything about getting naked."

"No, you didn't. And technically, you haven't gotten naked for me yet," he said, wrapping one arm around her and kissing the top of her head. "But we still have a few days, no need to rush."

She laughed. What else could she do? "I'm not getting naked for you, Trent. We do not need to have sex, because it would only complicate things. But really, I should be the one apologizing. I shouldn't have started that."

"You're not hearing me complain, are you?" he said, smiling. "And personally, I bet you dream about it tonight, you know, everything that just happened, and where it could go if you let it. Then eventually, you'll decide to let this thing go . . . as far as it can."

She splashed him playfully. "I've never met a guy so cocky."

"Confident." He pushed against the ledge to stand, then stepped out of the tub. "But obviously, we're done with our—bonding—tonight; however, I should warn you, this is far from over, just so you know." He grabbed one of the towels and wrapped it around his waist, but not before Marissa saw the evidence of his unfulfilled desire.

"I'm sorry," she said again, and he had the nerve to laugh.

"Sure you are," he challenged. "I'm betting you left me this way just so you could size me up." Then, to her complete shock, he opened the towel to give her a better look at his hardened length, pressing against his suit. "Well, how do I measure up, darling?"

"Very well," she said automatically, then her cheeks flamed, and his laugh filled the night air.

"You know, you're as feisty now as you were when we were kids." He secured the towel again, then he held a hand out to help her exit the tub.

"We did have a lot of fun together back then, didn't we?" she asked, taking a towel from him and drying off.

"Yeah, we did, though I'm suspecting you've forgotten a lot of that in your teenage fury over that dance thing.

I'm going to make that up to you," he said, turning off the switch that controlled the hot tub jets.

"Trent," she started, but he kept talking.

"And eventually, we're going to get to more of those not-so-kidlike things that will also take advantage of the fiery spirit you're trying to tame. You let go tonight, Rissi, and like it or not, I helped it happen."

"That kiss went too far," she said. "And you're wrong. I won't let it happen again. I can't."

He acted as though she hadn't said a thing. "So, Ms. Kincaid, do you want to have sex now?"

"What?" she asked, tightening the towel around her, then tucking it in at her chest to make sure the thing kept her covered. No way did she need to get anywhere near naked again tonight, particularly when he'd ignored her declaration that they weren't going any further, and consequently asked her to have sex. She shivered again, and wasn't exactly sure whether it was due to the night air against her damp skin or the awareness that she did want to have sex with Trent Jackson, the guy who, merely days ago, was the enemy. *No sex with Trent, no weddings with Trent, no more kisses with Trent, no more semi getting naked with Trent.*

Her list was getting longer by the minute.

"I asked if you wanted to have sex now," he repeated.

"No," she lied. "And we don't need to kiss again either," she added, for good measure, as the two of them crossed the patio and she spotted Petie, dozing in the center of her bed.

"Lucky dog, in your bed," Trent said, and Marissa grinned.

"You really don't give up, do you?"

"Not if I can help it," he said. "So no sex tonight?"

"Looks like I already have a male in my bed."

"Uh-huh. Well, how about a run together in the morning?" he asked, shifting gears pretty darn fast, so fast that Marissa had to think about her answer.

"A run?"

"Yeah, a brisk run at dawn to start the day. I try to run every other day, and tomorrow's the day."

Marissa remembered his entering the apartment Monday morning in his jogging shorts. All hot and sweaty and hot and smiling and hot . . .

"Rissi? Want to join me? We can't leave the apartment alone, so either you go with me, or I miss my morning exercise. And I'll admit that if I go too long without something I'm used to, I get cranky."

She had no doubt he wasn't merely referring to running, but she didn't want to touch the other implication. "I've never been jogging in my life. There's no way I could keep up with you."

"Don't worry, I'll be gentle."

And again, she knew better than to touch that remark. "You really jog every other day?"

"Five miles minimum," he said, reaching over her shoulder to turn off the tree lights and leaving them in predominant darkness, with only a hint of moonlight filtering through the trees. Uncomfortable with the intimacy of their new environment, Marissa stepped inside her room and turned on the light. Petie growled and put a paw over his eyes.

"If you can keep the pace slow enough for me, and if you're willing to drop it to a walk if I need you to, then

I'll go." She didn't want him to miss out on his normal routine because she wasn't all that "into" exercising.

"Great," he said, then he kissed her forehead again, as a married man would kiss his wife good-bye before heading to work. Except Marissa wouldn't want a mere peck on the forehead from her husband. Oh, no, if Trent were her husband, she'd want a make-your-knees-weak gropefest each morning before he headed out the door, the kind of kiss she saw Amy and Landon enjoying beside his truck, and the kind of kiss she knew Trent was quite capable of giving, since she'd been completely lost in his kiss merely moments ago, in the hot tub.

She inadvertently glanced back at the tub.

"It was nice, wasn't it? Our soak in the tub," he asked, his words feathering against the shell of her ear.

When had he stepped so close?

Marissa sucked in a breath, swallowed. "Yeah, it was, but I really am glad we stopped things."

"Not we," he reminded. "You. And I'm not so certain you're all that glad about it, but I'll leave you alone about it, for now."

"Thanks," she whispered, still entranced by the way his warm breath felt against her ear. What would it feel like to have Trent nibbling on her lobe, or her neck? And she already knew what it felt like to have him paying homage to her breasts. It felt . . . right.

"Rissi?" he said again, still disarmingly close to her ear.

"Um-hmm?"

"It worked, again."

She squinted and tried to decipher his meaning. "What worked?"

"The Hershey's request. I asked for sex, and I'm getting a morning jog."

She pulled away from him and shoved him in the chest. "You *wanted* sex," she said. "And don't you even try to deny it."

"Hell, I wanted the big Hershey bar, too, but I'm no dummy. I'll take what I can get, and for the record, every time I asked for a bargain, I got closer to the prize." He touched a finger to her lower lip, then grinned. "Sleep well, Rissi. I'll wake you up, bright and early, and until then . . . dream of me."

Who in their right mind starts the day with a five-mile run?
—MARISSA KINCAID

~

Chapter 17

The next morning, Trent opened the door to the apartment and immediately heard the phone blaring. He really needed to turn the volume down on that thing. "Go ahead," he said, holding the door open while a panting Marissa stumbled through, and while her faithful silver puppy yapped happily at their return.

"Oh, Petie, it was horrible," she said, going straight to the kitchen. "Need water."

Trent chuckled, closing the door and watching her cute, sweat-covered body absorb yet another bottle of water. He'd carried two large bottles for the run. She downed hers during the first mile, then finished off his in mile three, which they walked. They'd also walked miles four and five, but Trent didn't mind. It was fun listening to her fuss, watching the sweat bead on her chest above her cute black sports bra, and seeing her try her best to make him feel like a total ass for making her start the day with a run. He had to give her an A for effort, but he didn't feel like an ass at all. He felt like the luckiest guy in the world. In spite of her grumbling professions to the contrary, he truly believed she was falling for him, almost as much as he was falling for her. It would happen; she'd see they were meant to be together. But if he didn't get her to realize it before Friday, she might not give him another chance. The woman was just stubborn enough to stay away from him for twelve months to win that ad campaign. And dammit if he didn't think her stubborn streak was cute, too.

He punched the speaker button on the phone, but only received a dial tone. "They hung up," he said. "But they'll call back. We're supposed to be on the air now."

"I hope they do call back," she said, wiping excess water off her mouth with the back of her hand. She'd tried to drink the entire bottle at once, and much of the liquid had dribbled freely. Trent wanted to lick her clean, but knew she wasn't ready for that. Yet.

"Looks like they left messages earlier," he said. "We've had six since we went jogging, and we're only five minutes late for the broadcast." He started to press the *Play* button, but stopped when the phone blared to life again. "We're on," he said, pushing the speaker button. "Liars and cheats."

"So you are still there," Speedy said through the line. "We were beginning to think you either killed each other or eloped. I was betting on the eloping, but most of our listeners seemed to be leaning toward a murder. In fact, we were in the process of starting a poll and we're about to take one call now."

"Go ahead and put her on the air. She's been waiting a while," Coleman said. "And then we'll start chatting with Trent and Marissa to find out where they've been."

"Okay," Speedy said, while Marissa dropped the empty

bottle in the trash, then grabbed another one from the fridge. She walked slowly to the living room and dropped into a chair near the phone, all the while glaring at Trent as though she'd vote the murder option if she were taking Coleman and Speedy's poll. Wicked short, black curls covered her head, with that sexy one Trent adored teasing her temple. And her eyes were fiery mad, even though he had stopped running each and every time she wanted and walked as much as she wanted.

"You'll feel better later," he mouthed.

She merely snarled, then drank more water.

"All right, we have our caller, who has been holding for a while, since we were waiting for our guests of honor to answer the phone," Speedy said, snickering.

"Sorry about that," Trent interjected.

"Not really a problem," Coleman said. "And we'll get more details later. Right now, we have Nan on the phone from Marietta. How are you this morning, Nan?"

"I'm fine, and I was going to vote on the murder option, but I heard on the radio that they've answered the phone, so I guess that one isn't a valid choice anymore, huh?"

"Well, you know," Speedy said. "Come to think of it, we haven't heard from Ms. Kincaid this morning. You still breathing, Marissa?"

Her snarl intensified, then she grinned sneakily, the little shit.

"Rissi," Trent warned.

Speedy cackled. "Don't tell me. She isn't talking to you, Jackson? What'd you do?"

"I know what he did," Nan said. "That's the main reason I called in to vote for murder, because when I saw the two of them this morning on my way to work, Ms. Kincaid looked like she wanted to kill him."

"You saw Ms. Kincaid and Mr. Jackson this morning?" Coleman asked.

"Yep. They were running near Powers Ferry Road in Marietta, near my office. I noticed him immediately, well, because, you know, I notice guys that look that good running. You do look good, not that I'm hitting on you, because I'm happily married, but you can still window shop, as long as you don't buy the merchandise," Nan said, then laughed.

"I agree with that philosophy," Speedy said. "So tell us about what you saw of our popular couple."

"Well, I stopped at a red light, and they ended up crossing the road right in front of me, and that's when I realized that it was Trent and Marissa. I thought it was so cool because there I was, trying to get to work in time to listen to the broadcast on my computer, and then there they were right in front of me. I've got to tell you, our whole office is really enjoying the fight on the air, but seeing it firsthand was even better. She was really pissed."

"Sorry, Coleman, I didn't realize where she was going until it was too late to beep it," Speedy said.

"Oh, shoot. I forgot," Nan said. "I'll watch my mouth. Anyway, she was obviously ticked off at him and actually stopped running and tossed her water bottle at him."

Trent grinned, remembering the moment vividly, while Rissi glared.

"He deserved it," she said.

"Aha, she does live," Speedy answered. "And *did* you throw a water bottle at him, Ms. Kincaid?"

"I tried."

"That's the truth," Nan said. "She flung it as hard as she could, but he just reached out a hand and caught it. Looked like a baseball player catching a line drive. Pretty impressive, if you ask me, but it didn't seem to impress her any. She stood there fuming and crossed her arms as though she wasn't going to move. Then he started laughing and twisted the cap off the bottle and gave it to her, and she drank it."

"Then what?" Coleman asked.

"Then he said something to her, and she nodded, and then they started walking, while she drank the water. Oh, and then the guy behind me honked his horn. I'm not sure how long the light was green before I started moving," Nan said with a giggle. "But I couldn't miss out on that show."

"I'd have watched, too," Speedy said.

"So," Coleman said, "why was she so ticked, Jackson? And what did you say to her to calm her down? I mean, there are lots of us married men out there who could use a pointer or two on calming down a wife when she's in the mood to throw something." He laughed, then added, "Just kidding, Margaret."

Trent cleared his throat. "See, I usually run at least five miles every other day, and since we can't leave the apartment alone, I asked if Rissi would run with me. She agreed, but she made some stipulations this morning, one of which was for me to tell her when we finished the first mile so we could walk the second one."

"And?" Speedy asked.

"And she was doing so well, hardly even breathing hard after the first mile, that I decided to wait and tell her after another mile."

"Oh, that'd get you the couch for sleeping quarters at my house," Speedy said. "*After* you got a hairbrush to the head."

"Well, he's obviously a rookie," Coleman said. "Listen, Jackson, if you tell a woman you're going to do something, then you better do it. It makes things easier."

"Yeah, things like breathing," Speedy added.

"Oh, so *that's* why you threw the bottle," Nan said through the line. "Well, I don't blame you, honey, I'd have thrown it at my man, too, even if his butt did look that good in gym shorts."

"Thanks," Marissa said, nodding. "I'm glad you understand."

"Hey, I understand, too. The guy should've told you after the first mile," Speedy said.

"Wait a minute, now," Trent said. "We were late to this broadcast as it was. Imagine how late we'd have been if I'd let her start walking a mile earlier?"

"Let me?" Apparently exhausted, Marissa had been slouched in the chair throughout this little interchange, but now she straightened, put her elbows on the armrests, and leaned forward, obviously unaware of the intriguing view this position provided Trent of her cleavage. "*Let* me?" she repeated incredulously.

"Maybe that wasn't the wisest choice of words," Trent said, really enjoying himself . . . and the view.

"There's no maybe to it," Coleman said. "But you're young. There's still time to learn."

"And you're lucky she's got bad aim with a bottle," Speedy said.

"I have good aim," Marissa said.

"Yeah, she aimed real well," Nan said. "He just has a good arm."

"You know, I've got a buddy who has been trying to get me to join his recreational baseball league," Trent said. "Keith, if you're listening, go ahead and sign me up. Evidently, I've got talent."

"You may have talent, but you haven't got a big interest in self-preservation," Rissi snapped. "Or you wouldn't have lied to me about how far we'd run."

Speedy again did his best cat-fight impersonation, and Nan added, "You go, girl!"

"Okay," Trent said, smiling at Rissi. She really was cute when she was mad. And when she was excited. And when she was merely breathing. "I apologize for not telling you when we hit that first mile, but you were doing so well, I figured I should let you keep going. I actually thought you'd be kind of excited when I told you that you ran two miles straight without needing a break, after you told me that you hardly ever exercise. That's quite an accomplishment, Rissi."

She opened her mouth, then closed it.

"What do you say to that, Ms. Kincaid?" Coleman asked.

Rissi turned toward the machine, as though staring at it would make the two DJs go away.

It didn't.

"Yeah, did it make you feel good that you went that far?" Speedy asked. "Or did it simply make you want to deck him with a water bottle?"

"Obviously, I wanted to deck him with a water bottle," she said, then laughed. "But I'll admit that it did feel pretty good to know I went that far on the first day."

Trent leaned back in his chair, stretched his legs in front of him, and laced his fingers in a triumphant I-was-right-and-I-knew-it stance.

She narrowed her eyes, screwed the top on her water bottle, and then pegged him in the chest.

"Ouch!" he said, when the bottle collided with his heart.

"Whoa, Nellie, I'm thinking she didn't miss the mark this time," Speedy said. "Am I right, Ms. Kincaid?"

"I'll let Trent answer," she said smugly.

"Yeah, Speedy," Trent said, rubbing his sternum and trying not to look too excited by the fact that he was with the most spirited woman he'd ever met in his life. "She didn't miss the mark."

Nan squealed in delight. "Oh, I wish I could get that kind of spunk when my husband and I are fussing. You hit him with a bottle?" she asked.

"I did," Marissa affirmed, grinning like a kid.

"Was it open or closed?" Nan asked. "I mean, the bottle. I'm just wondering if you're now sitting there and looking at him all wet. You know, that's not a bad image, given I saw him in that T-shirt and shorts this morning." She giggled. "Lord, I hope my husband isn't listening to this."

"It was closed," Rissi said, but then her head tilted slightly, and Trent had no doubt she was wondering exactly how he'd have ended up if it had been opened. Then again, she'd seen him completely wet last night, and completely aroused, too, for that matter. Was she remembering that now?

She licked her lips.

Yeah, she was. Trent smiled broadly, feeling mighty sure of himself, and of the fact that he'd have her soon.

Rissi evidently noticed. "Cocky."

"What was that, Ms. Kincaid?" Speedy asked.

"Lucky," she said, her cheeks flaming. "He'll be lucky if any baseball team wants him if he can't catch any better than that."

"Really?" Trent asked, stirring up trouble and loving it. "You sure that's what you said? Because I could have sworn . . ."

"I—said—lucky."

"Oh, right," Trent said in his best patronizing tone.

Speedy cackled. "Well, Nan, it seems our couple is having an interesting morning, and while I believe they're perfectly content throwing things at each other, we really need to find out about Ms. Kincaid's assignment from last night and let them both know what we need them to do for tomorrow's broadcast."

"Okay," Nan said, "I've got to get back to work, anyway. But I have a quick question for Trent."

"Go ahead," Coleman said.

"If you run every other day, does that mean the two of you will be running again on Friday morning? Will I see you on my way to work?"

"Don't count on it," Rissi said.

"We'll see," Trent countered.

"Great. I bet I can probably talk some of my coworkers into carpooling that day," Nan said, then the line clicked as she hung up.

"We got a late start, but we still have a lot of listeners who are wondering about Trent's hopes and dreams," Coleman said. "We found out about Marissa's yesterday, thanks to Trent, but now we've got to see if these two got closer than bottle-throwing since yesterday and whether she actually found out whether the CEO of Jackson Enterprises has interesting aspirations."

Trent watched her face closely. His truthful admission of what he wanted most out of life had instigated that heated kiss in the hot tub, and everything that followed. This morning, she'd awakened with a determination to play it cool, as though none of that had happened. She ran with him, and they fought, but it was a playful, friendly fight. Rissi wasn't really mad, and what's more, Trent thoroughly believed that she was actually flirting with him, even when she flung a bottle his way. She'd enjoyed last night as much as he, but she didn't want him to see that now. However, could she tell Coleman and Speedy about his hopes and dreams without remembering what had happened when he told her?

She grazed her lower lip with her teeth, then slowly brought her left hand toward her mouth. Trent shifted in his chair, leaned forward, then gently caught her wrist and lowered it to the armrest. "You can do it," he mouthed.

He expected her to push his hand away, or to wait for him to let go, but she didn't. Instead, she slid her wrist through his fingers, then, when her palm reached his, she stopped and softly squeezed. The gesture was as intimate as anything they had shared last night, or more, because Rissi was accepting strength . . . from him.

"Marissa?" Coleman prodded. "Can you tell us about his hopes and dreams?"

She gave Trent a soft smile, then said, "Yes, I can. Basically, he wants what any other guy wants," she said, using the same introduction Trent had used when telling her his goals last night. "He wants to do well in his business life and to live up to the expectations his father had for him before he died, and he wants to do well in his personal life, to have a wife who's meant for him and children who look up to him and respect him." She paused, then added, "That's the short version, of course, but that's pretty much it." She tried to sound dismissive, but Trent knew her better. He'd seen the heartfelt emotion in her eyes last night. She'd been touched by his sincere goals, and he'd been touched by her response to them.

"Sounds good," Coleman said. "And I'm betting you learned that in as few words as possible, hmm? Since you claim you don't want to talk to Mr. Jackson any more than necessary this week?"

"It didn't take a whole lot of words," Trent said, and gave her another wink. She squeezed his hand, then released it.

"That's right," she said. "It didn't take that many words, and then we didn't have anything left to talk about."

Trent cocked a brow, but chose not to argue the point. Truthfully, he hadn't talked much more than that, but he had done plenty of other things, like kissing her neck and fondling her breasts. His attention dropped to the two swells against the clingy sports bra. They weren't overly large and, in fact, were closer to the small classification, but they were, in Trent's opinion, perfect, from the gentle slope outward to the taut, ultrasensitive nipples that had instantly budded beneath his tongue and hand. Trent shifted in his chair and attempted to will the beckoning hard-on to subside, but what normal guy wouldn't get turned on remembering how responsive Rissi had been at his command, especially while looking at her, still heated from their run and still wearing the gray athletic shorts with peekaboo notches at each outer thigh and the black sports bra that only emphasized her pert breasts, flat abs, and narrow waist.

Damn, he wanted her, and he couldn't have her. Yet.

"Well, today's assignment won't involve a whole heck of a lot of talking," Speedy said. "But it should still be fun."

"Yeah, it should," Coleman added. "I mentioned it last Friday, you may recall. Today, Trent will need to come up with a menu for tonight's dinner. If you need anything that isn't in the apartment, and I assume you probably will, fax the list of items to us by noon, and we'll have someone deliver it to you in plenty of time for you to start cooking. Tonight, you're going to prepare a meal for Marissa and then the two of you will dine together."

"Sounds good," Trent said, and was inwardly pleased that he was, according to Keith and all of the women he'd previously dated, "quite talented in the kitchen." Of course, being raised by Anna Boudreaux Jackson didn't hurt. His mother was proud of her Cajun heritage and determined that the legacy of preparing seasoned cuisine wouldn't die when she passed on. Thanks to her, Trent could cook one mean étouffée, and tonight, he'd prepare it for Rissi. "I'll fax everything I need shortly."

"Sounds good," Coleman said. "And Marissa, you've probably already figured this out, but tomorrow will be your night, just in case you need to prepare."

Her right hand eased toward her mouth, but then she noticed Trent watching and ran her fingers through her short curls. "Sounds good," she said.

"Fine. Then we'll wait for the list and send the things over. And tomorrow, Marissa, you can let us know if Trent Jackson can hold his own in the kitchen," Coleman said.

"Well, I don't know about you, but I'm betting our listeners are also wanting to know if he can hold his own at the dinner table, as in whether she ends up stabbing him with a knife before it's over," Speedy said. "Trent, maybe you shouldn't serve anything that requires a knife. You know, they have meals at those theme shows where you eat everything with your fingers. Isn't that right, Coleman? Where is that place again? You and Margaret took the grandkids there last summer."

"The Dixie Stampede," Coleman said. "Dolly Parton's place in Pigeon Forge. And yes, you eat everything with your fingers, but Trent, I'm betting you'll earn a lot more points with the lady if you fix something that at least requires a fork."

Trent laughed. He really liked the two DJs, and he was pretty sure they were both rooting for him to win major points with "the lady" before the week ended. "Don't worry, Coleman. She'll use a fork, or a *fourchette*, as my mother always said."

"Your mother was French?" Coleman asked.

"Cajun, and proud of it," Trent said. "As a matter of fact, I believe I'll prepare a taste of bayou cooking for Rissi this evening, so she can get a taste of my mother's heritage."

"Do the rules say that we can't go over there for dinner?" Speedy asked.

"Yes," Coleman answered. "The one that says only the two of them shall inhabit the apartment until Friday morning. But if you want to fix us some of that Cajun food another time, Jackson, we'll be more than happy to sample it."

Trent grinned. "Count on it."

"You want to give us a hint of what you'll be preparing tomorrow night, Marissa?" Speedy asked.

"It's a surprise," she said coyly.

"Might want to add a bottle of Mylanta to your shopping list there, Trent," Speedy said.

Chuckling, Coleman reprimanded Speedy under his breath, then said, "Well, folks, it's been an interesting show, and we know all of you are enjoying these morning visits with our resident liar and cheat, but for today, we're going to have to let them go. In the meantime, if you want to check out Trent and Marissa's feud online, you can access all of our previous broadcasts, as well as all of their sites, AtlantaTellAll.com, DieHard Atlanta.com, TheGuyCheats.com, and TheGirlLies.com, through our station's home page. And Trent and Marissa, we'll talk to you tomorrow morning."

"Yeah," Speedy said. "Maybe next time you'll answer the phone." The theme music for their show filled the line, and then they disconnected.

"So," Trent said, turning from the phone to look directly at Rissi, "you can't cook, can you?"

"Of course I can," she snapped. "It's just that I didn't feel the need to go bragging about the amazing meal I'll prepare tomorrow night. Besides, today is *your* cooking day, so the question should be whether *you* can cook, and I guess I'll find out tonight, won't I?"

"You certainly will," he said, eager to show her that his talents extended beyond kissing in hot tubs. Of course, he really wanted to show her that they extended in lots of ways, beyond the kitchen, too, but all in due time. "Until tonight, what would you like to do?" he asked. Sure, he had a ton of work for DieHardAtlanta and Jackson Enterprises to keep him busy, but he was more than happy to play hooky if she wanted. Hooky in the hot tub, in the shower, in the bed, on the couch, in the kitchen, on the table . . .

He'd contemplated endless possibilities all night, and he was pretty sure she had, too.

"First I'm going to shower," she said.

"Need help washing your back?"

"No."

"The front?" he asked, smiling.

"Definitely not."

"Can't blame a guy for trying."

"What happened to the old Hershey game? You forgot to ask if I wanted to have sex first."

"Hell, if I washed your back or your front, darling, we'd have sex before it was over."

"You're terrible," she said, leaning down to rub Petie's head on her way to her room and giving Trent a nice view of her behind in the process.

"Damn, you are one hot lady, Rissi Kincaid," he said, and then realized that he probably should have kept that comment internal.

But she turned around and delivered the sexiest, most provocative smile Trent had ever received. The effect was extremely potent. "Change your mind about that back wash?" he asked hopefully.

"No, I haven't," she said, still moving toward her bedroom, but at a slower pace. "But you do know how to flatter a girl."

"I'm only stating the facts, ma'am."

"Well, facts or not, you do make me feel good, Trent Jackson, and for that I thank you. But as far as what I'm going to do until dinner tonight, I'm going to shower—solo—and then I'm going to check out the system at work and make sure that everything is still up and running. If it is, then I'll get back to the program I was writing when the system crashed and work on that until late this afternoon or this evening, whenever your dinner is prepared. Then I'll eat dinner with you, and then I'm going to bed, again, solo. That's it."

"You don't even plan on chatting with me anywhere in there? I mean, it'd be kind of odd to go the whole day without speaking, given we're living together and all, not to mention I've sucked on your breast."

Her eyes widened, but then her laughter rolled forward and made Trent laugh, too. "You are wicked. Completely, utterly wicked."

"Does that mean you're going to talk to me today? Because I've got to tell you, yesterday, with you in there banging on those keys and paying me no attention whatsoever, well, that was quite the blow to this guy's usually swollen ego."

She paused at the door to her room, then Petie ran to her feet and she opened it to let him pass, apparently en route to the patio. "Okay," she said. "This is probably one of the dumbest things I've ever done, but I'm going to tell you the truth."

"Beats the hell out of lying," he said, which caused one side of her mouth to curl up in a snarl. "Okay. Sorry," he said. "Tell me what truth?"

"I can see myself being friends with you," she said. "And I think it's kind of sad that after this week I won't be able to go out with you, as friends, to dinner or to hang out, or whatever. I think being friends with you would be fun," she said, then shrugged. "But we simply can't. I want that ad campaign, and—I know this is hard for you to understand—I also don't want any type of relationship with you beyond friendship. It wouldn't work."

Trent really wanted to argue that last point, but he knew this wasn't the time for it, so he focused on the positive part of her statement. "I can live with that, that you'd like to be friends, only we can't. However, I do have a suggestion for the short-term part of that scenario that might make the rest of this week a little more comfortable, for both of us."

"I'm listening," she said skeptically.

"That friends part, hanging out and having dinner, enjoying each other's company—as friends—we could do that this week. True, we wouldn't be able to carry it forward into the real world when the contest ends, not if you want that ad campaign, but we could still take advantage of the fact that we click well together, at least while we're here. And we could have a lot of fun in the process, maybe even make it through a day without you throwing something at me."

"I've already thrown something today," she reminded him. "Twice."

"So we'll start that part of the new and improved co-existence tomorrow. But today, friends it is, deal?"

She sighed, then grinned. "Okay, deal."

Trent waited until her bedroom door closed and the shower water started running, then he leaned back in the desk chair and gloated. He'd played the Hershey bar game again, and this time, he'd gain his biggest prize yet.

Never admit the effect of a man's kiss on your libido,
particularly when he could be listening.
— MARISSA KINCAID

Chapter 18

"Okay, tell us what he's fixing you for dinner," Amy instructed, while Marissa opened the French door for Petie, then followed him onto the patio. His nails clicked softly on the pebbled concrete as he headed toward his favorite spot on the grass. Marissa inhaled the warm July night air and thought of how hot it had been out here last night, when Trent fondled her beneath the canopy of trees.

"Yeah, tell us," Candi insisted, pulling Marissa back into the conversation. "I've got to leave for work in fifteen minutes, and I'm dying to hear what's happening over there, starting with tonight's menu, and then ending up with whether the two of you are having dessert."

Marissa laughed, sat in a patio chair, and settled in for a fun conversation with her friends. She'd been pleased when Amy's name displayed on her cell phone's caller ID, and even more pleased when she learned Candi was also on the line via speakerphone. She hadn't talked to them since Monday, and she missed their chats.

"I have no idea what he's cooking," Marissa said, "but if it tastes as good as it smells, I'm in for the best home-cooked meal I've had in quite some time."

"Gotta admit, though," Amy said, "the bar for accomplishing that isn't very high. When was the last time you even ate a home-cooked meal?"

"Yeah," Candi said. "We were talking about that after this morning's broadcast. Have you thought about what you're going to do tomorrow night? I mean, does he know about your, er, experience in the kitchen?"

"Or the lack thereof?" Amy added with a giggle.

Marissa shot a look at the open patio door to make sure Trent was still safely tucked away in the kitchen and busy with dinner, then she smirked toward the phone. "I can do it. I've been on the Internet today and found complete menus that are supposed to be simple enough that a child can do it."

"Uh-huh," Candi said sarcastically.

"You know, maybe you should just tell him you can't boil water," Amy said helpfully.

"Right, she messed that up, too, that one time," Candi said. "Remember? She decided to take a shower and forgot about the pot on the stove. Took at least a week before we could go back into her apartment without smelling it."

"Ew," Amy said. "I do remember, but that wasn't because of the boiling water. She had eggs in there, too. Talk about nasty."

"You two are doing wonders for my self-esteem," Marissa said, but they were right, after all. "However, I'm determined to pay attention to the recipes and get it right, and I'd appreciate it if you'd wish me luck."

"I'll do better than that," Amy said. "I'm going to send over some chicken and sides from Boston Market. Take them out of the containers and act like you fixed it. He'll never know. Do you think he'd like the creamed spinach? And what time do you want me to send it? Maybe you can suggest he take a shower, and then while he's doing that, I'll sneak in with the goods."

"I think she was some sort of conspirator in a prior life," Candi said. "But I admit, the idea does have potential."

Marissa patted her lap and waited for Petie to get his running start and jump. He did, then plopped down for a thorough back rub. While her hands stroked his soft coat, she chastised her friends. "If the two of you really want to support me in this whole contest thing, you'll encourage me to do things right. Do you really think I want Trent to go on the radio and tell everyone that he recognized my creamed spinach from his last trip to Boston Market? I don't think so."

Amy laughed. "Hey, I was trying to help, in my own way. And if you do get a package from me tomorrow, make sure he's not around to smell the evidence."

"Don't," Marissa warned.

"She's messing with you," Candi said. "Aren't you, Amy?"

"She'll find out tomorrow," Amy teased. "Anyway, give us the scoop on how things are going. Oh—wait a minute—I nearly forgot. Did Mona get in touch with you this morning?"

"No," Marissa said. "She left six messages, though, while we were out for that horrid morning run. I didn't get them until after our broadcast, then I called her back on her cell phone and only got her voice mail. I left a message for her to call me, but she hasn't. Did she call you again?"

"Yeah," Amy said. "She said she was really wanting to talk to you this morning, but couldn't get through. I don't know why she didn't answer her cell. Maybe she's busy. In any case, I told her you were doing fine. Oh, she said her trip was going fabulous, by the way."

"Go on and tell Marissa how fabulous you think it's going," Candi said, then barely paused before adding, "Amy thinks your mother has found a man in that seniors group."

"What?" Her mother, with a man? While Marissa would love to think it was possible, Mona Kincaid's history, and her admission that she 'just couldn't get over her husband,' made her hooking up with a stranger about as probable as snow in Atlanta . . . in July. How many times had Marissa tried to talk her mother into at least considering the idea of dating again? And how many times had Mona said she couldn't do it?

"I'm telling you, I heard a guy in the background," Amy said. "And then she giggled, you know, like he was tickling her—or something."

"Right," Marissa said. "You sure you were talking to my mother? The woman whose entire day revolves around calling me?"

"But you haven't talked to her much lately," Amy reminded her. "I mean, sure, she's in Branson, but has her traveling ever stopped her from needing her 6:00 A.M. phone fix before?"

Marissa swallowed. She'd thought the same thing all

week. Her mother was acting odd, and she *hadn't* called every morning. In fact, she had gone several days without calling Marissa at all. Of course, that was what Marissa had always wanted, for Mona to find happiness beyond her daughter, and she really wanted her to find love again, someday. Had it happened? This week? And if it had, what would Marissa do if this guy hurt her mom, the way Marissa's father had? Could Mona go through that again?

Could Marissa?

"I think it's sweet," Candi said. "And it's high time Mona found some happiness with a man. Personally, I think it's high time all of us found happiness with a man, and I'm doing my part to make that happen."

"Speak for yourself," Amy said. "I've got my man, but I agree on the rest of it. By the way, Candi has been with your buddy's financial advisor the past three nights. And last night, when she worked late, he picked her up and drove her home, at three in the morning. Now if that isn't a man who's smitten, I don't know what is."

"Keith Parker?" Marissa questioned.

Candi laughed loudly. "I know, it's wild, isn't it? I just met him Friday, or officially met him, since we'd seen each other before at his ballgames, but—what a guy. And he's the first one I've been out with since Cal who really understands where I'm coming from on the whole cheating thing. His ex-wife cheated on him—with her boss. And that's absolutely ludicrous, because what woman in her right mind would cheat on him? Not only is he to-die-for, but he's got a heart of gold, too."

"She's whooped," Amy said. "And shoot, I like him, too. He really does seem like a good guy."

"Yeah, he's a good guy," Candi echoed, then her voice

dropped to a whisper, as Marissa pictured her leaning close to the speakerphone. "*And* he likes Landon's massage oils."

"Just wait till you try some of the toys made for two," Amy said, while Marissa gasped. She'd only been gone three days, and already Candi had not only become "whooped" over Trent's financial advisor, but more than that, she was trying out Amy and Landon's products with him.

"Candi, are you sure, you know, that he's—" Marissa started, but didn't know quite how to finish.

"Not going to hurt me?" Candi completed. "No, I'm not sure, but trust me, he's worth the chance. I'm crazy about him. Wait until you meet him. Well, meet him again, since you met him briefly already. You'll see him when we all go to Landon's games. They're on the same team, and I thought we could start going to them regularly, all of us, particularly since Trent said on the radio that he wanted to be added to the roster. Keith was thrilled. He's evidently been trying to get him to play for a while."

Marissa blinked. Was this really Candi, her typically cynical friend, not only falling for a guy herself, but insinuating that Marissa and Trent would get together, too? As in give-up-the-ad-campaign-and-forget-he-could-break-her-heart? "In case you've forgotten, I won't even be seeing him anymore after Friday. I can't, at least for twelve months, or I forfeit the campaign. And you both told me to make sure I didn't let anything happen to get in the way of winning that prize and boosting our business, remember?"

"That was before," Candi said.

"Before what?"

"Before we decided that you should forget the prize and go for the guy. I mean, he's loaded. If you two end up together, you could get all the advertising you want, or even better, you both may decide to combine your e-zines, or put the two of them out with the same publisher, or, well, I don't know how it'd work, but I think you should try it. Amy and I can tell listening to the two of you over the radio that you're made for each other."

"We've fought every morning," Marissa said.

"No, you've flirted every morning," Amy corrected. "And even your mother can tell. That's why all of Atlanta is talking about it."

"All of Atlanta is talking about what?" Marissa asked, not sure she really wanted to know.

"Aren't you getting the paper at the apartment?" Candi asked.

"No."

"Doesn't matter," Amy said. "The *Atlanta Journal* is online. Pull it up on your computer. You and Trent have been on the front page of the Living Section every day this week. I'm betting you're probably on the site's home page. Everybody's debating whether you can pull off hating him long enough to snag the prize, or whether you'll end up with a ring on your finger when all is said and done. You know, based on his hopes and dreams that you gave on air, he wants a wife."

"I've got news for you," Marissa said. "He probably wants someone who wants to *be* his wife."

"Come on," Amy urged. "Admit it. You're attracted to him."

"You know I am. That's why you packed Pinky for me,

to keep me from being too tempted. When did you change your mind?"

"When I decided that your happiness is more important than advertising for the e-zine. And besides, everybody's already talking about our sites, and our subscriptions continue to skyrocket every day the two of you are on the radio or in the paper. We're going to be fine."

"She's right, you know," Candi said. "I'm betting all three of us will be able to work at home on the e-zine, and a whole lot sooner than we planned, all because of the publicity you're getting with the contest. We really don't need the big prize."

Marissa leaned her head back so her neck rested on the top edge of the chair and could literally feel the tension building in her muscles. A good soak in the hot tub was probably in order, but right now she had to convince her friends that she didn't need to go for Trent. "Listen. I'll tell you the truth. The two of us have admitted an attraction, and we even crossed the boundary—a little—last night."

"I knew it!" Amy said.

"But," Marissa said, determined to make her point, "we've talked about it, and I've told Trent, in no uncertain terms, that while I like him as a friend, I am not ready for a new relationship that could end up with me getting cheated on again." Marissa knew her own pattern. She'd watched it happen to her mother and had dealt with the fallout ever since.

"There's nothing wrong with the two of you being friends, of course, but as long as you're both under one roof, and admittedly attracted to each other, I think you should investigate the possibility that he may be worth the risk," Candi said.

"I agree," Amy said. "But I'll put it more bluntly. Get to know him as a friend. See if you think he could indeed stay true to one woman, if he loved her with all of his heart. I've always said that I'm not at all certain a cheater can't change his stripes. And while he admitted to cheating on that Lily person, he also said it was in college and that he hadn't settled down. So, he could have changed, you know, grown up and learned that's not the way to treat women. I mean, I don't have a problem exposing cheaters for what they are on the site. If they've cheated, then the world needs to know. But if they see the light, and want to treat a woman the way she should be treated, then I think they should get another chance."

"You told me to use Pinky instead of Trent," Marissa said. "Merely two days ago!"

"That was before I realized that you two have something going. Now I want you to get rid of Pinky for the rest of the week and get into Trent's pants," Amy said matter-of-factly.

Marissa's eyes widened. "Get into his pants?"

"Sleep. With. Him," Amy said, each word slower and stronger than the one before.

"Yeah, I think you should, too," Candi said. "You have chemistry. Everyone can hear it, even over the radio. I can only imagine what you're like in person. Go for it."

"We do have chemistry," Marissa said, shocked at where this conversation had headed. They'd been all for her maintaining her distance from Trent, and now they were trying to convince her to go to bed with him? "But that chemistry is volatile, trust me. Sometimes all I want to do is jump his bones, and other times, I want to throttle him. And I know that the best thing I can do is keep things at the friendship level."

"Wow, sounds like you've got it bad," Amy said.

"I've got to tell you," Candi said, "and no offense to Amy's prize product, but Marissa, Pinky doesn't hold a candle to the real thing. For a while there, I'd have argued for the battery version, too, but after being with Keith, I realize I'd forgotten how damn hot it can be."

"Tell me about it," Marissa said, entranced by the bubbling water in the hot tub . . . and the memory of Trent's body on hers. "I nearly came when he kissed me. I can only imagine what I'd do if we did more."

"Well, if you'd like to do more than imagine it, darling, I'm happy to help," Trent said.

"Oh!" Amy squealed into the phone, while Marissa's chest burned, then her neck, then her cheeks, and she turned to view Trent, standing in the doorway with a satisfied grin on his face and a chef's hat on his head.

"Dinner is served."

*Any man worth his salt knows how to cook
a good meal . . . and give a great massage.*
— TRENT JACKSON

Chapter 19

Trent's chest swelled as Marissa took another bite of étouffée and hummed her contentment with his cooking. She made the same sweet sound with every bite, and Trent had to wonder if he wouldn't hear something similar when they made love. And now that he knew he could nearly get her there with a kiss . . .

She took another bite, then caught him staring. "There's no need to look so smug."

"I thought you said you didn't want to talk about it." After he'd overheard her admission on the patio, she'd issued a pointed warning that if he muttered one word, she'd make him rethink his decision about providing her with silverware.

She pushed her plate forward, then took another longing look at the food and pulled it back in place. "You should be ashamed of yourself, both for eavesdropping on my private conversation and for cooking something that I can't stop eating. I was full five minutes ago."

"I wasn't eavesdropping. I came out to tell you that dinner was ready and happened to hear you mention something rather *interesting*." Before she had a chance to respond, he continued, "And I'm glad you like the meal. You can't beat my mama's recipe for crawfish étouffée. And just wait until you try her bread pudding, our dessert. I'm assuming we'll probably have to wait until later for that, since you're full."

Her mouth stopped chewing, then she swallowed. "Crawfish?"

"Yeah. What'd you think?"

She eyed the remainder on her plate, then slowly took another bite of étouffée. "Can you teach me how to make it?"

He grinned, not surprised that Rissi Kincaid didn't balk at crawfish as a Cajun cooking staple. She wasn't the type to back away from things that were different, or a challenge, like the run this morning, or his cooking with "mud bugs" tonight. Not that he'd tell her the Louisiana nickname for his favorite crustacean. "Sure, I'll teach you. In fact, I'll teach you lots of things, if you want, like what 'more than a kiss' would do for you."

She took a bite of French bread. "You know, it's very tacky to listen to other people's conversations. I'd think you would know better."

"If I had known you were talking sex, I'd have come out sooner," he said. "As would any other normal male. Listening to a woman talk about sex, particularly about the fact that I can merely kiss her and nearly give her an orgasm, is quite the ego booster."

"As if your ego needs boosting." Pink tinged her cheeks

as she continued to eat. This time, she didn't look up, but kept her eyes focused on her food.

He pushed his plate away, put his elbows on the table, and leaned forward, thoroughly enjoying this conversation. He'd waited throughout dinner to see how long it would take her to bring up her steamy admission. She'd maintained her cool throughout the meal, chatting with small talk in much the same way they'd chatted all day, as friends getting to know each other better, but now, the conversation had turned to that snippet he heard on the patio, and Trent couldn't be more pleased. If she was talking about it, then she was thinking about it. And if he could keep her thinking about it, chances were, she'd want to do more than talk and think. Trent was ready for that, too.

She took another bite, finishing off her étouffée, then pushed her plate forward before looking up. "Oh, man," she said, leaning back. "I think I ate more than you."

Okay, she changed the subject. Trent would let her, for now, but he'd make sure to eventually get her mind back on the conversation he had overheard . . . and on him. "Oh, there's no thinking to it. You ate more than me."

"A gentleman wouldn't have agreed," she said with a laugh. "But you're right; I did. It's just that I'm not used to good cooking." The color in her cheeks intensified. "I should probably forewarn you that tomorrow night won't be like this. In fact, Amy may send food from Boston Market tomorrow," she said with a guilty smile. "I can't exactly cook, or rather, I can't cook at all. Since we're friends and everything, I feel I should let you know. That, and because you may actually want to invest in some of that Mylanta Speedy mentioned."

He laughed. "Okay. How about I help you tomorrow night? I'm a decent cook. My mother said she didn't want me living on takeout through college, and I think she saw teaching me how to cook not only as passing on her heritage, but also as a way of bonding. Dad had my attention with business; she got it with good food."

"I remember seeing your parents a few times when we were kids," she said. "But I didn't even realize how big your dad was in the business world."

"That's because he wanted it that way. He liked living a fairly normal life, in spite of the money, and he wanted to raise me like any other kid."

"You were really close to them," she said, and Trent could tell she wanted to say more, so he waited. But she remained silent.

"Yeah," he said, fishing for what she wasn't telling. "You're close to your folks, too, or you wouldn't get six messages from your mother in one day."

She laughed at that. "Normally, Mom calls every morning, religiously."

"And she's refraining from that because we're here?"

"I don't think so. She's on vacation this week, one of those bus trips to Branson with the Gwinnett seniors group. In fact, that was part of what Amy and Candi called to tell me; they think my mother has found a man there and that's why I haven't heard from her." She paused, as if deciding whether to say more. "My parents divorced twenty years ago, and she hasn't really gone out with anybody since, so this is a first." She gave him a forced smile. "About time, huh?" She didn't seem happy about it.

"Were you hoping your folks would get back together?"

"Oh, no, definitely not. I mean, don't get me wrong. I still talk to my father, on birthdays and Christmas," Rissi said instantly. "But I've never had any hope, or even a desire, for the two of them to get back together. That's the thing that kind of catches me off-guard about all of this. She said she didn't want to date again, because she couldn't get over my dad. Back then, it didn't matter what he did, she always took him back. Then, he didn't want to come back. He said he'd fallen in love, and we moved to Florida because she couldn't bear the thought of running into them out in public, my dad and his girlfriend."

"But you came back here."

"Eventually, but a lot happened in the middle. They got back together once," she said, then nibbled at her index finger.

"It didn't work?" he asked.

"No."

Trent nodded, and all of the pieces settled into place. The first cheater in Rissi's life wasn't even listed in her database. "Sounds like it might be good that your mother has met someone else."

She took a deep breath, let it out slowly. "That's what Amy and Candi think, but what if she ends up with someone else who does the same thing?"

Aha. And there was the hold-up in Rissi's relationships with men . . . and with Trent. Unfortunately, the fact that Trent had cheated on Lily put him in the same classification as her father, the kind of guy she described on her website as a "serial cheater." How was Trent supposed to prove to her that he was worth a chance?

"Sorry," she said, between nibbles on her finger. "Kind of brought a downer to our nice dinner."

Trent stood, moved his chair around the table, and sat beside her. He wanted Rissi Kincaid, wanted her in his bed, and in fact, wanted her in his life, but convincing her was a bigger challenge than he'd previously realized. Good thing Trent liked a challenge. He took her wrist and gently pulled her hand away from her mouth. "There are no nails left to bite," he said, bringing her finger to his lips and kissing it softly. Then he eased to the next finger and did the same, distributing feather-soft kisses to each of her fingertips, before moving to her palm. He licked the sensitive center, then blew warm air over the damp skin, while she shivered. "You're so tense, Rissi," he said. "Let me help."

Her laughter broke the silence, and he looked up to see her dark eyes glistening. "Trent Jackson, your mouth is lethal, and I want you to keep it off of me. I was trying to talk to you as a friend, and your tongue on my palm definitely goes above and beyond the call of friendship."

"This isn't what you do with all of your friends?"

She shook her head. "Hardly."

"Seriously, Rissi, I realize that you're worried about your mother, and I really do want to help you relax."

"You want to help me out of my clothes."

He released her hand, looked into those intriguing eyes, and grinned. "Do you *want* me to help you out of them?"

She shoved him. "No, thank you. And for your information, friends typically don't offer to help each other out of their clothes either."

"No, but a friend would offer to help you relax."

"True, with a trip to a salon for a manicure and pedicure, or a massage, or something like that. They don't offer to remove my clothes."

"I can do that," Trent said confidently.

"What? Take me to a salon? Tonight?" she asked, then leaned around him to look at the clock. "It's after eight, and I don't even know where one is around here."

"No, *I* can do it. Not the manicure and pedicure thing, but the massage. I can give a damn good massage."

One dark brow curved on her forehead. "*You* can give massages? Something else you learned from your mother?"

"Trust me, she wasn't my mother," he said with a wink, while Rissi smirked.

"I'm not even going to ask," she said. "Seriously? You can give a massage? As in something near professional, and not merely running your hands all over my body because you want to?"

"Hell, I do want to, but yeah, I seriously know how to give a semiprofessional massage. I know we don't have a masseuse table around here anywhere, but I can always use your bed."

"I just bet you can."

He held up his palms. "I promise, I'll give you a great massage, guaranteed to relax you enough that you sleep like a baby, and that's it. Unless you *want* more than a massage, and then I'm happy to oblige."

"I knew that idea was in there," she said, pointing to his temple. "Friends wouldn't offer more than the massage, but I appreciate your willingness to go above and beyond once more."

"No problem," he said. "Does that mean you're going to let me give you that massage?"

"What about dessert? Your mother's bread pudding, remember?" she asked, once again attempting to change the subject away from things that made her think about sex with Trent.

"I thought you said you were full."

"I am, but *you* said we'd have it later, and if you give me a massage, I'll probably end up so relaxed that I go to sleep right after, and we won't have dessert. I'm sure you wouldn't want that, so we shouldn't do the massage thing."

The massage thing. A funny way to put it, particularly if she knew exactly how well he planned to massage her tension away, not stopping until she had at least one orgasm. If he almost got her there with a kiss, his massaging talents would definitely take her over the edge, at least once, which was exactly what he wanted. Rissi Kincaid, letting go, for him.

"We can have the bread pudding for breakfast," he said. "It'll be just as good, and you can still get that massage."

She swallowed, lifted one hand toward her mouth, then let it detour to run through her soft curls. The action caused her sexy black swirl to tease her temple.

"Petie is asleep on my bed," she said, as though this would change Trent's plans.

"Then we can use my bed."

She darted a look toward his bedroom door, opened enough for her to see the king-sized bed on the other side. "No sex, right? A massage, something any friend would do for another friend?"

Trent's heart kicked up the rhythm. She was about to say yes, and he was ready. If he had his way, he'd put all worries out of her mind with the mere touch of his fingers, and he'd have her do more than say yes. He'd have her screaming it before the night ended. "No sex," he said. "A massage, from a friend."

"Just a massage," she said.

"Just a massage," he repeated. *Guaranteed to make you come.*

Marissa settled against the soft comforter on Trent's bed and closed her eyes.

"With a deep-tissue massage, your results would be much better if you were naked," Trent said.

"Sure they would," she said, keeping her eyes closed. He stood beside the bed, and more than likely, if she opened her eyes, she'd be approximately eye-level to his crotch. She wasn't about to go there. "But we'll have to get the best results we can in a tank top and shorts."

"Suit yourself, darling."

"I will," she said, grinning. It was bad enough that she'd forgone wearing a bra, since the tank top had a built-in liner. She wasn't about to rid her body of all clothing and then have Trent's hands on her. That wasn't what she wanted at all.

His fingertips pressed against the back of her neck, then slid out toward her shoulders, and a shiver of sheer delight shimmied down her skin.

Who was she kidding? Getting naked and having Trent's hands all over her was *exactly* what she wanted. And now she wondered . . . could she make it through this massage without asking him to give her what she wanted? She squeezed her eyes tighter, while those fingers continued kneading and probing and delighting. Good thing he'd already asked her about removing her clothes; she'd have a much more difficult time explaining why she shouldn't get naked now.

"You're so tight." He applied more pressure, making a gradual path down her back with his hands. "Knotted," he said, and then put what felt like his elbow against one side of her back and pressed down. Hard.

Marissa opened her eyes, turned her head to the side and sucked in her breath. "Ow!" And yes, her eyes were directly even with his crotch, so she jerked her attention to his face, and cracked her neck in the process. "Ow!" she yelled again.

He moved one hand to the back of her neck and gently pressed her head back against the comforter. "You're going to hurt yourself, Rissi."

"No, *you're* going to hurt myself," she corrected. "What did you do to my back?"

"Deep-tissue massaging has been proven to be the most effective type of massage for removing muscle tension, and you've got some serious muscle tension," he said smoothly. "I was serious when I said I know how to give a good massage."

"Maybe I don't want a good one," Marissa said. "Maybe I want a bad one. What was that, anyway, your elbow?" she asked. Her head rested on the bed, but her eyes were looking as high as possible, rather than at what was dead center in front of them.

"Yes. Deep-tissue massaging involves using fingertips, knuckles, elbows, and forearms. So far, you've only had one elbow to one knot."

"You mean there's going to be more?" she asked, unable to control the rising panic in every word of the question.

His laugh rumbled from his stomach, and he sat down on the edge of the bed. Petie darted in from the other room and cocked his head as though wondering if he should bark, or run.

"It's okay, Petie," Trent said. "She's fine."

His silvery head bobbed to the side once more, as if he were trying to judge for himself, and then he evidently decided Trent told the truth, because he turned tail and headed back out the door.

"Some guard dog he's turning out to be," Marissa grumbled, while Trent laughed again. Then she looked up at Trent, now sitting beside her on the bed. "You actually learned how to give this massage from a real masseuse?"

"Yep."

"I'm assuming you were dating her at the time," she said.

"Yeah, but it didn't last long."

"Why's that?"

"Seems the only thing we had in common was a love of deep-tissue massages," he said with a shrug.

"Well, I don't know if I can handle an entire deep-tissue massage, if it involves your elbows bearing down on my back."

"Elbows, forearms, knuckles . . ."

"Right. Do you not know how to give a good old-fashioned massage, the kind where it's your hands—and only your hands—and pressure applied? I think that'd be fine for my muscles, without all the deep-tissue extras."

He looked down at her and smiled. "I planned on trying to work out the knots in your back first, then move on to something like that, but I can start there if you want."

Marissa swallowed. Something about his tone gave her

the impression that she wasn't sure what she'd asked for. "Trent?"

"Yeah," he said, his voice raspy as he put his hands on her back and started working his fingertips down her spine.

"What exactly are you going to do?"

"Help relieve your tension, with an old-fashioned massage," he said. "Exactly what you asked for, Rissi."

His hands, now kneading the lower portion of her spine, inched lower, pushing the waistband of her shorts down in the process. In fact, she was fairly certain that he moved them low enough that the sides of her thong were visible. She glanced down her right side and saw the thin strip of red satin on her hip, and then she saw one of Trent's long fingers slide beneath that strip, as those magical hands moved outward from her spine to the curve of her bottom.

Marissa's top teeth grazed her lower lip. She should stop him now, even if this was totally a friendship kind of thing to help relieve her tension, because right now, her only thought was seeing what else those talented fingers could do. She should stop him. She should.

His hands moved up her sides, sliding up her waist, while Marissa closed her eyes and enjoyed the feeling of a man's hands, of Trent's hands, against her flesh. Maybe she should stop him, but no way was she going to. His fingertips grazed the curves of her breasts before continuing up her back to her shoulder blades, then repeating the pattern. Down the spine slowly, pressing outward. Marissa could actually feel the bunched muscles relaxing, could sense her back heating up beneath the pressure of his hands, and could feel her very center craving some of the attention he gave her back.

"Okay if I do your legs?" he asked, his tone husky and deep.

Marissa nodded. Like any woman in her right mind would say no. Not in this life.

Trent's hands cupped her bottom as he moved to the backs of her thighs and eased her legs apart. His hands slid simultaneously down both legs, fingertips moving in small circles as he progressed slowly down her thighs, then to her calves, while Marissa moaned her contentment. This was wonderful. Magical. And downright erotic. She breathed in deeply, enjoying the feel of those fingers as they moved slowly back up her legs, then she moved her hips and inched her legs out farther.

"Rissi?"

"Mmm?"

His hands returned to the tops of her legs, and his fingertips, moving in luxurious circles, eased under the edge of her shorts. She let them. In fact, she raised her hips to give him better access, wanting him to touch her everywhere.

"I need you to roll over now," he said, his voice thick and hungry, definitely aroused. "So I can do the front." He moved his hands to her waist and slid them under her to lift her body and help her turn.

She stretched as she rolled over, then looked into those smoky eyes. His hands moved to her stomach, thumbs dipping beneath the waistband of her shorts.

"Rissi?" he asked, and his fingers stopped moving.

"Yes?" Her hips lifted slightly from the bed. She

wanted those hands to start again. In fact, she didn't want him to stop. Ever.

"I want to have sex with you," he said honestly.

A small tingle of excitement—or was it panic—singed her flesh. She wanted that, too, didn't she? Yes, she did, but could she have "just sex" with Trent? In all honesty, particularly now that they'd started their friendship bonding, she didn't know. While her body might want merely sex, what if her heart got confused, and thought it was more? And she didn't want more with Trent. Really.

"But," he continued.

She was grateful she hadn't already responded.

"I know you aren't ready for that yet, so—" He let the word hang.

"So . . ."

"So, until you are ready, I want to give you a taste of how good it would be, how good we would be, together."

She licked her lips. "How?"

He slid his hands up her sides, then over her shoulders to rest them beside her head. Then he leaned down and brought his mouth to her ear. "I want to get you naked, completely naked and completely accessible, and then I want to massage you thoroughly, all over, where no part of your body is left untouched, and then, I want to make you come, repeatedly."

She sucked in an audible breath, then turned her head enough that her lips almost touched his. He edged forward and softly kissed her mouth, then waited, his eyes studying hers.

"Say yes, Rissi."

As if *no* even entered the equation. "Yes."

He kissed her again, but this time, there wasn't anything gentle about it. His mouth claimed hers with a hunger she hadn't anticipated, and her body responded by lifting off the bed, her very center burning to experience everything he'd described only seconds ago.

I want to massage you thoroughly, all over, where no part of your body is left untouched, and then, I want to make you come, repeatedly.

While his tongue teased hers, his hands slid beneath her tank top and slid over her breasts, rubbing her sensitive nipples until her core clenched hard in direct response, then he broke the kiss and eased the fabric up, over her breasts, over her head, then tossed it to the floor.

"Perfect," he said, boldly eyeing her nipples, erect and waiting to be caressed again. He didn't make her wait. His mouth kissed one tip, then pulled it within his teeth, until Rissi gasped at the delicious pain. Then he moved to the other and did the same. The intensity of it, the hunger and the desire, started a spiraling sensation beneath her belly, and lower. She moved her legs apart and lifted her hips. "Trent, please."

He rose above her and looked down at her, waiting and oh so ready. "Please what, Rissi. Say it for me."

"Please make me come."

"With pleasure." He trailed a finger from the lower curve of her breast down her abdomen. She sucked in a breath and held it as that finger moved past the waistband of her shorts, then down toward her thigh. "But I want to make sure you're ready." His finger met the top of her thigh, then eased toward her clitoris.

She willed him to go ahead and put her out of this aching misery. She wanted to climax, needed to, had to.

His finger moved down her swollen labia to push

slowly into her vagina, while his thumb passed over her clitoris in a teasing circle that made her hips buck completely off the mattress.

"You're hot," he said. "And very, very wet." He moved his hands to the top of her shorts and slid them down her legs, the friction of the fabric against her flesh providing yet another erotic sensation that had her hips undulating wildly. Trent dropped the shorts to the floor and moved to lie beside her on the bed. He was completely clothed, and Marissa wanted to tell him that this wasn't fair. She was wearing nothing more than a red satin thong, and he was still in a shirt and jeans. However, telling him would require speaking, and right now, in the state her body was in, she could do no more than moan, or scream.

"This is so sexy," he said, running a finger beneath the thin red strap on one hip. "I almost hate taking it off." He moved his hand toward the center of the shiny red triangle, then slid his fingers down to cup her with his palm. "But then again, it's so wet. Surely you want it off." Those fingers pressed against her, and it was almost enough to get her there. Almost.

"Yes," she whispered, and within two seconds, the panties were on the floor and she was naked, exactly the way he said he wanted her.

"I had planned on the first time being with my mouth," he said, while he rolled toward her on the bed. He was on his side now, and Rissi was on her back, with one leg trapped between his thighs and the other spread as far as she could manage. "But I want my first time having oral sex with you to last a while before you come, and you're not going to last long this time, are you?"

She shook her head. If he kept talking like that, she

was liable to climax before he laid a hand, or a mouth, or anything else, on her.

"Then let's start you out easy," he said into her ear, his warm breath teasing her senses, while he put one hand on her belly, then slid it down to her clitoris. His thumb moved over the burning nub, then circled it again, while he kissed the shell of her ear, then flicked his tongue over her lobe. The friction of his thumb against her clitoris increased, in perfect rhythm with the kissing and sucking and nibbling on her lobe. "Come for me, baby," he said. "Come for me now."

Her heels pressed into the mattress and her hips arched upward, pushing her clitoris against his thumb as she screamed through the most intense orgasm she'd ever experienced. Her body shuddered through the power of it, and she lost herself in the magnificent, perfect feeling.

She licked her lips, determined to speak, to let him know that she'd never had anything as good as that, but all that came out was, "Wow."

He leaned over her, gave her another hungry kiss, then winked. "Honey, that was only the beginning. I said repeatedly, remember?"

Then, while Marissa watched in sheer amazement—and delight—he moved down the bed. "Perfect," he said again, as he brought his mouth to her center and licked her clitoris. "Now, darling, try to hold on. I want this to last."

She gripped the fabric of the comforter in each hand and prepared to try to do that, to hold on, and to make this last. But her body was so eager to experience another earth-shattering orgasm, she wasn't sure how much she could take.

Trent's tongue eased downward to lick her wet opening, then back to her clitoris for a maddening assault of tiny little flicks that had her hands clenching against the comforter, then he closed his mouth and sucked. Her second climax was even more potent than the first, with Marissa screaming out his name as thrilling waves of release claimed her senses.

"You're—too—much," she whispered, her head thrashing on the pillow. "Incredible." Had she ever had two climaxes so close together? Or so powerful that she felt as if her body wasn't hers to control? "I—don't know if I can take any more."

He kissed her clitoris again, and her body instinctively arched toward that marvelous mouth. "Oh, honey," he whispered against her most sensitive flesh, "sure you can."

No matter how thoroughly you've lost control, you should always pay attention to where your underwear falls.
— MARISSA KINCAID

~

Chapter 20

Marissa's delicious dream of Trent bringing her to a fifth toe-curling, eye-glazing orgasm was brutally interrupted by Petie's barking, and a loud thumping. She eased one eye open to see the object of her desire exit the bathroom with nothing but a turquoise towel covering his to-die-for frame. He crossed the room and, to Marissa's delight, dropped the blue covering to give her a glorious show of his perfect behind, then he grabbed his jeans and stepped into them. "I'll get it," he said and left the bedroom.

Marissa smiled. So Trent was a commando kind of guy. Good to know.

The thumping continued, and Petie's barking intensified, while Marissa put all of the pieces together. Number one, that wasn't merely a dream of Trent bringing her to five orgasms; it had happened, last night, and it was amazing. Number two, the thumping wasn't merely a thump; it was a knock, and someone was now entering the apartment. And last, but certainly not least, number three, she was totally and completely naked.

She scanned the floor in a panicked search for clothing, then leaned off the bed to grab her shirt and shorts from the spot where Trent had tossed them last night. There was no sign of her red thong, but she didn't have time to worry about it. Someone, a female someone, was chatting with Trent. Marissa used the comforter as a privacy shield and shimmied beneath it to dress, since Trent had left the bedroom door open and anyone could walk in, then she hurriedly slid her top on and wiggled into her shorts. Breathing a sigh of relief, she emerged from the comforter to see her red thong . . . in Petie's mouth.

"Hey, Aunt Rissi," Bo said, entering the bedroom behind her panty-stealing dog. Thank goodness he hadn't seemed to notice what was hanging from her dog's mouth.

"Hi, Bo," she managed, then held her hand out toward the furry thief. "Come here, Petie." To Marissa's shock, the dog appeared to be smiling.

Amy stuck her head into the bedroom and grinned. "I know we aren't supposed to be here, and we didn't plan on coming inside," she said, and then added, "well *I* didn't plan on coming inside."

"We were leaving a surprise by your door," Bo said, "but I wanted to see you and Petie, so I knocked."

"I was going to leave it and then call you after your broadcast to tell you it was out there," Amy explained. "I kind of figured you would be getting ready to go on the air, since you're on in thirty minutes."

"What?" Marissa said, jerking her head toward the side

of the bed, where the clock declared she'd slept late. Very late.

"I was about to wake you," Trent explained, edging against the opposite side of the doorframe from Amy. He looked very good, his chest bare and jeans dipping low in the front, enough to see that sexy tad of hair starting above the waist and leading to his commando self. Bare feet completed the scrumptious, appealing look of the man who'd satisfied her totally all night long. "You were sleeping so well," he said. "I thought I'd let you sleep in."

"Mighty sweet of you." Amy gave him that I-know-what-you-two-did grin before turning to Marissa with the same knowing look. "You must have been *very* tired, and *very* relaxed, to sleep so long. Oh, and it looks as though you lost something during the night," she added, pointing to Petie's treasure. "You might want to get it, before *someone* realizes what it is." She pointed to the back of Bo's tiny head. Then she said, "Bo, why don't you go check and make sure Petie has water in his dish. He looked kind of thirsty to me."

"In the kitchen?" Bo asked, still oblivious to the underwear in the dog's mouth.

"Yep," Trent responded, and then he smiled as Bo turned and headed toward the kitchen to check.

"Give me that, Petie," Marissa said, grabbing at the tiny piece of material and pulling until the dog relented and released his hold, but not before her underwear ripped loudly. Sighing, she tossed the panties into a small wicker trashcan near the bed.

"Guess they served their purpose, huh?" Amy asked.

"Did you honestly come over here with Boston Market?" Marissa asked, eager to change the subject. "And are they even open this early?"

"No, I don't think they are, but I brought you something else you can use," Amy said, as Bo squirmed between Amy and Trent to re-enter the room.

"He's got water. Come on, Petie. I'll take you to get a drink." Bo scooped up Petie, then left again.

"And Bo, we need to go," Amy called to him. "I told you Aunt Rissi can't have visitors this week. We'll find out about how much fun she's had here when she comes back home tomorrow. Or rather, I'll find out."

"Can Petie come with us?" Bo asked, halting his trek toward the kitchen to turn around and plead his case. He stepped toward his mother, so Marissa could see his pleading little face. "Please?"

"Oh, honey," Amy said apologetically, squatting down to his eye level. "I told you on the way over here that Petie is Aunt Rissi's puppy. I know you got used to seeing him each day and you've missed him this week, but he's coming back to live by us again tomorrow, when Aunt Rissi comes home."

Bo's lower lip trembled, and he looked longingly at the puppy. "I'd take good care of him till she comes back."

Marissa got on her knees beside Amy on the floor, then ruffled Bo's sandy curls. "You know what, that would really help me out. I forgot his leash, and he hasn't been able to run outside and play like he's used to doing at home. Do you think you and your mom could get his leash from my apartment and take him out today? Then he can stay at your place tonight, and you can take care of him until I get back tomorrow. How does that sound?"

"That sounds great," he said, sniffing a little from the

near-cry, but smiling at his victory. And Marissa did think Petie would be happier if he could go outside for more than mere trips to the patio.

"Come on, sport," Trent said. "You can help me get Petie's things together."

"Okay," Bo said, snuggling Petie as he followed Trent toward the kitchen.

"You slept in, huh?" Amy asked, getting up from the floor, then taking Marissa's hand and pulling her up as well.

Marissa glanced out the doorway to see Trent and Bo chatting in the kitchen. "I came five times," she whispered.

"Quit it." Amy's green eyes glittered in absolute delight.

"I'm serious. But we didn't have sex. In fact, I still haven't even seen him naked, well not from the front anyway. The whole world knows I've seen his behind, thanks to him telling them on the air."

Amy laughed. "Yeah, I think that had a lot to do with the ratings boost Coleman and Speedy keep mentioning this week. Everyone is tuning in to see when Trent admits he's seen yours."

"He wouldn't," Marissa said, and prayed it was true.

"Oh, of course he wouldn't. He wants you, and any guy knows a woman isn't going to swoon over him if he kisses and tells, especially if he does it on live radio. Then again, he did admit you saw his ass," she added with a laugh. "Anyway, tell me about last night, and hurry. We don't have long."

"He was completely and totally set on satisfying me, and didn't ask for a thing in return. Nothing."

"Don't tell me it's this prize that's keeping you from having sex with him," Amy said. "I mean, come on. You two are great together. I can hear it on the radio, and I can see it now."

"But—"

"It isn't the prize at all, is it? It's the cheating thing."

Marissa swallowed thickly. "I wish I could forget how much that bothers me, but I can't. I don't think I'd ever be able to let myself fall for a guy who's cheated before. He'll do it again, and I don't want to be hurt like that." She'd seen how painful that could be, particularly for a woman whose life revolved around a man, and she didn't want to live her life that way, the way her mother lived hers.

Amy glanced at the kitchen, where Bo and Trent were wrapping up their conversation. "Forget falling for him, then," she said. "Just enjoy being with him. Have sex with him. Give him an orgasm, or five, too," she said with a wicked grin. "I'm serious. Enjoy having a mouthwatering man who wants you, and who can give your body everything it needs, and give him what he needs right back. You have one more day. Make the most of it. And when all is said and done, if you can honestly say you haven't fallen for him, then fine. Walk away. But if you have, then why don't you give him a chance? People do change, you know."

"I'm not so sure about that." Marissa had never seen any evidence of it. "But you're right about one thing."

"What's that?"

"I only have one more day, and then, if I do accept that prize, I won't see him again for at least twelve months."

"That's right. So, if I were you and that was the case,

I'd make the most of that day." Amy hugged Marissa, and whispered in her ear. "And with the surprises I brought you, you can make the most of it several times, in very unique and inventive ways."

Oh. Man.

"We're ready to go, Mom!" Bo squealed.

"Yes, we are," Amy said, entering the living room with Marissa. "And so are you," she whispered to Marissa. Then she said good-bye to Trent and left with Bo and Petie in tow.

Trent closed the door behind them, then turned to face Marissa. "Sleep well?" he asked.

"What do you think?" She shifted from one foot to the other, feeling oddly shy about idle morning chitchat with a guy who had licked most of her body, thoroughly, last night.

"If you didn't, then I must have done something wrong, and I really don't think I did anything wrong," he said with a sly smirk. "Did I?"

"Surely you knew I wasn't faking."

"Oh, yeah, I knew," he said. "Particularly that last time. It took a lot of work to get you there, darling, but trust me; it was worth it."

"I'll say it was," she said, then inhaled a sweet, buttery aroma wafting from the kitchen. "Oh, my, what is that?"

"Bread pudding with rum sauce," he said proudly. "I promised we'd have it for breakfast, remember? But it isn't quite warm yet." He glanced at the coyote clock on the wall. "You know, if you want to go shower first, it should be ready by the time you're done, but we may have to wait and eat after our broadcast, all depending on how long it takes you to shower."

"I won't be long." Turning, she went to her room, grabbed a T-shirt and shorts and headed to the bathroom. She purposely forwent all undergarments. If he was going commando, then so was she. While she'd gone without a bra before, going without panties wasn't exactly her forte, and the fact that she was doing it today, for Trent, sent a tingle of anxious excitement down her spine. Marissa Kincaid, commando. She giggled as she started the shower water and climbed in. The hot water teased her already-sensitive skin and reminded her of the blazing kisses Trent had bestowed on her last night, causing her to writhe and scream and completely lose herself in his caresses, in his talented touch, and in his determined goal of making her climax . . . repeatedly. He'd given her the most exquisite sexual experience of her life, and yet he'd remained completely clothed throughout the process and hadn't asked for anything in return. He'd merely stated that giving her orgasms would please him. And Marissa had no doubt that he took immense pleasure in controlling her so completely.

But what Trent Jackson didn't realize was that Marissa would also take immense pleasure in controlling him. Completely. She'd told Amy the truth; she didn't want a relationship with Trent. She was going to have a difficult time trusting *any* man, let alone a man who had cheated in the past. And while Amy might have been right, that people do change, Marissa wasn't willing to risk her heart on something she didn't completely believe. However, she also wasn't willing to throw away the undeniable attraction, the incredible connection, she'd found with Trent. And if she only had that for one more day, she was going to make the most of every minute.

She turned off the shower water and heard the phone ring. Was it time for Coleman and Speedy's call already? She wrapped a towel around her, tucked it in at her breasts, then quickly brushed her teeth. Her hair was wild and curly, and would take too much time to dry, so she ran some peach-scented hair gel through it and left it wild. It suited what she had in mind, after all. Seducing Trent Jackson and making *him* climax, repeatedly. Hey, she wasn't about to give less than she got; she was a girl who played fair, after all, and Trent would get his fair share today, and then some. And if Amy's surprise package was what Marissa thought, she'd have no trouble giving him plenty of everything he deserved, and have a whole lot of fun in the process.

She started to put on her T-shirt, but then thought of another idea, one she liked much better. And one Trent Jackson would like, too. What man wouldn't?

Trent sat in the desk chair and punched the speaker button on the clanging phone. "Liars and cheats."

Speedy's trademark cackle echoed through the line. "You know, I'm really going to miss hearing that next week. So, how's it going, Jackson? Your dinner pass muster?"

"She ate every bite." Trent smiled at the memory of Marissa humming through each nibble of étouffée. And as he had suspected, the sweet sound had been very similar to the sound she made when she was close to orgasm. It wasn't, however, the sound she made when her body actually found its release. Then, she abandoned all mild, sweet tones and screamed through the event as though her entire body were exploding. It was an incredible thing to witness, Marissa letting go, and Trent dearly hoped to see the beauty of it again. Soon.

"Is that so, Ms. Kincaid? Every bite? Can he really cook?" Coleman asked.

Trent looked at the closed bedroom door, then back at the speaker. "She'll have to tell you in a minute. I'm afraid she slept a little late and hasn't finished her shower yet."

"Well, I suppose it's a little much to expect a woman not to be late at least one day a week, huh?" Speedy asked.

"I'd watch it if I were you," Coleman warned. "Last time you said something like that on air, you had a brush mark on your forehead the next morning."

"Just kidding, honey," Speedy said. "You take all the time you want getting ready. But as for Ms. Kincaid, the only way we're really going to know what she thought of your talents in the kitchen is if she tells us herself. I mean, we believe you and all, but still . . ."

The bedroom door opened, and Marissa stepped out, while Trent tried to remember if Speedy had asked him a question. She was wearing one of his white dress shirts, and from the look of where it fell on her thighs, and the way her nipples pressed against the cotton, that was all she had on.

Trent went hard. Rock hard and ready.

"Yeah, no offense, Trent, but we really need to hear it from Marissa," Coleman said.

"What do you need to hear?" she asked silkily, walking past Trent and then sitting in the other chair. She crossed her legs, but not before he caught a glimpse of what he wanted, and he immediately remembered the way her intimate center pulsed when she climaxed, and the way she tasted on his tongue.

"Did you enjoy last night's dinner?" Speedy asked, while she slid her hands to her neck, unbuttoned the top button and smiled at Trent.

"Yes," she said. "It was incredible." Then she leaned toward Trent, gave him a provocative smile, and unfastened his jeans.

Have mercy.

He tried to listen to Speedy, but it was difficult, with Marissa slowly sliding his zipper down. Then she wrapped her fingers around his hard length and licked her lips.

"And what are you going to fix for Mr. Jackson tonight?" Speedy asked. "We'll need another list, if you need things that aren't in the apartment."

"Trent offered to teach me how to make étouffée," she said, getting out of her seat and lowering herself to the floor.

"You're going to fix the same thing as last night?" Speedy asked, obviously surprised.

"Yeah. This is our last night together," she said, moving her hands to the top of Trent's jeans and pulling them down. Trent lifted his hips and let her. There was no way he was going to stop Rissi Kincaid, not now, not ever, in spite of the fact that they were on the radio, broadcasting live. "If he's going to teach me how to do something, he'll have to do it tonight, right? Because we won't see each other after tomorrow morning."

Trent wanted to argue that point, particularly now, while she boldly eyed his penis as though she couldn't wait to take it all. But he couldn't form words at the moment.

"Okay, if you say so, though Speedy and I still think something's up with you two," Coleman said.

Oh, something was definitely up.

"So, do you want us to get the exact same shopping list as yesterday, Trent, or do you want to change it up a bit?" Coleman asked.

Rissi brought her mouth to the base of his penis, ran her tongue across his balls, then sucked. Hard.

"Trent?" Coleman repeated, while Trent's jaw clenched tight, and Rissi continued thoroughly torturing him.

"Yeah," Trent finally said through gritted teeth. "The same." He had to get off the phone soon, because Rissi Kincaid was going to get him off. Soon. And he'd never been more ready in his life. Forget making it last. He wasn't going to make it through the rest of this phone call, with her tongue doing some kind of magical dance against his balls. Then her mouth started up his length, sucking and nibbling until Trent wanted to yell. He slid his fingers into her sexy, wispy curls and guided her mouth to the tip, then she licked the first drop away.

Trent was going to die. Right here. Right now. And there was no doubt about it; he'd die happy. If he could hang up the phone and let go.

"Just a reminder," Speedy said, and Trent vaguely realized that Coleman and Speedy had continued talking while Marissa's tongue kept moving, and he was clueless about what they'd said. He hoped it was nothing that required a response, because the only part of his body currently responding was the part that Marissa was sliding into her mouth, and letting her teeth graze along the way. "Tomorrow we'll broadcast from your apartment, and we'll award that prize, if the two of you can still claim that there's nothing more than fury between you. You know, I think we're going to have a lot of listeners who will be disappointed if you haven't mended fences, and even decided to try this cohabitation thing to a larger degree."

Trent didn't think he could get any "larger" than he was right now. But Marissa was trying to take every inch, and doing a damn good job.

"You know, since you've mentioned it, Speedy," Coleman said, while Marissa moved back up Trent's length, then slid back down again. Up and down, sucking harder and harder. "I'm surprised that the two of them haven't, you know, found something mutually appealing in each other throughout the week. And I'll tell you the truth, I'm still thinking that tomorrow morning, they'll tell us they don't want the prize, and that they've decided to give a relationship a go, feuding websites and dueling webzines and all." Then Coleman spoke directly to Trent and Marissa. "You two have to admit, you'd have plenty to talk about at the dinner table each night," he said. "Do the two of you really think you'll be able to walk away tomorrow and not even talk again for a year? That's the deal, you know. Twelve months of no interaction, or you'll forfeit the prize. I mean, this is a guy who's willing to teach you how to make étouffée, Marissa," he said jokingly. "And in all honesty, the two of you haven't seemed to be fighting this week in our broadcasts. In fact, I'd say flirting was the more accurate term."

"I agree," Speedy said. "And that's the consensus of our listeners, too. Go on, Marissa, admit it. You two really want to see where things can go, and you don't care about the prize. Trent's already admitted that he doesn't want the prize; he wants you. And like he says on the phone, liars and cheats. They go together." Speedy laughed loudly.

She moved her mouth off of Trent long enough to answer. "Sorry, Speedy," she said. "But today *is* our last day together. It has to be." Then she pulled the tip of Trent's penis into her mouth and drew the entire length in again.

"Well, I guess she's made up her mind, huh, Jackson?" Speedy asked, while Marissa's fingers clutched Trent's hips and she began to move faster, up and down his length, running her tongue around the tip with every pass. Trent closed his eyes and lost himself in the intoxicating pleasure of her mouth and tongue and teeth. "Is that what you think, Trent? That she's decided what she wants, the prize, and she's going for it?"

"Yeah," Trent said, the single word painful to produce while he was holding back on the orgasm.

"But you said you want Ms. Kincaid. Is that still the case?" Coleman asked. "And are you going to try to change her mind today?"

Marissa's fingers dug in deeper, mouth clamped down harder, and Trent answered. "Yes."

"Care to tell us how?" Speedy asked.

"No." Trent slammed the speaker button to disconnect, then lost himself in the power of his release. And in the power of Rissi.

Slow and easy is very overrated.
—MARISSA KINCAID

~⌒~

Chapter 21

I still can't believe you basically hung up on them."
Marissa scraped the spoon against the bottom of her
bowl, then licked the last bit of bread pudding away. It
was a good thing she was only going to be with Trent
another day; any longer and she'd gain twenty pounds.
The guy could seriously cook. She smiled at him, then
dished out another spoonful of his delicious creation. "By
the way, this is amazing."

He took another bite of his, swallowed, then finally
spoke. And it was about time. He hadn't said a word since
she'd pleasured him and then pronounced it was time for
breakfast. Obviously, he wasn't used to a woman getting
him off while he conversed on the phone. Then again, he
didn't do a whole lot of conversing, did he? She grinned
again. She'd never done anything like that before in her
life, and there was something mighty empowering knowing she could bring the CEO of Jackson Enterprises to
his knees. Or rather, bring herself to her knees and render
him practically speechless in the process. Very empower-

ing indeed. In fact, she might do it again. She licked the spoon.

"Now who's cocky?" he asked, taking her attention from the food, and back to the man who tasted just as good.

"Me," she answered.

He laughed. "What would you have done if they'd figured out exactly what was happening on this end of the line?"

"I don't know," she said with a shrug. "I wasn't exactly thinking; I was too busy doing."

"I'll say you were." He shook his head, then took another bite of his pudding. He was still on his first bowl, and Marissa was on her second, or was it her third? Who'd have known that having five orgasms through the night and then giving Trent one really would work up her appetite? "I take it we're forgoing working for our respective companies today?" he asked.

She smiled. "I called Gary and told him I was taking the day off."

"When?"

"After my shower," she said easily, and enjoyed watching the way his eyes smoldered as he processed this information. She'd slated out the whole day for sex, with him, and he appeared to be pleased. "Called him from the bedroom before I came out, since I wasn't sure exactly how long that—phone call—would take. Didn't take all that long," she said, smirking, and knowing *that* would get a response.

Trent didn't disappoint. "Trust me, darling, when I'm not trying to carry on a phone conversation, on live radio, and when I'm not shocked out of my mind with your choice of clothing, or your unexpected approach, that—phone call—will last much longer."

"We only have one more day for you to prove that," she said, both to remind him that she really planned on this ending tomorrow, and to remind her heart of the same thing.

"So you say." He leaned back in his chair and watched her lick her spoon. "I suppose you're expecting me to take the day off, too?"

"You do own the company."

He grinned at that. "Yeah, I do. And if I take the day off, what do you plan on us doing?"

"That depends."

"On?"

"On what Amy sent. Why don't you get it and see what we got?"

Obviously perplexed, he stood and left the breakfast nook, then returned with the brown box and placed it on the table. "This isn't a Boston Market care package?"

"Oh, it's a care package all right, but it's not from Boston Market," she said, anxious to see what Amy had packed, and to see Trent's reaction. "Open it."

He lifted one end of the thick strip of packing tape holding the top in place, pulled it across, then lifted the lid.

"Well?" she asked, lifting her hips off the chair as she attempted to peer over the top. "What do we have?" She felt like a kid on Christmas morning, except in this case, the biggest present was the guy opening the package.

Trent lifted a bottle that Marissa instantly recognized. "That's Landon's newest edible massage oil. Caramel apple flavor."

"Edible massage oil," he said appreciatively, placing it on the table. Then he removed a big purple glove covered in tiny nubs, put it on one hand and rubbed his other palm over the stubby extensions. "Dare I ask?"

"You don't read my e-zine, do you?" she accused. "AtlantaTellAll. Have you *ever* read it?"

He frowned slightly. "I've looked it over, since our web war began."

"Did you read Amy's column?"

"Where she answers sex questions? Yeah, I may have skimmed it."

Marissa laughed. "You read it, and you liked it. You may have noticed that she usually recommends a product or two from Landon's company, which was where she worked, too, before she had Bo." She pointed to the glove. "That's a smitten, and she described it in one of last month's issues. You cover it with the edible massage oil, give your partner a massage that feels like tiny butterflies covering his or her skin, and then, you lick it off."

"You sound like you have firsthand knowledge," he said, then lifted a brow while he waited for her answer.

"Hah," Marissa said, shaking her head. "I've thought about using Amy's recommendations plenty of times, but haven't met the right guy for the part. Now, some of the items for solo performances, like Pinky, I've tried."

"Since she brought this care package to us, she must have dubbed me the right guy for the part, as far as you're concerned?"

"Evidently so," Marissa said. "But we've only got a day, so we shouldn't waste time."

"And this is the same woman who said she didn't want to have sex with me?"

"It's difficult not to want to have sex with the guy who gave you the best orgasms of your life," she said honestly. Might as well put it all out there, since she wouldn't see him after tomorrow.

"The best, huh?" Then he grinned. "Well, in all honesty, Ms. Kincaid, I've never had an orgasm like the one you gave me this morning, either. Something about trying to carry on a normal conversation while you're using your talented tongue on me ranks that orgasm at the top as well."

She lifted her nose in the air and smiled triumphantly. "Mission accomplished."

"And the fact that you entered wearing my shirt didn't hurt the prelude aspect either," he added. "I almost came just looking at you."

"Flattery will get you everywhere," she said, as he lifted a small package from the box. "Ooh, those are the flavored ones," she said, eyeing the multicolored condoms.

"Flavored," he repeated.

"They make musical ones, too, but I don't guess she included any of those."

"Musical ones?" he questioned, and Marissa giggled. She was instructing him on sex toys. How cool was that?

"Yeah. You can get Happy Birthday, or the Wedding March, but the most popular in Atlanta is still Dixie."

"I have to say I'm glad she left those out," he said, stifling his laughter.

"They're really very popular," Marissa said, "according to her column in my e-zine, which you should read, by the way."

"Trust me, I won't miss another of Amy's insightful

columns." He lifted the last item from the box. "Okay. I'll bite. What do we do with this?"

Marissa smiled. She'd always wanted to try the two-person vibrator that Amy labeled the "thriller," and now was her chance. "You see that ring, with all the hard little nubs around it?"

"Yeah."

"Put your fingers through it," she instructed, her excitement growing at the prospect of everything they could do—would do—before the day ended. "Amy showcased this one in our first issue of AtlantaTellAll."

Trent slid three fingers into the center of the circle, while Marissa unwound the cord from the remote control. "This part will rub against me, directly on my clitoris," she said, pointing to the gel-covered tiny vibrator, "and that will surround your penis." She pointed to the circle currently encasing his fingers. "Now check this out." She pushed the switch on the remote and slid the control to high, while the entire thing pulsated wickedly in his hand.

"You ever used one of these before?" he asked, his voice raspy and undeniably aroused.

"No, but I've always wanted to."

"No time like the present." He grabbed the box of flavored condoms, took the remote from her, and then grabbed her hand.

"Does that mean you're going to take the day off?" she teased, as he led her to the bedroom.

He grabbed both sides of the shirt she was barely wearing, since only two buttons in the center held it on her body, and he yanked them apart. The buttons popped obediently off and landed softly on the floor, and the shirt quickly followed.

"Oh, no you don't," Marissa said. "This time, you're not starting on me until you're naked, too."

"Gotta love a lady who gives orders," he said and wasted no time unfastening his jeans, then dropping them to the floor. His erection held her momentarily speechless, and she reached out to stroke the hard length that she'd tasted only moments ago.

"I want you inside me," she whispered.

"Which is exactly where I want to be." He picked her up and laid her on the bed, and while she watched, he sheathed his penis with a condom. Marissa squinted at the wrapper. "Oh, no," he instructed. "Don't even think about investigating the flavor of this one. I can't wait long enough to let you taste it, not this time. I've wanted inside you all week, and besides, you've already thoroughly tasted me."

She licked her lips. "You were delicious."

"You're going to be the death of me, Rissi," he said, grinning as he climbed onto the bed and boldly eyed her nudity. He moved between her legs, then leaned over her, those smoky eyes drinking her in as Marissa sucked in a breath and waited for him to push inside. It'd been a long time, way too long, since she'd had a man inside her, and more than that, she'd never had Trent, and that was what she wanted more than anything. Bracing his weight on one arm, he ran his fingers through her hair, then softly kissed her lips. "Rissi?"

"Yeah?"

"I know you want to try that vibrator, and I do, too," he said, running the back of his hand down the length of her neck, then trailing his fingertips across her right breast. He caressed it, then leaned down and kissed the aching tip. "But this time, our first time, I want it to be just us."

Oh. Wow.

Rissi nodded. Sure, she wanted to try out all of Amy's things, but what she really wanted, more than that, was to be one with Trent, without any more obstacles than a condom between them.

"And," he said, his voice almost a growl.

"And?"

"And I'd planned to take the first time slow and easy, to show you how much it means to me that you're letting me have you, completely . . ."

Rissi waited, knowing a "but" was coming.

He took a deep breath, let it out slow. "But I'm afraid this time won't be slow, or easy. I want you so bad it hurts."

She pressed her elbows against the bed and leaned up, kissed him passionately, more than merely exploring him, but feeding on his desire, and hers. Her tongue mated with his, as his body rolled on top of hers and his penis nudged her center. Then Rissi broke the kiss and trailed her lips along his jaw, to his neck, and she sucked the sexy curve between his neck and shoulder, then bit him hard. "I don't want slow and easy," she said, arching her hips to put her hot center against his rock-hard length. "I want hard and fast and fierce, and I want it now."

Trent pushed her shoulders against the bed, then claimed her mouth with unreserved intensity, his lips pressing almost painfully against hers, but her body reveled in the torture, and in the undeniable sensation of his penis pushing against her wet opening, and then forcefully pressing inside. She pushed against the sweet invasion and screamed in hot, delicious pleasure as he moved powerfully within her intimate core and set her climax free.

*The only thing better than hot and spicy food is
a hot and spicy woman to share it with.*
— TRENT JACKSON

Chapter 22

Marissa inhaled the zesty aroma of green onions, yellow onions, and bell pepper, as the vegetables sautéed in a big glob of butter that definitely proved Cajun chefs didn't count fat grams. Her personal chef leaned against her and pressed his pelvis against her behind.

"How's it going?" he asked against her ear.

She wasn't completely certain he was talking about the food, since they'd been "going" very well all day. They never stopped for lunch, instead deciding to christen every room of the apartment, and the hot tub, and make certain to try out each and every one of Amy's marvelous toys. Marissa still tasted a hint of caramel apple massage oil on her tongue, along with more than a hint of Trent. In fact, their only brief break occurred when the delivery guy brought the groceries, and even then, Trent pinched her behind every time the guy wasn't looking.

He wrapped his arms around hers and gently moved her wrist to help stir the veggies, while she rocked against him and hummed her contentment. So this was what cooking with a man was like. She definitely had waited too long to try it. Then again, she rarely cooked at all, with a man or without, but she vowed to change that. This was fun, preparing her own meal, and something that was actually edible at that. Or she assumed it would be. They weren't done yet.

She tilted her head toward his, which was covered in the tall white hat he'd worn last night. "Where did you get that?" she asked, a giggle creeping forward at the end of the question. He looked hilarious with that Pillsbury doughboy thing sitting above his fine chiseled face. It looked extremely odd . . . and undeniably charming.

He smiled, kissed her cheek, and then winked. "Go on, admit it. You like me in a hat. Women find hats sexy," he said. "I read that somewhere."

"I don't think I'd consider that the type of hat we find sexy," she said. "When I think of a sexy hat, I think of a Stetson, or a baseball cap, or even a derby kind of thing, but I can't say I've ever thought of anything remotely like this when I thought of a guy in a hat. And I definitely have never considered a chef's hat in the sexy category," she said, turning back toward the pot and stirring.

He stepped away from her, and she heard a familiar rustle of clothing, and then something hit the floor. Before she turned to look, she suspected she knew what she'd see, but it didn't make the vision any less surprising. Or outrageous.

"You are absolutely crazy," she said, staring at the naked man in the kitchen, particularly at the most prominent part of him. Then it moved. "Oh, my."

"Dare you," he said.

"To what?"

"Cook. Naked." He turned and opened one of the kitchen drawers and withdrew another chef's hat. "Or, you can wear this, and we'll match."

She laughed. "And what will I do if any of this pops out on me?" she asked, pointing to the hot bubbling butter and veggies in the pot.

He grinned, dropped the hat back in the drawer, then scooped up his jeans and slid them on. "Okay, you've got a point, but someday, we're going to cook naked together."

Marissa smiled and decided not to tell him, again, that this was their last day together. She'd enjoyed spending time with him, having sex with him, learning how to cook with him, and basically, doing everything with him for the past few days. But that was all it could be, a few days of no-strings sensual entertainment, because no matter how much she tried to convince herself that she could actually give a relationship with Trent Jackson a go, she knew she wouldn't.

He moved beside her, then added garlic powder and paprika to the mixture in the pot. "Okay, darling, since we're cooking with our clothes on, we might as well keep this show rolling. Stir that for me."

Marissa did, but she also wiggled her behind against the front of his pants in the process.

"Hey now, you were the one who didn't want to cook naked," he reminded her, opening a can of golden mushroom soup, pouring it in, then adding a can of water. "Keep stirring."

"Yes, sir, Chef Trent."

He nodded his approval at the rich brown mixture in the pot, then added a pound of crawfish tails. "Looks perfect. Now we let it simmer twenty minutes, and then we'll be ready to taste your first crawfish étouffée."

"You don't mind having it again tonight?" she asked, stirring the crawfish into the gravy.

"Are you kidding? I could eat étouffée every meal of every day for a week, and still want more. That's the Cajun in me, I guess."

"Amy and Candi won't believe it when I cook for them."

"Or when we cook for them," he said and gave her that sexy smile that made her knees turn to jelly.

"Trent," she started, but stopped when her cell phone rang in the living room. "Can you take over?" she asked, kissing him softly before edging away.

"Oh, sure. I knew somehow you'd turn this around and have me cooking for you again, darling. I'm learning how you operate, and just so you know, I'm onto you."

"Yep, I've been planning for the phone to ring at precisely this moment all night," she said, punching the *Talk* button. "Hello."

"Marissa?" Mona said, her voice barely audible over the loud music and squealing voices in the background. "Is that you, dear? Can you hear me, honey?"

"Mom?" Marissa sat on the couch and pressed the phone closer to her ear. "I can hear you, barely. Can you speak up? Are you at one of the shows?"

Mona giggled into the phone. "Oh, baby, we left Branson last night." She laughed some more.

"I thought the senior center bus wasn't heading back until tomorrow." Evidently her concern was evident in her tone, since Trent switched off the stove, shoved the pot to the back burner, and came to sit beside her on the couch.

"Something wrong?" he asked.

"I don't know," she whispered. "Mom? Are you still there?"

"Yes, baby. You know, I shouldn't have called. I'll tell you all about it tomorrow. It's just that I'm so excited. The happiest night of my life, really, and I wanted you to know."

Marissa swallowed, tried to control her racing pulse. "Mom, you've been drinking, haven't you?" Mona Kincaid couldn't handle alcohol, at all, which was a big reason that Marissa never drank more than a margarita. She'd seen what happened when her mother did, but every time before, Mona had ended up crying as though she'd lost her best friend. Or, more accurately, like she'd lost her husband. Every time Daniel Kincaid had waltzed out of her life—correction, *their* lives—Mona had turned to a drink, or five, and Marissa ended up having to help her mother through the pain. But there had been years without her mother getting upset and smashed over Marissa's father. And Mona wasn't upset now. In fact, she was laughing hysterically. "Mom!" Marissa repeated with conviction, "Tell me where you are."

"I'm at my wedding reception, honey. In Gatlinburg. Remember that little white church on the mountain, the one where I said if I ever got married again, I'd get married in that church? Well, that's where we got married, and now we're celebrating. I'm sorry, sweetie. I wish you could've been here for the wedding, but we were so anxious"—more giggles—"and it's such a dream come true."

Marissa's breath came in sharp, harsh pants. Her

mother was married? To whom? "Mama," she said, working hard to keep her voice calm. "Who did you marry?"

Trent leaned forward as though trying to hear the conversation through the tiny phone, but Marissa couldn't look at him. She closed her eyes and prayed for a miracle. *Don't say you've done it again, Mama.*

For some reason, her simple question caused a fit of belly laughter to echo through the line. "Oh, baby, you know better than to ask that," Mona finally said. "But here, I'll let him tell you."

Marissa held her breath, and listened to her mother calling to her new husband. *Her husband.*

"Honey!" Mona yelled, then lowered her voice as *Honey* apparently neared. "Did you get me another piece of cake? Oh, thank you, dear. Butter cream is my favorite, you know. Hey, come here, baby. I've got someone on the line who wants to talk to you."

The distinctive chorus of "You Make Me Wanna Shout" filled the air, and a loud clunk indicated that Mona had either dropped, or thrown, the phone.

"Hang on. Sorry about that," the deep baritone said into the line. "I apologize. My—my wife called you by mistake, I believe. May I ask who I'm speaking with?"

Marissa's head pounded feverishly. She didn't have to ask any more questions. She knew. And the realization pierced her like a knife to the heart. It was starting again. No, it *had* started again. And, as always, she would be the one picking up the pieces.

"Hello?" the familiar voice repeated. "Is anyone there?"

She swallowed, frowned at Trent, then answered. "Hi, Daddy."

"Oh. Rissi," he said, clearly at a loss for words, something rare for Daniel Kincaid. "Mona, you called Marissa?"

"I wanted her to know how happy we are, honey," Mona said over the music in the background. Then Marissa heard the smacking of her mother's kisses. She was probably swooning all over him, something that he was used to, when it came to her. The whole idea of it made Marissa's stomach churn.

"Listen, sweetheart," he said into the line. "I know what you're thinking, but this isn't like before. Really. There's a lot going on here—a lot that's been going on—that you, well, you don't know about yet. We were going to wait and talk to you in person tomorrow, but your mother wanted to celebrate with champagne, and I guess she decided to call you while I went for more cake."

"Daddy," Marissa said, her head throbbing. "Are you sure that . . ." She couldn't even finish the sentence.

"I won't hurt her, Rissi. I swear it."

"Let me talk to her, hon," Mona said, and apparently took control of the phone. "We'll tell you all the details tomorrow, sweetie. But I wanted you to know how happy I am, how happy we both are. This has been the best week of my life. A dream, really."

Marissa nodded. This had been the best week of her life, too, a dream, with Trent. But now, with one phone call, it'd turned into a bit of a nightmare, and one she'd had before. "I'll talk to you tomorrow, Mom. I'm glad you're so happy."

"Thanks, sweetie. And tell that sweet Trent hello for me, okay?" She disconnected, and Marissa dropped her cell phone on the couch.

"My parents got married."

Trent's face was solemn. Obviously, he'd picked up on the fact that this wasn't exactly a joyous occasion, at least not for Marissa.

"I don't think she can handle it if he does it again."

"You mean if he cheats on her again?" he asked, apparently trying to offer supportive conversation.

While she didn't exactly need support, she did need to talk to someone, and through the past couple of days, she had bonded with him, not only sexually, but emotionally as well. They were learning about each other again, in a different way than they had as children, and right now, he was about to learn plenty about Marissa, and her crazy family. "That was why we moved that year, when I was thirteen. His cheating. I think I told you before," she said, her mind fumbling over their conversations the past few days. "Anyway, we left, and they stayed apart until I graduated from high school. Then Daddy came down to see me graduate, they ended up in bed together, and before you knew it, she married him. Again. She moved back to Atlanta, and I stayed in Florida, thinking my life was finally taking a turn toward normalcy. And then, halfway through college, she calls me from Atlanta crying, saying he'd found someone else. Again."

Trent nodded, and frowned. "What did you do?"

"Moved out of the dorm and got an apartment near campus, so she could come back down and live with me until I got my degree. Then after school, I got a computer-programming position in Tallahassee, and Mom stayed there with me. She got a job working at the *Tallahassee Democrat* as an ad rep, but she never really adjusted to

Florida. However, she said she didn't want to move back to Atlanta, where her friends were, by herself."

"She wanted you to move back, too."

Marissa nodded.

"And you did."

Another nod. "I know it sounds crazy, but she really needed me. She needed to know someone wasn't going to leave her."

"The way your father did."

"Yeah."

Trent took an audible breath, eased it out, then wrapped his arm around her and gently folded her into his embrace. "Maybe it'll be different this time," he said, his hand gently moving over her spine. He was trying his best to make her feel better, to make her find a glimmer of hope that perhaps this situation was a good thing, perhaps her father wouldn't cause another heartbreak and run. But Marissa couldn't get over the truth of the past.

She shook her head against Trent's chest. "I can't even think that way," she whispered. Then she eased away from him and fought the tears burning for release. "I'm sorry, Trent. I really want to be alone and think. If it's okay with you, I'm going to take a hot bath and go to bed."

"You don't want to eat something?" he asked, and even though Marissa hadn't had a bite since breakfast, she suddenly had no appetite whatsoever.

"No."

"And I suppose you don't want company, a friend, to hold you while you sleep?" he asked, and the concern in those smoky eyes touched her heart.

"No," she whispered, then stood and walked away.

*The transition from having sex to making love is
part exhilarating, part terrifying. The transition from
broadcasting on live radio to live TV is similar, except there
is no exhilaration involved; it's just plain terrifying.*
—MARISSA KINCAID

Chapter 23

Marissa rolled over and peered through the French
doors to see moonlight spilling over the bubbling water
in the hot tub. She'd slept, some, but not peacefully.
The tangled comforter and sheet, in an ugly pile on the
floor, provided proof of the fact. How she wished she
could convince herself that her mother's phone call was
merely a dream, but she knew better. The sick feeling
in her stomach and the overpowering throbbing of her
head were evidence to the contrary. And to think, she'd
planned on a relaxing evening with Trent, sampling her
first attempt at étouffée, visiting with him, and then
spending the night in his arms. She missed those arms.
Needed them.

Before second-guessing her decision, she slid off the
bed, then moved toward the bathroom door, the coarse
Berber carpet making her bare feet tingle. She entered the

bathroom, and the cool tile provided another sensation to the soles of her feet, like a splash of ice water intended to wake someone up. In this case, Marissa saw the chilly awareness as a warning, telling her that if she moved beyond the cold tiles and into the opposite bedroom, she had better be prepared for the consequences. Tonight, if she were with Trent, it wouldn't merely be sex.

She swallowed, and kept moving. She wanted him, and she wouldn't let fear stand in her way, not tonight, when she needed his warmth, his friendship, and more. Her hand reached for the knob on his door and turned it. The soft click of the cylinder sliding free confirmed what she'd known. Trent hadn't locked the door. She slowly pushed it open and entered his room. The carpet tickled her feet once more, reminding her that she'd crossed the barrier now and that there was no going back. And she didn't want to stop now. She wanted the man whose deep breathing was the only sound in the room.

Marissa inhaled the scent of him, and her nipples budded into hard points against her white silk gown. She moved a finger to one of the spaghetti straps at her shoulder, pushed it off her arm, then shifted so the other side also fell free. The sleek fabric whispered over her skin on its way to the floor.

"You're beautiful."

His voice startled her, and she gasped. Had he been watching her the entire time? Had he been waiting for her tonight, knowing that she wouldn't be able to sleep, because her heart ached to be comforted? And because her very soul ached for him? She realized that the moonlight spilling freely into her room had followed her through the small passage between the two and was now silhouetting her frame. He'd watched her enter, had seen her undress, and now viewed her, standing before him, completely nude. He'd seen her this way for most of the day, as they explored their sexual desires together, but now, it seemed different. More sensual, more intimate.

"Come here, Rissi," he said, and sat up in the bed; then he leaned toward her, taking her hand in his. "Let me love you."

She moved to the bed, then lay beside him, his powerful, male body radiating strength against her shivering flesh. His arms encircled her, pulled her close, while he kissed her hair, then her forehead, the bridge of her nose, her eyelids, and finally, her mouth. Marissa curved instinctively into him, relishing the feeling of something so perfect, so right. His fingers caressed her, moving over her breasts, then easing down her abdomen in whisper-light touches that had her body quivering deep inside, while his intoxicating kiss overwhelmed her worries and left her thinking only of this moment, of his touch, of the two of them.

He gently slid his leg between hers, opening her center as he moved his fingers lower, to her most sensitive place, then kissed her and touched her and loved her until her body blissfully lost all control.

She slid her hand down his side, across his hip, and to his hard length. Then she arched her hips and guided him to her center. "I want you. Please."

Trent reached over her to the bedside table, and Rissi heard the soft tear of foil as he prepared to give her what she wanted—needed—*him*. He entered her slowly, filling her completely. "I've wanted you all night, Rissi," he said, moving inside her, while he kissed her cheek, then her neck, making Rissi's entire body squirm against him. She wanted to feel him lose control inside her, wanted to know that she could do that to him, and that he could do this to her, make her forget everything but the two of them. "I've wanted you all my life," he said against her ear. "I've been waiting to find you, and now I have."

Her body responded as much to his words as to the sensation of his deep penetration. She convulsed around him, her orgasm fierce and powerful, and brought him to the edge as well. He pushed deep within her, then growled through his release, while Marissa's intimate center clenched around him, determined to keep him inside, a part of her, for as long as possible.

He settled beside her as her body shuddered through the aftershock of her intense climax, and her intense realization. This was so much more than sex.

"Oh, Rissi," he whispered, moving his mouth against her cheeks . . . and kissing her tears away.

Merely a few hours later, Marissa opened her eyes to see that moonlight had changed to blinding sunlight, and Trent's body was still cradling hers, holding her, protecting her. She could get used to waking up like this.

"Hey," he whispered, his words tickling her ear.

"Hey to you." She tilted her head to look at him and smiled easily. It was natural to smile at him, to feel better with him.

"I'd really love to stay here and hold you all day, but if we wait too much longer, Coleman and Speedy will be in here with us."

Her eyes widened, then she quickly looked at the clock: *8:07.*

"What time are they coming?" she asked, sitting up in the bed in a semipanic. She and Trent were supposed to be ready for the broadcast and packed by nine. She knew that much. What she couldn't recall was how early the entire production crew would be here to get ready for the show.

"I believe they said eight-thirty, but I'm sure they'll understand if you're still getting ready," he said. "Besides, you look terrific when you first wake up, and the people listening won't be able to see you anyway. It'd suit me fine if you went like that," he said, while Marissa scooped her nightgown from the floor and held it in front of her nudity.

"I'm sure it'd suit Coleman, Speedy, and the crew fine, too," she said, "but it isn't happening." She grinned at him. "I'm going to take a quick shower then get busy packing. You go ahead and pack, then you can shower second."

"Listen to you, giving orders," he said. "You know, we could shower together, to save time."

"No time would be saved, and you know it."

"Wouldn't be able to keep your hands off me all hot and wet and soapy?" he asked.

"You're terrible."

"And I'd bet money that you like me that way," he said, smiling. Then he scooted up in the bed, leaned against the headboard, and studied her. "You're feeling better now?"

She nodded. True, she'd have to face her parents in a little while, but sharing last night with Trent had taken the edge off the apprehension. "I am feeling better," she admitted. "And I have you to thank for that." She turned to go shower.

"Rissi?"

She could tell by the tone that she wasn't ready to answer the rest of his question. "Yeah?"

"What are you going to tell them this morning? When they ask about the two of us?" He waited a heartbeat, then added, "I don't want this to end, and I don't believe you do either."

She looked at him, the sexy man who had made her happier in the past few days than she'd been in a very long time, and she told him the truth. "I don't know." Then she turned and entered the bathroom, determined to prepare for the upcoming interview and to try to control her battling emotions, one side wanting to ask Trent to take her away from everything, to run away together and get married and ride off into the sunset, the exact picture of happily ever after that she believed her mother had seen, again, when she eloped with her father last night. And the other side wanting Trent to go away, to take away the temptation to give in, to forget the fact that he could end up like her father, but instead of hurting her mother, he'd be hurting Rissi.

She couldn't handle that, but she also couldn't handle losing something that felt so perfect. The hot shower water stung her skin, but she moved the knob to make it even hotter, to blaze reality back to the forefront of her thoughts. Life wasn't perfect. Her family wasn't perfect, and Trent wasn't perfect. She scrubbed her skin, then washed her hair, while her tears joined the scalding water trickling down her flesh. What to do. Her heart wanted him. Her body wanted him. But her mind kept reminding her of the pain, and she did have a propensity for picking guys who cheated. Amy said so, and so did Jamie. What if she were merely picking another one, and if by starting a relationship with Trent, she was merely setting herself up to follow her mother's pattern of handing over her heart, then having it broken?

"Marissa? They'll be here in a few minutes," Trent said through the door.

She twisted the knobs to stop the shower water and sniffed. "I'm done," she said. "Be out in a sec." She quickly brushed her teeth and decided to forgo drying her hair. Trent had admitted that he liked it wild and curly, and she liked giving Trent what he wanted. She'd do that today, for sure, since she wouldn't see him after this broadcast.

Within minutes, she'd dressed and tossed her additional clothes into her suitcase, while listening to the shower water echo from the opposite side of the bathroom door. She and Trent had taken advantage of the space in that shower yesterday, yet another location to try another position, and Amy's waterproof vibrator. Marissa's throat clenched at the memory. Would she ever let go so powerfully with anyone else? Would she ever want to? No. She only wanted Trent, and that thought brought on a fresh batch of tears.

The water stopped running at the same moment that a pounding began on the front door. Marissa glanced in the mirror, wiped her eyes, and moistened her lips, salty from her tears. She took a calming breath, then nodded at her reflection. This was it. She had to do this interview, and then she'd be done with letting Coleman, Speedy, and all of Atlanta in on her daily events. She'd be done with everything, Trent included.

If she could make it through this interview.

She crossed the living room and opened the door, still rattling from a hard knock on its other side.

"So you are here," Speedy said, shuffling hurriedly in, while Coleman and a huge production team brought up the rear. Marissa had expected the three people she'd seen last Friday, but there were at least ten men, and four women, bustling through the door in an effort to claim space. And unlike last time, this crew had cameras.

Cameras?

"Coleman?" she questioned. "Who are all of these people?"

"A little surprise we have for both of you. It'll add even more exposure to your websites," he added quickly, as though he knew she wasn't going to like whatever they'd done.

What had they done?

"What kind of exposure?" she asked, while Trent emerged from his bedroom in a pale blue button-down and khakis. He looked . . . delicious.

Marissa did not need to keep staring at him, or picturing him naked and above her, below her, beside her, inside her. She cleared her throat and forced her attention back to Coleman while she waited for his answer.

"Television," Speedy said, interrupting with a big, triumphant grin. "We really hit the jackpot this time, and all of Atlanta wants to know what you're going to decide."

"What I'm going to decide," Marissa repeated.

"Whether you're going to take the man or the advertising," Speedy said. "There are polls about it all over the Net, and our morning broadcasts this week have been downloaded and replayed more than ever before,

particularly the one where Trent accused you of checking out his ass."

Her cheeks sizzled, and there was no way she could
control the color that she knew blazed there.

"Are you wearing makeup?" Speedy asked pointedly.

Marissa had no need to worry about the fire in her
cheeks anymore; she felt the color drain from them completely. "Makeup," she said. "I was about to do that."

She started to her room, while Trent stepped toward
her and whispered, "It'll be fine, just a couple of cameras.
No big deal."

Marissa nodded, but moved mechanically to her room.
How had she forgotten makeup? And had she ever put any
on yesterday? No, she hadn't, and Trent hadn't seemed to
care. And on top of that, he'd told her she was beautiful
more times than she could count. She was really going to
miss that.

Within ten minutes, she returned to the living room
with her eyes accented in brown shadow and mascara,
and her lips glossed raspberry. She had also changed
clothes, swapping her red cotton blouse with a turquoise
tank set with an inch of sparkling silver sequins above her
chest. It would look nice with Trent's shirt, and for some
bizarre reason, she wanted the two of them to match. Marissa didn't want to spend a whole lot of time analyzing
that desire.

"Right here," a man in a ragged T-shirt and jeans said,
ushering her to one of the two chairs by the speakerphone
that she and Trent had used each morning. Trent was already seated in the opposite chair and gave her a reassuring smile as she sat down. "We're on in ten," the guy
continued, holding up both palms.

"Minutes or seconds?" Marissa asked, then figured it out as his left hand retreated, then the right one popped up and he mouthed, "Five, four . . ."

"I love you, Rissi," Trent said firmly.

All eyes turned to Trent, and the man's last finger rolled toward his palm.

"Hello, I'm Coleman from the Coleman and Speedy show, and we're live in Atlanta, Georgia, with Trent Jackson and Marissa Kincaid, the battling web duo forced to live together for a week, with the prospect of winning a seven-figure ad campaign. We'd like to thank our local NBC affiliate for broadcasting the outcome of our contest."

"Yeah, I'd like to thank them, too," Speedy said, "but right now, I'm wanting to know if I heard correctly. Trent, you said something to Marissa right before we went on the air, didn't you?"

"I did." Trent's eyes never strayed from Marissa's face.

She put a hand on her stomach and prayed she wouldn't hurl on live TV. What was she supposed to do now? He loved her? Trent Jackson loved her. *"Let me love you."* His words from last night drifted over her thoughts, as well as the sweet, tender kisses and touches, the way the two of them had bonded so intimately, so completely.

"Let me love you."

Have mercy, she shouldn't love him. She shouldn't. He *had* cheated in the past, only once, but still . . . thanks to her father, she'd seen firsthand how hard it was for a cheater to change, and how painful it can be for the innocent party. It had nearly killed her mother, and Marissa.

She should *not* love Trent Jackson.

But she did.

Her throat closed in, while Speedy trudged ahead.

"And what was it, again, that you said to her?" he asked.

"Speedy, we really need to follow our outline for the show," Coleman interjected in his best supervisor tone. "And first we need to ask Trent what he thought of Marissa's cooking."

"She was amazing in the kitchen," Trent said smoothly, and Marissa envisioned them, yesterday afternoon, her bottom naked on the counter, legs spread wide and Trent pushing deep within her while she climaxed. *He* was amazing in the kitchen.

"So she can cook?" Speedy asked. "You taught her how to make that étouffée?"

"Yeah, I taught her," Trent said, and gave Marissa that crooked, sexy grin that she adored. She wanted him, and she wanted to love him.

"Let me love you."

"Okay, so we've got the scoop on the cooking deal," Speedy said. "I'd say we're ready to move on to what Trent said."

A big black camera crept in, eerily close to Marissa's face, and she felt her cheeks heat up. They were moving on to what Trent said. Was she ready?

"Okay," Coleman relented. "Trent, I heard you as well. Before we went on the air, you made a comment to Marissa. Would you care to repeat that now?"

"I love you," Trent said again, with no doubt whatsoever in his tone. He loved her. He did.

And she loved him.

Marissa quietly cleared her throat, licked her lips. She

had never planned on this, but she'd be lying if she said it hadn't happened. Yes, he was a cheater, or he had been before, but she couldn't help that now. She loved him.

"Marissa," Coleman prodded.

She couldn't deny the truth. She'd been a fool to think she could walk away from Trent today, or any other day. She inhaled, and prepared to admit that she'd fallen for a former—she prayed it was former—cheater, but then a loud knock echoed from the apartment door, and Mona Kincaid bustled in, with Marissa's father in her wake.

"Oh, dear," Mona said. "I never set my watch back when we left Branson. I thought we were getting here early." Then her eyes widened at the cameras, and Coleman and Speedy. "Oh, no, you're on the air?"

"Mom?" Marissa questioned.

Speedy chuckled. "Well, for those of you who are listening on the radio, we've turned this happy little occasion into a family affair. You're Marissa's mother?"

Mona nodded, then whispered, "Oh, honey, I'm sorry. We'll leave."

"Nonsense," Coleman said. "Come on in. Chances are, you'll be interested in what's happening on our broadcast." He leaned around to view Daniel Kincaid, still tall and broad-shouldered, looking fifty, in spite of his birth certificate reporting his true sixty-eight. "And you are?"

"I'm Marissa's father," he said.

"And my husband," Mona beamed, turning to wrap an arm around him, then giving him a soft kiss on the cheek. "As of last night."

"Oooh, this is gonna be good for ratings," Speedy mumbled.

"As of last night?" Coleman questioned.

"Yes," Mona said, still glowing with happiness. How long would that last? "Third time's a charm."

"This is your third time to marry?" Speedy asked. "Or your third time to marry him?"

"Both," Mona said. "This was the first time we eloped, though." She looked past Coleman to view Trent, handsome as ever, sitting in the chair and waiting for this odd little scenario to end. "You're Trent."

"Yes, ma'am." Trent stood and extended his hand. She wrapped both of her palms around it and held it tight. "You really are a nice young man, aren't you?"

"I try."

"Hello, son, I'm Daniel Kincaid, Rissi's—I mean Marissa's—father." He also extended a hand. Retrieving the one Mona had captured, Trent gave Marissa's father a firm, business shake.

"What do you know, we have newlyweds and a family reunion and a proclamation of love, all in one show," Speedy said. "We should call Oprah."

"A proclamation of love?" Mona asked, her head turning to view Marissa and Trent.

The round camera lenses zoomed in, snake eyes sizing up prey.

"Trent told Marissa that he loves her," Speedy relayed, "and we're waiting for Marissa's response."

"Well, technically," Coleman corrected, "we're asking the two of them if they want to continue seeing each other, or if they want the prize, a seven-figure multimedia ad campaign. That's a mighty nice prize," he said. "And may cause one to really consider whether he or she is in love."

"You're not seriously trying to talk him out of it, are

you?" Speedy asked his partner. "Because it sounded like he meant it to me."

"I did," Trent said. "And, like I said earlier this week, I don't want the prize. I want Marissa."

"Ohhhhh," Mona moaned, her lip trembling as she stepped closer to Marissa's father. Her new husband. The guy who had cheated so long ago, and then again, and would probably continue the pattern.

Marissa's heart stilled in her chest. She couldn't look at them. She shifted in her chair to look at something else, and saw Trent. She looked away; she couldn't look at him either. Seconds ticked by. Cameras zoomed.

"He doesn't want the prize," Coleman repeated. His tan, golfer's face formed several thick creases as he smiled, believing he knew what her response would be. "Marissa, how about you?"

"I—" She took another glance at her mother, practically drooling over the distinctive presence of Daniel Kincaid. The man whose promises she believed, always, no matter what. The man who hurt and cheated again and again, and the man she couldn't stop loving, because he was her first, and her only, love. Marissa wanted to hate him, but she couldn't; he was her father, and she couldn't get past that to hate him. She loved him, too. They all loved him, and it didn't matter. He hurt them all, again and again. Because that's what cheaters do.

"He said he wants you," Speedy repeated, as though she hadn't heard Trent at all. "He doesn't want the prize."

"I'm sorry," Marissa said, locking eyes with Coleman, so she didn't have to see her mother, or her father, or Trent. "I understand he doesn't want the prize, but I do."

In adulthood, there are times when familial roles are reversed. The child assumes the role of caregiver, and the parent assumes the role of dependent. However, there are times when, even if the parents have relinquished the role of caregiver, they need to step up to the plate and do their jobs once more. Now is one of those times.
— MONA KINCAID

Chapter 24

The backseat of her father's Lexus SUV was probably plenty big enough for hauling whatever he needed on a daily basis, but currently, with all of his and Mona's luggage, as well as Marissa's suitcase, and Marissa, packed within its boundaries, the space was rather cramped. Add to that her mother's continual neck swivel and bless-her-heart smile, and Marissa felt a bout of carsickness gearing up. And she didn't even know she got carsick, but evidently, she did.

"I thought you went to Branson on a bus," Marissa said.

Mona cleared her throat guiltily. "Well, if you'll remember, I said the seniors were going to Branson on a bus. I went to Branson, but I didn't ride with the seniors.

We rode together." She moved her hand across to stroke the back of her husband's head, then she let her fingers twirl in the pale waves ending at his neck. Marissa's father had great hair, and Mona had always been a sucker for it. She still was, obviously. Mona's hair was also gray, but hers had that silver thing going, where Daniel's was Kenny Rogers white.

Marissa attempted to inhale extra air, since there seemed to be too little of it in the backseat. "And I thought Amy was picking me up," she said, watching the buildings lining I-285 fly by the window. Her stomach churned. It was not smart to watch buildings flying by, not with so little air.

"I called Amy to find out how to get to the apartment where you were staying, and she said she was going to pick you up. Since I thought you'd want to—talk—your father and I offered to pick you up instead." Mona did her neck swivel to see Marissa's reaction, and obviously got more than she bargained for. "Oh, my, you're green."

"Yeah." It was all Marissa could manage. Was she sick because of the car? Maybe. Or was she sick because she'd just turned down and humiliated the first guy she ever really loved, and the very first one who professed to love her back, on live TV and radio? Definitely.

"Daniel, get off at the next exit," Mona instructed.

He nodded, accelerated, and the car quickly veered up a ramp off the interstate. Marissa tried to remember if there was some sort of technique to breathing. In and out, in and out. Yeah, that was it. But the new-car smell of the Lexus was creeping into the mix, and she really didn't think she was going to make it much longer before she christened Daniel Kincaid's latest retirement perk with this morning's breakfast. Wait. She hadn't eaten breakfast. Or dinner last night. Or anything since yesterday morning's bread pudding. Oh, well, nothing like dry heaves to make your day complete. Her stomach pitched, as though telling her that was exactly what was about to happen.

"Daniel, pull in right there!" Mona demanded, and again, he obeyed. Well, what do you know, some things do change.

The car rolled to a stop, and Marissa fell out. Literally. She was on the ground before Mona had time to circle the car and see her daughter crawl to the curb, then immediately put her head between her knees.

"There you go, baby. Take deep breaths. Heavens, I should have let you sit up front. I never realized that you get carsick. You never did when you were little."

"I never have, until now." Marissa breathed in the warm July air and quickly began feeling normal. In, out. Nice, clean air. No new-car smell. This was good.

"It isn't the car, is it?" Mona asked, sitting beside Marissa on the curb and waving Daniel back into the SUV when he tried to approach. "We can handle this," she said, and again, he nodded, and got back into the car.

Was this really Marissa's father? Or some twin uncle Marissa didn't know about who didn't mind listening to his wife and doing what she asked, twice in one day?

"It's Trent," Mona continued. "You love him, don't you?"

"Yes." Easy question. Easy answer. The fact that she loved him wasn't up for debate. Whether she could trust a guy who might be like the man currently driving her across Atlanta was another story.

"Then why did you let him go, honey?" Mona asked, sincerity etched across her face. Amazing that this was the same woman who undeniably had had one champagne too many last night.

"No hangover?" Marissa asked, choosing that subject over the one her mother had initiated.

"It's bizarre, but I've never had a hangover on a night I had sex. I think all of the expended energy must counteract the effects of the alcohol, or something."

This was said with such a matter-of-factness that Marissa didn't know whether to point out the *eww* factor of hearing that her parents had had sex last night or to discuss the possibility of sex reducing the chances of a hangover. Neither really seemed like an option Marissa wanted to take. Luckily, Mona kept talking without waiting for input.

"Do you think you can get back into the car for a block? I know where I want to go. I'll let you ride up front, if that will help."

"Okay." Marissa got up and wobbled around the car, then let her mother help her in.

"Better?" her father asked, as she buckled her seatbelt, adjusted the air vent to blow directly on her face, and settled in.

"Yeah, better." She smiled at him. He did care about her, and Mona, too, for that matter. Marissa never had doubted that. The problem was that, occasionally, he cared about other women, too, way too much.

"Honey, make a right. I'll show you where to go," Mona said, getting in behind her husband.

He did as he was told, again, and then waited for her next instruction.

"Right there. Pull in and park, please," Mona said, and he did. She leaned over the seat and kissed him on the cheek. "Would you mind taking a drive or going to a nearby store or something for fifteen minutes or so? I believe we need to have a little time for girl talk."

He smiled, kissed her on the lips, then nodded. "Sure, dear."

"And when you get back, we'll swap, and the two of you can chat."

His face lost a tad of color at that, but again, he nodded. "You're right. That's definitely in order."

Marissa opened the door and was pleasantly surprised that she could stand on her own two feet without the least bit of wobble. Then she saw the red-and-white-striped awning and grinned. "Bruster's."

"Best ice cream around," Mona said. "Do you think you can eat some, with your queasy stomach?"

"I can always eat Bruster's," Marissa said, and oddly enough, her stomach did feel better, ready for ice cream. Bruster's had been a major source of comfort when she was a kid. Great report card? Head to Bruster's for cherry vanilla. Skinned your knee? Bruster's banana chocolate chip would fix you right up.

"What flavor?" Mona asked, nearing a side window of the old-fashioned ice cream stand.

"Hmm," Marissa pondered aloud as she read the large billboard of over thirty unique treats. What kind would help you feel better after you turned down the guy you love in front of most of Atlanta? "White chocolate turtle." No, it wouldn't fix things, but it couldn't hurt.

"White chocolate turtle in a waffle cone," Mona said. "And I'll take a banana split."

Within minutes, mother and daughter were sitting at an umbrella-covered picnic table and eating ice cream the way they had many years ago. Marissa licked hers and sighed at the way the caramel teased her tongue. It reminded her of . . . caramel apple massage oil.

"Thinking about him, huh?" Mona asked, ever watchful of her daughter's every move and every expression.

Marissa nodded, and took a bite of the cone. This felt rather strange, having her mother appear to take care of her again, the way she had so long ago. For the past two decades, their roles had been reversed, with Marissa being the stronger of the two. The realization that they'd switched places again sent a lump directly to Marissa's throat, and it had nothing to do with the ice cream. A single tear pushed forward and trickled from her right eye. Mona reached out and wiped it away.

"Why didn't you tell him, honey?" she asked, merely moving the banana split around with her spoon. This wasn't about her, after all.

This was Marissa's pity party, so she took another big bite of her ice cream . . . and got brain freeze. She put her fingers to her temple and winced.

"Oh, I hate it when that happens," Mona said, sympathetically watching her recover from the ice-cream-induced brain freeze, but continuing with her interrogation. "Okay, honey. Tell me. What did he do?"

"He didn't do anything," Marissa said honestly. "It's what Daddy did, and how often he did it. And the fact that I seem to attract guys who do the same."

Mona nodded knowingly. "I thought that might be it."

"How am I supposed to trust any man not to cheat? And how do you?" There, *that* was the kicker. Obviously, it was in Marissa's genes to fall for cheaters, and obviously, it was in her genes to let them walk all over her, time and time again, and take them back.

"I listened to that radio broadcast, when that woman said Trent cheated on her in college," Mona said, and she finally started eating the dessert. "That's what this is about, isn't it? You think the fact that he cheated back then means he'll do it again, and you're basing that on my history with your father."

Marissa swallowed, then nodded.

"So one time he cheated. And he was in college, still playing the field, as they call it," Mona said. "He wasn't married, sweetie."

"How do I know that it wouldn't spill over into marriage—not that he's asked me or anything, but—"

"If he hasn't asked you yet, he will," Mona said, appearing very certain of the fact. She smiled, then dug into the banana split, humming her delight with the medley of chocolate fudge, vanilla ice cream, cherries, and bananas.

Marissa licked her ice cream and stared at her mother, this extremely confident woman who ate ice cream, discussed sex and hangovers, and gave her husband orders. "Who are you, and what have you done with my mother?" Marissa asked.

Mona laughed, in much the same manner as she had last night over the phone, when she was at her wedding reception, or whatever it was. They might have called from a topless bar for all Marissa knew. "I've wanted to tell you about everything for a couple of years, sweetie, but I didn't want to hurt you again. So I waited until I was certain he was in it for real this time, you know, committed and all. He is. Truly."

Marissa's head throbbed. There was a whole lot of information in that little spiel, but one factor well surpassed all others. "A couple of years?"

"That's how long we've been dating, dear. Oh, I wasn't going to let him just waltz back in and take control anymore. I'm a woman of the twenty-first century, after all. No more of this eighties lady kind of thing for me."

"Eighties?"

"Oh, okay. I guess I was a sixties lady, but eighties sounds better. Anyway, he came back a couple of years ago, wanting to start up in my life and in my bed, and I said no. Flat no. No questions asked. And then, of course, he came back again, and I made him court me, the old-fashioned way. And I made the turkey wait until we got married again until he got me in the sack," she said, while Marissa's eyes popped.

"Mother!"

"Oh, shoot, darling, this doesn't even get close to water-cooler talk at work, and you know it." She smiled. "Anyway, when I told him I was going on the senior center bus trip, and he knew that Vernon McDaily was going—Vern has had his eye on me for some time—he really got his tail feathers ruffled and put his butt in gear, and it was high time. I'm not getting any younger, and Amy's toys can only take you so far."

Marissa had no control over the brain freeze that came when *that* bit of information hit her ears at the same time a big gulp of ice cream hit her throat. She slapped her head. "Amy's toys?"

"Phffft," Mona said, waving away Marissa's expression.

"We're not going to talk about them today, though she's got some really amazing things. Right now we need to talk about you and that hot CEO who professed to all of Atlanta that he loves you and who you turned your nose up at like he was something nasty that you stepped in."

"I didn't," Marissa argued.

"Just telling it the way Atlanta saw it," Mona said, now enthusiastically finishing her banana split. "I was going to save half of this for your daddy, but I believe he'll have to get his own," she said with a grin.

"Mom."

"Yes?"

"Do you really think Daddy has changed?"

Mona laid her spoon on the edge of the paper boat holding her treat and shrugged. "Honey, I believe he has, and I truly hope that he has. Can I tell you that I'm a hundred percent sure that he won't find a younger model and trade the old one in again? No, maybe not a hundred percent, but I'd say a solid eighty-five now."

"And is that good enough? He hurt you so much last time," Marissa said. *And he hurt me.*

"Honey, I didn't go into this with my eyes closed. I know the chances of getting hurt again are there, but you know what, I love that man, and I believe he's worked hard to get me back for the past two years. Last night was beautiful. My dream come true. And if he has changed, and I don't give him a chance, or give myself a chance to really have us back together again, I'd never forgive myself. True love is worth that chance, don't you think?"

Marissa didn't answer, because a car horn right behind her caused her to turn and see Daniel Kincaid, climbing from his SUV.

"My turn?" he asked, approaching the table cautiously.

Mona nodded. "Well, shoot, I guess he'll get half of it after all," she whispered with a wink. Then she turned toward him. "I saved you half of my split, baby!"

Marissa giggled. Who would have known? Her mother took a while to find it, but she'd definitely located her sass.

"I'm going to hope that smile is a good thing," he said, sitting beside Mona and giving her a sweet peck on the cheek.

"I think it is." Mona took the keys out of his hand. "Now, I'm going to see if I can find something interesting in that little boutique across the street." Humming, she sashayed toward the car.

"I was a fool to ever treat that woman wrong," he said, waving to her as she backed the Lexus out of the space and headed out of the parking lot.

"Yes, you were."

He sighed deeply, then started finishing off Mona's banana split. "We used to go to this place called Zack's and eat a banana split at the end of every one of our dates, back when we were teens," he said.

"I know. She told me, every time she ordered one when I was little."

"I'm guessing that's probably the reason she ordered one today, to remind me," he said, smiling.

"I'd guess you're right," she said, still feeling a bit odd at having this conversation, but knowing it was necessary. "Daddy—" She halted when he held up a hand.

"Wait. Let me talk first, if you don't mind. I have something to say to you, and I don't want to wait any longer." He pushed the ice cream away and looked directly at Marissa, his dark eyes sincere and solemn. "I know I hurt your mother, and I've done my best to convince her that I am sorry, and that I'll never do it again. I love her, truly I do, and I was incredibly stupid to ever let her get away. But it wasn't just your mother that I hurt back then, and I don't think I really saw that until recently, with your new business venture and all. That cheater site, and all of those pages where you talk about how it feels to be done wrong. I mean, I know that you were talking about those guys, but there was more to it than that, maybe even more than you realized. You were also talking to me, about me, and publicly reprimanding me for what I did. I left you and your mother at the very beginning of your teen years, when you needed me so much, and I can't ever get that time back. I'll never forgive myself for that, for hurting her, and for hurting you. But I've proven to her that I'm the man she fell in love with, and can be the kind of husband she always wanted, the kind she deserved. People can change, Rissi, and I have. I swear it. I know it'll take time for you to believe me, but I want to take that time, the same way I've taken that time with your mother, and I want to eventually believe that you trust me again, that you trust me not to hurt her ever again, and that you trust me not to hurt you."

He cleared his throat. "Rissi, honey, I know this will be hard for you to believe, after everything I've put your mother—and you—through, but I *have* changed. Back then, with you and your mother, I had everything a man could want, a beautiful wife who loved me more than any woman should, and a daughter who would make any father proud. Yet, for reasons I still can't understand, I

messed around with other women, and I hurt the two people who cared the most."

"But you didn't care about us back then," Marissa said.
"Not the way you should have, or you wouldn't have
cheated on Mom."

His chin trembled, mouth dipped at the corners, and
he slowly shook his head. "No, I didn't, and I'll spend the
rest of my life regretting that, honey, and trying to make
things right. Your mother deserves that, and so do you."

"But what's different this time?" she asked. "You said
the same thing before, when you came to Florida for
my graduation and then got back with Mama then. But
you did it again, found someone else, and hurt her." She
paused, then whispered, "You hurt both of us."

A heavy tear trickled down his cheek, and he rubbed his
palm down his face to wipe it away. "I'm so sorry for that,
Rissi. I hate that I hurt you, both of you. I never want to
hurt either of you that way again, and that's why I waited
so long before contacting Mona." He shrugged. "I never
told you before, because I didn't think you would want to
know, but none of the other relationships ever made it beyond a few months. The last one only lasted a few weeks
before I realized that I'd messed up—again—and ended
it. I knew I wouldn't be satisfied with Anita, because I
still loved Mona."

"But you cheated on her."

"I know, which is why I didn't try to get back with
her then. I kept hurting her, and I wasn't going to let myself hurt her again. So I didn't call her, didn't try to see
her, or to do anything that would give me the opportunity
to hurt her again. But Rissi—this is important—I didn't
see anyone else either during that time. I'd decided if I

couldn't have Mona, and trust myself to treat her right, then I didn't want anyone."

"For how long?" Marissa asked. "How long did you go without seeing anyone?"

He gave her a soft smile. "Nine years, from the day we divorced until the day I called her and begged her for another chance to treat her right, which was two years ago."

"But you were already seeing Anita when you and Mom divorced."

"No," he said, shaking his head. "Like I said, the thing with Anita only lasted a few weeks, and was over before the divorce was even final. I knew I'd messed up, and I did still love Mona."

Marissa frowned. "Then why didn't you try to stay with her?"

"Because I was afraid," he said, his voice barely a whisper now, and completely losing its typical confident air. "I was afraid I'd hurt Mona and you, again, and I couldn't let that happen. I'd put you through too much already."

"Then why *did* you finally call her again, two years ago?" Marissa asked, needing to see the full picture and needing to know whether her father had really changed.

He smiled. "I guess the best way to explain it is to tell you that I flat-out didn't want to live the rest of my life without your mother being a part of it. I was miserable without her, Rissi, and miserable that I'd let her get away. So I called her and told her that no matter what it took, I was going to prove to her that I'd changed, that I understood how lucky I was to have had her in my life before, and that if she'd just give me another chance, I'd be the loving *faithful* husband she deserved." He laughed. "Do you know what she said to that?"

"No, what?"

"She said for me to prove it," he said, then laughed again. "And I've been doing my damnedest to show her that I have changed—and that I deserve her—for two years. And finally she said she'd marry me again." He shrugged. "I wanted you to be there, honey, but once she said yes, I didn't want to wait." He sighed. "I love her, Rissi, and I won't hurt her again."

Marissa's chest clenched tight. He'd said it all, everything she kept tethered for twenty years, and evidently, he'd worked for two years to prove himself worthy of her mother's love. "I want to believe you," she whispered.

"And I want you to," he said, "but I'm not fool enough to think that it won't take time. I'm just asking for you to give me a chance, and to support your mother's decision to take me back, if you can. She doesn't want to do anything that would make you unhappy, and she was so concerned that she'd upset you last night, with her telephone call, that she woke me up at three this morning so we could get to you before your show."

Marissa grinned. "When she gets something on her mind, she can't exactly concentrate on anything else."

"I'm lucky that I'm still on her mind."

"Yeah, you are," she agreed, then licked her quickly melting cone.

He also turned his attention back to his ice cream, and, having said all that needed to be said, the two of them sat in companionable silence until Mona returned in the SUV. She pulled into a nearby parking space and held up the "okay" sign, then gave them her questioning wince, as if asking, "You two all right?"

They both nodded and smiled.

"I do love you, honey," he said, patting the top of her hand. Then he gathered their trash and tossed it into a can on their way to the car.

"I know. I love you, too," she said softly, walking beside him.

"And that young man that I met this morning. Trent. What about him?" Daniel asked.

"I believe I blew it, don't you think? Turning my back on him on television and radio probably isn't the best way to start a relationship," she said, as they neared the SUV.

"The way I see it," her father said, climbing into the backseat so Mona could drive and Marissa could ride shotgun, "anything worth having is worth working for, even groveling for, if the occasion calls for it. Isn't that right, dear?"

"It didn't kill you," Mona said with a laugh.

"You know, you're right," Marissa said, pulling her phone out of her purse and dialing Candi's cellular. "And it won't kill me."

"Marissa? I'm so glad you called! Where are you? Are you okay?" Candi answered, obviously taking advantage of her caller ID.

"I'm with my folks, and they're taking me home. Listen, I don't have a lot of time. Can you tell me where Trent lives? I mean, can you find out from Keith and let me know, by the time I get home?"

"Oh, I don't know if that's such a good idea. He was really pissed, or maybe hurt is a better word. Keith brought him over here a little while ago, but he wasn't exactly in a talkative mood. In fact, he looked like he was ready to hit something."

"Keith brought him where?" Marissa asked. "Where are you?"

"At Amy's place. We've been working on next week's issue of AtlantaTellAll, since we thought you'd probably be preoccupied this weekend with all the radio and television fallout, which has netted us a ton of new subscribers, by the way. I have to tell you, I'm still shocked at what happened this morning. Amy said the two of you were getting hot and heated when she came over there. What went wrong?"

"Me," Marissa said miserably. "I went wrong. I messed up, and I need to try to fix it. Now tell me why he came to Amy's."

"Trent asked Keith to find out where you live, and Keith had been to Amy's with me a couple of times this week already, when Amy and I were working on the site, so he and Trent came on over. Trent left a package for you, said it was something you left at the apartment and that you'd want it. Amy's got it here at her place."

"Is that all he said?" she asked, as Mona pulled into Marissa's apartment complex.

"That's it."

"Well, I'm nearly home. Meet me at my place with that package."

"And then what?"

"Then, I'm going to grovel."

*When all is said and done, never settle for
less than the king Hershey bar.*
—TRENT JACKSON AND MARISSA KINCAID

Chapter 25

Trent leaned back in his recliner and closed his eyes, exhausted physically from lack of sleep, since he'd spent all of last night waiting to see if Rissi would come to his room, then making love to her after she did, and exhausted emotionally, since she'd drained him completely of *all* emotions with her declaration this morning. She wanted the prize. Fine. Let her have it.

He'd spent most of the day postbroadcast with Keith, who, ever the faithful friend, had invited Trent to deliver his little "package" to Amy's apartment complex and then spent the remainder of the afternoon at Trent's townhouse drinking Jack and Coke and listening to Trent vent about the woman who had thoroughly trampled his heart on live television. Amazingly, the venting gave him much more satisfaction than the alcohol. He closed his eyes and decided to give sleep a go. Keith had left only a few moments ago, and while Trent had been glad for the company, he'd also been painfully aware that his body needed to shut down. Completely. As in, turn off the pain of Rissi walking away. And hell, he couldn't deny that part of him was really disappointed she hadn't shown up, telling him she'd made a horrid mistake and begging his forgiveness.

He let his neck relax against the back of the chair and tried to steady his breathing. He needed to calm down, relax, and forget her.

Yeah, right.

A knock sounded at the door. Since no one had requested to be buzzed in, he knew who was on the other side. Keith. He'd never made it out of the building. Probably changed his mind about leaving. He was a good friend, but he was going above and beyond the call of duty. Trent climbed out of his chair, walked to the door, and opened it. "I'm okay. You can go on and—" His words stuck in his throat.

"Keith was on his way out and let me in," Rissi said, those big dark eyes studying his face.

He snarled, not about to let her off the hook easily, if she even wanted off the hook. "That was big of him."

She frowned.

Trent frowned, too. "What do you want, Rissi? Or haven't you done enough damage today?"

"I deserve that," she said. "But I would really—well, I'd like to come in."

He stepped back and waved her through, then inhaled her sweet scent as she entered. God help him, he wanted her, even after this morning. He was a fool, and he needed to get a grip.

She turned, and he saw that she held an item in each hand. In one, her purse, clutched tightly, and in the other, the small box he'd left with Amy, also clutched tightly. She was nervous. Good. Trent closed the door, walked past her en route to his recliner, and sat down.

"Can you explain this?" she asked, moving to sit on the couch, merely a few feet away from Trent, then holding up the box.

"I brought you what you left behind."

"Yeah. I got that. You could have left the batteries in, you know."

He smirked. Removing Pinky's batteries had been his own attempt at a little jab, and he was rather impressed that it had worked.

"I see you smiling," she said. "And for the record, Pinky wasn't what I was asking about. It's the other item in the box."

Trent closed his eyes. He really was tired. Plus, he didn't want to give her the impression he cared . . . too much. "The other item?"

"This," she said, and he wedged one eye open to see her holding the tiny silver-wrapped drop of chocolate.

"It's a Hershey's kiss," he said, then let his eyelid fall back into place. Damn, it felt good to close his eyes, and to see her here, in his townhouse, where he wanted her. But he wouldn't let her know that. Not now. The sting from this morning was still a little too raw, and he wanted to hear what she had to say about it. So he'd listen . . . with his eyes closed.

"I know it's a Hershey's kiss," she said. "But Amy said you were bringing me something I left at the apartment, and I didn't leave a Hershey's kiss."

"I was talking about Pinky."

"O-kay," she said, and even though he didn't open his

eyes, he could tell she'd moved closer. How close was she? It didn't matter. He wouldn't give her the satisfaction of caring enough to look.

"Then why did you give me the kiss?" she asked, and dammit if he didn't feel her breath against his right ear and smell her peach-scented shampoo.

He opened his eyes and turned his head to face her, which put their lips mere centimeters apart. "I gave you the kiss to remind you."

"Remind me of what?" she asked, not backing away from the close proximity, and even moving a fraction closer.

"That a kiss is never enough to satisfy. That a kiss will only make you want more, and you'll never be happy with less than what you want. I gave you that to prove that what you really want is the big king Hershey bar, and you gave that up. You're settling for the kiss." He was suddenly very awake, and very pissed. He wanted to make her hurt, the way she had hurt him this morning. And he wanted to kiss her and hold her and love her, the way he had last night. The woman was going to be the death of him.

"That's what I thought you'd say," she whispered, those dark eyes drinking him in as she looked down at the purse still clutched in her hand. She opened it, then slid her hand inside and withdrew . . . a king Hershey bar. "A kiss *isn't* enough," she said. "And I was a fool to think I could settle for anything less than what I want."

"What do you want, Rissi?"

"I want you. I wanted you last night. I wanted you this morning. And I want you for the rest of my life. I was scared, I'll admit it, because of what I've seen my father put my mother through. I don't want that for me."

"I'd never do that to you, Rissi. I've wanted to throttle you all day, but I've loved you the entire time. I can't stop loving you. I won't."

Her chin quivered. "You know the guy on the site, the one who said I cried when—"

"I know," he said, interrupting her, because he couldn't bear to think about any other bastard who might have been lucky enough to sleep with Rissi.

"Well, that time, I cried because I *thought* I was making love for the first time." Her eyes shimmered with fresh tears. "But last night, I cried because I *knew*. I love you, Trent, and I've never been in love with anyone else. This is real, and I don't want to live without it, not anymore." She sniffed, then inched so close that her warmth penetrated the tiny distance between them. "Can you forgive me for this morning?"

So much for making her wait. He wrapped an arm around her and pulled her onto his lap. "It won't be easy, but if you work at it, really hard, I might be able to find it in my heart to forgive you for humiliating me royally on live TV and radio."

"Ouch," she said. "I really am sorry. What more do you want? Just tell me, and I'll do it." Her throat pulsed, and one tear spilled free.

He brushed the tear away with his hand. "Oh, well, I thought you might want to make it up to me in, let's see, unique and inventive ways." He turned his head toward his dining room, where a big brown box sat in the center of the table.

She blinked, then squinted toward the dining room.

"What is that?" she asked, climbing off his lap and moving toward the box. Then she looked inside and laughed. "Wait a minute. You didn't know I was coming over here."

He puffed out his chest. "Hell, I knew you'd come to your senses eventually."

"You *are* cocky!" she exclaimed, lifting a bottle of massage oil, cotton candy flavored, from the box filled with goodies from Landon's company. "And do you really expect us to go through all of these?" She held up an industrial-sized box of flavored condoms.

"Actually, there's a particular one I wanted to try first, whenever you came to your senses," he added, getting out of the chair. He came up behind her in the dining room and wrapped his arms around her, then nudged her bottom with his pelvis.

"And which one would that be?" she asked.

He reached around her, into the box, and withdrew the condom he'd asked for specifically.

"Oh, my," Rissi said, as he held up the unique item, designed to look like a man in a tuxedo.

"Squeeze his top hat," Trent instructed, a bit of pride in his tone that *he* was actually teaching *her* a thing or two about a sex toy.

Laughing, Rissi squeezed the hat, and the condom promptly belted out the Wedding March. She stopped laughing, tilted her head to look at him. Okay, this wasn't the traditional way he had envisioned proposing to a woman, especially on an afternoon following a public dismissal on morning television and radio. A condom shaped like a groom that played the Wedding March? But then again, this was no traditional woman. This was Rissi

Kincaid, e-zine owner, cheating-guy-basher, noncooker, belly laugher . . . sensual, sexual, maddening . . . the woman he loved.

"Are you—or, well, does this mean what I think it means?" she stammered.

Trent got down on one knee. "I haven't got a ring yet, darling, since I was rather tied up this week, living in an apartment with a woman who professed to hate me, but I'm hoping we can shop for one soon, because I don't want to wait any longer than necessary to be your husband. And, for now, *that* was the most unique way to show you what I want. I want you, forever."

She pressed the hat again and laughed. "I can't believe it. He's playing the Wedding March!"

"Well, he's not just whistling Dixie," Trent said with a grin. "And you still haven't answered me, darling."

"Just a second," she said, and barreled through the other bizarre items in the box.

Trent waited. And waited. And waited. "You realize I don't plan to stay on my knees forever."

"I'm looking to see if Amy has what I need."

"What you need?"

She nodded, then shrugged. "I guess I'll have to let Landon know there's a condom that would be very useful, particularly for occasions like this."

"Care to describe it?" he asked.

"It'd be in the shape of a bride, and when you squeezed her veil, she'd scream, *Yes, Yes, Yes!*"

Trent grabbed her and they tumbled to the floor. Then he kissed her thoroughly, lovingly, the way he planned to kiss her every day, from this day on. "You realize, since they don't have one like that yet, we'll have to improvise."

"Improvise?"

"I'll let that groom play the Wedding March," he said slyly, "and you scream *Yes, Yes, Yes!*"

The top three things in a man's priority list—a sharp car, a close game, and a hot woman . . . not in that order.
—KEITH PARKER

Chapter 26

Swing, batter, batter, batter. Sha-wing!" Candi Moody chanted from her position on third base. Then she turned, looked at Keith in the opposing dugout, merely feet away from her, and blew him a kiss. "We're going to beat ya, big boy," she said.

Keith merely shook his head and laughed, then he turned to Trent, grabbing a batting helmet in preparation to face the fierce pitcher on the girls' team, and a woman who would be his mother-in-law in two days.

"Daniel's having a rough time at the plate today," Keith said.

Trent watched as Daniel Kincaid took a swing and missed. He'd struck out every time he'd been at bat.

Amy, decked out in full catcher gear behind the plate, screamed, "Stu-rike one!"

Landon, currently on second base and ready to run, heckled his wife. "You call that a strike?"

"Hey, buster," she warned. "Keep that up, and I'll throw you out of this park!"

"You better be nice, Daddy!" Bo yelled from the girls' dugout, where he and Lettie's daughter, Ginny, were playing in the dirt.

Landon smiled, then geared his yell toward the man at the plate. "Come on, Daniel. Don't let her strike you out again!"

Mona did some kind of little dance on the mound—the same dance she'd done with every strike she'd achieved throughout the "rehearsal game"—and Trent laughed so hard he snorted.

It'd actually been Mona's idea that Trent and Marissa should have something unique for their wedding reception, and then Amy's idea that a baseball game would do the trick. Naturally, they wanted to play a "rehearsal game" before the fact, just so they'd have the whole shebang down pat. And because they had so much fun playing. And flirting. Right now, Mona was getting in her share of flirting with her husband, doing his best at the plate, but failing miserably. Bill, Lettie's husband, was also getting in a bit of flirting. He was on first base, and should have been prepared to run when Daniel hit the ball, but he was kissing the first baseman (first basewoman?), his wife.

"I could hit the ball if your shirt wasn't so tight," Daniel complained from the plate, and Mona, totally thrilled that he'd noticed her snug T-shirt, stuck her chest out.

Marissa giggled from her spot at second base, and Mona gave her the thumbs-up sign.

"I've still got it, don't I, baby?" Mona called to Daniel. "Go on, admit it. I do."

He straightened his batter's helmet, then laughed. "I doubt you'll ever lose it, dear."

Keith, thoroughly enjoying having all of their friends playing his favorite sport, turned to Trent and grinned. "Mona's got a pretty good arm."

"I'm not so sure it's that her arm is so good, or that his swing is so bad."

"Show 'em what we've got, girls! Work it, now," Mona instructed, and all of the women on the field mimicked her celebration jig. Marissa put a bit more wiggle in her hips, though, and consequently, Trent's pants became extremely tight along the crotch.

She'd decided that the two of them should abstain from making love for the final month before the wedding. So far, they'd made it twenty-seven days, ten hours, and twenty-two minutes.

Trent had counted every second.

Candi, with her blond ponytail pulled through the back of her baseball cap and dangling down her back, added a shimmy move to her celebration dance that was totally geared toward Keith in the dugout.

"You're killin' me," he told her. Then he looked at Trent and said, "Damn, she's cute."

"Yeah," Trent said, "she's definitely cute," though he was looking at the woman who'd marry him in merely two days, on the one-year anniversary of their first day in Coleman and Speedy's apartment.

"So tell me something," Keith said, still eyeing Candi, while Daniel fouled another ball, and Lettie stopped kissing her husband long enough to chase after it.

"Tell you what?" Trent asked.

"How'd we get so damn lucky?"

Trent grinned. "I think it all started when you were try-ing to help me move DieHardAtlanta into print format, and then you found my name in a cheating database, or something like that."

Keith smiled, obviously recalling that day a year ago when he'd shown Trent the cheater site. "And the whole time, I was just doing my job as your financial advisor. Hell, I was simply trying to see if we could get your name out there for the world to see." He put on his bat-ting gloves, then grabbed an aluminum bat. "Coleman and Speedy sure took care of getting your name out there, didn't they?"

"I'll say they did." Trent had even invited the duo of DJs to the wedding, and had even given them permission to post the highlights on their website. It was the least he could do, given they'd done so much to help all of his dreams come true with Rissi Kincaid.

He watched her take her cap off, blow her rogue curl off her forehead, then put the cap back on. Then he laughed when that adorable curl snuck back down to tickle the edge of her brow. She shrugged, and left it alone this time.

"Think about it. Because of everything that happened back then, I found Candi," Keith said. "Hell, I'd nearly given up on finding a woman I wanted."

"I know." Trent felt the same way about finding Rissi again.

Trent and Keith were the only two in the dugout, since Landon and Bill were on first and second, respectively. During the entire engagement period, Keith hadn't said much about the whole wedding thing, or the fact that he was serving as Trent's best man, since Trent's father had passed on, or the fact that he and Candi were also coming up on their one-year anniversary of dating each other. But evidently, he now decided that the confine of a baseball dugout was the perfect place to get all sentimental.

"You know what's even better about it, about everything happening the way it did?" Keith asked.

"No, but I have a feeling you'll probably tell me."

"Basically, I helped you find the woman you're going to marry."

"That's true," Trent said. "And I'll always owe you big-time for that, won't I?"

"Not really, because I'd say we can call it even."

"How's that?" Trent asked.

"You helped me find the woman I'm going to marry, too, and you even paid me while you were doing it. I did charge you my regular fee for all of that insight back then, you know. And my fee's pretty damn high."

"You're pathetic," Trent said, laughing.

But Candi had vacated her spot on third base, even though Daniel had finally managed to hit the ball, and Amy's husband, Landon, was now rounding second and heading directly toward where Candi should have been.

"What did you say?" she asked, apparently listening in on this bit of male bonding occurring in the dugout. Guys never really got a handle on the fact that those chain-link fences weren't exactly soundproof. Typically, they were only caught cussing in the dugout, but this time, that wasn't what Candi had overheard.

"Busted," Trent said, while Keith shrugged.

"What do you mean?" he asked, playing dumb, and doing a pretty pitiful job of it, as she entered the dugout and poked a finger at his chest.

"You know what I mean, Keith Parker. Did you say what I thought you said, just now, and in the dugout, to Trent, instead of to me?"

"Heard that, did ya?"

Daniel Kincaid was huffing and puffing as though he wished someone would tag him out, but that wasn't happening, since the ball was currently boogying down the third-base line, and the third baseman (basewoman?) was currently interrogating her man in the guys' dugout. Nevertheless, Daniel continued to run, and his wife actually cheered for him from the pitcher's mound.

"Yes, I heard," Candi said, not caring one iota that Daniel was about to score a home run. "And I'm wondering . . . exactly when were you going to say something, well, similar, to me?" she asked.

"Similar to what?" Keith asked, and now both teams began to converge by the guys' dugout, with Mona helping her husband make the walk. He was breathing way too hard to handle it on his own.

"You said Trent helped you find the woman you're going to marry," Candi said, and she eased closer to him. "Is that true?"

"I also said that he paid me at the time," Keith said, "though that doesn't seem to be the part that you're interested in, huh?"

"I've never been interested in your money, though it does make life easier," she answered with a grin. "But I am interested in that other part."

"Which part was that again?" he asked, and she grabbed his chest—more specifically, from the look of things, his nipple—and pinched it hard.

"Damn!" he exclaimed, then grabbed her wrist, and held it.

"I'm waiting," she whispered, their faces merely inches apart.

"We all are," Rissi said, as she moved closer to Trent and grinned at Candi and Keith.

"You really want me to ask you here?" he asked.

"Unless you want me to grab the other one," she said, moving her other hand toward the opposite nipple.

"You got a feisty one there," Daniel said, finally catching his breath. Then, when Mona elbowed him, he added, "And feisty ones are the best kind."

Trent wrapped an arm around Marissa and squeezed her tightly. His future father-in-law was right; feisty ones *were* the best kind. She responded by snuggling against him.

"What's happ'nin'?" Bo asked, edging his way into the dugout with his cousin Ginny beside him. They'd obviously noticed there were more interesting things happening over here than in the girls' dugout.

"Yeah, what's happ'nin'?" Ginny echoed.

"Keith needs to ask Candi a question," Amy told her son, while Landon moved next to her, then scooped Bo up as they watched Keith grow nervous.

"Well, you gonna ask her?" Bo asked, and they all laughed.

"Yeah, are you?" Trent joined in.

Keith grinned. "Candi, will you—" he started, then stopped when Candi held up her palm.

"Uh-uh," she said. "I've waited a long time for this, and if you're going to do it, you'd better do it right."

"The ring is at home," Keith said, obviously baffled.

She smiled. "That's not what I mean by doing it right. On your knees, mister."

Keith's dark brows inched up a notch, then he nodded, and lowered to his knees in the dugout, which was getting pretty crowded now.

"Will this do, my dear?" Keith asked, and though everyone probably wanted to comment, or laugh, or applaud, no one said a word. Everyone was merely watching their special moment take place.

"Yes, it's perfect now," Candi said, smiling through the tears currently slipping down her cheeks. "This is the way I've always pictured it, the man I love proposing to me on one knee."

"I bet you didn't picture him in a dugout, and with a dozen people huddled around him at the time."

"No," she whispered, shaking her head, "but having our friends here just makes it better." She swallowed, paused, then let him take her hand. "Ask me, Keith. Please."

"Candi Moody, will you marry me?"

"Yes," she said, her tears flowing steadily, then she cupped his face and lowered her mouth to his.

"Mom, does that mean I get to go to another wedding, too?" Bo asked, his big green eyes watching Keith and Candi hug and kiss. "And wear another zedo?"

"Tuxedo," Amy said, laughing. "And I imagine that's exactly what it means."

"Cool!" he squealed, and clapped.

"Yes," Keith said, hugging his new fiancée. "Very, very cool."

There's nothing like a good old-fashioned feud to boost ratings, except, maybe, a good old-fashioned wedding.
—SPEEDY

Chapter 27

(Highlights of the Wedding, Courtesy of ColemanAndSpeedy.com)

Since we understand that many of our online listeners weren't able to make the trek to Atlanta for the event of the year, Trent and Marissa's wedding, we have included some of the highlights here on our site. Click the links below to view the invitation, interviews with guests, reception highlights, and last but not least, the famed recipe for Trent's crawfish étouffée, prepared a year ago when he and Marissa spent that famed week in our corporate apartment. And since we want to support our fabulous duo (who landed us the number-one spot in ratings for the week they appeared on the show), we'll also ask you to visit their respective e-zine sites, AtlantaTellAll.com (hers) and DieHardAtlanta.com (his), and don't forget that you can now purchase both in print! Oh, and the sites that started it all, TheGuyCheats.com and TheGirlLies.

com. Both are still open for business, though the primary liar and cheater are now hitched.

Enjoy the highlights from the wedding, and continue to tune in each weekday morning to Coleman and Speedy!

THE INVITATION

Coleman and Speedy cordially invite you to the marriage uniting the previously feuding couple of Trenton Jameson Jackson and Marissa Leola Kincaid. This celebration of love (a love that started courtesy of the Coleman and Speedy show) will be on the eleventh of July at four-thirty in the afternoon.

(Okay. The wedding is actually on the Fourth of July, and we're merely broadcasting the tape on the radio on the eleventh, and no, this isn't the actual invitation. Do you really think we could fit all of our listeners into one location for this ceremony? Which is why you can listen to the ceremony via the radio or your computer.)

INTERVIEWS WITH GUESTS

Mona Kincaid.

"And you're the mother of the bride?" Speedy asked.

"Yes, and I'm thrilled to be here," Mona gushed.

"Would you like to say any words to the happy couple?"

"Of course. Marissa, I'm so glad you've got the man of your dreams. And I'm proud of you, honey, for putting the past where it belongs and looking to the future. That's what your daddy and I are doing, and I couldn't be happier that I'm going after my dream, too."

Daniel Kincaid.

"Any words for the newlyweds?" Speedy asked.

"Trent, we want to welcome you to the family, but if you do anything to hurt her, you're dead."

"Daniel!" Mona scolded.

"Oh, okay, dear. Trent, welcome to our clan. We're glad you're here." He lowered his voice. "And don't you dare mess up."

Landon, Amy, and Bo Brooks.

"We hope Trent and Marissa will be as happy as we are, and we truly expect that to be the case," Amy said.

"Especially with the interesting wedding gift we've provided them from Adventurous Accessories," Landon added with a chuckle.

"I can only imagine what that is," Speedy said, snickering. "And what's your name, little man?"

"Bo. Bo Brooks, and this is Fella."

"Fella?"

"My dog. He's like Petie, Aunt Rissi's dog, but littler. He was just borned two months ago, but he'll get bigger."

"I'm sure he will," Speedy said. "And are you having fun at the wedding?"

"Yeah, but I'm ready to play baseball."

"He's talking about the reception," Amy informed Speedy.

"Right. And if you're tuning in, we'll cover that, too, in a little bit," Speedy said.

Candi Moody and Keith Parker.

"Any words for the happy couple?" Speedy asked.

"Yes," Keith said. "We want to wish you both the best."

"And we want to thank you," Candi added. "Your web

war brought the two of us together, and we'll be walking down the aisle at our own wedding this Christmas. Thanks for helping me find this amazing man!"

"Wow, all you listeners out there, I wish you could see this! I've never seen a clinch like this!" Then Speedy cleared his throat. "Okay," he said. "Moving right along."

Jamie Abernathy and Gerald Hopkins.

"I'd like to congratulate Marissa for finding that perfect guy. There's nothing like finding the right man," Jamie said.

"I agree," Gerald added. "I'd never have met Jamie, a guy who appreciates both me and my love of the symphony, without Marissa's site. Thanks again for helping me see the light."

"And we have another clinch, folks!" Speedy said, then cleared his throat again. "And we'll keep going."

LaDonna Farraday, Robin Grenade, and "Crazy Irene."

LaDonna: "I am really happy for them. I mean, I never really meant all that stuff about him having bad breath. He just dropped me, without warning, and I was pissed, so I wanted to make him look bad. But that morning when Marissa turned him down on live TV, I felt vindicated. And I didn't mind all that much when they worked things out and got together. Besides, I got an invite to the wedding, and they've got great cake."

Robin: "Okay, I'll admit I lied about his less-than-favorable anatomy, but that's all I'm going to say about that. Like LaDonna, I was pissed, and when women get pissed, they get even. Take that to heart, all you men out there listening."

Crazy Irene: "Well, I worked for Trent, and I never dated him or anything like that, but I sure would have if he had asked. He's the kindest, most thoughtful, sweetest, most handsome—"

"Um, Irene, is it?" Speedy interrupted.

She sniffed, loudly and grossly. "Yeah?"

"We're going to have to move on."

RECEPTION HIGHLIGHTS

"We're at the most unique wedding reception I've ever attended," Coleman said. "What do you think, Speedy?"

"Never been to one like it," Speedy said. "Not that I mind. I've always loved baseball."

"Well, for our listening audience, let me describe what's happening. The bride, bridesmaids, and the bride's mother are gathered in one dugout and wearing white uniforms. The groom, groomsmen, and bride's father are in the other and wearing black uniforms. And Bo Brooks, son of Landon and Amy Brooks, is getting set to throw out the first pitch of the game," Coleman said.

"And there it is. A nice throw, for a four-year-old," Speedy said.

"Since the ladies wanted the home-team advantage, the guys will be the first at bat," Coleman relayed. "Ladies, can I ask you a few questions before you start?"

"Sure!" Marissa answered, giggling.

"We're talking to the bride, who will be playing second base."

"And letting my husband get to first base tonight," she said. "Then second, third, and definitely home."

Laughter rang out around her, while Coleman cleared his throat. "Family show, dear."

"Right," Marissa said. "Sorry, I'm excited."

"No problem," Speedy said. "So Marissa, tell us why you decided on a baseball game for the reception. I heard it was your idea."

"It was actually Amy's idea. She thought of it one night while we were working on our e-zine," Marissa said.

"And drinking a few margaritas," Candi added.

"Care to enlighten our listeners?" Coleman asked.

"Sure," Marissa said. "Are all of you ready?" she asked her cohorts.

"Baseball tickets, ten dollars," Amy said.

"Hot dog, two dollars," Mona said.

"Coke, a dollar-fifty," Candi added.

"Guys in baseball pants . . ." Marissa said, then whistled.

The men laughed from their dugout, while the women yelled in unison . . . "Priceless!"

AND LAST, BUT NOT LEAST, THE RECIPE

Trent Jackson's Crawfish Étouffée

1 pound crawfish tails
1½ to 2 blocks of butter
½ cup chopped green onions
1 chopped onion
1 small chopped bell pepper
½ cup chopped celery
1 tablespoon parsley
1 can golden mushroom soup
½ teaspoon garlic powder
½ teaspoon paprika

Sauté crawfish tails in butter. Remove tails, add chopped vegetables, and sauté until tender. Add garlic powder and paprika, stir well. Add soup, one can of water, and crawfish tails. Cook about 20 minutes. Serve over cooked rice, pasta, or broiled fish.

(Trent's recipe provided by amazing Cajun chefs Doug and Gay Duhon of Grand Point, Louisiana.)

About the Author

Kelley St. John's previous experience as a senior writer at NASA fueled her interest in writing action-packed suspense, although she also enjoys penning steamy romances and quirky women's fiction. Since 2000, St. John has obtained more than fifty writing awards, including the National Readers' Choice Award, and was elected to the Board of Directors for Romance Writers of America. Visit her website, www.kelleystjohn.com, to learn the latest news about recent and upcoming releases and to register for fabulous vacation and spa giveaways!

The lovin' ain't over!

~

Please turn this page for
an excerpt from
Kelley St. John's
next sexy novel,

*The Trouble
with Men*

available in mass market
November 2008.

Chapter 1

Throughout her thirty-three years, Babette Robinson had sported eight hair colors (red, blond, brunette, platinum, strawberry-blond, auburn, black, and pink), obtained four college degrees (Accounting, Business Administration, Computer Information Systems, and Photography), and held a total of twenty-two part-time jobs (way too many to list). However, in none of those positions could she ever recall getting hit on by an eighty-two-year-old in a wheelchair.

"Mr. Wiggins!" she scolded, turning to view his sneaky little grin, nearly hidden in a sea of wrinkles, and two wiggling wiry silver eyebrows.

"Got your attention, didn't I?" he asked, holding up the thumb and forefinger that had just pinched her behind.

"Yes, you got my attention. But trust me, *that's* not the way you want to get my attention." She lowered her voice. "I fight dirty."

Another eyebrow wiggle. "Tell me more."

"In other words, I know where they keep the poppy seed container in the kitchen," she continued smartly.

He brought a weathered hand to his cheek and obviously recalled his lunch two days ago, when a poppy seed had ended up between his gums and his dentures. "Ouch. You didn't do that, did you?"

"No, but you didn't pinch my butt that morning either." Babette smiled and squatted at eye level with him in the wheelchair. "We understand each other?"

He straightened in his seat and leaned forward, then blatantly attempted to peer down the front of her camisole.

She slapped a hand between her breasts to hold the fabric close. Have mercy, if he was that eager to take a peek at her tiny excuses for boobs, then he really was in sad shape. "Mr. Wiggins, you're playing with fire here."

"Any chance of me getting burned?" he asked. "You know, your grandmother said you were originally a redhead." He indicated her hair, currently straight and blond. "Redheads are known for fire, aren't they?"

"Ethel, we still have plenty of poppy seed in the kitchen, right?" she called to one of the assisted living center's cooks, currently leaning against the door frame and shaking her head at Lambert Wiggins.

Ethel answered loudly. "Yes, we do, and I ain't afraid to use it, Lambert."

He stuck his tongue out at the cook, then turned back to Babette. "Oh, all right, I give, and I'm going to have to agree with the other old farts around here. You're more like her."

Babette followed his gaze to see her grandmother, currently engrossed in a game of Canasta with three of the women who resided at Shady Pines. Gertrude Robinson didn't live here, but she visited regularly, partly because she liked the socializing, but mostly because she and her partner Maud were the reigning Canasta champs. Consequently, she'd gotten Babette this new job, a part-time deal where she simply made sure all of the residents had some type of activity that they could participate in during their free time. She was kind of like a cruise director, without the ship, and with a bunch of passengers who no longer had their teeth.

But Babette enjoyed the job and had already been employed at the center for a whopping two weeks. If she made it six more, she'd break her all-time employment record. "Are you talking about Granny Gert?"

"Yep, and the guys were right. You're more like her. I met the other one, your sister. She comes here every now and then with the kids. Folks round here love little kids. The guys"—he pointed to the group of men gathered in the television area of the recreation room watching *Wheel of Fortune*—"they said she was the sweet one, and that you were the feisty one, like Gertrude."

Babette swallowed, then nodded. The story of her life. Clarise was the sweet child; she was the hellion. Clarise was the stable one, the one who went to college—once—got the degree, made a career choice, and stuck with it. Then she found the perfect guy—and again, it only took once to find the right one—settled down, and had a beautiful set of twins. And now Clarise was visiting the assisted living center on her own time, without having to get paid for it, and earning the admiration of the older crowd, including Lambert Wiggins.

Meanwhile, Lambert Wiggins was pinching Babette's bottom.

Something that she appreciated even less now.

"Hey, wait," he said, his tone shifting gears faster than her beat-up CRX, and that sucker could fly. He held up his palms defensively. "I didn't mean anything bad by that. Shoot, I like feisty better, myself." He grinned again, then looked toward the women now fussing over who had played what during the last hand of cards. "Being like Gertrude isn't a bad thing," he continued. "Not bad at all."

This time, Babette's brows lifted. "You want to hook up with my grandmother, don't you?"

"Nope, I tried that already. You think I'd have wasted this much time before asking a pistol like her out? Shoot, I gave it a go the day I moved in here. She turned me down flat. Would've hurt my ego, if I was a normal man."

"A normal man?"

"Ask her what she calls me," he instructed. "It should bother me, but I like it." He winked and clicked his tongue against the roof of his mouth. "It suits me."

As if knowing she was the main topic of this conversation, Granny Gert waved at them. "Babette," she called. "Come here, honey." She curled hot-pink-tipped fingers urgently, which sent her multitude of charm bracelets clanging, and Babette heeded the instruction.

"I'll talk to you later, Mr. Wiggins, and you'd better learn to keep those hands to yourself." She walked away, but could hear him laughing behind her.

"Honestly, what are we going to do with him?" Granny Gert said to the other women at the table. "He just pinched my granddaughter's butt." She looked up at Babette. "Didn't he? I saw it, out of the corner of my eye, and I swear that's why I botched that last hand."

"Oh, stow it, Gert," Flora Halliday said, then she motioned toward her cards on the table. "We beat you, fair and square, and you're just looking for excuses. Admit it."

"Now, you know me better than that, Flora," Granny said. "I'll admit no such thing."

Babette pulled up a chair and sat at the table while Flora, still grinning smugly from her victory, shuffled the cards for another round.

"You needed me, Granny?" Babette couldn't deny that Lambert had pegged Granny Gert correctly; she was definitely feisty, from the way she spoke to the way she dressed. Today's apparel was perfect for the July weather, a hot pink silk dress with a shiny white collar and cuffs. She looked as if she belonged on the cover of *AARP* magazine. Babette aspired to look that good when she hit retirement status. Then again, would "retire" be the right word, since at her current rate, she'd never be at one job long enough to warrant retirement? Granny smiled, plumping up her cheeks, embellished a little too brightly with pink glitter blush, the exact same hue as her glossed lips.

"Actually, Flora wanted to ask you something," she said.

Flora's silver brows puckered and she pursed her lips. "I did?"

"Oh, for Pete's sake," Maud Lovette, Granny Gert's Canasta partner, spouted. "Come on, Flora. You just said you wanted to hear how she hitched up those two." She pointed to the other side of the room, where an elderly couple Babette recognized as Sara Tolleson and Jed Lackey sat cozily near the window. They were holding hands and chatting, the picture of young love, even if they were both well past seventy.

"That's right, I did," Flora said. "Gertrude said you're good at matchmaking, that you helped Sara hook up with Jed. She's been trying to get the nerve to talk to him for a year, and now they're all settled in over there, flirting even. And Gert said you made it happen. Is that right?" She shuffled the cards wildly as she spoke and wasn't disguising her interest in Babette's matchmaking abilities. "Well, is it? Did you do that?"

Babette, along with the rest of the women at the table, watched Jed tenderly stroke a hand down Sara's cheek, while she promptly blushed. "He wanted to meet her, too," Babette said. "They just needed someone to set the wheels in motion. That's all I did."

"Uh-huh," Flora said. "Well, we've needed somebody like you around here for quite some time, a very long time, in fact." She smacked the deck of cards on the table and pointed a finger at Babette. "I'm next."

"Next?"

Flora nodded. "Fix me up with Hosea. I've tried everything known to man to get him to look my way, and nothing works. I've been signing up for two beauty shop days every week, I've kept my nails painted—but then again, I always did that."

"Yep, you're real good with your nails," Maud said, leaning over to inspect Flora's latest color, a dusty rose, not nearly as bright as Granny's polish, but then again, none of the women at the center wore anything nearly as bright as Granny Gert.

"I've even signed up for Bingo on Tuesdays and Thursdays, and I don't even like Bingo," she said, then glanced at Hosea. "But he really seems to enjoy it. I just wish that he'd glance up from his game card every now and then to socialize. I mean, I'm sitting there hoping that some-time between B-1 and O-60, he'll notice that I'm across the table." She shrugged. "Hasn't happened yet. But then again, he really gets into the game. We play for money, you know."

"I know." Babette had sat in on the Bingo games the previous week and did agree that Hosea came to life dur-ing the game, particularly last Thursday, when he won the jackpot, a whole twenty-seven dollars and thirty-four cents.

Flora leaned around Babette to view the man in ques-tion. "He's got a whole lot of energy, and is a whole lot of fun, when he's awake."

Babette twisted around to view Hosea, his long legs crossed in front of him and his hands folded on top of his belly as he slept in one of the loungers near the television. He wore his trademark attire, old navy Dickies workpants and a matching button-up shirt. He looked as if he'd been plucked out of a Norman Rockwell painting, the sleeping old man enjoying retirement to the fullest. Babette tried to remember if she'd ever seen the man awake when he wasn't playing Bingo. If she had, she couldn't recall it.

"Does he only wake up for Bingo?"

Granny Gert laughed, then stifled it when Flora shot her a look of warning. "Sorry, Flo," she said.

"He's kind of funny that way," Flora said. "He's up with the birds, like me. I usually see him in here before breakfast, and he stays awake for Bingo, naturally. But during the rest of the day, he naps a bit . . ."

"A bit?" Maud interjected, and again, Flora sent a look

of elderly venom her way. "Okay, okay. I'll hush. Don't get huffy."

"Then he's up at night in time for the shows."

"The shows?" Babette asked.

"*House*, *CSI Miami*, *CSI Las Vegas*, *CSI New York*, *ER*, you know, the shows. Tonight is *CSI Miami*, you know, since it's Monday."

"Ohhh, right," Babette said. "And you want me to . . ."

"Do whatever it is you do to let him know I wouldn't mind being courted."

"Have mercy, I had no idea when I set Babette up with this job that she'd become the eHarmony of Shady Pines," Granny Gert said, but Babette was still looking at Hosea, sleeping peacefully, and Flora, smiling like a schoolgirl as she gazed at him.

"I'll do my best." Babette was also surprised that the men and women here, most in their seventies and eighties, found it difficult to simply express their feelings toward each other. She had merely mentioned to Jed that Sara found him "rather interesting" and to Sara that Jed "felt the same" and then the two were "courting," as they called it, which she found endearing.

She had no doubt that she could probably help Flora and Hosea the same way and truthfully looked forward to making it happen. It'd been a while since she'd felt really good about something she did on the job, and although matchmaking for the elderly wasn't technically part of her job description at Shady Pines, it did make her feel as though she was doing something worthwhile. True, she always felt a smidgen of pride when she viewed a Eubanks Elegant Apparel catalog and saw the photographs she'd taken gracing every page, but this was different.

That work affected the company's sales, but this—this affected people's lives.

She could get used to having that kind of impact.

"Fine then," Flora said, with a sharp single nod that said she considered the matter taken care of; then she dealt the cards.

Four hours later, after waiting for *CSI Miami* to start and verifying that Hosea had heeded Babette's advice to ask Flora to sit with him for the show, Babette climbed into the passenger's seat of Granny Gert's Camry. She could have driven herself to the center, but Granny played cards here every Monday during Babette's work hours, and Granny Gert loved to drive. There weren't many of her friends still driving, so she felt rather special that her family hadn't required her to hand over the keys. And why should they? Gertrude Robinson was still sharp as a tack and had perfect vision and a perfect driving record. Plus, if they even attempted to take her keys, she'd probably fight them to the finish, and with her "gumption," as she called it, she'd probably win.

"You didn't mind staying here this long?" Babette asked.

"Shoot, I enjoyed watching you in action. And to see Flora do something other than snarl for a change was worth a few hours of my time. Typically, I only see her smile when she beats me at cards, and Lord knows, that's a rare occurrence." She cranked the car and backed up, then headed out of the center. "Wanna pick up some Boston Market? I'm craving creamed spinach."

"Sure." Babette watched the woman Lambert had deemed "feisty" drive her car with her trademark air of confidence. He'd said Babette was like her. Babette would have to agree, for the most part; however, when Gertrude Robinson was Babette's age, she'd been married for a good thirteen years. Not that Babette wanted to get married or anything like that, but if they were so alike, why hadn't she at least considered the possibility?

Evidently, Babette was staring, because at the next red light, Granny turned and tilted her head. Her bold platinum curls glistened beneath the streetlamp. "Go on. Tell me."

"Tell you what?"

"What's on your mind, child. You're never this quiet, and you should be talking nonstop after your matchmaking went so well. Flora was absolutely beaming."

"Yeah, but Hosea looked like he could fall asleep at any moment," Babette reminded her.

Granny Gert lifted one shoulder. "Phfft, he always looks like that. Well, unless he's won a game of Bingo, but I could tell there was a twinkle in his eye. Hey, when's your next workday at the center?"

"Wednesday."

"I bet by the time you go back, they'll be officially courting, and it'll be your doing. Flora was giving it her best shot by flirting with him, but you know, after sixty, flirting just doesn't come as easy. Matter of fact, after sixty, lots of things don't come as easy," she said, smiling.

"I'm really happy things seem to be working out for Flora."

"And yet you look like something's wrong. What is it?"

What was it? Granny Gert was right; she should be

feeling pretty good right now. She'd helped two couples get together at the center, and without all that much effort on her part. Now they were courting, and there were four fewer people in the world feeling alone.

Well, hell. *That* was it. Babette was feeling alone. Why? She'd had plenty of dates lately. No more than three with the same person, except for Jeff Eubanks, and that'd been, well, a while—nearly a year, in fact. But all of the guys she'd dated recently would have gone out with her on a regular basis, if that's what Babette wanted, which it wasn't.

So why did seeing all of the single people at Shady Pines bother her so much?

Simple. A part of her was starting to wonder if she'd be old and single and lonely one day, simply because she didn't feel the need or desire to connect with someone, to rely on someone, to give her heart to someone. Hell, she'd never even committed to a job for longer than eight weeks; why would her dating life be any different? And maybe she was the type that wouldn't mind going solo throughout life. She was having fun, after all. And if those folks at the assisted living center were alone, they obviously wanted to be that way.

No, not true. Flora wanted Hosea, and Sara wanted Jed. How many others at Shady Pines had met someone there whom they'd like to know better, yet were afraid to go for what they wanted? And why wouldn't someone go for the person she wanted, especially if that person was right in front of her nose?

Babette always did. When she wanted to get to know a guy better, she found a way to make it happen. It wasn't all that difficult. Again, Jeff came to mind, and again,

Babette pushed him out. Now was not the time to try to figure out what had happened then.

"Babette?" Granny Gert questioned, as the light turned green and she continued toward Boston Market.

"What do you call Lambert?" Babette asked, both because she wanted to know, and because she didn't want to try to explain what she was currently thinking.

"Lambert? *That's* who's on your mind?" Her doubt was evident in her tone.

"Yes." *And Jeff Eubanks.* "He said that you call him something, and that it should bother him, but he likes it. What do you call him?"

She grinned, and even though it was dark outside, Babette could tell Gertrude Robinson's glittery cheeks were a little more rosy than usual.

"What?" Babette asked.

"I call him a player with a heart."

"A player?"

"Surely that term is still around, isn't it?" Granny Gert asked. She parked at the restaurant and turned off the car.

"Yes, we still say player. But what do you mean by a player with a heart?"

"Lambert Wiggins flirts with every lady at that center, every one of them, and he acts as though he could care less whether any of them get hooked on him or not, that it won't change the way he's acting, or make him settle down. But there's a sweet spot in that man, and while he tries to come across like he doesn't care, he does. And I'd venture to say he cares quite a lot."

"You like him?" Babette wasn't quite certain whether she was asking a question or stating a fact. It'd been over ten years since Grandpa Henry had passed on, but still, she didn't really think of her grandmother as "available."

"Heavens, no." Granny Gert shook her head and caused her big, bold waves to shift against her temple. "I've had his type before, and while it was good the first time, that isn't what I want again. I don't want to mess up the memory of the original." She climbed out of the car, while Babette's jaw dropped. She'd had his type before? What did that mean?

"You are going to explain that, aren't you?" she asked, following Granny Gert inside.

Her grandmother placed their order, knowing Babette well enough to know she'd want a vegetable plate, and even picking the very vegetables Babette would have selected, creamed spinach, corn, and green beans. Then, ignoring Granny Gert's protest, Babette paid for their food.

"You wait until your money situation is better," Granny said, but Babette shook her head.

"I may not be rolling in it, but I'm not going to have you buying my dinner." Truth was, dinner at Boston Market was the extent of what she could provide her grandmother now, but she wasn't about to take a handout from Granny Gert or anyone else. Besides, she should receive her check for the last Eubanks catalog she had shot any day now, and even though she only took photographs for them a couple of times a year, it still paid pretty well. Or rather, it paid more than most of her part-time jobs, not that that was saying much.

"I asked you a question." She grabbed the to-go sack and followed Granny Gert out of the restaurant.

"Well, I couldn't very well tell you in there, with

those people listening and all," Granny said as she got into the car.

"Tell me what?"

"That your Grandpa Henry was like Lambert Wiggins, quite a lot like him, in fact. He was a big flirt, and he acted like he didn't care about anyone but himself."

Babette remembered her grandfather, the way he always looked as if he was on the verge of laughing, and the way he teased and flirted with her grandmother, right up until he died. They would give Sara and Jed a run for their money in the cuddling department, but Henry and Gertrude Robinson had been together for years, where Sara and Jed were still in the courting stage.

"He was a player, you know, kept all the girls hanging around and pining for him, every one of them thinking she was his one and only, when he didn't want to settle down, or that's what he wanted everyone to think."

"But you saw through that."

"Sure I did. I'm nobody's fool, and I sure wasn't a fool when it came to Henry Robinson. Sure, the man was hard to get, but I always liked a challenge." She opened her hands on the steering wheel and wiggled her fingers, then held out her left hand and let her tiny diamond catch the moonlight. "And all it took was proving to him that he couldn't live without me. I snagged him that way when we were teens, and I kept him that way until the day he died." She laughed softly. "He didn't want to care about a girl that much—he told me so—but he did, and I can honestly say that I never regretted a bit of the effort it took to make him realize that."

"You said you didn't want that type *again*," Babette

pointed out as they pulled back onto the highway. "Are you thinking about dating again?"

Granny Gert's mouth twitched a little, then she whispered, "I'd be lying if I said the thought of spending time with a man again hasn't crossed my mind. I mean, living next door to Clarise, and now you, means I've always got someone to talk to, and I do have my visits to Shady Pines to occupy my time, but there's just something different about living with someone, having that person be a part of everything you do. And don't get me wrong, no one could ever take Henry's place in my heart, but I really don't think he'd have intended me to live alone forever, do you?"

Babette heard the concern in her grandmother's voice, as though she were wondering whether Grandpa Henry would have in fact wanted her to stay single the remainder of her life, even though, by all appearances, she still had quite a lot of life left to live. How long had Granny Gert been thinking about dating again? And how long had she resisted admitting it? Did she feel guilty about it? Because she shouldn't; she was right, after all. Grandpa Henry wouldn't have wanted her to be alone, and perhaps he'd have wanted Babette to help her out.

"He definitely wouldn't have wanted you alone," she said. "He wanted you happy, and he'd want you happy now." She paused, then asked, "Is there someone at the center that you're wanting to meet, Granny? Because, you know, my track record with matchmaking there is running a hundred percent." She smiled, and so did Granny.

"Oh, no, child." She waved at Milton in the guard station as she pulled into their apartment complex. "I mean, I haven't got anyone in mind. I've just been thinking that it might be nice, if I happened to run across an interesting man."

"Someone who isn't a player with a heart, this time," Babette said.

"Right. It—well, that was your granddaddy's place, and I wouldn't want to try to have someone compete with him there. There's no way to compete with Henry anyway. He's the love of my life and the father of my kids, you know. But somebody different, perhaps."

"Well, if you figure out who you'd like to meet, and if I can help . . ."

"That's what I was thinking. If I do meet someone, I may actually take advantage of your talent in that area, because you really are good at matchmaking, dear. You've got a way of putting the right people together, whether you realize it or not. And someday, I may just put that talent to use for myself, if I do ever meet a guy who suits my fancy." She parked the car, grabbed the food sack, and climbed out. "But for now, I'm quite content living next door to my granddaughter and letting you keep me company."

Babette smiled, but inside she wondered how Granny Gert would ever handle it if Babette eventually met someone who "suited her fancy" and ended up moving away. Granny had spent a lot of her time visiting with Clarise when Clarise had lived next door, and now she spent that time with Babette, since Babette had moved into Clarise's old apartment. Truthfully, Gertrude Robinson didn't like being alone, at all, and so far, the situation had never required it. But what if it did? What if Babette found the "right guy" one day and settled down and got married, perhaps moving away from here?

Babette blinked. What was she talking about? She hadn't even thought of any guy as "right" before. Usually, she simply thought of all of them as wrong. So Granny's constant need for companionship was covered, for now. Besides, at the rate Babette's love life was going, barely sticking with a guy for a third date, Granny would probably find her perfect fellow way before Babette did.

"You know," Granny said, unlocking her apartment door and heading inside, "I've got a dentist appointment Wednesday, so I won't be going to the center the next time you work, but Maud said she wanted to talk to you about getting together with Lloyd Tinsley, and believe it or not, Lambert said he needed to talk to you about something 'confidential,' too."

"Lambert?"

"I'll admit that he looked like he was up to something," Granny Gert said. "But who knows, maybe he really does have his eye on someone special there. Stranger things have happened." She put the food bag on the table, then gathered utensils. "You want to fix the tea?"

"Sure." Babette soon had two big glasses of sweet tea with lemon next to their plates. They sat down, and Granny Gert quickly started on her chicken, but Babette didn't have food on her mind. She was wondering about the men and women at Shady Pines, and about men and women in general.

Granny stopped eating, wiped her hands on her napkin, and looked at Babette. "What is it?"

"Why is it so hard for them to just tell each other how they feel? I mean, they've obviously lived for quite a while, and they don't have tons of time to waste . . ."

Granny laughed softly. "You realize I'm in that category."

"Oh, sorry."

"Don't be. You're simply stating the facts." She placed her napkin on the table. "And it's true. Life would be easier if we'd simply find enough gumption to come out and say, 'Hey, I like you, and neither of us is a spring chicken. Why don't we spend some time together?' That'd be easy enough to ask, if we had the nerve." Granny turned, looked at the black-and-white wedding portrait centered on the wall above her mantel, and at the ornate urn beneath it. "But even back then, as crazy as I was about Henry, I was still a little nervous about letting him know how I felt. I don't know if it's that normal fear of rejection or something else, but people are kind of timid about putting their heart out on the line, aren't they? With Henry, though, I simply decided he was worth it, and I cornered him one day in his barn and told him that I had a mind to kiss him, and then after that, I planned to marry him."

Unfortunately, Babette had just taken a big sip of tea and nearly spewed it all over the table. Finally, she managed to swallow and then laughed. "You didn't."

"I most certainly did," Granny Gert said with a nod.

"And what did he do?"

"He asked me what I was waiting for." Her glossy pink lips grew fuller with her grin, and Babette suddenly found it very easy to see why her grandfather had always said he married Granny Gert for her gumption.

"Why didn't either of you ever tell us that story? I just assumed he courted you the old-fashioned way—you know, spending a little time together, then he asked you out, then you dated awhile, and then, eventually, you got married."

"Why waste all that time, when you know what you want?" Again, Granny Gert's attention drifted to the portrait on the mantel and the urn that held Grandpa Henry's ashes. "I suppose I never mentioned how I caught him because that was our little secret. But now that I'm thinking about perhaps seeing someone again, I realize that it was very hard to put myself out there, and really try to gain Henry Robinson's attention." She shrugged slightly. "I'm not sure that I can do it again, and after hearing the other women at the center talk about how they have a hard time meeting the men they want to meet, I realize that most people never do venture out of that comfort zone. I guess now I feel rather proud that I did it, even once."

Babette pondered the guys she'd dated and tried to determine whether she'd *ever* ventured out of her own comfort zone for any of them. No, she hadn't. Did that mean she hadn't met the guy who was worth that venture, or did it mean she hadn't inherited Granny Gert's gumption after all?

"I don't think I could do it again," Granny said. "Be so blunt with a man and tell him what I want. I'm thinking most people can't, because if they could, then those people at the center wouldn't need your help, would they?"

"I guess not."

"It's funny, though. I mean, we're all mature—very mature—adults, and you'd think that we'd be able to handle pretty much everything by now. But while I may be seventy on the outside, inside I still feel like I'm seventeen. Still get nervous around men, still get excited about driving a car, still like getting all gussied up with my hair and my makeup and my clothes, still—well—seventeen."

"How old were you when you propositioned Grandpa Henry in that barn?"

Granny Gert laughed. "Propositioned. It sounds so risqué, doesn't it?" Then she smiled, and her cheeks turned rosy. "I like that idea. Me, risqué and daring and full of gumption." She paused. "I was seventeen."

"You know what's really funny, Granny? I'm thirty-three, and I don't believe I've ever had nearly the amount of gumption that it took for you to approach Grandpa Henry that day in the barn. I've never put myself out there for a guy like that, and I'm nearly twice the age that you were when you did. What does that say about me?"

Granny Gert's grin climbed even higher into her cheeks and she winked at Babette. "I believe it says that it's high time you give it a try."

THE DISH

Where authors give you the inside scoop!

♥ ♥ ♥ ♥ ♥ ♥ ♥ ♥ ♥ ♥ ♥ ♥ ♥ ♥ ♥

A Note to Readers from Paige Darlington
(SEX & THE IMMORTAL BAD BOY)
and Marissa Kincaid
(TO CATCH A CHEAT)

Marissa: We want to talk to you about liars and cheats. Wait—no—something more positive.

Paige: Oh, fantastic idea! I'm all about being positive. How about being turned into an evil wraith who answers to Satan? Or about being caught in a turf battle between Satan and his sociopathic son, Satan Junior? No? I guess that still isn't very positive, is it? Tell you what, you tell me something positive about liars and cheats, and I'll tell you something positive about being consumed by evil and groomed to destroy the world.

Marissa: Okay, I've got it. Let's talk about a woman who has been cheated on by every man in her life and is finally going to make them all pay. Yeah, that's a positive spin on it.

Paige: You sound as if you're speaking from experience.

Marissa: Who, me?

Paige: Okay, to make them pay, what exactly does she do? Because my idea of making people pay—well, we're probably talking about two different kinds of making people pay.

Marissa: I—um, she—created a cheater database where women could list the guys who've cheated on them in the past and could also check potential dates to see if they'd cheated before.

Paige: Hmm . . . sounds like a database Satan could use. Brilliant idea.

Marissa: Yeah, it would've been, if the first cheater listed had actually cheated. And if he hadn't retaliated with his own Web site identifying women who lie. And if he hadn't put me—I mean, her—as the liar of the month.

Paige: Oh, wow. I'm feeling your pain, girlfriend. Is he hot? Because if he is, I'm thinking maybe you could have fun making him pay . . .

Marissa: Anyway, what about something positive about "wraithhood" and Satan?

Paige: Well, I guess that it's helping me organize my career goals. I've crossed being an evil being who kowtows to Satan off my list. But I'm thinking I need to hire someone tough enough to handle me and keep me from turning wraith while I try to get things resolved.

Marissa: Got someone in mind?

Paige: Oh, yeah.

Marissa: Then your problems are solved.

Paige: Not exactly. Satan Junior's holding his brother hostage, and Junior won't release his brother until he delivers the goods.

Marissa: The goods . . . as in you?

Paige: As in me.

Wouldn't it be nice if life (and wraithhood) was easy?

So, readers, let our authors know what you think about liars and cheats, Satan (and Satan Jr.), and the men who complicate all of the above or anything else. They love hearing from you!

Sincerely,

Stephanie   *Kelley St. John*

Paige Darlington, of   Marissa Kincaid, of
SEX & THE IMMORTAL   TO CATCH A CHEAT
BAD BOY
By Stephanie Rowe   By Kelley St. John
(Available now)   (Available now)
www.stephanierowe.com   www.kelleystjohn.com